The
Third
Time

Books by Helen McKenna

The Beach House Series
The Beach House
The Perfect Proposal (short story)
The Third Time

Other Novels
Room 46

Short Stories
Flashback (includes The Perfect Proposal)

All titles also available as e-books.

The Third Time

HELEN MCKENNA

The Third Time

By Helen McKenna

Published by Lightning Source

ISBN 13: 9780648264170

Website: www.helenmckenna.com.au

Email: info@helenmckenna.com.au

It is a wise father who knows his own child.

William Shakespeare

It was always a treat to come across him accidentally.

While she spent many an hour plotting ways to catch a glimpse of Daniel from the anonymity of a crowd, it was a bonus when she could gaze at him close up, absorb his familiar features and feel great pride at the fine, strapping young man he had become. Not that she deserved to feel proud – after all she'd had no hand in his upbringing and had only met him on a couple of occasions when he was a small child – but still, the pride was there.

As he stood on the sand in his red and yellow surf patrol uniform, intently scanning the water, she had to resist the urge to reach out and touch him. Silly old woman, she chided herself. Imagine how that would go down? While she knew him to be a polite young man, he would surely be a little alarmed to have his arm stroked by a random beach goer. It was fortunate that her sunglasses and hat hid her face, allowing her to study him surreptitiously.

For a mad moment she considered wading out into the water and raising her hand to signal she was in trouble. She imagined being rescued by Daniel and having the opportunity to speak to him and to hold onto him. But, just as quickly, the thought left her. It was a ridiculous notion. While she walked along the beach every day she never swam there, she didn't even own a pair of swimming togs. They would think she was senile, going swimming fully clothed.

Nobody knew of her secret obsession. If it ever got out she'd be branded a stalker, even though she never made contact, she just watched from a distance. Still, to an outside observer, it would seem strange for a woman of her age to be so invested in a teenage boy who didn't even know her. Most would wonder at her being so fixated on this boy simply because he shared the same name as the boy she had lost. And others couldn't hope to understand how she had pinned all her hopes on this boy making it through to adulthood, unscathed, and to life the life she had dreamed her son would live.

Standing still for a moment, she grasped the silver locket that hung around her neck. It was her most precious possession. The tiny photograph it contained was like the missing piece of her heart. From this talisman she gained great strength, but also moments of crushing sorrow. The pain was often still as raw as it had been twenty-five years ago. Today was a good day, though. She felt that her son had brought her here to this place at the right time to see his namesake, to cement the decision she had been tossing up. As much as it might burden Daniel temporarily, in the long term he was the only one who could do something about it.

If it were possible she would have stayed there all afternoon, but, of course, that was not to be. Another patrol member came up to Daniel and slapped him on the back. 'Race around the cans?' the boy challenged.

'Yeah, sure,' Daniel replied with a grin.

She had to move then, to avoid looking suspicious, but it didn't stop her watching from a distance. The two young men ran across the sand and splashed into the waves, dolphin diving as the water got deeper then swimming effortlessly out into the surf, their red and yellow patrol caps bobbing up and down as they headed further out. It didn't escape her notice that Daniel was the better swimmer and reached the red and yellow buoy first. Surely, he would be the first one back to shore.

Finally breaking her gaze, she headed back across the

sand to the beach car park. After unlocking the door of her ageing Daihatsu Charade, she reached inside and pulled out an envelope. She looked at it one last time and walked across the street and deposited it into the red mailbox outside the Post Office.

CHAPTER ONE

It was a beautiful school.

Set on a leafy thirty acres, the century-old timber buildings formed the centrepiece of the campus, while the modern brick additions were positioned on the lower side of the site. It was a pleasant contrast from many other schools that had expanded in a much more ad hoc fashion in the seventies and eighties. A statue of Saint Joseph, the school patron, stood in a small circular garden just inside the front entrance.

Jack's footsteps echoed on the wooden veranda as he made his way to the administration wing. It had been a long time since he'd been summoned to the principal's office, and even then, it had been to receive congratulations for outstanding results on his HSC trials. He could still remember the look of pride on Brother Anthony's face. Jack shook his head, suddenly feeling old. It couldn't have been over twenty-five years ago, surely?

The sharp trill of the bell sounded, startling him. Jack picked up his pace and made it into the office just before the hordes of students erupted from the classrooms and swarmed over the campus heading to their next class.

The front part of the office was empty but the adjoining

print room was a hive of activity. Through an open doorway Jack could see several women congregated around a long table apparently in the throes of preparing a mail-out. Not wanting to interrupt what was clearly a complex process, Jack held back from ringing the bell on the counter. Looking around, he saw the usual collection of photos and trophies that often featured on school office walls, including a large black and white print of what must have been the original school house. He recognised it as one of the buildings he had walked past outside. Jack read the caption under the photo – it was taken in 1905. He liked visiting places with a history, especially one where the buildings had been preserved so well.

Caught up in his photo gazing, Jack was startled when a voice behind him said, 'Mr Nolan?'

Spinning around, he came face to face with another woman. Looking young enough to be a student herself, she was wearing a vintage-style red dress with chunky yellow beads and had a hibiscus clip perched over her right ear. Apparently surprised at the sight of a good-looking man in a designer suit, she smiled warmly.

'Yes, that's right,' Jack replied, returning the smile, surprised to find someone outside the normal school secretary demographic.

'Fabulous!' she replied. 'Adrian is on a bit of a tight timeline today, so it's great you're early. Just go on through,' she added, indicating a short hallway to the right. 'The door is open.'

'Thank you,' Jack said, before making his way to the office at the end of the corridor. He took a deep breath before walking in. He wasn't sure if he was ready for teenage rebellion yet. His own children were much younger, the oldest only six. And Danny had been such a good kid to this point, too caught up in his numerous sporting pursuits to get into any kind of trouble.

Adrian McGregor looked up from his computer as Jack entered the room. 'Jack, how are you?'

'Well thanks, and you?'

'Can't complain. Please have a seat,' Adrian said, reaching over to shake Jack's hand, then indicating to the padded office chair on the opposite side of his desk.

Jack sat down, reaching into his inside coat pocket as he did so. Pulling out his phone he flicked it to silent, then put it back away before glancing over at Adrian 'Well?' he asked, eyebrows raised.

'Well, indeed.' Closing his laptop, Adrian removed his glasses and pinched the bridge of his nose. 'First of all, thank you so much for coming all this way. I know we could have had a phone conference, but as you can appreciate it is much easier to deal with these things face to face.'

'It's no problem. I meant what I said when I committed to this whole deal in the first place. I will do anything for Danny and that includes the hard stuff. I just thought we were going so well.'

'We were, we really were. We got him through to year ten with solid results and prepared him the best we could for his senior schooling. You know, I really thought we were on the home straight.'

'Well, I guess that's teenagers for you. Never count your chickens, hey?'

'No, definitely not.'

'How did you know something was up?' Adrian asked.

'Well, I didn't, not until I spoke to you.'

'But you rang first, asking how he was going. I was glad you did, I'd been in two minds whether to get you involved at this stage…'

Furrowing his brow, Jack shook his head. 'I know we had a bit of phone tag, but I initially got in touch because I got a message from the school saying I needed to ring you regarding Danny.'

Adrian was frowning now. 'This was before you rang me?'

'Yes, definitely. Like I said, I wouldn't have known otherwise.'

The two men looked at each other in confusion. Eventually Adrian shrugged. 'It's a bit puzzling but let's not worry about it now. Maybe one of the office staff got confused or rang for another reason.'

Jack nodded in agreement, even though the lawyer in him didn't like the unanswered question. Still, Adrian was right, it wasn't worth worrying about now. 'So, what are we dealing with here?'

'I really don't know, Jack. He started the year out so well, but in the past month there has been a serious decline in his general attitude and schoolwork. He's been turning up late at times, his homework isn't always done, his first English assignment wasn't handed in and he's had several days off. His mother did call the absentee line saying he was sick, but you know the situation there, so I'm guessing he just hasn't bothered coming in some days and she's covered for him.'

'Not a great way to start year eleven.'

'No, absolutely not.'

'And you've got no idea why?'

'None at all. I had a chat to him but that was pretty

futile, so I got him to talk to the counsellor. Of course, she couldn't reveal what they spoke about, but she did agree it was a pretty one sided conversation. I think Jim has tried to talk to him as well, but no dice there either.' Adrian shrugged helplessly.

'And that's where I come in?'

'Uh huh. Have you spoken to him much lately?'

'No, not for a month at least. You know teenagers, they've got every means of communication possible within reach, but when they want to be invisible, they can. He must be screening my calls and I've had no reply to my last few emails.'

'I don't suppose you're a Facebook friend?'

Jack shook his head. 'I don't do Facebook.'

'I'm with you on that.'

Both men were silent for a moment. Jack could feel his phone vibrating in his pocket but ignored it, knowing this issue required his full and immediate attention. 'So, what do we do now?' he asked, finally.

'Yes. That's the big question.' Adrian leaned back in his chair for a moment. 'I think the best plan for now is for you to talk to him and see if you can get him to open up. You're here for the weekend, right?'

'Yep.'

'I know he might not be forthcoming with anything, but see how you go and let's say we touch base on Sunday. What time's your flight?'

'Not til seven.'

'Good, that gives us more of a window. Look, Jack, as you can appreciate, it's not the end of the world yet. First semester year eleven is only a minor portion of the final result, so there is still time to fix things. But, as we know,

Danny needs prompting to stay on task, so if we don't act now, then it could be a downhill slide.'

'Yeah, that's what I'm afraid of.'

'He's a great kid and I hate to see any student not make the most of their educational opportunities, especially one with such promise.'

'Tell me about it. We'll get it fixed, Adrian. There's no way Danny isn't going to graduate.'

Guessing that a sixteen-year-old wouldn't want to be greeted at the front gate, Jack waited down near the bus stop. It didn't take long to spot Danny in the sea of navy, white and grey uniforms, as he towered above the crowd. At 180 centimetres, Jack had always considered himself tall, until Danny not only matched, but exceeded, his height by a full fifteen centimetres in the space of two years. He had also filled out, leaving behind the thin, wiry build he'd had since childhood. It wasn't surprising given how much of Danny's time was taken up with sport but it was still hard for Jack to assimilate that this young man was the boy he had formed such a close bond with almost eight years before.

When Danny got closer, Jack climbed out of the hire car. 'Hey, Dan!' he called.

Danny looked up, his light brown eyes widening in surprise to see Jack on the opposite side of the street. He waved uncertainly, then said goodbye to his friends before crossing the road to the Corolla sedan.

'Hey, Jack, what the hell?' said Danny, stopping near the left front headlight. His mid brown hair seemed to have lightened since their last meeting and it was more closely cropped. Jack wondered if the short cut was due to school rules or convenience for all the time Danny spent in the water.

'Nice to see you too,' Jack replied.

'Sorry, it's just a bit random. What's going on?'

'I just thought I'd pop up for a visit.'

'Oh yeah?' Danny eyed him warily.

Jack motioned to the front passenger door. 'Hop in, we can talk on the way home,' he said, climbing back into the driver's seat.

Danny slung his school bag into the back before slouching onto the front passenger seat. 'So, what's the go? Why are you here?' he asked, as he put his seat belt on.

Jack started the car and nosed his way onto the street that was busy with school traffic. 'What? I can't just drop in for a visit?'

'Yeah, you can, but you don't. You always tell me when you're coming and you don't usually come by yourself.'

'Well, you didn't answer my phone messages or texts or emails.'

Danny shrugged. 'I've been busy.'

'Yeah, those thirty second texts, they really eat up your time.'

'Jeez, lay off, Jack. You always say kids today spend too much time on technology.'

'Yeah, well, you do, but there's a happy medium. I know when I'm being ignored,' Jack said, looking over his shoulder as he merged onto the main road.

Danny ignored that comment, adjusting the seat to a semi-reclined position and exhaling loudly before speaking again. 'What's with the lawyer clothes?' he asked, casting an eye over Jack's charcoal suit.

'I was going to change before I left work, but my last

meeting ran late and I barely made it to the airport. I did ditch the jacket and tie but I spilt coffee on my shirt when I went through the drive through on my way here so I put them back on to look presentable when I met…' Jack's voice trailed off when he realised he'd said too much.

Glancing back over at Danny, he waited for a response, but none was forthcoming. Danny remained in the same position with his eyes closed, feigning sleep.

Jack reached over and nudged him on the arm. 'Come on, Dan, I make a special effort to come and visit and you don't even want to talk to me?'

'I don't want to talk to you because I know you came to see Mr McGregor. About me.'

'And just how do you know that?'

'Because I'm not quite as dumb as you all think I am.'

'I'm not going there, Danny. You know we don't think that.'

Danny opened his eyes and extended his arm to touch the roof. 'Oh yeah? Then why all the special treatment from Grego? The "Go Danny! You can do it!" speeches? Like I need special encouragement to even show up for school every day.'

Jack drummed his fingers on the steering wheel. 'Mr McGregor is concerned that you're falling behind after making a really good start. He's worried that something might be going on with you, that you need help with.'

'What kind of something?'

'I don't know, you tell me.'

'There's nothing to tell. School just sucks. And year eleven sucks majorly. You don't get time for fun stuff and all the teachers go on about is how important everything is. I don't even want to be there anymore.'

As he gathered his thoughts, Jack concentrated on the road. He had loved the academic challenge of school. So it was hard for him to get into the headspace of somebody who didn't feel the same way.

'Look, I know it's a step up when you hit your senior years. It can take time to adjust, that's all. Once you get more organised and settle down a bit, it won't be so bad.'

'I don't want to settle down. You know I've never been good at schoolwork and it's only going to get worse. Let's just accept it, I'm dumb and going to a nice, private school isn't going to fix that. I'm going to start looking for a job.'

Jack's stomach plummeted but outwardly he didn't flinch. Okay, Jack, he told himself, he's just testing you, don't react too strongly. 'You sure about that?' he asked. 'It's a pretty tough job market out there for unqualified sixteen year old's.'

Danny sat up straighter and glanced over at Jack, obviously disappointed that his remark hadn't drawn a stronger reaction. 'I could be a lifeguard, or a swimming teacher or a surfing instructor.'

'Yeah, you could, and there's nothing wrong with any of those jobs. But, just say in five or ten years' time, you decide you want to do something else? Having year twelve behind you offers way more options.'

'I don't want options; I just want to be out of here. And nothing you or Grego or Jim or anyone else can say is going to change my mind.'

Even though Danny seemed to have changed overnight, Sunset Point still looked the same as Jack drove around the southern cliff and caught his first glimpse of the ocean. He wound down his window a little and took a deep breath of

15

the fresh, salty air, and smiled. Sunset Point, the town that had changed his life almost a decade ago, would always have a special place in his heart.

After a revolving conversation about the pros and cons of leaving school, he and Danny agreed to disagree for the time being. If he kept pushing, Jack knew he might just lose the battle then and there. The one thing he had in his favour was the "learning or earning" rule that meant Danny either had to be enrolled in some kind of educational course or actually have a paid job. He couldn't just leave school and go surfing every day.

After dropping Danny off at home, Jack headed to his motel and checked in. Although not in the mood for friendly chit chat, he engaged in polite conversation with the receptionist before accepting his key and locating Room 10. He wheeled his suitcase inside and resisted the urge to have a shower. Instead, he changed into board shorts and a t-shirt and walked the two blocks to the beach.

Wandering across the sand, Jack smiled at the familiar sight of Jim Stewart standing in front of the south patrol flag, arms crossed and feet firmly planted in the sand, watching the ocean intently. Jim had handed over the role of head lifeguard and was now supposedly semi-retired, but by all accounts, he still spent almost as much time in the job as before. Jack knew he would keep doing it until he was physically unable to. Although still in amazing shape, Jim was nudging sixty-five and his wife, Gloria, had aspirations to travel and take things a bit easier. The first time Jack had visited Sunset Point, he had worked as a lifeguard and whenever he came back, he always felt like he could slip the uniform back on and do the job again. At the time, he had been seriously contemplating a career change, but in hindsight, he'd known deep down he could never quit law. It was too much a part of him. Yet, on occasion, he had considered how he might combine the two jobs.

Jim smiled as Jack approached him. 'Always good to see you, Jack,' he said, extending his hand.

'You too.' Jack shook Jim's hand. 'I thought you only worked part-time these days.'

'Ah, you know me, Jack, can't keep me off the beach. But I'm learning to step back and let the young boys run the shop. I'm just an employee now, part of the gang.'

Jack nodded and smiled, knowing that while the new head lifeguard, Steve, did all the admin work, he would always defer to Jim when he was there.

'So, where's the boy?' Jim asked.

'I just dropped him home. I presume he'll be down here soon.'

'Uh huh. There's a decent swell out past the lighthouse, you won't keep him away.'

'So, if we're going to talk about him, we'd better do it fast?'

'Yeah, spot on.' Lifting his hat off, Jim smoothed back his hair before plonking it back on. 'So, any joy?'

'After a twenty-minute car ride? Not even close. We got as far as him telling me he's leaving school.'

Jim nodded. 'I got the same spiel. He keeps asking me if there are any openings here. I've tried to tell him he needs a good education, but all I get from him is how I left school early and it didn't do me any harm.'

'I know teenagers all go through this stage of non-communication and all the rest, but this whole bad attitude just isn't like him. Let's be honest, he's never going to love school, but we've talked endlessly about how important it is.

17

Plus, he's always dreamed of going on the overseas rugby tour St Joseph's run at the end of year twelve. If nothing else, I thought the idea of that would keep him there.'

'I'm with you, Jack, something's just not right with him. He's even been funny with Gloria and you know how well the two of them get on.'

'Yeah,' Jack agreed. Gloria treated Danny like one of her grandsons and they had always shared a special bond. She still packed lunch for him every day and washed and ironed his school uniforms.

Jack looked down at the sand before speaking again. 'Anything different at home that you know about?'

'Well his mother's latest boyfriend has moved in.'

'Could that be it?'

'I dunno. She's had plenty of boyfriends over the years and it's never affected him like this.'

'Yeah, but if he's moved in that must mean it's pretty serious, right? I don't think any of the others have lived with them have they?'

Jim shook his head.

'So, what's he like then?'

'Who, the boyfriend?' Jim asked.

'Yeah.'

'Well, I would say Danny's mother definitely has a type, you know big and burly, lots of tatts, the kind you wouldn't want to meet in a dark alley.'

'Scary kind of character then?'

'Well, in fairness, I've never exchanged two words with the bloke. He's not from around here. And he rides a Harley, which in itself raises a few eyebrows around town.' Returning his gaze to the ocean, Jim scanned the patrolled area and beyond, an action so natural for him it was barely noticeable to a bystander.

Jack, however, knew him well enough to spot a diversionary tactic. 'That's all good info but, come on, there's something else isn't there?'

'I don't know how the hell you do that.'

'Do what?'

'Sniff out information.'

Smiling, Jack looked out to sea. 'It's what I do. I like to think I'm good at it.'

'All right. Gloria will kill me for saying anything but she reckons Danny might soon have a sibling.'

'Oh, wow, really? Now we're getting somewhere. Is she sure?'

'No, it's not official but Gloria saw her at the doctor's and said she was "glowing", whatever the hell that means.'

'Far be it for me to doubt a woman's intuition. It certainly puts a new spin on everything. I'll see if he'll open up and tell me.'

'Just do what you've got to do, Jack, because we don't have a lot of time.' Glancing over his shoulder Jim motioned with his eyes further along the sand to where Danny had just appeared, surfboard under his arm.

Jack exhaled sharply. 'I'll just go for a dip while he's out there, then I'll see if he'll have dinner with me. Maybe some lobster will loosen his tongue.'

Jim shrugged. 'I dunno, Jack, but good luck.'

'Yeah, thanks.'

Leo's seafood restaurant was an institution in Sunset Point and throughout regional Queensland. Since featuring in a segment on *The Weekender*, tour buses would often stop there for lunch to sample the exquisitely cooked seafood. A step up from the café and Chinese restaurant in town, Jack always loved to eat at Leo's when he was visiting Sunset Point.

He didn't like pulling rank to get Danny there on Saturday evening, but in the end, he had no choice. Danny had declined his invitation the night before, claiming a prior family engagement. Given that Danny's mother had pretty much left him to his own devices from early childhood, a cosy family get-together on a Friday night didn't seem likely. Still, Jack hadn't pushed it, and they made plans for breakfast instead. But predictably, a "sorry can't make it" text had arrived five minutes before the agreed meeting time. When Jack tried to ring Danny, his phone was switched off, so he spent the morning on the beach waiting for Danny to emerge, but he didn't. Eventually Jack gave in and got Jim involved. While Danny might be in the throes of some major teenage rebellion, he didn't dare defy Jim and had arrived at Leo's as directed. But, the kid wasn't giving in easily. Standing by the bar as they waited to be seated, Danny kept his attention focused on his phone, sending and receiving numerous texts without looking up once.

'You know you're not allowed to use your mobile in the dining room,' Jack said, sipping his mineral water. He would have preferred a decent glass of wine, but it didn't seem appropriate somehow.

He got a shrug in response.

'You remember the first time I brought you here?'

'Yeah,' Danny mumbled, as his fingers worked the touch screen. 'One of your first great acts of charity.'

Jack knew he was being tested, but the barb still stung. He was pondering how to respond when the maître d appeared to escort them to their table. Threading their way through tables in the softly lit restaurant, Jack steeled himself for the evening ahead, hoping desperately that he could get through to Danny. They had always got along so well and although the hero worship had died off as Danny got older, Jack knew Danny still looked up to him. Or he had until recently.

They were seated near the front window that boasted a stunning ocean view. 'Enjoy your meals, gentlemen,' the maître d said. 'Marco will be your waiter. He's just transferred out from the kitchen, so if you have any questions, he's your man.'

A teenaged boy appeared from the shadows and handed them menus. 'Good evening. Have you dined at Leo's before?' he asked, his voice quavering a little.

Danny and Jack nodded.

'Great! Then you know you're in for a real treat.'

Sensing the young man's nerves, Jack smiled

encouragingly. 'Did you cook in the kitchen?'

Marco shook his head. 'Uh, no. I was just a dish pig, I mean kitchen hand. But you still learn a lot about the meals out there.'

'I imagine you would,' Jack said.

Becoming more relaxed as he ran through the specials, Marco then poured two glasses of water. Glancing at Danny he said, 'You go to St Joseph's, don't you?'

Danny eyed him warily. 'Yeah.'

'I thought so. I saw your rowing team at the regatta a few weeks ago. You guys were poetry in motion! The way you came right up at the end and just smashed the Hervey Bay team, it was awesome.'

'Thanks,' Danny replied with a smile. 'Our coach is really into the backend of the race and even though it sucks to start behind, it's cool to just cruise on past like that.'

'Yeah, totally. So do you get to go to State's or anything?'

'Well, we're still in the heats, but yeah, hopefully we'll get through. Our senior crew won last year.'

'Nice. Well, I'd better get back to it. I'll come back to take your order soon.'

'Cool,' Danny replied easily.

'Yeah, thanks,' said Jack. He studied Danny's face, watching as it shut down again as soon as Marco left. 'Great table,' he said, shaking out his linen napkin and placing it on his lap.

'Yeah,' Danny grunted before turning his attention to the menu. Jack did the same, although he wasn't sure he was going to be able to eat with the knot of dread that was forming in his stomach. He had never imagined having a stilted, awkward conversation with Danny. Their friendship, although a little unconventional, had always been strong. They had never had a cross word between them.

'Have you done any driving since your got your Learner's permit?' Jack asked, trying to open a dialogue that might run to more than yes or no answers.

Danny shook his head. 'Mum drives a Getz. I can't even fit behind the steering wheel properly.'

Remembering Jim's comment about Danny's mother's boyfriend riding a Harley, Jack didn't bother asking if he could teach him instead. 'They are pretty small,' he agreed.

'Mum said she couldn't teach me anyway, it would make her too nervous.'

With great self-control, Jack didn't react to that statement. As a rule, he refrained from talking about Danny's mother, Tamara, other than general enquiries about how she was. He still found it difficult to understand how a parent could leave her child to largely bring himself up. Sure, Tamara had provided a roof over Danny's head and had fed and clothed him, but she had also been quite happy for Jim and Gloria to babysit him endlessly without any kind of official arrangement, nor any acknowledgement or thanks.

Similarly, he'd found Tamara's indifference about Danny's secondary education hard to comprehend. When Jack had broached the subject of Danny applying to attend St Joseph's to make the most of its specialised PE program, she'd simply shrugged before replying, 'Sure, he can go there if he wants to. It doesn't bother me.'

Jack had wanted to shake her to try and instil some enthusiasm and yes, he was willing to admit, some appreciation for the fact that he and Jim had jumped through plenty of hoops to get Danny's name bumped up a waiting list, then through two interviews. He wanted Tamara to try and understand what a great opportunity her son was being handed and that he would need to be encouraged to embrace it fully. Although Jack knew Gloria didn't mind washing and ironing Danny's school uniforms for him and packing his lunch each day (in fact she loved doing it), it rankled that Tamara blithely accepted somebody else taking responsibility for tasks she should have undertaken, or at least supervised, herself.

The arrival of Marco snapped Jack out of his reverie. Although he'd been staring at the menu, he had paid no attention to it. 'Oh, uh, the lobster, thanks,' he said, closing his menu and sliding it to the edge of the table.

Danny flipped to the back of the menu. 'So, the swordfish and caviar combo, is it all it's cracked up to be?'

'Oh, yeah, totally,' said Marco. 'But, uh, you know how much it costs, right? I mean it's an awesome dish, but…'

'Oh, I don't have to worry about the cost,' Danny assured him. 'Jack here is paying and he's loaded.'

'Right,' Marco said uncertainly, his nerves returning. 'Sure, that's fine. I was just checking.'

Danny gave Jack a level gaze. 'That's okay, right? Or do you only throw money at me when I'm being nice to you?'

Jack held his hands out palms up. 'Have whatever you want.'

Danny studied the menu for a moment longer, then snapped it closed. 'I'll have the seafood basket, thanks,' he said, holding the leather-bound book aloft for collection.

'Great choices, guys.' Marco dropped the order pad in his apron pocket and topped up their water glasses. 'Your meals won't be long,' he assured them as he collected the menus, obviously relieved not to have been caught in the middle of anything and apparently keen to get away, in case they changed their minds.

'The basket always was your favourite,' Jack said when Marco walked away.

'Yeah,' Danny mumbled.

Jack exhaled deeply. 'Come on, Dan, what's wrong?'

'Who said anything's wrong?'

'You're just not yourself. Is it your mum's new boyfriend?'

'Colin? Nuh, what's Colin got to do with anything?'

'I don't know, you tell me. Do you get on all right with him? He lives with you, right? That must be a big adjustment. Jim tells me he's a bit scary looking.'

Danny shook his head. 'Like Jim can talk. He can be pretty scary when he wants to be.'

'Oh, yeah,' Jack agreed with a chuckle. 'But seriously, is Colin making things hard? Is he violent or does he drink or something?'

'You've got it all worked out, haven't you? Big bad Colin moved in, so it must all be his fault.' Danny looked up at the ceiling for a moment and shook his head again.

'Dan, I'm really trying to understand here. So, you're telling me it's all okay with Colin?'

'Yeah, it's totally okay. You know Colin might look and sound rough, but he's actually the most genuine guy Mum has ever dated. He's got a job, he does normal stuff like put the bins out and fix things in the house and he's really into family stuff like eating dinner together every night.'

'Oh, right,' Jack replied, taken aback. Whatever Danny's problem was, it didn't seem to be Colin. The kid wasn't that good an actor.

'But you know what the best thing is?'

Jack shook his head.

'He's made Mum really happy, like proper happy. She doesn't go out all the time anymore and she's stopped smoking,' he said in wonder. 'And drinking too. She hardly even has wine now.'

'Well, yeah, that's probably because of the bab—' Jack's voiced trailed off when he saw the look of complete shock on Danny's face. Great! he thought, I've really put my foot in it. Maybe Gloria has got it completely wrong. Or perhaps there's a problem of some kind.

'The *what*?'

'Dan, I'm sorry, I shouldn't have said that. It was just something Jim mentioned and it was absolutely not my place to repeat it. It could be wrong anyway, I don't know for sure.'

Danny was still staring at him in disbelief. 'Did you say baby? Mum's having a baby?'

'Well, that's the thing, I really don't know. Gloria suspected she might be pregnant. Honestly, please forget I said it.'

But Danny was nodding his head now. 'Now I get it. Ladies get sick when they're pregnant, right?'

'Uh, yeah, most of them do.'

'And really tired and stuff?'

'Yeah.'

'Oh man, I can't believe this!'

'Seriously, Danny, I'm really not sure that it's true. Please don't get upset until we know for certain.'

'Upset?' Danny said. 'Why would I be upset? I think it's awesome.'

Jack's heartbeat slowed a little. 'You do?'

'Of course! I've always wanted a brother or a sister.

27

Well maybe a brother more than a sister, but I really wouldn't care. It sucks being an only child.'

'Yeah,' Jack agreed with a smile, 'I always wanted a brother or sister too.' Their eyes met for a moment and for a second the real Danny was back, the eager nine-year-old he had met so long ago.

'I hope she has two babies,' Danny said.

'What, twins? There's a lot of work with twins,' Jack said, speaking from his own experience. His daughters were eighteen months old now and past the small baby stage, but the first year had been a blur, even with family support and hired help.

'Well, yeah, that would be cool. But what I meant was I hope she has another one too, so they'll have someone to play with. I *always* wanted that.'

'I'm hearing you, Dan,' Jack replied. And he was. As a child, he had felt the same way and even as a small boy had sensed his parents' regret at not being able to provide him with a sibling. Thrilled to have the normal Danny back, even if only temporarily, Jack was happy to keep the conversation centred on the pregnancy as they ate their meal. The lobster, as always, was superb and Danny demolished his seafood basket in the way only a growing, athletic teenager could. Danny revealed Colin was working on a garage conversion to extend the house.

As much as he hated to do it, Jack had to continue his fact-finding mission. 'Look, Danny, I really am sorry I spilled the beans about all this. It's great you're so excited, but it wasn't my news to tell. I was totally out of line.'

Danny shook his head. 'You're *so* law abiding.'

'And that's a bad thing?'

'No, I guess not.'

'There is probably a really good reason why they haven't told you yet and I've ruined that.'

Danny picked up his glass and upended it into his mouth, emptying it of ice cubes, mint leaf and all. He didn't speak for a moment, concentrating on chewing the ice. Jack spun his coaster in his hands while he waited for a response.

Finally, Danny spoke. 'They have tried to tell me,' he admitted. 'Lots of times over the past week they've said we have to talk, but I've kept avoiding them. I can be pretty good at that.'

'I noticed,' said Jack. 'But why? What did you think they were going to say?'

Danny shook his head. 'I thought they'd found out about something else.' Before Jack had a chance to interject and ask him what the "something else" was, the wall came up again and Danny's expression went back to closed. Jack was surprised when Danny spoke again without being prodded. 'So, this baby is like a half brother or sister, right?'

'Well, yeah, but you don't need to get too hung up on the label. They're still your brother or sister.'

'Yeah, but the half thing is actually good, for them, that is. It means their DNA might be okay, not screwed up like mine.'

'Screwed up?' Jack said. 'What are you talking about? What makes you think there's anything wrong with your DNA?'

'You get half from your mum and half from your dad, right?'

'Yeah, that's right.'

'Well, Colin has got normal DNA, he's a good guy so that will make up for it.'

'Make up for what? Dan, please. What's wrong?'

'You wouldn't understand.'

'Try me, mate. Whatever it is can't be that bad.'

Danny stared up at the ceiling for a moment, then lowered his gaze and studied the starched linen tablecloth. But finally he spoke. 'It's my dad, my *biological* father,' he mumbled. 'He's in jail.'

Half an hour later the story came tumbling out. Jack had suggested leaving the restaurant and going for a walk on the beach so they could talk. It was a full moon and almost like daylight as they strolled along the deserted shoreline.

'I was watching this TV show last year about people finding their lost relatives and stuff and I started thinking about Dad. I haven't seen him for five years. He used to ring me randomly sometimes, but not since about three Christmases ago.' Danny sighed. 'You probably think why bother, right? I mean clearly he doesn't care much about me if he can't even call me on my birthday or even just to see how I'm going.'

Jack weighed his answer carefully, knowing Danny was right in what he was saying, but also understanding that the parent/child bond was strong from a child's point of view, even when a parent clearly didn't care about their offspring. 'You know, Dan, different people have their own way of relating…'

'Forget the lawyer talk, I know what you think of him and that's okay. But he's still my dad and sometimes I just want to talk to him, maybe even ask him why he doesn't care about me.'

'I understand; you don't have to justify it to me.'

'So anyway, they were saying on this show how much easier it is to track people down these days because of the internet and social media and all that. So I looked him up on Facebook and, weirdly enough, he was on there. I was pretty surprised, as from what I remember he didn't seem the type that would be into computers. I checked out his profile, but it was a bit of a dead end. He only had, like, ten friends and he hadn't posted anything on there for ages. It looked like he'd just been on there to try it out, and had lost interest. I sent him a message but I didn't get any response.'

'And there wasn't any clue on there about where he was, an email address or anything?'

'Nah, he'd listed Sydney as his current city and his email address was hidden.' Danny bent down and picked up a pebble from the sand and skimmed it across the flat surf before speaking again. 'I kind of forgot about it for a while then. It wasn't like it was that big a deal to get in touch. But then a few weeks ago, I got this letter in the mail. I was so shocked, I mean who sends letters anymore, right?'

Jack nodded and smiled inwardly, thinking about the numerous letters he signed every day at work that were mailed to clients. But Danny had a point, for his generation snail mail was a rare beast. 'Who was it from?' he asked.

'That's the thing, I don't know. It wasn't even a letter. Inside the envelope was a newspaper clipping with a story about an employee of a home alarm installation company who had been done for a string of robberies of the houses he worked on. How dumb is that? He didn't even wait that long after he installed the alarms, so it took the cops about five minutes to figure out he did it. His name was Russell Anderson.'

'And that's your father's name?'

'Yeah.'

'Are you sure it's him? There could be lots of guys with

31

the same name.'

'No, it's him, there was a photo. When I read the rest of the story I found out it's not the first time he's been in jail. It's actually the third time. He was charged as an illegal bookmaker and was implicated in that huge derelict factory fire in Sydney that burned down a whole block of shops.'

'I guess that explains why you didn't hear from him for so long.'

Danny gave a bitter laugh. 'Yeah.'

'Who do you reckon sent the article to you?'

Danny shrugged exaggeratedly. 'Stuffed if I know. It's creepy, actually. It feels like someone is trying to blackmail me.'

'It is a bit unusual. You haven't had any other letters or phone calls or anything else?'

'No, nothing.'

'Maybe it was just a nosy local person wanting to make sure you knew about it.'

Danny made a face. 'Could be. But it was from a Sydney newspaper. How would someone from Sunset Point have even seen it?'

Jack shrugged this time, trying not to show his unease. Danny's father had never really been part of his life, so why had someone taken the time and effort to alert the teenager of his criminal status? Had Russell got himself into a situation where someone would intimidate his family members to deliver some kind of sinister message?

When he spoke again, Jack made sure he kept his tone normal. 'Dan, it's not great news to hear something like that, but I don't think you need to be concerned about blackmail. Maybe a friend of your dad just wanted you to know that's why you haven't heard from him. Getting so worried about it that it's affecting your schoolwork isn't good mate. You were doing so well before.'

Danny shook his head vehemently. 'Don't you get it Jack? It's not just the potential blackmail that's affecting my schoolwork, it's the science.'

'Science?' Jack asked, still trying to process the blackmail angle.

'We're learning about genetics at school, DNA and all that and how you inherit characteristics from your parents. While the other guys at school talk about their dads being lawyers like you and doctors or a builder or plumber, well, I've got to live with the fact that my father is a criminal and I'm probably gonna end up just like him because I've got his genes and I'm not smart. So it doesn't matter if I go to a fancy school or do well at sports, because under it all I'm still a loser, like him.'

'Danny,' Jack began.

But Danny just shook his head and stalked off towards the sand dunes, leaving Jack staring at the moonlit ocean.

CHAPTER THREE

It was almost midnight when they arrived at Jack's house. Having slept most of the way during the ninety-minute drive from Sydney airport, Danny stumbled into the house and headed straight up to the guest bedroom, leaving Jack to haul the suitcases inside. He did it as quietly as he could, but wasn't surprised to see his wife, Erin, appear in the entrance hall. She always worried when Jack was out on the road late at night and would often wait up for him.

Although she'd been napping on the couch and was still half asleep, Erin managed to look alert and excited to see Jack. The middle child in a family of five siblings, Erin possessed an inbuilt ability to adapt to just about any situation and roll with the punches. As a busy mother, she never seemed to spend much time in front of the mirror but always pulled off a casual, yet put together style. While other women might look frumpy in tartan pyjama pants and an Elmo t-shirt, Erin carried it off. Although she declared herself to be plain, to Jack, with her blue eyes, tawny blonde hair and fine features, Erin possessed a wholesome beauty that had captivated him right from their first meeting.

'Big weekend?' Erin asked, stepping past the suitcases to hug and kiss Jack. Close to the same height, Erin liked that she had an excuse to ditch high heels these days.

'Oh, yeah.' Jack returned the embrace, holding her slender body tight. 'How about you, were the kids okay?' he asked.

'Yeah, totally fine, although we all missed you,' Erin said, leaning her head wearily against Jack's shoulder. 'Izzy stayed over. She loves our guest room.'

Jack smiled, glad as always that Erin's large extended family could be called upon to help out with childcare when required. Her fourteen-year-old niece Izzy was a particular favourite of their children. 'It is a cool room,' he agreed.

'Don't worry, I did a doona and accessories change, to masculinise it a bit.'

'Dan's so tired tonight he wouldn't have noticed if it was a fairy princess theme.'

'Are you hungry?' Erin asked, taking Jack's hand and leading him into the lounge room.

'Definitely not,' he said. 'Gloria stuffed us to the gills at lunch and then packed snacks for the plane. Between her cooking and eating at Leo's, I've gained about five kilos since Friday.'

'Cup of tea?' she offered. 'Nightcap?'

'I know you're kidding about the nightcap, but I reckon I could go a small scotch,' Jack said, as he collapsed onto the couch.

'It must have been a big weekend,' Erin said, taking a crystal glass and the bottle of Johnny Walker out of the china cabinet. A gift from the partners at Jack's work, the scotch was cracked open only very occasionally. 'So,' she said as she poured a measure into the glass, 'Do you reckon you can help Danny's dad?'

Jack shrugged. 'Honestly, I really don't know if there's much I can do. Obviously, I haven't seen the paperwork yet, but going by the newspaper article it sounds pretty cut and dried. There were fingerprints and stolen property found in his possession, it's pretty dumb even for a petty crim.'

'Well, maybe it was just too much of a temptation.' Erin handed Jack the glass.

'Thanks,' he said, taking a sip. 'Yeah, I guess that could be it. It seems like his boss went out on a limb to give him the job in the first place.' He shrugged. 'I guess some people steal just for the hell of it, because it's there.'

Erin sat down on the couch, folding her legs under her. 'Dare I ask *why* you've decided to take on the case?'

'I had to. Dan is so cut up about it. Not to mention there's a chance he is being intimidated by someone.'

Erin's face showed her concern as Jack explained about the newspaper article. 'Is this something we need to be worried about?' she asked.

'No, not at all. The official story is that Danny has gone to Perth to stay with his aunty. Only the Stewarts, Adrian and his parents know where he is.'

'Oh, that's okay then. What's happening with school?'

'Well, seeing there's only three weeks until the Easter holidays, and one of them is volunteer week, Adrian agreed to let him come here, as long as I get him caught up on his work.'

'And *your* work?' Erin asked, covering her mouth as she yawned.

'I'll see what I can sort out. I should be able to put off some of my non-urgent stuff and I'll just have to juggle the rest. One good thing is that Regent Park is close by, it would have been a major pain if I had go to a Sydney prison to visit him.'

'Yeah, that is lucky. How long does it take to get there?'

'About twenty minutes. It's out near Begonia.'

Erin yawned again. 'The kids will be excited to have Danny here.'

'They will. And it will be good practice for him.'

Despite his exhaustion, and the scotch, Jack couldn't sleep. Sick of staring at the ceiling, he eventually got up and stepped out onto the balcony that adjoined the master bedroom. The full moon was stunning, illuminating the bushland that surrounded the house as well as the town in the valley below. Jack loved their house. Purchased in unfinished condition in a fire sale ten years ago, he had spent a considerable amount of time and money transforming the two-bedroom cottage into a spacious, split-level five-bedroom home, with a wide veranda that showcased the awesome view. Perched on the top of a range, it was private and quiet, yet still only a ten-minute drive down to the regional city of Millvale.

Jack leaned on the railing, shivering a little in the cool night air. The fact it was guaranteed to be at least two to three degrees cooler up here than the valley could be both a good and bad thing, depending on the season. Tonight though, it wasn't just the temperature that was making Jack shiver. In his efforts to get Danny on board with Adrian's deal, Jack had assured him he could help his father. It was an easy enough thing for a teenager with no knowledge of the legal system to believe, but, in reality, Jack had never mounted a criminal defence case before. Starting out in wills and estate planning, he had moved on to employment law before several years in a small firm that dabbled in pretty much everything except criminal cases. When Jack joined his current firm, Kendall and Masters, he had initially specialised in personal injury but was now a mediation consultant who focussed on settling cases out of court. It was an impressive resume to be sure, but not very helpful for a seasoned criminal facing burglary charges.

The touch of Erin's hand on his back startled Jack.

'What are you doing out here? It's a bit chilly,' she said, leaning her head against his back and wrapping her right arm around his waist.

Jack grabbed her hand and held it against his chest. 'Just trying to get my head around it all. Criminal defence is not something I thought I'd ever attempt and the stakes are high, for Danny at least.'

'If anyone can do it, you can.'

Jack chuckled mirthlessly. 'I'm not so sure about that, but I'd hate to let Danny down.'

'You could never do that.' Grabbing Jack's hand, Erin lead him back along the balcony. 'Come on, we both need to sleep.'

Nodding wearily Jack followed her back inside.

CHAPTER FOUR

It took Jack a while to find Regent Park Detention Centre. Deliberately situated off the beaten track, it was also located in a valley, making it almost impossible to see until you were practically upon it. A low security facility with no razor wire in sight, it didn't look as intimidating as Jack had imagined. Given that he had two previous jail terms under his belt, Russell was lucky he had ended up there, rather than one of the bigger, high security prisons. Considered to be a progressive facility, Regent Park focussed on rehabilitation and retraining, although this was only available to those serving a sentence.

After finally completing the lengthy first-time sign in process, Jack was instructed to wait in a small outer office. Too nervous to sit, he paced around the confined space before stopping to examine his reflection in a mirrored window. Outwardly he looked the same as always, his expression affable, clean shaven with his full head of dark brown hair neatly combed, although he'd held off on the styling wax that morning, not wanting to appear too corporate. Similarly, he had decided against his suit jacket but had stuck with a tie, feeling he shouldn't look too casual. As always, it was Jack's eyes that gave him away, their dark depths reflecting how out of his comfort zone he was. He was so keyed up that he flinched when the door opened and a corrections officer appeared to escort him to the meeting room.

A bland, rectangular space with high windows, the meeting room housed several long, plastic topped tables, with chairs on either side. Given the low security status of the facility, face-to-face meetings were conducted at the tables, with guards in attendance scattered around the room. Although grateful for this relative liberty, Jack still found the atmosphere of the room gut-wrenchingly depressing. While an optimist might look at the inmates and see the potential for rehabilitation and the gaining of new skills, those who knew the system realised that many of them would spend the rest of their lives in and out of such institutions.

There were five men at different tables, apparently waiting for visitors. Three of them were just kids, in their late teens or early twenties at most. Another must have been at least sixty years old. Skinny as a rake, he was sucking on a cigarette like his life depended on it. Hunched in his chair, his wary eyes met Jack's gaze and then looked away. The final inmate sat alone at the furthest table, as if daring anyone to approach him. Also puffing on a cigarette, his feet were extended onto the neighbouring chair, while he blew smoke rings into the air. The short sleeves on his khaki prison uniform did little to hide the extensive web of tattoos extending down both well-muscled arms and his brown hair was long and straggly, hanging down well past his collar. Jack wasn't sure what he'd been expecting, but Russell's appearance didn't surprise him and he realised that Jim was right, Tamara apparently did have a type.

Raising his eyebrows at the man who had escorted him,

Jack sighed wearily. 'That's him, right?'

The heavyset balding man nodded. 'Uh huh. Good luck is all I can say. He wasn't very impressed about coming here when he just had a legal visit on Friday.'

'Great,' Jack said, wondering if it was too late to back out. Clutching his briefcase handle like a drowning man clinging to a life rope, he exhaled slowly and made his way over to the table.

Up close, Russell Anderson was even more intimidating. His muscular chest and broad shoulders dwarfed Jack's lean build and the thick, ropey scar that wound its way around his right forearm also made a statement. His right thumb sat awkwardly, as if it had been broken and healed without being properly re-set, and three of his top teeth were missing. His hazel eyes were flat and hard and gave nothing away.

When Jack tentatively placed his briefcase on the scarred plastic table, Russell stared him down. 'I don't know what your story is, but I reckon you've got the wrong guy.'

Jack shook his head, hoping the rapid beating of his heart wasn't as audible as it felt. 'Russell Anderson, right?'

'Depends who's asking.'

'I'm Jack Nolan. I'm a solicitor with Kendall and Masters and I'm taking over your case. I've already spoken to Legal Aid and they've approved the transfer if you agree.' Jack's voice sounded normal but he was sure Russell could sense his unease.

'Why would you want to do that? I'm totally skint. Got about two bucks in the bank,' Russell said, not breaking his stare while he took another puff on his cigarette.

Jack was sweating now, but pushed on. 'There will be no charge for my work. I'm here at the request of another

43

party, who wished to see that you had proper legal representation for your upcoming trial.'

Still bewildered, Russell frowned. 'Totally missed all that. *What* are you doing here?'

'I'm here because of Danny, okay? As much as you don't seem to care about him, the fact that you're in prison has upset him a lot and I promised I would help.'

'Danny?' Russell said. 'Danny who?'

Jack shook his head, his nerves morphing into incredulity. 'Unbelievable. Who do you reckon? How about your son? The one you haven't spoken to for three years?'

Finally, Jack had Russell's attention. 'My son?' he repeated, dropping his feet to the floor and swivelling around to look Jack in the eye. 'My son's name is Daniel.'

It was only a small chink in Russell's armour, but it was all Jack needed. The mention of Danny had triggered a reaction. That meant he might have a shot. He pulled out the grey plastic chair on the other side of the table and sat down before facing the other man again. 'Sorry, Daniel it is. I've just always know him as Danny.'

'I told Tamara to never shorten his name. No doubt she did it just to spite me.'

'I really don't know about that, maybe it was a school thing?'

Russell shook his head. 'Nuh, it's just the kind of thing she would do. She always thought she was too good for me.' He took a final drag on his cigarette before crushing the butt in an overflowing plastic ashtray.

'All right, I'm sorry if that's the case, but the main thing is that Danny, uh Daniel, asked me to help you. And I'd really like to.'

'Like to?' scoffed Russell, 'Yeah, sure you'd *like* to. You're about as happy to be here as I am.'

'Okay, fair point. But here's the deal, Russell. Daniel is a good friend of mine, a really good friend, and I'm doing this as a favour for him. So let's just go with that.'

'What's it to him? It's not like we're best buddies.'

'Despite the fact that you've shown so little interest in him, Daniel cares about you,' Jack said, hoping he didn't sound insincere. He wasn't sure if Danny *did* care, it was more his shame about having a convict for a father that had stirred up his emotions.

Russell crossed his arms and fixed Jack with a hard glare. 'Listen, *Jack*, don't you be coming here and judging me. Tamara gave me the flick about three months after Daniel was born and she made it almost impossible for me to see him. Eventually, you just get to the point where you think, why bother?'

'Didn't you have a custody arrangement? You're entitled to regular visitation even if Tamara…'

Russell cut him off. 'I was a kid with a police record and Tamara knew stuff about my family that wouldn't have gone over very well in the court system. What chance did I have of getting regular visitation?'

'Each case is based on individual circumstances.'

'You've got nooo idea.'

Heat suffused Jack's neck and face as he busied himself opening his briefcase. It was all very well to debate how equitable the legal system was, but the reality was often very different. And unfortunately, sometimes those who needed Legal Aid most, had no idea how to access it.

'There's another reason I backed off with contact,' Russell muttered.

Jack was glad to have a change of topic. 'Oh yeah?'

'About five years ago, Tamara told me Daniel wasn't mine. Said she was on with some other bloke at the same time.'

'And what was your reaction to that?'

Russell shrugged. 'Didn't seem like that big a deal. I never saw the kid anyway and I'm sure she slagged me off to him every chance she got. So it wouldn't have surprised me if she'd done the dirty on me.'

Jack nodded slowly, while studying Russell's face. His words belied his feelings. It was clear that the idea Danny might not be his *was* a big deal to Russell. Jack saw it all too often in his line of work, that is, women using paternity as a weapon when things got nasty. As a father, he understood how much that must hurt. So, it gave him a small measure of satisfaction to say, 'I can arrange a DNA test if you like, but I really don't think it's necessary.'

'Why not?'

'Because Danny, sorry, Daniel, is the spitting image of you. Same face shape, same eyes and hair colour. How tall are you?'

'About 194.'

'He's even pretty much the same height.'

'You serious? He's as tall as me? Last time I saw him he was a little, skinny thing.'

'He shot right up.' Which you would know if you had bothered to keep in touch, Jack thought.

'I did the same at that age.' Russell pulled another cigarette from the packet on the table and lit it. 'I'm guessing you don't want a smoke?'

Maybe I should mess with his head and say yes, Jack thought as he arranged several documents in front of him.

'No, thanks anyway,' he replied. 'We really need to get on to the details of your case and I need you to sign these forms. They're pretty straightforward, the first two are to terminate your contract with Legal Aid and the other two are to engage me as your solicitor with no payment required.'

'I don't know why you're botherin'. They've got me stitched up.'

'Russell, I've already told you why I'm here. If you want my help, I need you to cooperate.' Jack wasn't surprised to hear the denial, but he would get to that later.

Russell glanced at the forms. 'Where do I sign?'

'I'd really advise you to read them first.'

'The way I see it, I can't be any more screwed than I already am.'

'All right, sign at the bottom of all four pages where the tags are.' Jack held his pen out and the other man took it and wrapped the fingers of his left hand awkwardly around the barrel and scrawled his name.

Feeling Jack's gaze, Russell looked up. 'What?'

'Daniel's a lefty too and he holds his pen the same kooky way.'

'Sounds like a slam dunk then.'

'Yes, I reckon so. So, you're going to work with me then, Russell?'

'I just signed the forms, didn't I? And you can knock off the Russell crap, everyone calls me Rusty.'

'All right, Rusty it is. Just one more question before we get started. Do you know anyone who would try to intimidate Daniel to get to you?'

For the first time, Jack knew he had his new client's full attention. Rusty abandoned his slouched position and sat up straight. 'What the hell does that mean?' he growled.

Holding out his hand out in a calming gesture, Jack explained about the newspaper article. 'It's just a bit random and I want to make sure I'm not getting myself into some kind of underworld scene here.'

Rusty shook his head and laughed mirthlessly. 'You watch too much TV. I can assure you I'm no Underbelly character and, besides, most of the people I hang around with don't even know I've got a kid, let alone where he lives.'

'That's good to know. It's still a mystery as to who sent him the article and why, but not something we need to be too worried about.'

'Yeah,' Rusty agreed.

Danny was the only one there when Jack arrived home. Monday was swimming day and Erin and the kids weren't usually home until about five. Jack was happy to see him sitting at the dining room table with his laptop open and textbooks scattered haphazardly around. They had spent an hour that morning going over Danny's school work and made a rough plan of attack, starting with the easiest things first to get some momentum going. Jack would help him with the more difficult things as needed. That was the least of his worries though. If this whole mess was only about school work, it would be a walk in the park.

'Hey, Dan,' Jack said, dropping his briefcase on the kitchen table.

'Hi,' Danny replied. Although doing his best to appear nonchalant, Jack could see the unasked questions in his expression. Despite saying his father was a loser, the hope was still there that it was all a big mistake.

'Good to see you working so hard. You could have

used the study you know. I cleared my desk for you.'

'Nah, it's more interesting out here.'

'So, you been hard at it?'

'Yeah, pretty much. I finished my first IT assignment and I'm just working on my PE training log.'

'That's great.' IT and PE were two subjects Danny could tackle alone; he just needed some focus to catch up on them.

Danny closed his laptop and stretched. 'Man, the kids have grown.'

'Yeah, tell me about it. You blink and they're ten centimetres taller.' Jack loosened his tie.

'Still cute though. I can't believe Sam is in year one now.'

'Yeah, he still seems way too little,' Jack replied as he filled a glass to the brim with filtered water. 'He loves school though.'

Danny eyed Jack's briefcase. Jack sat at the table and drained his glass.

'I guess you want to know how it all went?'

Jack got a teenager shrug in response. The type that said yes, I desperately want to know, but there's no way I'm going to come out and say it.

'Well, the good news is that Russell agreed to me representing him. And he asked after you.' Jack felt justified in stretching the truth a little, believing he had seen enough reaction from Rusty to indicate at least some interest in his son.

'What, after three years he suddenly remembers me?'

Jack sighed. 'It's complicated, Dan. Obviously things between him and your mum aren't very good.'

'Yeah, she hates him,' Danny said. 'And I reckon I can

see why.'

'Well, I don't want to get into that now,' Jack hedged. He didn't doubt that Tamara had made it hard for Rusty to see Danny, but, then again, the man was hardly a paragon of virtue and could be lying through his teeth. Their past relationship was a murky topic that Jack was happy to sidestep for the time being.

Danny made a fist with his left hand and pounded it into the palm of his right. 'So, you said that's the good news. Now what's the bad?'

'Well, I don't know if it's bad as such, more like a confirmation of what we thought. The charges are pretty iron clad and there's reasonable evidence against him.'

'So it's all over then? There's no hope?'

'No, I didn't say that. I've got a lot of background work to do and I'll need to get advice from my cousin, you remember Julia, right? This is a bit outside my area of expertise but she's done lots of criminal work.'

'Great! Now you're gonna involve other people and you won't get your own work done. I told you Jack, he's not worth it. You don't have to help him. Just let him stay in jail.'

'Dan, I told you I'd do everything I could to help him and I will. For what it's worth he says he was set up. As his legal representation, I have to work with that.'

'Even if he's lying?'

'Well, yeah, unless he tells me otherwise.'

'What a loser.'

'Dan, he's still your dad, so just try and respect him a bit hey?'

Danny folded his arms and stared at him in a fashion eerily similar to Rusty. 'Respect? I don't reckon he deserves my respect.'

Jack stayed up late that night, going over the file that Legal Aid had released to him. He did a double take when he saw Rusty's date of birth. At thirty-four, Rusty was a whole decade younger than him. Doing the maths, he realised Rusty had been barely eighteen when Danny was born. It wasn't a great surprise, Tamara was a year younger than that, but if he'd had to guess Rusty's age just by looking at him, he would have estimated mid-forties at least.

Unsurprisingly, Rusty's childhood and home life offered many clues to how he had ended up in prison. With a father who had been jailed seven times for varying petty offences and an older brother who did his first stint in juvenile detention at age fourteen, it would have been more surprising if Rusty had stayed on the straight and narrow. His criminal record had officially begun aged fifteen and ten months, when he was charged with vandalism at a video arcade that refused entry to him and his friends after they had been found rigging the machines to score free games. Let off with a warning for his first offence, Rusty was not so lucky six months later when the same gang was caught trespassing after hours at the local pool. This transgression led to a community service order. He incurred five further charges over the next two years with varying community service punishments. A relatively crime free phase followed until he was charged with DVD piracy at twenty-two years of age. Striking a decent judge, Rusty was ordered to complete a work training program with the Green Corps, which had apparently kept him out of trouble up to age twenty-five. He had then changed tack, going to work as an agent for an illegal bookmaker and this eventually led to his first jail term of six months, aged twenty-seven. His most serious criminal act had occurred aged thirty, when he was found to be part of an arson-for-hire gang that torched ageing buildings for insurance purposes. As Danny had mentioned, they had been behind a huge factory fire in Sydney that had also destroyed six surrounding businesses. For this he served two years and three months behind bars.

Scanning the file further, Jack noted that Rusty's employment history was decidedly patchy. He had worked a series of unskilled jobs after leaving school at fifteen, from labouring on building sites, crewing on a fishing boat, delivering pizza and working on a council road gang. An apprenticeship as a concreter had lasted a mere six weeks before he was dismissed for chronic absenteeism. The Green Corps training led to a landscaping job; however, he was let go when one of his friends stole his boss's ute. In between his first and second stints in jail, Rusty didn't appear to have worked at all. Jack could only be grateful that Danny didn't know the true extent of his father's criminal history, as third offence didn't quite capture the true picture.

On a positive note, Rusty had apparently been telling the truth about the kind of criminal he was. He had no known links with organised crime, no ties to selling drugs, and no violent offences. His prison records noted that while his general attitude and body language might come across as defiant, he wasn't considered a troublemaker and he had served his time incident free. By all accounts he was a petty criminal, an opportunist who saw the chance for a quick buck and took it without first thinking through the consequences. While the newspaper story still niggled a little, Jack felt reasonably confident it wasn't as sinister as he first thought. His original take on it was probably right, that it was some local busybody who wanted Danny to know his father was a loser.

Suddenly weary, Jack snapped the file closed and pushed it to the other side of his desk, as if physically distancing himself from it could similarly remove Rusty from his own personal space. He had jumped headlong into this whole mess way too hastily. Seeing it all laid out on paper was bringing home to him just how far over his head he really was.

CHAPTER FIVE

Jack put in a solid morning at work the next day before pulling Rusty's paperwork out to make a proper start. He could work through lunch, plus another half hour or so, to at least get the ball rolling. He had told Danny it wasn't a problem, but the reality was that he couldn't just drop his other cases and, after taking a day off to visit Russell, he was already behind on existing work. He had postponed what could be put off for the moment, but in the meantime, he would need to burn the candle at both ends for a while. It wasn't like Jack didn't know how to be a workaholic – he'd been there and done that – but he'd been younger then and single. Still, being a consultant afforded him more freedom than the other senior associates and he would do his best to snatch every spare moment he could over the following weeks.

Unwrapping the Subway Club sandwich his secretary had picked up for him, Jack took a bite and picked up the first stack of documents in the file, which turned out to be Rusty's arrest report. According to the paperwork, Rusty's boss, Cameron Melville, had been fully co-operative with the police, even though it meant negative publicity for his business, Melville Security. They specialised in keyless house security systems, allowing home owners to unlock their door either via a remote control or a keypad on the property.

Rusty had been approached for questioning at his residence, a ground floor unit in Parramatta. Upon seeing the police at his door, he had immediately become aggressive and initially refused to let the two detectives enter, but had eventually relented when they produced a search warrant and said they would use force to enter if necessary.

A search of the premises had revealed the stolen property hidden in a plastic storage tub in the garage. Rusty had immediately declared his innocence, informing them that the junk stored in the garage belonged to the landlord and he did not have a key to the garage. (The detectives had gained entry with a key provided by the Real Estate agency). When asked why he didn't have a key, Rusty explained that he had agreed to no garage access in exchange for a small reduction in rent, as the space was being used for storage by the owner. Rusty also pointed out that the lock on the ageing tilt-a-door was old and flimsy and could have easily been jimmied by anybody who applied a bit of force. The detectives agreed to take this into consideration, but informed Rusty that he was under arrest for seven counts of burglary.

Upon checking out the landlord, the detectives found he worked in the mines in Western Australia, on a month on/week off roster but had not returned to Sydney for the past three months as he had spent his time off in Broome and Bali, respectively. Work attendance log-ins, airline tickets and credit card receipts proved this to be true. This meant he was away from Sydney at the time of each of the burglaries. The other items in storage in the garage were found to be relatively worthless, such as boxes of ski gear, books, CDs and DVDs, roller blades, golf clubs and other miscellaneous household items that appeared to be second hand. Apparently, the landlord had never even met Rusty, as the rental was arranged through an LJ Hooker real estate agency. And the detectives could find absolutely no affiliation between Rusty and the landlord. The twenty-seven-year-old landlord was, by all appearances, a hard working young man with no criminal record, who had sought out work in the mines due to the higher salaries offered in the hope of getting ahead financially. The unit in Parramatta was his first property purchase and he had lived there only six months before heading west. The investigators could find no possible reason why the landlord would want to frame his tenant for the burglaries.

Looking through the records from Rusty's initial court appearance, Jack couldn't fault Victor Kingston, the Legal Aid lawyer who had been assigned to represent Rusty. Victor's first task was to give Rusty adequate legal representation through his police interview and initial court appearance and that had happened. His attempt to get Rusty released on bail had been unsuccessful and with a stack of other cases requiring his attention, Victor had only just started preparing for Rusty's trial and had made little progress. He had been more than relieved to sign Rusty over to Jack.

Taking his last bite of sandwich, Jack scrunched up the wrapper and dropped it in the bin, before checking his watch. One thirty. He still had a bit more time. Jack pulled the stack of papers out of the cardboard wallet and shuffled through them, looking for the list of stolen property he had glanced at briefly last night. Pulling it out, he studied the form, looking for something beyond the obvious among the various items.

> 1 TAG watch (this was determined to be a fake when it was recovered, although it was listed as genuine for insurance purposes)
> 2 iPads
> 1 Dell laptop
> 1 Macbook Pro
> 1 set of Stirling silver candlesticks
> 1 Nikon SLR digital camera plus six specialist lenses and camera bag
> 1 JVC video camera
> 1 Panasonic DVD/HDD recorder
> 1 Sony Blu-Ray player
> 1 Coach handbag
> 3 gold necklaces
> 1 Pandora bracelet with ten charms
> 2 pairs of diamond earrings
> 1 Garman multi-sport watch
> $750 cash

The police noted that the items stolen were the usual type of electronic and jewellery items targeted in burglaries. The one anomaly, in Jack's opinion, was the Coach handbag. It seemed an odd item for Rusty to steal. It could be argued it was for the cash or cards inside, but if he was already in the townhouse in question, it wouldn't take more than a few seconds to empty the bag and take anything of value inside and leave the bag.

Jack assumed that Rusty, like most men, would be unaware of the cash value of a Coach handbag, or other designer handbag, for that matter. He only knew himself after a rather painful shopping experience the previous month, while in Hawaii. On the second last day of a week-long trip, he had agreed to a "quick" visit with Erin to the Ala Moana mall in Honolulu before an afternoon of surfing. Just as they were about to leave the mall, Erin received a text from her sister, Arianne, asking Erin to purchase her a Coach handbag at Macy's. Although mildly annoyed, Jack had agreed to the detour. After all Arianne was part of the babysitting team, allowing him and Erin a child-free holiday. Of course, by the time they got inside the packed store and realised Macy's was having a one-day sale, it was too late to back out.

Mild annoyance turned to crankiness as Erin rummaged through piles of stock, leaving no bag unturned until she finally found the specific handbag Arianne had requested, which looked much like a dozen other bags Erin had rejected. Jack could almost feel the steam rising out of his ears as they queued for half an hour to pay for the bag, then a further twenty minutes as the cheerful, yet clearly inexperienced, sales clerk searched in vain for the correct price on a paper stock list. When she finally announced it was a mere US $350, Jack had assumed Erin would balk at the price. He couldn't believe it when she started gushing to the sales clerk about what a bargain that was. To him, it seemed an awful lot to pay for a very small bag, but in the interests of salvaging what was left of his surfing time, he had said nothing.

Circling the handbag on the list, Jack smiled wryly at the memory. Given that the house contents in question were uninsured, it seemed unlikely that it was a false claim. This was backed up by the police report that noted the young woman was much more upset at the loss of the designer handbag than of her iPad and even more upset when it was revealed the bag had not been recovered with the other stolen items.

Jack pondered this for a moment, then re-checked the list for other things not recovered. The rose gold necklace was the only other item still outstanding. Again, the handbag was the anomaly. Anyone would know that jewellery could be quickly fenced or easily stashed away to be sold later. But the average man would not know the value of a handbag. Reading further down, Jack saw a notation where the victim had provided a credit card receipt and a printout from the website from which she had purchased the handbag. Listed as a special edition, it had cost US $2700. Jack shook his head in disbelief, both that the handbag, which was even smaller than the one Erin had bought, could cost so much and that Rusty would know the cost.

Flicking over to the next page of the report, he read that the young woman had contacted Cameron Melville and threatened to sue him for the value of the handbag and the financial stress it's loss had caused her. Somewhat surprisingly Cameron had capitulated, paying her out in cash a few days later. Jack scratched his chin as he considered this. Maybe it was a false claim after all? It seemed silly to have such a valuable item in your home without contents insurance. But then again, the installation of the alarm system should have largely negated the risk of theft. It was a hard one to judge.

Caught up in his musings, Jack was startled when his phone buzzed. 'Jack Nolan,' he said absently, his mind still wrapped up in the stolen property list.

'Hi Jack, your two o'clock is here,' the receptionist announced.

'Thanks, Maddie, send them up,' he replied, gathering the contents of the file together and shoving them in his bottom desk drawer. Rusty was just going to have to wait for now.

CHAPTER SIX

Jack had been an early riser for as long as he could remember. In addition to his day job in a hardware store, Jack's father had been a milkman and, as soon he was old enough, Jack had gone on the daily run with him. While his friends had been aghast at the idea of getting out of bed at dawn, Jack had developed a special appreciation for daybreak. He and his dad had agreed it was even more sacred because so few people bothered to get up and experience it.

In his teens Jack's parents had insisted that school was his priority, so he no longer did the milk run, but he had still risen early, finding he studied better before the sun rose than after it set. It was a practice he continued through university and into his working life. He was always amazed at what he could get done by coming into the office early, before the rest of the staff arrived.

As much as he still loved experiencing the delights of early morning, the practicalities of having four young children (and the inherent sleep deprivation that involved) meant that Jack didn't see as many sunrises these days, even at the tail end of summer when first light was arriving later each day. But he was still a light sleeper, so the sound of the pool filter coming to life at five thirty on Wednesday morning woke him. He lay there for a moment, puzzled, wondering if the timer had somehow malfunctioned. It was only when he heard the muted splash of someone in the water that he realised it must be Danny.

When Jack had first installed his pool, he had swum every morning without fail. But since the kids came along, his efforts were a bit patchier. While he still spent plenty of time in the water, not too much of it was dedicated to swimming laps. Given that he was awake, he decided he should get up and go for a swim too, but it took another five minutes for him to push the covers back.

Danny was surprised to see him. 'Hey, Jack,' he said, pausing between laps. 'You coming in?'

Jack draped his towel on a deck chair and rubbed his arms in the brisk morning air. 'Yeah. I'm a bit rusty though, I haven't done a serious session for yonks.'

'I'll go easy on you,' Danny replied, with the confidence of a sixteen-year-old athlete who trained every day.

'Gee, thanks.' Jack dipped his toe in and gasped at the coolness of the water.

'Don't be a wimp, just dive in,' Danny said.

'It's cold!'

'Come off it, it's heated.'

'Yeah, but I didn't have the cover on last night.'

'It's really warm once you start swimming, I promise. Stop being a baby and get in.'

Rising to the challenge, Jack put on his goggles and dived in.

They swam for half an hour. At twenty metres long, the pool was long enough to provide a reasonable workout. It had been a deliberate decision on Jack's part; while he still enjoyed being part of a squad at the local pool, he didn't see the point of having a pool at home if he couldn't train in it when he needed to. He was a latecomer to swimming training, only taking it up when he had to give up running in his mid-thirties, but had come to enjoy it over time.

Jack was happy to go along with Danny's suggested sets as they swam, although he quickly gave up trying to keep up with him. Having learned the correct techniques early and having put in enough sessions to build speed and endurance, Danny was the quintessential child swimmer. Although not quite in contention for regional or state representation, he wasn't far off it and it showed as his pace held up over the session, while Jack's dropped off steadily. When they finally stopped, Jack did his best to hide his fatigue, although given the length of time since his last proper training session, he was pleasantly surprised at his form, far from his best as it was.

'I know, I know,' he said as Danny glided to a stop and looked over at him.

'I didn't say anything.'

'Yeah, but I know you're thinking what a slowcoach I am. My disclaimer is that the last serious training I did was for my surf proficiency, back in October.'

'Well, in that case, you did all right then, for an old guy.'

'Yeah, yeah. Thanks for the positive reinforcement,' Jack said, as he climbed out of the pool.

'You're welcome.' Danny grinned as he pulled his goggles off and climbed out too. He wrapped his towel around himself and sat on the sun lounger. 'So, I guess it's more school work today, then?' he asked, his lack of enthusiasm obvious as he used the corner of his towel to dry his hair.

'You got it,' Jack said, draping his oversized towel around his shoulders and pulling it tight around him.

'But I've done heaps already.'

'Yeah, well, you slacked off in a big way mate, it's going to take some effort to make it up. You okay with it? Or do you need some help?'

Danny lay back on the lounger and looked up at the sky, which was beginning to brighten as the sun rose. 'Nah, I'm good for the moment. I'll finish all the stuff I can do first.'

'Good plan.' Looking over at his young friend, Jack smiled. 'Tell you what, you put in a big effort today and I'll give you a driving lesson this arvo. You brought your Learners Permit, didn't you?'

Danny sat back up at this announcement. 'Yeah, I did, I always have it in my wallet. Will you really take me out for a spin?'

'Of course. I'll grab some L plates at the newsagent today.'

Danny leapt to his feet and followed Jack to the gate. Amused, Jack held it open and then followed him back to the house.

* * * * *

Jack managed to squeeze in a visit to Regent Park in at midday. He grabbed a coffee at the service station on his way out of town and ate a banana as he drove, trying to ignore the growling of his stomach. Between his pre-dawn swimming session and an early start at work, he hadn't had time to pack lunch. If dealing with Rusty wasn't already hard enough, now the guy was going to give him an ulcer from too much caffeine and not enough food.

Rusty was still claiming innocence. And he was getting tired of discussing the finer details. Twirling one of Jack's pens on the plastic table top, he was getting to the point of being annoying, both in action and attitude. 'We've already been over this ten times!' he said, as he spun the pen like a top.

'And we'll go over it ten more times if necessary,' Jack replied, reaching over to snatch the pen and put it back in his briefcase. 'The key to a successful defence strategy is nailing every single detail so they can't trip us up with something unexpected.'

'It's getting boring.'

'Sorry about that, but it's kinda necessary if you want any chance of getting out of jail.'

With no comeback to that, Rusty gave Jack a withering glare before leaning forward and cupping his chin in his hands. 'If the cops had done their job properly, they would see that I don't nick other people's stuff,' he said.

'What?' Jack looked over at Rusty in obvious distrust.

'You heard me, I don't nick other people's stuff.'

'Rusty, you were part of a DVD piracy operation.'

'Yeah, but that was only ripping off a big company that already made huge profits. I've never broken into someone's house and nicked their stuff.'

'What? You've got some kind of morality scale where some crimes are okay but others aren't?'

'I'm just telling you I don't do that. I never have and I never will.'

Jack wasn't sure what to make of this information. 'All right,' he said finally, 'I'll note that down. Unfortunately, moral stances can be hard to prove in court. But it's good to know.'

'Yeah, whatever. I'm sure you don't believe me anyway.'

'I didn't say that.'

'No, you're really careful what you say, aren't you?'

'Yes, I suppose I am.'

'Can't you tell the jury I've never been convicted of burglary before?'

'No, hopefully we won't disclose your previous convictions, if the magistrate agrees. It's for your own benefit because it means they don't take that into consideration when deciding on your guilt or innocence.'

'Oh, yeah, that sounds fair. They can pin me for something I didn't do but you don't want to say something that might get me off the hook.'

Jack focussed on his notebook for a minute and counted to five in his mind, determined not to lose his cool. 'Rusty we're already on a pretty tight time frame here. I can assure you my time will be much better spent working on your defence, rather than debating the legal system.'

'All right, fine, what's next?'

Jack slid a printout of the Coach handbag across the table. 'What kind of bag is this?'

Rusty made a face and shrugged. 'I don't know. A red one?'

'You've never seen it before?'

'Yeah, you got me. I like ladies bags. I've got a big collection of them so I can make sure they match all my clothes.'

'I'm actually shocked you know handbags are supposed to match clothes.'

'I went out with this chick for a while who used to spend, like, an hour choosing which bag matched her outfit.

She had about fifty bags.'

Jack raised his eyebrows. 'That does sound a bit excessive.'

'More like obsessive. And not only about bags,' Rusty muttered.

'What do you know about Coach?' Jack asked, wanting to stay on track.

'What, like a football coach?'

'No, the brand Coach. Have you ever heard of it?'

'My old man used to smoke Coach cigarettes. Some hippy guy from Nimbin used to drive around and sell them in bulk. They smelt like cow dung.'

Jack reclaimed the picture and slid it into the file. 'And that didn't put you off smoking?'

'Nuh.' To illustrate his point, Rusty pulled a cigarette out of the packet in his front pocket. Sticking it in his mouth, he paused before lighting it. 'Anything else?'

'I think we're just about finished actually. You are hereby categorically denying that you used the keyless entry codes previously set by yourself to gain access to seven properties in the suburbs of Manly, Cremorne, Neutral Bay and Seaforth?'

Rusty lit the cigarette. 'Yes, I deny it.'

'You have no knowledge of how footprints matching your boot size and style were found in varying locations outside one of the properties in question several weeks after the alarm installation took place?'

'No, I don't.'

'You did not leave cigarette butts containing your DNA at any of the properties?'

'No, I didn't. I had a butt bin I kept in the van. Believe it or not, I'm actually a bit of a neat freak.'

'Okay, good on you, but what about when you were at work before and after installations? Did you dispose of butts there when you had a smoke?'

'Well, yeah, in the big bin outside. I had to smoke around the back.'

'And where did you empty your butt bin?'

'Sometimes at work, sometimes at home.'

'So, it would have been pretty easy for someone to get hold of your cigarette butts then, even if they were disposed of correctly?'

'Yeah, I guess. Is that good?'

'Well, yes. It shows how the butts could have been planted.'

'That's something, right?'

Jack nodded. 'It is but we've still got lots of other evidence to explain away. Continuing on, you are saying that fingerprints matching yours found at the houses were left when you were working there?'

'Yeah, I am, and they can't prove any different.'

'That's true, they can't. But they will question why items such as a TAG gold watch, an iPad, a camera and a set of sterling silver candlesticks had your prints on them.' Jack paused after he said this, raising his eyes to meet Rusty's in a questioning manner.

'Fine, I'll admit I might have picked some stuff up, just to take a closer look, but I never nicked it. I just told you I don't do that. And, by the way, how can I be charged with stealing all the stuff if only some of the items have got my prints on them?'

'The fact that all the items were found together would suggest the same person stole them. You might have worn gloves on some occasions. It's a point I can argue but that's a long way off yet.'

Rusty just shook his head.

'On that topic, though, how did you touch those items if there was someone in the house with you?'

'People don't normally hang around and watch you work. They go outside, watch TV, make phone calls. Sometimes they nip down to the shops.' Rusty shrugged. 'It wasn't like I picked stuff up at every house.'

'Thank goodness,' Jack mumbled under his breath, coming back to the sticky question of how the alleged framer would know what Rusty *had* touched.

Rusty gave one of his best glares. 'What did you say?'

Shaking his head, Jack kept writing. 'Nothing. You didn't tell anyone you picked stuff up?'

'No, I didn't. That would be stupid.'

As opposed to picking the stuff up in the first place, Jack thought, suddenly weary with the whole situation. Looking up from his notes he said, 'Okay, to wrap up, you are saying that the stolen property located at your place of residence was not put there by you?'

'That's exactly what I'm saying. Someone planted it.'

Jack sighed. 'All right.'

'You think I did it, don't you?'

'I didn't say that,' Jack replied, gathering his papers into a pile.

'No, but you don't need to say it, I can tell by the way you're acting.'

'Oh really?'

'Yep, I can. You might think I'm dumb, but I'm not.'

'I don't think you're dumb.'

'Sure you don't.'

Jack opened his briefcase and stuck the papers and his

pen inside. 'Rusty can you just work with me rather than all this posturing?'

'Whatever,' Rusty mumbled.

'All right, I think I've got enough to go on for now. I'll see you on Saturday.'

'Yeah, see ya.'

Arriving back at work by two, Jack put Rusty out of his mind and concentrated on getting his own work done. He couldn't help but think that fate had smiled upon him when his three o'clock appointment was cancelled, allowing him to leave the office at four o'clock. It was something he never would have done ten years ago.

Driving home, he let his mind drift back to Rusty. Jack still had no idea if he was dealing with a skilled liar or a genuine miscarriage of justice. More than anything, Danny's father was his own worst enemy with his continuing need to be combative. He smiled wryly as he remembered Rusty's assurances that he wasn't dumb, which echoed Danny's words from the week before. What was the old saying about the apple not falling far from the tree?

Pulling up at the lights next to a woman with a red handbag, Jack thought about the missing Coach bag again. Rusty had seemed genuinely confused by the picture, further cementing the fact in Jack's mind that, if nothing else, he hadn't had anything to do with its disappearance. Jack didn't like loose ends, but this was one he would have to let go, as he had no time to pursue it any further. At this point he was leaning towards getting the lightest sentence possible, with a promise of an approved rehabilitation program after release. That was something he might be able to manage.

With Erin and the kids visiting her parents, Jack didn't need to feel bad about spending his early mark time with Danny. Normally home by five, he did his best to give Erin a break and do the baths and pre-dinner play. On any day he got home earlier, he would usually take the boys for a swim or a run outside in the yard and he was relieved he didn't have to disappoint them today. In hindsight, he probably shouldn't have promised Danny a driving lesson today, but he'd needed something to motivate him.

Danny was on the phone when he walked inside, so Jack quickly got changed and made himself a thick chicken and roast potato sandwich from the leftovers in the fridge to quell his hunger pangs. He walked into the lounge room and motioned for Danny to end his call so they could get going, then headed outside. Autumn was definitely starting to set in, with the afternoon air already cooling down considerably. It was funny how March could be like that, Jack thought. Just last week they'd had a late summer heatwave and had been in the pool at this time of day. Hearing the door close, Jack headed over to the garage.

Danny stopped short when Jack walked over to his Audi and opened the driver's door.

'What?' Jack asked, looking over the top of the open door with one foot inside the vehicle. 'You can't burn off just yet, I'm taking you out to a back road without any traffic.'

'No, I realise that. I just can't believe you're letting me drive the Audi. I thought we'd be going in Erin's car,' he said, looking over to where the Honda Odyssey was usually parked.

'Well apart from the fact Erin's not here, her car is automatic,' Jack replied. 'You need to start in a manual.

Come on, jump in.'

'How come your car isn't automatic? Isn't it easier to drive?'

'I'm a purist, Dan. In my opinion if you drive a European car it needs to be manual. Besides the fact I like changing gears.'

Danny slid into the passenger seat and fastened his seat belt. 'I seriously can't believe you're letting me drive your car.'

'Why wouldn't I?'

'Well, because it's expensive. What if I crash it?'

'We won't be driving fast enough to crash today. Besides it's fully insured and it's not *that* expensive. If I drove a Lamborghini I might think twice about it.' Jack decided not to mention the hefty excess for young male drivers his insurance company had quoted him when he'd rung to put Danny on his policy.

'I remember the first time you took me for a drive in your car. It was, like, the coolest thing ever.'

Smiling at the memory, Jack nodded. 'That was actually my first Audi. I thought it was pretty cool too.'

'This is a different one though, right?'

'Uh huh. I've had two since then. I usually trade up every three or four years.'

'Why do you always get the same colour?'

'Again, I'm a purist. It has to be black.'

'You're sure about this?'

Jack shook his head before starting the car. 'Dan, stop stressing. You'll be fine.'

Danny looked out the window for a moment before responding. 'Thanks, Jack,' he finally murmured. 'For everything.'

'You're totally welcome.'

Jack joined Danny at the dining room table that night. Although Danny appeared to be making good progress with his schoolwork, Jack wasn't totally convinced he was working to full capacity. He figured that sitting with him for a couple of hours each evening would up his effort level.

Danny had his measure. 'You don't have to babysit me. I'm getting stuff done.'

'I know you are. I just thought it might be nice to hang out while we worked.'

Considering this for a moment, Danny nodded. 'Okay.'

Slipping his reading glasses on, Jack opened Rusty's file.

Danny set up his books and opened his laptop. 'Since when do you wear specs?' he asked.

'Since I hit my early forties. Pretty much everyone needs them for reading by then.'

'Really? I never knew that.'

'Neither did I until I had to hold everything at arm's length to read it.'

They worked in silence for a while, Jack watching Danny as unobtrusively as possible, happy to see he did seem to be working diligently. In fact, Danny was so engrossed in his work, he got a fright when Jack's phone vibrated on the table.

'Aren't you going to get that?' he asked.

Jack shook his head. 'No, it's a telemarketer. They call at the same time every night.'

'Oh, right.'

'On the subject of phones, though, thanks so much for changing my ring tone. I was in a meeting with a client when Bob The Builder came blaring out. I was so embarrassed.'

Danny burst out laughing. 'Sorry.'

'You don't sound very sorry.'

'I was just fooling around. Everyone does it. And Bob is pretty harmless. It's not like I put a rude song on or something.'

'Well, I guess I should be grateful for that. Luckily my client was a parent and could relate.'

'There you go, I helped you out.'

'I can do without that kind of help, thanks.'

Danny was still smiling. 'All right, fine.'

Shaking his head, Jack was smiling too as he got back to work.

CHAPTER SEVEN

Despite the effort required to get up and swim with Danny each morning, Jack embraced the challenge. He had forgotten just how beautiful it was to watch the sun rise while in the pool and, as Danny kept telling him, it really wasn't that cool in the water, once you got moving. He was reminded too, that it was a great way to start the day and he had so much more energy and focus as he headed off for work, rather than having to rely on coffee to kick his brain into gear.

On Friday, he managed to wake without his alarm and was in the water before Danny. 'Hey, sleepyhead,' he teased, as the tousle haired teenager trudged into the pool area.

Danny gave a half-hearted nod and rubbed his eyes. 'Hey,' he grunted, dropping his towel and heading for the deep end.

'What's up? Too much Facebooking when you're supposed to be sleeping?'

'Too much school work more like it,' Danny grumbled, before diving in.

Jack continued kicking on the kickboard for a while, waiting for Danny to warm up and wake up. He watched with envy as Danny completed lap after lap in his smooth, efficient freestyle stroke, with seemingly little effort. Despite having done swimming lessons as a child, Jack had come to realise his lack of squad experience was something that could never really be made up as an adult. He had done stroke correction and considered himself a decent swimmer, but his perfectionist nature still struggled with the knowledge that he would never match Danny's skill level.

By the time he'd knocked out a solid four hundred metres, Danny was in a more sociable mood. 'What kind of warm up is that?' he asked, pausing to watch Jack finish a lap of leisurely freestyle kick.

'A slow one. I didn't have your expert knowledge to go by.'

'Yeah, well, that's no excuse to turn into a geriatric. I reckon we're gonna do some distance this morning. Two eight hundreds, then three four hundreds. Twenty second rest interval and negative split for each one.'

Jack's eyes widened as he tossed his kickboard up on the side. 'You trying to kill me?'

'That's only two point eight k. I usually do four or five.'

'Righto, no need to rub it in. Tell you what, I'll just keep going until you finish.'

'All right but don't wimp out on the negative split.'

'No, I won't.'

Danny navigated to the stopwatch function on his watch, then paused to grin wickedly. 'See you on the other side,' he said, pressing the reset button then pushing off the wall in one smooth motion.

'Yeah, see ya.' Jack smiled as he programmed his own watch, then pushed off as well.

Jack and Erin had deliberated long and hard about how to achieve the best work/life balance for both of them while their children were small. Erin's job as a music composer for an advertising company was relatively flexible and, with family help, she could manage two mornings of work in her home studio but needed at least one full day at the office. It was when they were considering hiring a nanny that Jack had decided that he should be the stay at home parent for that day.

He had been nervous when he had put forward the proposal of working at four-day week to the partners at Kendall and Masters. Given that they had offered him a partnership only three months before, Jack didn't imagine they would appreciate him wanting to work less hours, rather than more. What he didn't realise was how invested they were in keeping him there. Relieved that Jack hadn't refused the partnership offer because he was looking to pursue employment elsewhere, the partners had accepted the proposal with open arms, even suggesting he should have permanent long weekends and take Fridays off.

Making his way to the kitchen after a long, leisurely shower, Danny smiled at the sight of Jack decked out in tracksuit pants and a t-shirt. Ensconced behind the kitchen bench, he was making a sandwich on a surface cluttered with breakfast paraphernalia. The boys were there too, each nibbling a slice of toast, Sam in his school uniform and Josh still in his pyjamas. Pausing to exchange a high five with Josh and to touch knuckles with Sam, Danny pulled up a stool at the breakfast bar and reached for a slice of raisin toast from the pile on the serving platter. 'Who said lawyers can't cook?' he joked.

'Ha, ha,' Jack said. 'And for the record, I can cook.' He started packing Sam's lunchbox and attempted, unsuccessfully, to fit carrot sticks in one of the compartments.

'*Dad,*' Sam giggled, 'they go in the green bit, the grapes go in the blue part.'

'Of course they do,' Jack agreed, scooping up the grapes and transferring them and the carrots to their correct section. 'Vegemite sandwiches are okay, right?'

'Yeah,' Sam said wearily, 'we're not allowed to have peanut butter anymore.'

'Allergies,' Jack said, sensing Danny's unasked question.

'Right.' Danny reached for the Nutri Grain and a bowl. 'Don't suppose there's any of that lasagne left from last night?'

'No, Erin grabbed the last bit for her lunch. Tell you what though, if you look after Josh and keep an ear out for the twins, I'll get us both a breakfast burger on the way home from taking Sam to school.'

'Deal.'

'Thanks, mate, it's so much easier if I don't have to pack the others in the car as well. I totally understand why school drop is my job every morning.' Jack filled a water bottle and packed it and the lunchbox into Sam's school bag. 'Right, Sammy, finish your milk and come and clean your teeth.' Dropping the school bag near the door he motioned for Sam to drink faster and said to Danny, 'Joshy has had some porridge, just see if you can convince him to eat the rest of his toast.'

'Sure,' Danny mumbled, through a mouthful of cereal.

When Jack arrived back forty minutes later Josh was watching Fireman Sam while Danny was engaged in a ball rolling game with Charlotte. 'You're a natural,' he said with a smile, dropping his keys on the hook near the door and putting their takeaway breakfast on the bench.

'I don't know about that. Sorry I had to put the TV on, but I couldn't keep both of them under control at the same time.'

'Totally fine, Dan, you've gotta do what you've gotta do sometimes. If you put Charlotte in the highchair now I'll give her some porridge, hopefully before Chloe wakes up. And you can have your burger.'

'Awesome. I'm starving.'

'Yeah tell me about it, you killed me with that session today. I got extra bacon and a hash brown on the burgers to fill the gaping hunger hole.'

Danny carefully deposited Charlotte into her chair before ripping the paper takeaway bag open. 'Let me at it. Which drink is mine?'

'The medium one, it's hot chocolate. You're smart enough not to drink coffee yet.' Jack put a bib on Charlotte then had a swig of his flat white and a bite of burger before turning his attention to making her porridge.

Attacking his burger, Danny didn't speak again until it was half gone. 'Man, that's good,' he said, pausing to mop up the egg yolk running down his hand.

'Angie's are the best,' Jack agreed, alternating between bites of his roll and stirring the porridge.

'I'm guessing we're not gonna get much done today.'

'All good, buddy, you work on in your room and I'll look after them.'

'But you won't get your stuff done and it's my fault. That's not fair.'

'Tell you what, you get stuck in now then you can help me take them for a swim at about eleven. It'll wear them out and all three of them will conk out for at least two hours.'

'All right, but how are you going to get everything done?' Danny's gaze took in the cluttered bench and the overflowing sink.

'I'm on it Dan, don't worry.'

Jack could see the shock on Danny's face when he emerged from his room at ten forty-five. Taking in the spotless kitchen, piles of clean folded clothes on the dining table and the sound of the washing machine in the background, the teenager stared at Jack as he sat playing trains with Josh while the twins played in the play pen.

'Something wrong?' Jack asked with a smile.

'What the hell, Jack? How did you get all that done?'

Before Jack could answer a small, grey-haired woman emerged from the laundry. Spying Danny, she broke into a warm smile and exclaimed, 'You must be Danny! I'm so pleased to meet you.'

Throwing Jack a puzzled glance, Danny managed an uncertain smile. 'Yes, I am.'

'Gosh, look how tall you are! You're right Jack he's not a little boy any more.'

Even more puzzled now, Danny looked closer at the woman. 'I'm sorry, how do you know me?'

The woman shook her head and placed a hand on her chest. 'Oh, forgive me, love, I've just heard so much about you and seen lots of photos. I'm Edna.'

'Right,' Danny said, still looking bewildered.

'Edna has been my cleaner for a long time, even before you and I met,' Jack explained. 'That's why she knows so much about you.'

'You changed his life,' Edna said. 'All he used to do was work. I barely had to clean anything because he was never here. Now I've got my work cut out for me with all this chaos, and I love it,' she added, still beaming at Danny.

'Oh, yeah,' Danny said. 'I do remember Jack talking about you.'

'It's great you could come and spend some time here while your mother is away.' Edna uncoiled the vacuum cleaner cord and plugged it in.

Danny shot Jack a grateful look. 'Yeah, it worked out pretty well for everyone,' he agreed.

'All right, let's get everyone organised for the pool and then I can get the vacuuming done,' Edna said. 'Their swimming things are on the couch there.'

Jack gathered the trains and put them in the toy box. 'I don't know what I'd do without you, Edna.'

The enclosed portable toddler ledge made swimming with the kids much simpler and safer. Having Danny there to help him made it seem almost easy. Jack enjoyed splashing with the twins on the step while Danny took Josh out into the main area and treated him to the kind of non-stop jumping and paddling three-year-old boys couldn't get enough of.

'He's a great swimmer,' Danny said, as he hoisted Josh up to his shoulders, ready for him to leap off yet again.

'Yeah, he's a real little fish and I feel bad when I have to keep him contained here in the enclosure with the twins. But I don't have enough arms to keep all three of them under control.'

As if to illustrate his point Chloe launched herself at Jack, knocking him backwards and under the water. Spying an opportunity, Charlotte hoisted herself onto his torso and toddled the length of his chest before tumbling off.

'Hey, easy, girls,' Jack gasped when he finally managed to sit back up. Giggling, Chloe got ready to launch herself again, but Jack was ready this time and caught her mid leap. 'More, Dadda,' she protested, her legs kicking furiously behind her.

'No, Daddy's had enough of that one,' Jack said, turning her around and setting her back on her feet. 'Here get the fish.' He picked up the bucket of sinkable toys and threw them in various positions in the enclosure. 'You too, Char,' he added as Charlotte started to climb up onto the edge.

As Jack hoped, the fish were a good distraction and the twins immersed themselves not only in the water, but in a toddler game of their own making, babbling to each other in what he and Erin was sure was their own special language. He loved watching the girls play together, knowing that being identical twins gave them a special bond that would hopefully continue throughout their lives. While they had Erin's facial features and hair colour, they had inherited Jack's dark eyes and he often saw glimpses of his own mother in them. It was a bittersweet thought, for while he was sure his parents could see their grandchildren, it wasn't the same as having them physically there.

Jack leaned back on his elbows for a moment, enjoying the warmth of the sun and the balmy temperature of the pool water. It was nice to step away from the stress of Rusty's case for a while and just embrace the moment. He was so glad he had made the choice to take Friday's off, allowing him this carefree play time that would all too soon be replaced with pre-school and other activities. It hadn't taken long for Jack to realise how much went into caring for three children under three while also keeping the household running, even for a day, so getting Edna in for a few hours to clean was a no-brainer. While she shook her head in mock horror at the work to be done, in reality she thrived on it and loved that her presence allowed Jack time to just enjoy the kids.

After an hour, the kids were still going strong but Jack and Danny were flagging. 'I don't think Josh has an off switch,' Danny said wearily, as he gathered up the little boy to be thrown like a ball for the tenth time. 'I'm ready for a serious nap.'

'Yeah, his energy levels range from very high to extreme,' Jack agreed, as he paddled across the shallow end, alternating each twin with piggy back rides. 'I reckon we're all ready for lunch and a sleep.' Stopping at the other side, he manoeuvred Chloe around to his hip and scooped Charlotte up with his other arm. 'Okay, time to get out now.' He ignored the girls' pleas of 'More! More!' and climbed the steps as Josh, ever the negotiator, bargained for three more jumps. 'All right, three and that's it,' Jack said in his best stern voice. 'Don't let him wheedle any more out of you, Dan.'

'Don't worry, I won't. I reckon I'm going to faint if I don't eat soon.'

'Yep, I'm with you.'

When he noticed the last of the three jumps was done, Jack spoke before Josh could begin his usual extended exit from the water. 'Out now, Joshua! It's lunch time.' Wrapping towels around the girls, he shepherded them out the gate and left Danny to wrangle Josh back inside.

As tempting as it was to snuggle down with the children for a sleep, Jack fortified himself with a strong iced coffee and made the most of the opportunity to get some work done. Danny wavered for a moment, eyeing the comfortable couch longingly before gathering his own books and laptop and joining Jack at the table.

'I can't believe how quickly they fall asleep. I reckon Josh was still chewing when his eyes closed.'

Jack smiled. 'He does that a lot. Swimming is a godsend. It's guaranteed to zonk them out no matter how hard they try to resist,' he said.

Even though he had his laptop set up and his books open, Danny wasn't in any hurry to start work. 'Erin doesn't know Edna comes, does she?' he asked.

Jack shook his head. 'I was going to ask you not to mention it. How did you know?'

'Josh showed me his sticker book and told me we can't tell Mum about Edna until all the pages are full.'

'I'm teaching him how to be discreet and confidential. You're never too young to learn that.'

Danny burst out laughing. 'Yeah, right.'

Jack laughed too. 'It's amazing what you can bribe a three-year-old to do and I'm actually surprised he's kept so quiet. Joshy is not known for his discretion.'

'So why don't you want Erin to know?'

'Well, it makes me look like a total failure if I can't do for one day what she does every other day. It took me one morning looking after the munchkins by myself to realise I needed help to make it all happen. So, I called in my trusty reinforcement.'

'Being married is complicated.'

'Yeah, it can be, but it trumps living in a clean, quiet house by yourself.'

'I guess that would be pretty lonely. Doesn't Erin realise

though when everything is so clean and organised?'

'No, because by the time she gets home the lounge is messy again and there are crumbs on the bench from afternoon tea and I leave the folded washing in the laundry to make it look like I just ran out of time.'

'Wow! Total stealth.'

'I know. I could be a spy, right?'

Danny laughed. 'Yeah, in your dreams.'

'I'm a bit offended by that statement. Can I get back to my work now?'

'Just one more question. What do you usually do when they're asleep?'

'It depends. If I'm really tired then I sleep too, but what I love to do is watch Survivor. I've got about three seasons taped and I'm working through them.'

'I can't believe you watch reality TV.' Danny widened his eyes in mock horror.

'Everyone's got a vice and I'm not ashamed to admit mine is Survivor. Have you ever watched it?'

'Nah.'

'You've gotta see it, I reckon you'd love it. Lots of ocean challenges.'

'Happy to give it a go. Can I watch it now?'

'Nice try. When your work's done, you can watch what you like,' said Jack.

Danny gave him a sour look.

'All right, sleep time is ticking away. Let's both get stuck into it.'

Watching Danny interacting with the boys and consuming vast quantities of pizza that night, Jack couldn't believe it was the same non-communicative teenager he had encountered just a week before. It always did his heart good to watch how easily Danny fitted in with his family and he was glad he had come to stay for a while. While the circumstances weren't the best, Jack couldn't help but be grateful for this unexpected chunk of time to spend together. Over the years, Danny had visited several times, but never for a month.

'I love pizza night!' Sam declared, reaching for another slice of ham and pineapple.

'We all do,' Erin agreed, as she assisted Sam to separate the piece he had his hand on.

'Here, here,' Jack nodded as he tucked into the last slice of Moroccan lamb. 'I made a standing order at Angie's so we don't have to wait any more. It's getting crazy busy there these days.'

'Well, they do the best pizza,' Erin said, wiping her fingers on a piece of paper towel. 'I guess a lot of people have the same idea on Friday night.' Noticing Danny looking longingly at one of the remaining slices of supreme, she laughed. 'It's okay, Danny, have as much as you want. We ordered extra.'

'Are you sure? I seem to have eaten double what everyone else has.'

Jack laughed. 'Enjoy it while you can. One of my fondest teenage memories is stuffing my face without even knowing what a calorie was.'

Needing no further urging, Danny devoured another slice.

Jack loved how much more relaxing a Friday evening was when he hadn't put a long day in at the office first. True, looking after the kids was just as busy, but it was a different kind of end of day exhaustion. He thought it had a lot to do with not having to leave the house except for school drop off and pick up. Plus, there was something decadent about having a weekday off when the rest of the world was toiling away. It wasn't that he didn't love his job, but Jack had realised he loved it no less by working four days rather than five.

'I got an email from Mr McGregor today,' Jack said, leaning over to pull the crust off Josh's pizza. Although Josh would insist on taking a full slice, he only ever ate the crust. Jack figured he saved lots of calories by eating Josh's crustless leftovers.

Danny stopped chewing. 'Oh.'

'Oh, no, it's fine. He was just checking in. I was happy to be able to tell him what good progress you're making.'

'Right. That's good. I thought you were going to say he'd changed his mind and I had to go home.'

'No, no, nothing like that.'

'You have been working hard,' Erin said.

Danny nodded. 'Yeah, I don't think I've ever studied this much in one week before.'

'I know I'm a broken record, Dan, but you're so capable. You just need to put your mind to it.'

Danny tore off a slice of garlic bread. 'So everybody keeps saying,' he murmured.

CHAPTER EIGHT

Saturday morning was taken up with the usual flurry of activity that accompanied having four small children. While Erin and Izzy took the girls to kinder gym, Jack headed to soccer with the boys. It was a great program that focussed on skill building and participation, rather than competition, and normally he enjoyed watching Sam and Josh play, but today Jack made the most of the window of time to make a phone call. He had been meaning to talk to Kit Smith, the LJ Hooker property manager that had handled Rusty's unit lease, all week. He dialled her mobile number and leaned his notebook on the seat next to him and clicked his pen on. Kit's phone rang and rang and Jack was getting ready to leave a message when she finally answered.

'Hello,' she mumbled, her voice thick with sleep.

'Kit?' Jack asked, a little confused at the unprofessional greeting.

'Yeah, who's this?'

'My name is Jack Nolan. I'm sorry, did I wake you?'

'Uh, yeah. But that's okay. I should be getting up anyway.'

'My sincere apologies. I just assumed that someone in real estate would be at work on a Saturday morning. Serves me right for generalising.'

'Don't worry about it. I *am* supposed to be at work but I decided to have a mental health day instead. Don't tell my manager,' Kit said with a laugh. 'She's the reason I need a day off.'

'Oh. Hard taskmaster, is she?'

'No, it's more of a personality thing. I think she's a bit threatened by me, you know being younger and all that. She doesn't want anyone else to be as successful as her.'

'Right,' Jack replied, wondering why Kit had told him all that. Saying she wasn't feeling well would have done.

'Sorry, I've gone off track. Why are you calling?'

'Uh, as I said my name is Jack Nolan from Kendall and Masters Solicitors and I'm representing Rusty Anderson. You remember him?'

'Um, let me think. Oh, yeah, that's it. From the place in Parramatta, right? Isn't he in jail?'

'Yes, he is, but he's only awaiting trial at the moment. I just wanted to verify a few things.'

'All right. Can you just hang on a sec, I'm googling you now.'

Jack was puzzled by this announcement. 'Pardon?'

'I'm just googling you to make sure I'm talking to a legit person.'

'Uh, all right. My mobile number is on the firm website if you want to ring me back.'

'No, it's fine, your voice matches your picture.'

'Excuse me?'

'I'm just looking at your photo now. I wasn't expecting someone so handsome. Nice suit, what is it, an Armani?'

'Uh, possibly, I can't remember what I was wearing the day they took the picture.'

'I know my designer brands and I reckon it's definitely

Armani. Great tie too.'

'Uh, thanks.' If she asks me what I'm wearing now I'm going to hang up, Jack thought.

'So, Jack Nolan, in the Armani suit, what can I help you with?'

Jack furrowed his brow, taken aback by Kit's flirty tone. Trying to sound more serious, he said, 'Like I said, I'm representing Rusty and I just wanted to verify a few things.'

'Sure.'

'Well, first of all, what were your impressions of him as a tenant?'

'Um, fine, I guess. He looked a bit rough and ready but he had the bond and he paid his rent on time. He had permanent employment at a reputable company. He kept the place pretty neat. There were no complaints from others in the block about noise or anything.'

'And you were aware he'd previously been in jail.'

'Uh, yes. I was a bit dubious about offering him the lease, but he'd been through a program and they give the agency a cash bonus if you take them. My manager gave the okay.'

'The one who's on your case now?'

'No, not *her*.'

Jack was surprised at the venom in Kit's tone. 'You really don't like her, do you?'

'No, I don't. But hey, that's the way life goes, right? The pretty girls get everything they want.'

'I suppose they do sometimes,' Jack said, realising he'd gotten off track again. 'Getting back to Rusty, were you surprised when you heard about the stolen property being found there?'

'Hmmm…'

'Kit?'

'Uh, I'm not sure if I should say this.'

'Please just tell me. I need to know all the facts.'

'Well, when I showed him around, I explained how the garage was not included and that he wouldn't be getting a key. He just laughed and said that if he wanted to, he'd be able to pick the lock in about five seconds.'

'Did that concern you?'

'Not really. I thought he was joking. But then after all this happened I realised maybe he wasn't.'

'Right. Thanks for telling me. Anything else?'

'No, I don't think so.' Kit paused a moment and laughed. 'Well, he did try and pick me up.'

'Really?'

She laughed again. 'Yeah. But it was fine. I just let him know I don't date clients.'

'You didn't feel threatened in any way?'

'Oh no, nothing like that. I just thought he was a bit cheeky.'

Jack sighed. 'Right. That's great. Thanks, Kit.'

Revelling in the silence of his work office, Jack felt a pang of guilt. After soccer he had dropped the boys at Erin's sister's house, having already told Erin he would head out to the prison and he wasn't sure how long he would be. He did see Rusty, but his visit was cut short by a fire drill. While driving back through town, the idea of dropping into work for an hour had occurred to him. While some of his colleagues worked on Saturday mornings to catch up, the place was usually deserted by lunch time.

Jack pushed the guilt away. The boys were being well cared for and would be having fun playing with their cousins. Danny was making good progress with his school work and didn't need constant supervision. And Erin and the twins were having lunch with her parents. So, having an hour to himself wasn't a crime.

Rusty had verified what Kit said about the lock, but had told Jack that he was actually pointing out that it was a security flaw in the building. 'I was just telling her that if I could pick the lock, then any other joker off the street could too,' Rusty had said. He had also confirmed he had invited Kit for a drink but she had declined.

Sighing, Jack underlined Rusty's words on his notebook. Checking through the reports again, he studied Rusty's criminal record and the various crimes he had been charged with: Vandalism, Trespass, Public Nuisance, Illegal Bookmaking, DVD Piracy, and Arson. They were hardly minor criminal acts but, what he was saying was true, he had never been charged with burglary of any kind.

Looking back through the notes Victor Kingston had made, Jack came across a highlighted paragraph. Having apparently told Victor what he'd told Jack, Rusty had further explained the reason why he did not, in his own words, "break into people's houses and nick their stuff".

RA: When I was a kid Dad bought this bike home one day and gave it to me. It was a real beauty and when I asked Dad where he got it he said it fell off the back of a truck. I was only, like, seven and I didn't know what that meant, so I thought cool, I've got a new bike.

VK: All right, then what happened?

RA: Well I'm riding it around one day, real proud that I've got this nice BMX and these big kids came up and starting yelling at me. They called me a thief. They dragged me off the bike and turned it over and sure enough there was a name on there. It turned out the bike belonged to their little brother. It had been stolen from their house.

VK: Stolen by your father?

RA: I guess so. Either by him or one of his mates.

VK: So what happened then?

RA: They told everyone at school and I got picked on so bad after that. I decided that no matter what I would never do that.

VK: You would never do what?

RA: Steal stuff from someone.

VK: Did you confront your father about it?

RA: Yeah. He just laughed at me and said, 'You win some and you lose some'.

Jack leaned back in his chair and put his feet up on the desk. It was something he would never dream of doing on a normal work day, but he liked the freedom of doing it when the place was empty. Staring out the window at the entrance to the Botanic Gardens he thought about fathers and sons. As he had learned in the past few years, being a father was a huge responsibility. Children watch and listen to everything you do and their characters are formed by what goes on around them.

Watching a family riding along the bike path into the gardens, Jack felt a dull anger build as he contemplated that Rusty's father had given no thought to how his myriad of irresponsible actions would adversely affect the lives of both of his sons. In that moment, Jack felt sympathy for the seven-year-old Rusty, who had been enrolled at the school of hard knocks long before he should have been.

Picking up the file again, Jack flipped through it idly, looking for, he wasn't sure, what. Near the bottom of the pile, he found a next of kin form, listing Rusty's parents as first contact at their address in Shell Park, which was a tiny village adjacent to Sunset Point. This information gave Jack pause for two reasons. Firstly, he had assumed, for whatever reason, that Rusty came from a broken home. It was bad form for a solicitor to assume such a thing and he acknowledged what a sweeping generalisation it was. Secondly, in the same vein, he had also believed that Rusty was not in regular contact with his family, but once again this was clearly not the case. He didn't know if either piece of information would have any impact on the case, in fact they probably wouldn't, but they did cause his thoughts about Rusty to shift a little.

Swivelling his chair slightly, Jack looked back over at the paperwork on his desk. Maybe it was time to give Rusty the benefit of the doubt and seriously consider the possibility that he had been framed. Looking at his watch, Jack decided he'd had enough for the moment and that he needed to spend an afternoon with his own children. And perhaps take them out to dinner for a treat.

Smiling, Jack dropped his feet back down to the floor and gathered the papers together, before picking up the phone to make a reservation.

The dining room was not the cosiest space in the house but it was the most practical place to spend time together while they worked. Sitting down at eight thirty for what had become their nightly ritual, Jack and Danny set up their laptops and notebooks on the table and immersed themselves in their respective tasks. Although both were left handed, they configured their spaces completely differently. While Jack kept his notes to the immediate left of his laptop and neatly stacked everything else he needed above that, Danny turned almost side on to write, creating a unique but cluttered arrangement, that took up a lot of room. Just as well it was an eight-seater table, Jack thought, as he rubbed his arms to ward off the chilly night breeze.

'You warm enough?' he asked Danny five minutes later.

'Yeah, totally fine,' Danny replied, engrossed in whatever he was looking at on his laptop.

Jack was actually feeling slightly cold now, but wasn't prepared to show Danny what an old man he was by putting on warmer clothes. While it had been quite a hot day, the temperature had dropped noticeably once the sun set. Considering Danny was the Queenslander, he should be the one rugging himself up, Jack thought in annoyance, trying to ignore the goose bumps on his arms.

'Want a hot chocolate?' he asked five minutes later, hoping that might warm him a bit.

'Yeah, thanks,' Danny replied.

Jack headed into the kitchen, flicked the electric jug on and grabbed the tin of Cadbury drinking chocolate from the pantry. Spying a hot water bottle on the top shelf, he paused for a moment. Erin often used hot water bottles to warm the kids' beds in the depths of winter and right now the one on the shelf looked pretty inviting. The kettle was boiling anyway, so it would be easy enough to fill.

Danny's voice stopped him in his tracks. 'Got any bikkies?'

'Yeah, sure,' Jack said. He picked up a packet of custard creams and stepped out of the pantry with a last wistful glance at the top shelf. He smiled, thinking of all the times he had told Danny and his own kids to do their own thing and not to worry what other people thought. He didn't feel middle aged and people told him he didn't look it, but watching Danny grow up made him much more aware he was almost forty-four and would soon be closer to fifty than forty. Right now, he was willing to freeze rather than exhibit any kind of weakness to his young friend.

Jack shook his head as he spooned chocolate into two mugs, enjoying the moment, despite the chill in the air. While he and Danny were both doing their own thing and weren't really talking much, it was nice to hang out all the same. The last time they had spent this much time together had been back at the Beach House, which seemed like a whole other lifetime now.

It wasn't until they'd been hard at work for an hour that Jack realised Erin hadn't come down to say goodnight. She always pottered around the kitchen and lounge room before bed and if he was staying up later, such as when he had work to do, she would always pop in to say goodnight … unless she was mad about something.

Jack paused in his typing and cast his mind back over then evening. They'd had a great time out at dinner, with no arguments or disagreements. The boys had behaved themselves, enjoying the novelty of taking Danny to their favourite restaurant. They had all laughed at Josh's off key rendition of Big Red Car and smiled fondly as Sam explained the finer points of kindy soccer. During the short drive home, he and Erin had talked, about nothing important, but nothing at all disagreeable.

Jack picked up his pen and tapped it on the writing pad next to his laptop. As happy as their marriage was, he and Erin didn't do conflict well. Jack prided himself on being even tempered and calm but when the pressure got to him, he would withdraw, rather than talk about it. Whereas Erin would go into a hyper façade, busying herself with any number of tasks so she didn't have to stop and admit something was wrong. The fact that she had gone the silent route tonight was definitely a concern.

It wasn't until Danny looked over at him that Jack realised how intense the tapping had become. 'Sorry,' he said, dropping the pen.

'Something up?' Danny asked, reaching for another biscuit.

'Maybe,' Jack replied. 'I think I'm in the doghouse, but I'm not sure why.'

'Yeah, I did notice a bit of a cold shoulder after Grandma left.'

Jack picked up the pen again and started doodling. Erin's mother, Evelyn, babysat the girls while they went out to dinner but hadn't stayed long after they arrived home. She had acted normally and bade Jack goodbye as warmly as she always did when he walked her to her car. While Evelyn could be a bit on the bossy side, she wasn't the kind of person to incite trouble behind the scenes. If she'd felt Jack had done something wrong, she would have come out and said it to his face, as she had done in the past.

'What did Erin do when I took Evelyn down to the car?'

'Nothing much, she was on her phone I think.'

'She didn't say anything to you?'

'Nuh, not really. Just thanks for putting the boys to bed.'

Jack stared at the concentric circles he'd just drawn. Come to think of it, Erin had been very quiet when he got back in, in fact, she hadn't even responded when he'd told her the neighbour's cat was sleeping on her car again. Assuming she hadn't heard him, Jack had gone to retrieve his notes from the study. Erin had remained quiet when she went into the kitchen, but again he had not thought much of it.

'I thought you guys didn't fight much.'

'We don't. But when we do, I usually know what it's about.'

Danny raised his eyebrows and shrugged. 'Maybe she's just tired,' he suggested, focusing on his laptop again. Jack wasn't convinced he was doing schoolwork, but figured he could cut him some slack on a Saturday night.

'Yeah,' Jack agreed, trying to reassure himself that was the truth. Deciding to worry about it in the morning, he waded back into the police report. Although Jack was now giving Rusty the benefit of the doubt, the fact he admitted touching things that had absolutely no bearing on the alarm systems he was installing was a major issue. It also raised the question of how the person who framed him knew which things he had touched. The discovery of cigarette butts with his DNA on them at three of the properties from which items were stolen was another serious issue, especially considering they were in pristine condition, making it highly unlikely they had been there several weeks. If Rusty had been framed, he had made it easy for the actual perpetrator by being careless. Jack could picture him at the pub, boasting about having access to people's valuables. That was the kind of talk that could get you into big trouble.

Losing himself back in the paperwork, Jack was startled when Danny exclaimed, 'Whoa!'

'I never knew researching a social justice topic could be

so exciting,' Jack said dryly without looking up.

'It's a bit of a side issue,' Danny said.

'Sure it is.'

They worked in silence a while longer before Danny spoke again. 'So, do you really not know what you did wrong?'

Shaking his head, Jack said, 'I have no idea.'

'Want me to tell you?'

'What, you're psychic now?'

'Maybe.'

'Dan, what are you talking about?''

Danny eyed Jack carefully for a moment before spinning his computer around.

'Facebook?' Jack glared at Danny. 'Are you seriously telling me Erin is angry about something to do with Facebook when I have absolutely no affiliation with it whatsoever?'

'Yep,' Danny confirmed. Coming around to the other side of the table he sat next to Jack and navigated to his timeline, then clicked on an entry halfway down the page. A photo popped up on the screen. 'Remember this?'

Jack looked at the picture. 'Yeah, of course I do, it was only a couple of weeks ago, at a Legal Industry awards dinner in Sydney. Several people at Kendall and Masters got excellence awards, myself included. Erin didn't even go. I told her not to bother because it was pretty boring if you weren't one of the recipients.'

Danny nodded, then clicked the arrow to the right of the picture. Another image appeared, taken at the same event. He continued to scroll through the photos and Jack grew increasingly impatient.

'Seriously, Dan, I'm not getting anything here. Apart

from the fact I don't know how you got these pictures, they are nothing special. And half of them are over exposed.'

Holding up one hand toward Jack, Danny said, 'Wait!' He moved on to the next picture, a shot of one of the Kendall and Masters partners holding up his award certificate. But equally as obvious, in the background was a clear image of Jack hugging a woman.

As he studied the image on the screen, Jack's stomach clenched, then started churning as Danny scrolled through the rest of the pictures. Although still only in the background of each photo, Jack felt like he was front and centre. The next photos showed him leaning forward to speak in the woman's ear and then the woman placing her hand on Jack's arm and finally rubbing something off Jack's face. The series of photographs blatantly suggested an intimate relationship between Jack and the woman.

'Unbelievable!' was all he could bring himself to say.

Danny shrugged sympathetically.

'So, are you saying Erin could see these?'

Danny nodded slowly.

'But how? Where did they even come from? And how can *you* see them?'

'All right Mr Facebook phobic, I'll dumb it down for you. You know how you have Facebook friends right?'

Jack nodded.

'Well, I'm friends with Erin, okay? Considering you won't embrace social media, she is nice enough to keep me in the loop.'

'Okay, I'm a weird freak because I'm not posting pictures of my lunch every day. But I still don't get what's happening here.'

'Well Erin is friends with Melanie from your work,

right?'

'Yeah, they get along well.'

Danny shook his head. 'No, I mean they're friends on Facebook.'

'All right, she never mentioned it, but fine, if you say so.'

'Well Melanie took these photos at the function and posted them on Facebook a couple of hours ago. I'm assuming other people from your work are also on Facebook and wanted to see her pictures. And given that you're not on Facebook, she tagged Erin instead.'

'Tagged?'

'Yeah it's like a label that goes on the photo so people know it's something they might want to look at. And that's why I saw the photos. Because I'm Erin's friend, I can see that she got tagged and I can see the photos.'

Jack's heart was banging against his ribs now. 'This is unbelievable,' he said again.

'Well not really, it's just photos on a website.'

'No, not the way it works although that pretty much confirms why I have a major aversion to Facebook in the first place. It's unbelievable that of all the background images she could capture she got that.'

'Want to talk about it?'

Jack gave a tight smile and shook his head. 'No, not right now, but thanks all the same. I can assure you it's not what it looks like but I'm going to have to do some major damage control right now.'

'Won't she be asleep?'

'No … she won't,' Jack replied with a sigh as he stood up.

'Good luck,' Danny offered.

'Thanks,' Jack murmured, taking another deep breath before heading across the lounge room and up the stairs.

Erin didn't even look up as Jack walked into the bedroom. Bundled up in flannelette pyjamas, she had the blankets drawn up high around her as she read a magazine. Ducking into the en suite, Jack cleaned his teeth, noticing as he did so, the collection of toys on the vanity unit. Two of Josh's trains were perched on the flat edge of the sink, along with Sam's Lightning McQueen car. The girls' baby monitor was in the mix too. Sam and Josh had obviously been playing walkie-talkie with it again. Jack shook his head, perplexed as to why Mum and Dad's bathroom had become such a fun play spot. Spitting out the toothpaste, Jack gave his mouth a quick rinse and grabbed the monitor, worried it might get wet. Taking it out with him, he deposited it on his bedside table before getting changed and diving under the covers, glad to finally get warm.

'Cold one tonight,' he said, turning on his side to look at Erin.

'Hmmm,' she agreed, flicking through the pages with more force than necessary and making no effort to look up.

'Danny showed me the pictures,' he said.

'Really?'

'Yeah. I know it looks suss.'

'Just a bit. You didn't think to mention that you ran into your ex "almost fiancée"?'

Jack rolled on to his back, trying to formulate the right response. 'I didn't mention it because I knew you wouldn't like it,' he said finally.

'Funny how you assured me I didn't need to come. Now I know why.'

Jack shook his head, even though Erin wasn't looking at him. 'No, no, it wasn't like that. I had no idea she was going to be there. How could I?'

'I don't know, you tell me.'

'There's nothing to tell. I was really shocked when she appeared.'

'I bet you were.'

'Erin come on, I mean it. I thought I was seeing things.'

'Why was she there anyway? I thought she was back in Tasmania.' Erin still hadn't looked up, but she had stopped flicking the pages, staring instead at a Calvin Klein perfume ad.

'She is, most of the time,' Jack said. 'Her brother runs a catering company in Sydney and sometimes she works functions for him as a waitress if she happens to be visiting.'

'A waitress? I thought she was a legal secretary?'

'She was back when I knew her.'

'So you have had no contact with her at all, then?'

'No, I haven't. Of course I haven't.'

'Looks like you had a great time catching up.'

Jack took the magazine from Erin and grabbed her hand. 'Erin, please let me tell you what happened.'

Erin withdrew her hand and refused to meet Jack's gaze. 'I'm all ears,' she assured him, arms folded and looking straight ahead.

'I saw her when we first arrived and tried to steer clear. But it was no use, she knew I was there and she made a point of coming over to talk to me.'

'And you hugged her.'

'No, she hugged me.'

'Oh, that makes it all right then.'

Jack sighed. 'I spoke to her for about five minutes, you

know, just to be polite.'

'Really? Polite chit chat with her touching your arm and your face?'

Jack hesitated. 'I wasn't comfortable with that but it's just her, she always does that. It used to bug me when she did it to other people when we were together.'

Erin's only response was a sigh.

'She also asked me to handle her divorce,' Jack said.

Erin chuckled mirthlessly. 'Oh, that's not concerning at all. The fact that she's single again and accidentally on purpose bumping into you. What did you say to that?'

'I told her if she's working as a waitress she couldn't afford me. And that I don't do divorces.'

'You really said that?'

'Yes, I did. Do you honestly think I'd take that on?'

Erin's face softened a little. 'You really had no idea she was going to be there?'

'None.'

'And you weren't excited to see her again.'

'No, I wasn't. I guess it was kind of interesting to see where she'd ended up but nothing more than that.'

'And where has she ended up?'

'Heading for divorce apparently. The cool musician she replaced me with turned out to be a bit of a slack husband funnily enough. He was off doing world tours and hanging out with groupies while she was home bringing up the kids alone.'

'You don't sound very sympathetic.'

'What can I say? You live, you learn. I think most people could have seen it coming. Of course I feel sorry for the children, but it sounds like they're used to their father being absent.'

'Nothing else, then?'

'Well, she did ask me if I was on Facebook. I took great delight in telling her I wasn't.'

'I was so jealous when I saw those photos.'

Jack sat up and gently turned Erin's head towards him. 'Why could you possibly be jealous of her?'

Erin still wouldn't meet his gaze. 'Think about it, Jack. You wanted to marry *her* once. That makes me your second choice.'

Jack took both Erin's hands in his. To his relief, she didn't pull away. 'I do not now, nor have I ever, considered you to be some kind of consolation prize,' he said, slowly and deliberately. 'Like I've told you before, Christine did me a favour by ditching me. Her actions eventually led me to you, in a very roundabout way. I've never doubted for a second that you and *our* children were my true destiny.'

A tear ran down Erin's cheek. Jack wiped it away.

'Do you really mean that?' she whispered.

'You know I do,' Jack replied.

* * * * *

Jack was woken by the girls chorusing, 'Mummy!' at six thirty. Charlotte and Chloe were good sleepers and always woke up happy, but they didn't like staying in their own room too long once their eyes were open. Pulling on some socks and a fleece over his pyjama pants and t-shirt, Jack slipped out of the master bedroom, closing the door behind him. Even though he and Erin both craved sleep these days, being the morning person, Jack didn't mind doing the early shift.

Happy to see Sam and Josh still dead to the world, Jack

headed into the twins' room. The two cots were pushed together, allowing the girls to maintain some of the closeness they'd previously had in their shared cot. Erin had struggled with separating them, but had finally agreed it was time.

Spying Jack, the girls made their way to the end of their respective cots.

'Dadda, up!' Chloe said, holding her arms out.

'Up! Up!' echoed Charlotte.

Jack bundled a child in each arm, dropping a kiss on each of their heads as he did so. The logistics of doing everything in unison had challenged him to begin with, but he had soon adapted. He and Erin often joked now about how easy it was to handle just one baby at a time. Jack looked at the pink walls of the room that used to be his home gym and shook his head. He still had moments when it all felt surreal, even when he had two wriggling toddlers in his arms, demanding his attention.

Urging the girls to be quiet, Jack headed down to the lounge room. Charlotte and Chloe loved playing with their teddy bear collection first thing in the morning. They would greet each toy with seemingly genuine affection and chatter away to each other. Placing them in their play pen with the bears, Jack headed out the back door to pick up the paper that the delivery man kindly brought up the driveway for them. With a bit of luck, he might get to read a couple of pages.

It wasn't until Jack came back through the kitchen that he noticed Danny sitting at the dining room table. 'Dan, what are you doing up so early?'

Danny looked up from his computer. 'Xavier asked me to go roller blading this morning. I didn't think you'd mind if I did some work first.' Danny and Erin's oldest nephew, Xavier, had always gotten along well and enjoyed catching up when Danny visited.

'No, of course I don't mind. You've been working really hard and you deserve to have some fun. I don't want you to feel like you're in prison or something.' It took Jack a moment to realise what he had said. 'Sorry, sorry, that was a bad choice of words.'

They looked at each other for a moment and burst out laughing.

'Really, Danny, I'm sorry. I didn't mean to make light of everything.'

'It's okay. I'm used to the fact my father is a jailbird now.'

Shaking his head Jack scanned the headlines of the newspaper.

Danny typed for a few moments before speaking again. 'So, you got yourself out of the doghouse, hey?'

'Yeah, I did,' Jack said with a smile. It was only when he glanced up to check on the twins that he noticed the baby monitor amid Danny's clutter on the table. It was the receiving end of the baby monitor. Which meant that the monitor he had rescued from the en suite last night was the transmitting one. The one they had paid a fortune for because it picked up even the slightest sound. Heat prickled Jack's face and scalp as he asked the question, even though he knew the answer. 'How do you know that?'

'How do you reckon?' Danny raised his eyebrows.

Jack's face flushed a bright red. 'Dan! You can't listen in on other people's private business,' he said. 'I know you kids today think it's normal to record everything and put it all over the internet, but it's just not right. I'm speechless you would stoop so low.'

Danny stared at him in surprise. 'What are you talking about?'

Jack jabbed a finger in the direction of the table. 'The monitor in front of you there.'

'What about it?'

'It's the receive end. The other end was on my bedside table last night, as if you didn't know.'

Danny picked the monitor up and held it out for Jack to see. 'It's not even on. Erin put it here yesterday to remind herself to change the batteries. Did you seriously think I would do that?'

Jack was even more embarrassed now. 'Well how *did* you know I sorted things out?'

'Easy. I figured if you were still in trouble you would have had to sleep down here.'

Feeling the heat leave his face, Jack breathed a sigh of relief. 'Fair call,' he agreed. 'No, actually I reckon I would have bunked in with you. That leather couch is comfortable but not very cosy.'

'It was a bit chilly last night.'

Jack shook his head. 'Believe me, it was arctic when I first got upstairs.'

'So, all is forgiven then? Facebook hasn't destroyed your marriage?'

'No, luckily. But it did cause unnecessary stress.'

'Facebook doesn't cause the stress; it's what people do on there that causes it.'

'You're quite the diplomat when you want to be, aren't you?'

'I try,' Danny said, with a smile.

'Sorry, buddy, I over-reacted without all the facts.

111

That's not a good look for a lawyer.'

'All good. And, Jack, even if it had been on I would have turned it off.'

'I know.' Jack started reading the front-page story for the third time, but gave up when he heard the boys clomping down the stairs. The news was going to have to wait.

CHAPTER NINE

Jack caught the early train to Sydney on Monday, planning to kill two birds with one stone. As well as a work meeting, he had arranged an appointment with Cameron Melville at his office in Mosman. Not knowing much about him, Jack used the travel time to research Rusty's former boss.

According to the bio on his website, Cameron had started his working career as a technician in a fly screen factory in Brisbane. Identified as a diligent worker with promise, he was given management training and had later stepped up and bought the business when it went into voluntary receivership. After relocating to smaller premises and paring down the staff numbers, Cameron managed to re-build the business, and soon expanded to open two other branches on the Gold Coast and Sunshine Coast. The business then merged with a larger company, specialising in high end security screens, at which time Cameron sold his shares and moved to Sydney.

There, Cameron started working in a small business that manufactured basic home alarm systems. Within two years he had purchased the business and then expanded it, and moved on to manufacturing and installing much more sophisticated home security systems. Renamed Melville Security, the company had developed a reputation as one of the best in the security business.

Scratching his chin, Jack looked out the train window. By all accounts, Melville Security specialised in high-end systems in expensive suburbs. Going by the staff photo on the website, the installers and technicians were clean cut and respectable looking. What he couldn't fathom was how Rusty had managed to get a job there.

Melville Security looked exactly as a security company should, with video cameras on the gate and main entrance, and signs announcing that the site was under constant surveillance. Greeted warmly at reception, Jack was offered tea or coffee, before being shown into Cameron Melville's office, right on his designated appointment time. Looking to be in his mid-thirties, Cameron had a thin, wiry build, close cropped sandy blond hair and piercing blue eyes. When Jack had rung and set up the meeting, he had led the receptionist to believe it was regarding a home surveillance system, but Cameron didn't seem overly put out when the real reason behind the visit was revealed.

'No offence, Jack, but I'm surprised Rusty has the means to afford a private solicitor,' Cameron said. 'Wasn't he a Legal Aid case?'

'I'm a friend. Well a friend of his son.'

Cameron eyed him for a moment before nodding slowly. 'Daniel, right? He'd be, what, fifteen now?'

'Sixteen.'

'And he's turned out all right?'

'Yeah, very well.' Jack took his notebook and pen out of his briefcase. 'The fact you just asked if Daniel turned out all right sounds like you are familiar with his background. Did you know Rusty before you hired him?'

Cameron nodded. 'Yes, yes I did. I assumed he would

have told you. We went to school together.'

'Oh, right. No, he didn't mention that,' Jack said, resisting the urge to shake his head in frustration.

'What can I say? Rusty was never one for social conventions.'

'Right, well, I've gathered that. Were you good friends?'

'Yeah, for a while there at least. We played rugby together, and knocked around on the weekends.'

'Uh huh. Did you remain friends after school?'

'Well, no, not exactly. Rusty got offered a rugby scholarship at the Grammar School when we were in grade ten. It was a pretty big deal at the time and he kind of went off in a blaze of glory. We drifted apart then, I mean teenage boys didn't write letters to each other and there was no email or texting of course.'

Jack frowned. 'But Rusty didn't finish school, did he? His file said he left school when he was fifteen.'

'Yeah, he did. For whatever reason the scholarship thing didn't work out and he decided to get a job instead.'

'And your friendship didn't continue when he was working?'

'Uh, not really. My parents thought he was a bad influence and they wanted me to concentrate on school.'

'So, you're saying he was in trouble back when you knew him?'

Cameron nodded. 'I guess. It wasn't anything major, he was just a bit of a tearaway, you know? His dad was a petty crim always on the make and his older brother spent time in juvenile detention and then in jail for burglary. It was pretty hard for Rusty to make his way in a small town. That's why the scholarship was a big deal. It was like his magic ticket out of his background and everyone thought it was a shame he didn't grab it with both hands.'

Jack nodded, torn between the thought that Rusty's life could have been so much better if he had stayed at school, and the reality that if that had happened Danny probably wouldn't exist. Giving himself a mental shake, he focussed back on the job at hand. He didn't have time for philosophical thoughts. 'Right, so how did he end up working with you here?'

'Believe it or not it was Facebook.'

'Seriously?'

'Yeah, I know, I know. If you're anything like me you don't want a bar of it, right?'

Jack's emphatic nod spoke volumes.

'I went to a business networking conference and they pushed social media pretty hard. They explained how it was almost impossible to be in business these days without it, so I reluctantly signed up. They had these teenagers as IT mentors helping us. Anyway, this young kid suggested a good way to make contacts was to find old school friends. Emphasis on the old, I'm sure he thought I was ancient. But I'd always kind of wondered what happened to Rusty so I typed in his name and up he popped.'

'Daniel found him on there too. But he said he'd barely used it.'

'Yes, that's right. When Rusty got out of prison last time they put him through a course that made sure he was up to date with internet and all that stuff. He set it up as part of the course and it just happened to be around the same time I joined. I suggested catching up for a drink and we did.'

'And you offered him a job even though you knew he'd been in jail?'

Cameron put both hands on his desk and laced his fingers together. 'I felt sorry for him. I mean, I've been pretty successful in my life, and here was he emerging from his second stint in the clink, with no prospects. He promised me he'd make a go of it.'

Jack nodded slowly and paused for a moment before asking his next question. 'So how was he as a worker then? Did he do his job properly?'

'Yeah, he did, as a matter of a fact. We provided him with full training, of course, and he picked it up really fast. His attention to detail was excellent.'

'And what was his pay scale like?'

'It was above award, $28.70 an hour, with the option of productivity bonuses.'

'So, definitely not too shabby, considering what most ex-inmates might hope to earn.'

'Absolutely.' Cameron chewed his lip before speaking again. 'Look, I'll be honest, when we got the first report of stolen property I was ready to give Rusty the benefit of the doubt. The customer was one of those tough old dames who finds fault with everything and I thought she might have somehow heard of his background and made a false report to cause trouble. I even offered to replace the camera in question rather than bring the police into it.'

'Did she agree?'

'No, she was adamant she was reporting it and then it wasn't too long before the other complaints starting coming in as well. It appeared the break-ins were done in a fairly co-ordinated fashion. Although, they weren't even technically break-ins because the correct entry codes – the ones Rusty set during installation – were used on the first attempt.'

'How do you know that?'

'There's a record on the system itself. It shows if and when codes are changed and if any incorrect attempts are keyed in.'

'Right. So, all the illegal entries were made on the keypad at the house and not the remote?'

'Yes, that's right. The system records that too.'

'And all these properties were still using the original code Rusty set?'

'Correct.'

'Why don't you just get the homeowner to set their own code during installation?'

'A couple of reasons. Firstly, they aren't always there. If people can't get time off work, they often get a friend or relative to wait while the installer works, or, for rentals, we sometimes get the property manager to let them in. Secondly, if the homeowner set it while the installer is there, it could be argued they have knowledge of the code. It's just more secure to get the homeowner to do it themselves afterwards. It's simple to do.'

'All right, understood. So, these affected people should have changed their codes?'

'Yes, they should have. We strongly advise them to do so on the day of installation. But you know how it goes, a lot of people don't get around to it, they get lazy. All the affected homes had not changed their codes. It's quite possible other homes were targeted but the attempt was unsuccessful because they *had* changed their codes.'

Jack sighed. 'Right. And Rusty was the only one who knew the codes?'

'Yeah, each installer sets their own codes.'

'And he always worked alone?'

'Yep, all our installers do. They each have their own

territory. Rusty hadn't even met the other blokes because they were all working out of the other office in Manly. That's the depot for the installers.'

'He working out of this office?'

'Yes, he was.'

'Why was that?'

'Well you've met him, you know how rough around the edges he is. I just wanted to take some time to try and make him a bit more respectable, you know?'

Jack nodded. 'Yeah, I hear what you're saying.'

'Is there anything else I can help you with?'

'One last thing. I saw you paid out the young woman whose expensive handbag was stolen. Why did you do that?'

Cameron made a face and shrugged. 'It just seemed like the decent thing to do, considering it was my company that allowed her premises to be robbed in the first place. It was damage control, I suppose.'

Jack nodded slowly. 'Fair enough.'

As well as his work meeting, Jack managed to squeeze in a quick lunch with his cousin Julia at her office in the city. Born in the same year, they had been great pals growing up and he affectionately referred to her as the sister he never had. Taking in the plush surroundings of Julia's office, Jack couldn't help but chuckle as they dined on hot dogs from the street vendor on Circular Quay.

'What's so funny?' Julia asked, as she squeezed more sauce from the takeaway sachet onto her hot dog.

'I was just remembering our early days back at McDonald and Wright.'

Nodding, Julia laughed too. 'Yes, that was quite an adventure, wasn't it?' After studying law at Sydney

119

University together, Jack and Julia had also worked for the same firm while doing their Articles. At a tiny premises in Pitt Street, McDonald and Wright had housed its article clerks in a small, windowless room at the rear of the office. They had both declared that if they survived the ordeal, they would go on to bigger and better things.

'I think we've done all right, Jules.'

Julia nodded, before wiping her mouth with a serviette. 'We have. Although I never thought I'd see the day when you took on a criminal case.'

'Well, as you know, it's not by choice. And I'm up to my neck now, so any advice you can give will be gratefully received.'

'I've got case notes here I can go over with you, but as you know, it's all about reasonable doubt. Not to be a big Debbie Downer, but without motive and a possible suspect or suspects, you're going to do it tough convincing a jury, especially with the fingerprints and DNA.'

'I know. But I think I actually believe him.'

'Have you considered a guilty plea and a push to keep him at Regent Park for rehab? Their program is one of the best in the state.'

'It is a decent facility and, yes, I have considered the guilty plea, but I just don't think he'll cop it. He's adamant he didn't do it.'

'Well, nothing is impossible, but it's a strange one all right.'

Finishing his hot dog, Jack crushed the cardboard holder and dropped it in the bin. 'Strange doesn't even begin to describe it.'

Jack and Julia talked strategy for the next hour. Having always had a similar approach to their work, they often

120

bounced ideas off each other and Jack felt at least slightly more confident by the time he had to leave.

'Speaking of McDonald and Wright,' Julia said. 'Did Erin show you those old staff photos I put on Facebook? We both look so young and innocent.'

Jack closed his briefcase and snapped the locks with more force than was necessary. 'She did show me, but don't talk to me about Facebook, Jules. It got me in big trouble the other night and as you know I don't even have an account.'

Julia put her hand to her mouth. 'Oh yeah, I meant to ask you about that! It was Christine in those pictures from the awards dinner, right?'

'Yeah, it was and I can't believe you saw them too! Is nothing private anymore?'

'Come on, Jack, most of Erin's friends wouldn't have even looked at them. And only you, me and Erin know about the Christine angle.'

Jack's only response was a withering glance.

'How did you both end up in the same room anyway?' Julia asked.

'Random bad luck I guess,' Jack said, explaining how his ex-girlfriend had come to be at the function.

'I'm sure she made a point of being there when she found out the guest list,' Julia said.

Jack rolled his eyes. 'I wouldn't put it past her. I couldn't believe it when I saw her there, but seeing nobody else knew her, I thought I'd gotten away with it. I didn't consider the possibility of getting sprung via social media.'

'So, was it all as innocent as what you told Erin?'

'Yeah, of course, on my behalf anyway. I didn't think it was necessary to mention that Christine invited me out for a drink afterwards or the suggestion that we should keep in touch, just to chat or *whatever.*'

Julia shook her head. 'She's got some front, that one, and I agree it's better to keep that under your hat. Don't worry I'll keep it under mine too.'

'I know you will, Jules, you really are as safe as the bank.'

'I am indeed,' Julia agreed, with a grin. 'As much as Christine destroyed your life for a while there, you know you dodged a bullet, right?'

'Yes, absolutely. You never liked her, did you?'

Julia shook her head. 'Nah. I tolerated her for your sake, but I knew she wasn't good enough for you.'

'What can I say? I was an idiot.'

'No, never that. She knew how to play you, that's all.'

'What was it that Grandma used to say? No experience is ever wasted?'

'Yep, that's it. You'll get something out of this case too.'

Jack laughed. 'I'm sure I will. High blood pressure and grey hair most likely.'

Julia opened the door to see him out. 'Well, possibly, but hopefully something else too.'

After catching the early afternoon train home, Jack was back at Millvale by three. In the commuter car park, he slid into the driver's seat of his car and hesitated after he put the key in the ignition. He had three options. He could drop into work and put in an hour or two, he could go home, or he could head out to see Rusty. As much as the third option was the least appealing, it was the one that made the most sense. This late in the day, he wouldn't get much done at work and he'd probably end up watching TV or reading the paper if he went home as the kids would be at swimming. Sighing, he started the ignition then turned left at the car park exit, heading out of town.

Half an hour later, Jack was in the now familiar meeting room at Regent Park. As a frequent visitor, his sign-in process had become much simpler, but he still couldn't stop the resentment that crept over him every time he had to make the trek out to the facility to work with an ungrateful client in a noisy, smoke filled environment.

As usual, Rusty had chosen the far end of the furthest table and he barely acknowledged Jack as he pulled out the chair opposite, his bored expression suggesting he had far more important things to be doing than dealing with his upcoming trial.

Rise above it, Jack told himself, as he sat down and pulled Rusty's case file out of his briefcase. Like Julia said, he would gain something from this ordeal. He fixed the most pleasant expression on his face he could manage. 'Good afternoon.'

'Hey,' Rusty grunted.

'I went to visit Cameron Melville this morning.'

'Good for you.'

'You didn't think to tell me that you knew him from school?' Jack said, biting back the sarcastic tone he was tempted to use.

He got a shrug in response. 'You never asked me that.'

'I know, but you didn't think it might be useful information to share?'

'Not really. What's it got to do with anything?'

'It might not be relevant but, still, it was something that I needed to know.'

'All right, so you know.'

'Well yeah, I know his side of the story. He said you were mates?'

'Yep, we were. Well, until I won the scholarship anyway. He was pretty pissed off about that.'

'Why? I thought a friend would be happy for you.'

'Not if they wanted what you got.'

'Oh, I didn't realise he wanted it too.'

'Yeah, he did, much more than me. I wagged school and went to the try outs for the hell of it and he'd spent all this time preparing notes for the interview, got new footy boots and all.'

'So how did you pull it off?'

'Simple. I was a better player than him. Cam tried his best, and he trained harder than anyone I know, but he was average at best. Those fancy schools, they want the best players they can find.'

'And you were one of the best?'

'Yeah. I know that makes me sound up myself, but I was. I reckon I coulda gone all the way.'

Jack leaned back in his chair and studied Rusty thoughtfully. 'So, why didn't you? Why didn't you stay on at school and get exposure to one of the feeder clubs?'

'You wouldn't understand.' Rusty looked down at the tabletop and shook his head.

'Try me.'

Rusty shook his head again.

'Was it the school work? Those schools are pretty academic, even if you're on a sports scholarship.'

Rusty crossed his arms and nodded slowly. 'Oh yeah, dumb old Rusty couldn't keep up with the schoolwork, I'm sure that fits right into the little box you've got me in.'

Heat crept up Jack's neck and face as he realised the

huge generalisation he'd just made. 'No, I'm not saying you're dumb,' he backtracked. 'I just…'

Rusty raised an eyebrow, clearly enjoying Jack's discomfiture. 'You just what?'

'Come on, Rusty, we don't have all day. I'm sorry for offending you. Please tell me why you left school.'

'I actually liked going to school there. Nobody knew me or my family and I got to play all the footy I wanted. It was so calm there at night, too. It sure beat fighting my brother for the leftovers in the fridge when Mum was at work, or rescuing Dad when he got himself into fights at the pub.'

'You were a boarder, then?'

'Yeah, it was part of the deal. The school work *was* kinda hard but they had tutors there to help you with your homework and stuff. And you could do all kinds of different subjects. For the first time, I realised that school could be interesting and that I wasn't as dumb as everyone had told me.'

Jack wrote some meaningless notes on his legal pad to avoid eye contact with Rusty and hopefully keep him talking. 'Uh huh,' he murmured.

'When we came back after the Easter holidays we started getting into some pretty serious training for the footy season. I made the firsts, which was pretty awesome for a kid from the wrong side of town.'

'That's true.'

'Anyway, one day the whole school got called to this big assembly. Nobody knew why. We're all sitting there and the principal comes out with this real serious face and announces that there has been a thief at large. Kids had reported that they'd had cash and other valuables nicked and that it was a very serious matter.'

'Okay.'

'So, it's the usual story, unless somebody owns up there will be loss of privileges for everyone.'

'Yeah, I know the way it goes.'

'Well, they gave a deadline for the Friday but nobody put their hand up. So, we had another assembly, lectures about honesty and promises of more severe action if nobody comes forward or at least anonymously returns the stolen stuff.'

Jack raised his eyebrows. 'And? What happened?'

'Nothing. Nobody owned up and stuff was still getting nicked. So, they got really severe and started interviewing everyone personally. And that's why I left.'

'*What*?' Jack was incredulous. 'Did they accuse you of something in the interview?'

Rusty shook his head. 'Nuh, I never had it. I left before they got to me.'

'Why would you do that?'

'Because I knew it would somehow come out. They'd find out that my old man and my brother had both been in jail and assume it was me. That's the way it goes.'

'Not always, Rusty. They have to be really careful in cases like that, they can't accuse you without proof.'

Rusty was shaking his head vehemently. 'You don't get it. That's exactly what they do. I just left and saved them the bother.'

The two men stared at the scarred tabletop, both lost in their own thoughts for a moment. Jack spun his pen around on his notebook for a moment before speaking. 'It just seems such a waste for something you didn't do.'

Rusty's shrug was one of defeat. 'Maybe. Or maybe it was all just a waste of time and finishing school there wouldn't have made any difference anyway. The stealing thing was just a reminder to me that I was somewhere I didn't belong.'

'I totally disagree with you, but I can understand how a kid without any kind of life experience could have made that decision,' Jack said, thinking about the way Danny had come to a similar conclusion. 'Didn't your parents try and get you to stay?'

'Nuh. Dad didn't care less and Mum, well, she thought it was a shame, but she liked having me home again. I was sorry I disappointed her, but it was just one of those things.'

Knowing there wasn't much else he could say, Jack moved onto other questions, contemplating as he did the way choices could have such far-reaching consequences and just how lucky his life had been.

As he drove home Jack pondered Rusty's family. Although his parents were still together, that didn't mean the marriage was a happy one and, going by his police records, Rusty clearly hadn't had much supervision at home. The comment about his mother working at night could have meant several things. Maybe she had no choice about the hours she worked or was only able to secure a position with unsocial hours? Or maybe the pay was much better? Then again, perhaps she deliberately absented herself in the evenings so she didn't have to deal with her deadbeat husband and wayward children?

The way Rusty talked about his parents had also caught Jack's attention. Comments about his father had been critical and judgemental, while his expression had softened considerably when he spoke of his mother. It was a hard one to judge because most boys, and indeed men, have a soft spot for their mother. Danny certainly did, even though Tamara, in Jack's opinion, had some obvious shortcomings as a parent. Was Rusty the same? Did he view his mother through rose coloured glasses, even though she'd let him down as far as providing a stable home life?

Dropping down a gear as the Audi negotiated the steep gradient of the range, Jack thought about his own mother, Alice. Although both his parents had doted on him, their long-awaited only child, his mother had been the stricter of the two, the one who meted out discipline when required and whose expectations he strived to live up to. But Jack had never doubted her unconditional love for him and they had become particularly close during the eighteen months he had cared for after his father's unexpected passing. Battling her second bout of cancer, Alice had remained stoic until her death and had never stopped worrying about Jack. She had continued to tell him that he worked too hard and that his potential wife wasn't going to come and knock on his door, so he would need to go out and look for her. He smiled wryly as he remembered that conversation, because Erin had arrived in his life via his office door. Then again, knowing how determined his mother could be, Jack didn't doubt she'd had a hand in arranging their meeting.

Checking his car clock as he came up to the driveway, Jack sighed in relief. He should just beat Erin home, allowing him to help out with the kids and be involved in family life for the evening. After all, he had a bit of a nerve criticising other people's parenting if he was slacking off himself. Pulling into the garage, he grabbed his briefcase and phone and headed inside, ready to face the onslaught of the crazy hour.

CHAPTER TEN

Like many legal firms, Kendall and Masters had become more family friendly over time, offering a range of initiatives to improve the work/life balance of their senior staff. Chief among these was a membership at the gym next door, as well as three hours per week on company time to use the facility. Jack made full use of the scheme, grateful to be able to maintain his fitness without encroaching on family time.

Gym fitness was different to water fitness, but Jack was surprised how quickly the latter picked up with the daily swimming sessions he'd been putting in. It also meant he didn't have to be concerned about sacrificing his gym time while working on Rusty's defence.

You've got to love muscle memory, Jack thought on Wednesday morning, when he noticed that the distance between Danny and himself was less as they swam. He knew Danny would always have him over the longer distances, but Jack did enjoy challenging the kid to a one lap sprint, occasionally. Levelling the playing field a little by restricting Danny to a push start with no underwater dolphin kicks, Jack could muster enough explosive power to finish only a couple of strokes behind. While Danny did not admit to being ruffled by this, Jack could tell he was, as they leaned against the wall of the shallow end, their chests still heaving.

'And you always say you're not competitive,' Danny said, his breathing still laboured.

'I'm not, I just like to finish first.'

Danny gave a sarcastic smile. 'Funny. You really upped your stroke rate.'

'Yeah, it's my secret weapon over a short distance. Sadly, I can't maintain it much beyond about fifty metres. So, don't worry, you will continue to smash me over any distance.' Jack didn't add that going all out in the sprint was also a great way to work out his frustrations with the case. Ten days and countless hours in, he still felt like he was getting nowhere. It wasn't something he shared with Danny though, instead he reassured him that things were going along okay.

Looking up at the beautiful orange and pink sky as they did some backstroke warm down laps, Jack pondered why, exactly, he was putting himself under so much pressure for such an ungrateful client. As much as he told himself, and everybody else, it was only for Danny, he couldn't deny that ego was also part of the equation. Back in his earlier years with Kendall and Masters, he had been their poster boy, the guy who never lost in court. Yet, Jack always acknowledged those stats were skewed, because he didn't take on cases he knew he couldn't win. He rarely made court appearances these days and the worry that he could have lost his edge in that arena added another layer to the anxiety he was feeling.

Coming to the end, Jack checked his watch and realised he had been dawdling through the backstroke. At this rate, he'd be lucky to fit in a shower, never mind have time for breakfast. Leaving Danny to finish his sprint session, Jack climbed out of the pool and jogged up to the house.

Noticing how stressed Jack looked, Erin told him she would take Sam to school, then handed him a cheese toastie, as well a lunchbox, when he rushed out the door at eight o'clock. Jack hadn't admitted he was missing meals to gain sympathy, but was nevertheless touched that Erin had found time to prepare food for him. The toastie hit the spot as he cruised down the range, relieved to avoid the need to negotiate the school drop off precinct. It wasn't that he didn't enjoy the one on one time he spent with Sam each morning, Jack just couldn't fathom why it took ten minutes to get in and out of a fifty metre stretch of driveway. When had getting children to school turned into such an ordeal? As a kid, he had walked to school, as did most of his classmates. There had been no such thing as the "kiss and go" zone, with only a handful of parents driving their children to the front gates in those days. And, those who lived beyond walking distance, rode their bikes or travelled on the bus.

Jack made good time to the office and met his secretary, Kelly, in the lift. 'You're early today,' she said.

'Dodged the school drop off.'

'Oh, lucky you. Did you swim this morning?'

Jack nodded, while lifting his hand up to smell it. While his shower had been quicker than normal, he thought he had used enough Alpine Forest shower gel to wash off the chlorine.

Kelly smiled. 'Don't worry, you don't stink. I can see your goggle marks.'

'Oh, right.'

'You okay, Jack? You're looking a bit stressed these days. I'm not spying on you, but your diary and billable hours aren't matching up with all the extra time you've been

131

working. I haven't seen you skip lunch for years and now you're doing it most days. And you haven't used your gym hours for the past couple of weeks.'

Jack sighed. 'Long story. It's a pro bono case I'm doing for a friend.'

'Wow, that's great. Go you.'

Jack forced himself to smile. 'Yeah, go me.' The lift stopped and he let Kelly exit first and they walked down the hallway towards his office.

'Well, if I can do anything to help, let me know. I like the idea of pro bono but nobody around here really does it.'

'Thanks, Kel. I might take you up on that.'

Opening his lunchbox at noon, Jack smiled at the kiddie lunch consisting of two mini quiches, a buttered dinner roll, a pile of carrot sticks and a bunch of grapes. Not that he was complaining, though. With some proper nutrition, he might actually make some progress, as he worked through lunch yet again.

Half an hour later, his stomach was satisfied, but the case was still doing his head in. Assuming Rusty was telling the truth, whoever framed him had to have known what alarm codes he used. Beyond having some kind of secret surveillance system, it seemed pretty impossible that anybody could guess not just one, but seven different codes. Jack paused for a moment, then looked back over his notes. Cameron had said that each installer set their own codes. As in codes plural. He had assumed that meant a different code for each house, but maybe it didn't. Picking up the phone, he dialled Melville Security and was put through to Cameron.

Cameron sounded distracted. 'Sorry, Jack, I'm due in a staff meeting in two minutes. Can I call you back later?'

'Just a really quick question,' Jack said. 'Do the installers use a new code for each job?'

'Yes, they do. Well, at least they're supposed to.'

'Do you verify that?'

'Well, no, it's too hard to. But we certainly hammer it home that they should do it. They initial their time sheet to say they've done it.'

'Uh huh, but beyond the honour system you've got no way of knowing if and when the installers change their codes.'

'No, we don't.'

'All right, that's all I needed to know. Thank you.'

'No worries. How's it all going anyway?'

'Slowly. But I'm not giving up yet.'

'Well, good luck. Keep me informed if anything happens, won't you?'

'Sure thing. Thanks again.'

Hanging up the phone, Jack was grateful that Cameron was not being obstructive. He certainly had the right to be, given that his previously very successful business had had its reputation unfairly tarnished. It was lucky people had short memories and that Rusty's upcoming trial was not interesting enough to still be making news all these months later.

Jack checked his watch and then mentally rearranged his afternoon so he could burn a bit more fuel and make another visit to his esteemed client.

After trudging through the main entrance to Regent Park and signing in, Jack was both surprised and pleased when the guard informed him that from now on he would be allocated a private meeting room to work in. Trailing the corrections officer down a hallway, Jack waited while the man unlocked a metal door and flicked on the overhead light. Sparsely furnished with a desk and two chairs, the office was nothing special, but it was a step up from the common meeting room, where noise and the ever-present plume of cigarette smoke were constant distractions and the presence of the guards was intimidating.

'I'll get Anderson,' the guard said.

Jack nodded. Taking a seat on the chair closest to the door, he pulled out his notebook and pen while he waited.

A few minutes later, Rusty appeared. Eyeing the room with some suspicion, he sat down on the opposite side of the table. Both he and Jack were surprised when the guard closed the door and left them alone. Jack raised his eyebrows in a questioning manner.

Rusty shrugged. 'Don't look at me. I dunno why we're getting special treatment.'

'Perhaps they have decided I'm trustworthy.'

'You definitely give off that vibe.'

'That's good to know,' Jack said, flipping through his notes until he got to a new page.

'What's the big question today?'

'The alarm codes you set at each house.'

'What about 'em?' While he was still not cordial or overly forthcoming, Rusty was becoming less belligerent when asked questions.

'Well, first of all, did you use the same code at every house?'

Rusty hesitated for a moment, but realised there was no point in lying. 'Yeah, I did.'

'You weren't supposed to do that though, were you?'

'No, it was meant to be a new one for each install. They

were supposed to be random. But it's a major pain in the arse. It's like when everything on the computer wants a new password, and you can't remember 'em all.'

'I do agree; however, by not changing your code you were ignoring company policy, correct?'

'Yes.'

'So basically, the person who allegedly framed you only needed to find one password rather than seven different ones?'

'Uh huh.'

'And did you tell anyone your password?'

'Only the customers, so they could access their system and change it later.'

'Nobody else?'

'No. Who was I gonna tell? You program the password on the actual house system when you set it up, you don't put it on the job log or anything.'

'All right then, was your password easy to guess? It wasn't your name or your birthday, was it?'

Rusty stared Jack down. 'Just because I've done time doesn't mean I don't know the rules about passwords. It's not my name or my birthday.'

'All right, fine, I just had to check. So, what was it?'

'25486 capital N.'

'You remember it just like that?' Jack wrote the password down and circled it, not seeing anything obvious about the digits and letter combination.

'It was the same one I use for everything. You know email, bankcards and all that.'

'You shouldn't have told me that. That's the problem with passwords, once you reveal them they're pretty pointless.'

135

'I reckon you're a pretty safe person to tell.'

'Well, yeah, I might be, but haven't you heard that saying "loose lips sink ships"?'

'No.' Rusty was being deliberately obtuse.

'Well, now you've heard it. Think about it before you share your sole password out to anyone else. Better still, change it when you get the chance.'

'Sure, I'll just pull out my personal laptop and use the free Wi-Fi we have in here.'

'Rusty, if you'd just drop the attitude for a while we might actually get somewhere with this.'

'Doesn't look like we've got anywhere so far.'

'No, maybe not, but the answer is always in the details so we've got to spend a lot of time getting lots of details. If I were charging you my normal hourly rate you'd be ten grand in by now.'

'Lucky I'm not paying then.'

'Yeah, lucky for you.'

Despite the many hours he was putting into Rusty's defence, Jack made sure that he was always available to help Danny with his schoolwork. Although the looming court case was the more complex problem, Jack didn't want Danny to feel he was being sidelined. In addition, he had given Adrian his word that the work would be done and he fully intended to honour that promise. He was glad he had the ability to think on his feet though, as some things needed a little bit of a memory jog before he could put on his teacher hat.

'Quadratic equations hey?' he said that night, as they sat at the dining table. Spinning the textbook around so he could study the example question, Jack nodded in a way that he hoped make him look wise.

Danny made a face. 'Yeah, yet another stupid mathematical idea. I still don't understand why we need to learn this junk. How is it going to help me if I decide to become a fire fighter?'

'You never know, Dan, someday you might have to calculate something fire related,' Jack said, as he scanned the lines of mathematical symbols. He was excited to hear Danny talking about his future career plans again but was careful not to show any reaction.

'I doubt it,' Danny grumbled.

'Mate, I don't design the curriculum; I'm only trying to help you pass the subject. Just accept you need to learn it and it won't be so painful.'

Finally accessing the corner of his brain to which quadratic equations had been filed away, Jack talked Danny through the example question, then through the first few problems, until he eventually caught on. Jack couldn't help but smile when he looked over and saw Danny working away, his mind replacing the teenage Danny's face with the eager nine-year-old he had spent hours drilling times tables with.

'It really wasn't that bad, was it?' he said half an hour later, when Danny closed the textbook and stretched.

'Yeah, yeah, whatever. I can't believe I'm actually starting to catch up.' Picking up the checklist he had made on his first day there, Danny ticked the maths column and scanned the rest of the chart. 'Now I have to write that dumb book review.'

Jack raised his eyebrows. 'I thought you liked books. That's what you told me that first time I bought you some.'

'I like *some* books, not the ones you have to read for

school,' Danny said.

'Again, sometimes you've just got to grit your teeth and do it, whether you like it or not.'

'I've still got them you know.'

'What, the original books I got you?'

'Yeah.'

'That's nice, I'm glad.'

'I might give them to my little brother or sister.'

'I'm sure they'd love them too.'

Danny doodled on his notebook for a moment. 'Why did you get them for me anyway?'

'What the books?'

'Yeah.'

'Because you needed them.'

'Yeah, but it wasn't your job to get stuff for me. I was just some random kid you happened to meet.'

'No, it wasn't my job, but I was in a position to help you and I wanted to do it. I really liked you, which was quite a revelation to me. I thought Jim was trying to rub my nose in it when he had us train together, I didn't expect to enjoy your company so much.'

'Really?'

'Yeah, of course. Why else do you think I hung around with you?'

'I just assumed you wanted to be my friend because kids think everyone wants to be friends.'

'Well, that was the beauty of it. You didn't look beyond the obvious, which gave me the opportunity to realise I could be friends with a child in a non-creepy way.'

'I never thought you were creepy. A bit strange because you couldn't catch a wave, but definitely not creepy.'

'That's good to know.'

'I'm really glad we're still friends.'

Jack smiled. 'Me too, mate. You're actually one of my closest friends.'

'Same here. I hope you don't think I'll ditch you because I've got a stepdad now,' Danny said.

Jack shook his head. 'No, I didn't think that and remember you've got your real dad now too.'

Danny made a face. 'I don't think we can quite put him in the same category.'

'Blood is blood Dan, don't forget that.'

CHAPTER ELEVEN

Thursday saw Jack taking his first lunch break in almost two weeks. Having decided to take a twenty-four-hour break from the whole Rusty debacle, he relished the chance to concentrate solely on his own work without feeling guilty. Heading out of the office at one o'clock, he treated himself to a deluxe burger from Angie's before picking up a paper at the newsagent. The lure of a coffee from the café next door was strong, but aware of how much caffeine he'd been ingesting lately, Jack picked up a bottle of water instead. Crossing the busy street, he headed over to his favourite seat at the Botanic Gardens.

Sometimes it was hard to believe that the bustling regional city of Millvale was the same country town he'd grown up in. Back then, the only café along the long, straight, main street had been of the greasy spoon variety, and the Chinese restaurant was about as exotic as takeaway food choices got. With a population of ten thousand it wasn't a tiny place, but it certainly lacked the sophistication of a city. Change had come gradually, spurred on by two major initiatives, the development of a regional university campus and the improvement of the highway to Sydney. Once it was within commuting distance, people began to see Millvale as a tree change kind of town and had started migrating there as new housing developments sprang up. Jack had never regretted moving back there after ten years away.

Reading the paper was luxurious. Unlike many of his colleagues who found it simpler to browse the news online, Jack still liked to hold the *Sydney Morning Herald* in his hands and flick through it at his leisure. These days he had no opportunity to do it at home, so he'd made it his lunch time ritual and realised just how much he had missed his "me" time activity since he had started on Rusty's case. When he finished, Jack folded the paper in half and pulled his phone out of his pocket.

'Hi, Babe,' Erin said, when she answered.

'Hey,' Jack replied. 'How's your day been?'

'Good. How about you?'

'Great. I've ditched my criminal defence case for the day and I feel liberated.'

'That's just what you needed. Did you eat?'

'I did indeed. How's Danny going?'

'Fine. He studied all morning and he's just in the pool with Joshy now. I tell you what, I'm going to miss my live-in babysitter when he goes.'

'Yeah, he's been a huge help. He'll be a great big brother I reckon.'

'Yes, he will.'

They chatted for a few more minutes and although they didn't talk about anything particularly exciting, Jack loved the normality of it and was smiling as he strolled back to the office.

The only glitch in Jack's Rusty free Thursday came at four ten pm when an email from LinkedIn landed in his inbox.

Frowning, he opened the message. "Nikita Blair would like to add you to her professional network." Rolling his eyes, Jack hit delete. He was about as interested in joining LinkedIn as he was in joining Facebook. While lots of the staff at Kendall and Masters had LinkedIn profiles, he had no desire to follow suit. And he didn't even know a Nikita Blair.

Leaning back in his chair, Jack shook his head. A few weeks ago, he had spoken at a conference and this wasn't the first LinkedIn request he had received since. Was the world officially going mad or was everyone chasing as many professional contacts as they could find to make their profile look better? Even if he had a LinkedIn account, Jack wouldn't have added Nikita, given that their only tenuous link was apparently being in the same room for an hour. It seemed inappropriate to develop some kind of social media relationship based on that.

Annoyed that the email had upset his equilibrium, Jack turned his attention back to the file on his desk, but struggled to regain the focus he'd had before. He just didn't understand social media. A reserved and private person, he hated the limelight and was very happy keeping his own business to himself. Beyond his picture and bio on the Kendall and Masters website, he had no intention of developing any other kind of internet presence.

But, later that night, as they sat at the dining room table, Danny was quick to shatter that illusion. Having vented about the LinkedIn invitation and his desire to remain invisible in cyber space, Jack was hard at work editing the first draft of Danny's book review when the teenager spun his laptop around and waited expectantly.

Jack didn't look up at first. 'Danny, what are you doing? I thought you were getting some quotes for this. You need at least three more.'

'Yeah, I am doing that, but I just want you to see this first.'

Reluctantly, Jack set his pen down and looked up. On the screen was a Google search box with his name and the word solicitor, followed by a full page of search results. Pulling the laptop closer, Jack studied the links, astonished to see that in addition to his work website, there were several newspaper reports about cases he had won as well as links to articles he had written for the *Law Journal.* Clicking on the Images link, he was further shocked to find a photo from the *Sunset Point Sentinel* from when they had saved the Beach House as well as his Kendall and Masters profile picture. He clicked on the latter image and studied it for a moment before murmuring, 'She's right, it was an Armani.'

'What?'

'Oh, nothing. All right, you made your point. I guess beyond living in complete hibernation it's very hard to avoid being online somewhere. However, I still maintain my aversion to social media where you are deliberately putting it all out there. What's wrong with just sending an email?'

Danny laughed. 'You're such a dinosaur. Nobody emails anymore.'

'I do. And you normally reply to me.'

'Yeah, only because I can't send you a Facebook message.'

'At least with email nobody else can see it.'

'You can keep your privacy settings high if you don't want everyone to see your stuff on Facie.'

'Still not convincing me, Dan. Thanks for the heads up,

but can we get back to your school work now?'

Spinning his computer back around, Danny closed the lid before picking up his book. 'Yeah, okay,' he sighed.

They worked mainly in silence for the next hour. With much prompting, Danny produced the required quotes and set about typing up the corrections. And Jack replied to some personal emails he had been too busy to look at recently. As he worked his way down the list of emails, he felt good, glad to have caught up on something. The final message was to his good friend, Dieter. Mates since school, they didn't see each other very often, but emailed at least once a month. Maybe I am a dinosaur, Jack thought as he hit send, but I like email. It was a quick and easy way to stay in touch, much more so than writing a letter or picking up the phone to call. Dieter was an Inspector in the NSW Police Service and, like Jack, kept himself very much off the social media grid. Without email they might have lost touch altogether.

Ready to call it a night, Jack looked over at Danny and realised he was no longer typing. 'Dan, I thought we agreed the book review was getting finished tonight.'

Danny looked up. 'It is done. I'll print it out tomorrow.'

'All right, that's good, but what are you doing now?'

'Checking out this Nikita chick.'

'Woman, Danny. Chick really isn't a very respectful word.'

'Okay, woman then. Do you want to hear all about her? I found her on Facebook.'

'No, not particularly. I told you, I don't even know her.'

'She just got a promotion at work and she must have got married because she made this big post about changing her name. Maybe you know her old name, I'll just have to scroll down a bit and see what it was.'

'I don't know anyone called Nikita, and I'm really not interested that she changed her name.'

Danny closed his laptop and folded his arms. 'Now you're being a cranky dinosaur. I was just trying to help.'

Closing his own laptop, Jack stood up and stretched. 'I know, Dan and I appreciate it. But I really don't have time for random people from LinkedIn or any other social media site. Like I said before, I still don't see anything redeeming about it. Now come on, let's hit the sack.'

Danny stood too. 'All right,' he agreed.

CHAPTER TWELVE

It was another hectic but enjoyable Friday morning for Jack as he played with the kids on the floor while Edna cleaned around them. He couldn't believe he had gotten away with his secret weapon for this long. They didn't call Joshua Mr Blabbermouth for nothing. In direct contrast to his father's reserved personality and ability to keep anything confidential, Josh loved to talk and did so whenever he got the chance. While he might not yet have mentioned Edna to Erin, Jack knew at some point he would unwittingly tell somebody. Still, that was something he would worry about when it happened.

Leaning back against the couch, Jack watched Josh drive his Thomas the Tank Engine trains in a convoy along the track they had just built. From a young age, Joshua had been fascinated with Thomas, and spent hours playing games with his collection of trains, each of which he knew by name, number and personality. Having been a train fan himself as a child, Jack could see the attraction, and he quite enjoyed watching the show on TV with the kids.

Danny meandered into the lounge room and stretched before lying down on the couch. 'He's so into those trains,' he said, lying on his side and watching Josh as he sent the trains up a hill backwards.

'Yeah I know. His face is so funny to watch; he gets this

really intense look when he's concentrating.'

Danny laughed. 'Talk about a mini me.'

'What?'

'Are you serious? He looks so much like you, especially the facial expressions. Now you know what it's like sitting across from you at the table every night.'

Jack was about to say something along the lines of pot, kettle and black but realised that might not go down too well. 'Really?' he said, instead. Although Jack could see the resemblance between him and Joshua when photographs of him at the same age were compared, naturally he didn't recognise his own expressions being mirrored back to him.

'He's totally got your eyes too. I think you're actually twins separated by time. Right, Edna?'

Edna looked up from where she was dusting. 'Absolutely. Except for the hair of course.'

Although gradually darkening from blond to brown, Josh's hair was a halo of curls unlike anyone else on either side of the family.

'The afro is awesome,' Danny said.

Jack laughed. 'It is cute. People comment on it all the time.'

Raising himself to a sitting position Danny looked out the door at the cloudy sky. 'I was just thinking it might be too cold for a swim today.'

'Nah, gotta do the swim,' Jack said. 'The cover has been on all morning and I cranked up the heat before. We're all set.'

Disappointed that his twenty-four-hour hiatus was over, Jack got back to work on Rusty's case once the kids were asleep. Taking up one of Julia's suggestions, he'd had a private investigator run a check on the other staff at Melville Security. Going by the thickness of the report, however, it didn't look like that angle would yield much. Still, needing to be thorough, Jack scrutinised the information closely.

The company employed six other installers, three of whom had been employed by the previous business. Of the six, five of them were from Sydney with no affiliation with Queensland whatsoever. The sixth was from Tasmania, also having no apparent links with anything from Rusty's background. It seemed that none of them even knew of Rusty's employment with the company, given that he had never even visited the depot at Manly. Cameron had trained Rusty himself, something that was unusual. Apparently, training was normally undertaken on the job with one of the other installers. Jack contemplated this for a moment, but eventually concluded that Cameron's explanation made sense. Rusty *was* rough around the edges and the other installers might well take exception to his somewhat abrasive manner.

Scanning the report further, Jack read the profiles of the staff at the Mosman office. As well as his secretary, Cameron employed a receptionist, IT specialist and an office manager. While the secretary, receptionist and office manager had no flags in their background checks, there was an anomaly with the IT guy, Sebastian. With a little bit of digging, the investigator had uncovered that Sebastian's father had also served time in prison for burglary. It had been a long time ago, though, almost seventeen years, and the prison was in Victoria. Linking that to Rusty was drawing a pretty long bow. But it did make Jack wonder about Sebastian, and it raised two questions. Had Sebastian taken some kind of revenge on Rusty in light of his own father's crimes or had the two been in cahoots somehow? Thinking about it further, Jack leaned towards the first possibility. Surely if they had been in some kind of crime partnership, they wouldn't have stashed the loot at Rusty's residence. Besides, why would a well-paid IT professional delve into petty theft? Reading further Jack could see that Sebastian shared a unit with his cousin at Manly and had no debts, having purchased his second-hand Mazda for cash. While not impossible, it seemed highly unlikely that Sebastian was the culprit. Still, it was something he would need to follow up, just to make sure.

Turning to a new page in his notebook, Jack was summarising his findings when he felt the gentle pressure of a little hand on his leg. Looking down, he smiled at the sight of Josh with his eyes still clouded with sleep and his hair a crazy tangle of ringlets.

'Play trains with me, Daddy?' he asked hopefully.

Lifting him up, Jack enveloped him in a hug. 'Sure, buddy. I'd love to.'

Another week, another pizza night, Jack thought as he dropped the boxes on the table and called everyone over. Setting out some plates and grabbing the roll of paper towel from the kitchen was his version of setting the table on Friday nights. Sometimes, as he did this, he would think of his mother. Always a stickler for doing things properly, he could hear her telling him to "make it civilised Jack" in her soft English accent. If there had even been a pizza shop in Millvale back in his childhood, Jack had no doubt they would have eaten it with a knife and fork, with a serve of vegetables on the side.

Smiling at the memory, Jack deposited the twins in their highchairs and gave them each a piece of buttered toast, which was their version of pizza. Erin always fed them their real dinner while he went to collect the pizza, allowing everyone to enjoy their meal without having to contend with mashed vegetables and stewed apple.

Danny tucked in heartily again, this time less shy about eating his fill and Sam kept them entertained with his blow by blow description of his day at school. Although not related biologically, Sam was not unlike Jack in looks, with brown eyes and hair and was more like him in personality than Josh, being quieter and more cautious. While Jack regretted that Sam would never know his real parents, he would always be eternally grateful for the way this little boy had brought Erin and him together.

'So, Danny, it looks like you've had another productive week then?' Erin said, as she tore her crust off and gave it to Josh.

'Yep, I reckon I have,' Danny replied, smiling proudly. 'I can't believe I got my maths finished, finally.'

'Mr McGregor was impressed,' Jack said. 'I emailed him yesterday.'

'I guess he's not bad, for a principal,' Danny said.

'Too right mate, he's one of the good guys. And limiting Facebook to nights only hasn't killed you, has it?'

Danny made a face. 'I don't go on Facebook that much normally. I was just winding you up.'

Erin rolled her eyes in sympathy. 'Jack won't look at it but he's always asking me what's happening on there.'

'I think always is overstating it a bit,' Jack said. 'I was just asking about the pictures Julia said she put up.'

'So, you're against it in theory but not so much in

practice then?' Erin asked, taking a sip of water.

'Yeah, yeah, gang up on me. I'm so old fashioned, blah, blah, blah. I'm happy to leave it for the young'uns.'

Danny and Erin exchanged a grin across the table.

'How much younger are you than him?' Danny asked Erin.

'Two years and three months.'

Jack gave a sarcastic smile. 'There's got to be a cut off somewhere.'

'I know someone older than you who's on there,' Danny said to Jack.

'Yeah, who's that?'

'Edna. She just sent me a friend request before.'

Jack's eyes widened. 'Edna's on Facebook?'

Danny nodded. 'Yep, she is.'

Jack shook his head. 'We've obviously stumbled into some kind of alternate reality. If you tell me Jim's on there, I'll really lose it.'

'No, you know Jim hates computers. Mrs Stewart is a bit more open minded but she's not on there either.'

Reaching over to re-fill Sam's cup, Erin furrowed her brow. 'Have you met Edna then, Danny?'

'Yeah, I met her. It was a bit weird because she…' His voice trailed off as he realised what he'd done. 'Oh, shit, sorry, Jack, I forgot.' Danny's face flushed red.

'Language, Dan,' Jack said, motioning with his eyes to the boys.

'Oh, man, sorry, sorry.'

Erin looked over at Jack and raised her eyebrows. 'Edna's been here recently?'

'I love Edna,' Josh chimed in. 'She made me banana sandwiches for lunch today.'

Jack studied the tablecloth to avoid making eye contact with Erin. 'Would you believe she popped in to say hello?'

Danny had his head in his hands now. 'Jack, I'm really sorry, I didn't mean to say anything.'

'It's okay, Danny, I already knew Edna works here on Fridays,' Erin said.

Jack looked up. 'What do you mean?'

'Come on, Jack, don't do your lawyer answer a question with a question thing. I already knew.'

'Mr Blabbermouth told you?' Jack asked, inclining his head towards Josh.

Erin shook her head. 'No, surprisingly he didn't.'

'You've got the house under surveillance?'

'You really want to know?'

'Of course I do. I went to a lot of trouble to cover my tracks.'

'Well, there were two things. Firstly, the vacuum cleaner. You never put it away properly. But Edna does.'

'I would if it actually fit in the cupboard.'

'It fits if you detach the hose first.'

Danny watched their interaction with interest, stifling a smile.

Jack picked up the last piece of garlic bread and bit into it savagely. 'All right, what was the other thing?'

'The lint filter on the washing machine. I'll freely admit I'm slack about cleaning it out, but it is always cleaned out on Fridays and I'm fairly sure you don't even know where it is, let alone how to empty it.'

Jack held his hands out palms up. 'All right, you got me. I call in reinforcements in your absence. I'm a failure as a house husband.'

'Seriously, Jack, I'm not grading your efforts,' said Erin.

'And I definitely don't mind that Edna comes. It means the house gets cleaned properly once a week, at least. She even wipes the fingerprints off the TV screen.'

'She is the best. I went through a series of cleaners before I found her.'

'I actually recommended her to one of Mum's friends just recently.'

'Why didn't you tell me you knew?'

'I don't know, you took steps to keep it secret. I figured there must be a reason behind it, although I'm still not sure what the reason is.'

'I don't know - male pride?'

Erin just shook her head and smiled.

CHAPTER THIRTEEN

Jack was grateful he didn't have to go through the same charade to get an appointment with Cameron Melville on Monday afternoon. While the ruse had worked the previous time, Jack disliked dishonesty of any kind when dealing with clients. He couldn't very well lecture them for not disclosing all the facts if he had danced around the truth himself. Having contemplated the Sebastian angle over the weekend, Jack knew there was no other way to get the required information than to ask Cameron himself.

Once again Cameron was polite and met Jack's gaze in a seemingly open and non-combative way. 'So, how's it all going?' he asked, after inviting Jack to sit down.

'Not great, to be honest. As much as it's a circumstantial case, the evidence is rock solid. I'm struggling to crack open any portal of reasonable doubt.'

'Not to sink the boot in, but Rusty should never have touched stuff in the houses. I absolutely hammer that home during the initial training.'

'I know, I agree completely.'

'So how exactly can I help you today then? I think I told you pretty much everything the last time.'

Jack pulled his notebook out of his briefcase and set it on the desk. 'Yes, you were very helpful and I really appreciate that. I've just got a few more things to go over.'

'Sure. You want a coffee or anything?'

'No, thank you. I'll try not to hold you up too long.' Writing the date on the top of the page, Jack circled it before looking up at Cameron again.

'How often is your rubbish collected here?'

'Once a week.'

'And who has access to your industrial bin?'

'Well, anyone really. Generally, the cleaner empties all the inside bins but the dumpster is just out the back. It's not locked or anything. Is this about the cigarette butts?'

Jack nodded and made a note on his page before launching into a further series of trivial questions about the general running of the business before wading into the murkier territory he knew would be harder to pull off. While it was a ploy that worked with unsuspecting clients, he could see that Cameron was becoming suspicious.

'I reckon we've covered all the minute details here, Jack, I'd really appreciate it if you'd come to the point. We're both busy men and we don't need to waste any more time.'

'Okay, fair call. As we previously discussed, each installer sets their own codes at the specific job site.'

'That's correct.'

'Right, so is there anywhere that these codes are physically recorded back at the office?'

'No, we really emphasise to the installers that they keep their codes secret.'

'So, you didn't know Rusty used the same code for each install?'

'No, I did not know that. Knowing Rusty, I'm not that surprised but I liked to think that he had done as I asked.'

'What do you mean by "knowing Rusty"?'

Realising his answer might come back to haunt him in

some way Cameron chose his words carefully. 'Rusty was never one to play by the rules. If the teachers told us not to use the bottom oval at lunchtime that was the first place he headed. He made a point of wearing the wrong shoes or hat to school and he was always late to footy training. He doesn't like to conform.'

'All right, so isn't it fair to ask that if you knew that about him, why did you hire him?'

'I told you last time,' Cameron said, impatience creeping into his tone, even though he was clearly doing his best to remain calm and measured.

Jack made a show of flicking back through his notes even though he knew Cameron's response by heart. 'You wanted to give him a chance to get his life back on track?'

'Yes, that's correct. I hadn't seen the guy for nearly twenty years and I thought he might have grown up a bit.'

'Did you get that impression when you interviewed him?'

'Well, yeah, he seemed on the up and up, like he really wanted to make a go of things.'

'But you believe now that he was just saying what you wanted to hear?'

'Yeah, I guess so. Anyone can act the part.'

'True. All right, I'm nearly finished … just a few more things to clear up.'

'Ask away.' The impatience in Cameron's expression was giving way to anger. It was a slow burn, but Jack could see he had an idea where the questions were heading.

'You stated before that you had no way of knowing what the installers codes were, but surely there must be some way they can be retrieved on your IT system? What if you had some kind of problem with a house alarm and needed to access the code and you couldn't get hold of the installer? I saw a case on the news where the alarm went off in the middle of the night by mistake and couldn't be shut off and they had to wait for the alarm company to come and disable it.'

Cameron eyeballed Jack, the slow burning anger bubbling closer to the surface. When he spoke, his tone was clipped and deliberate. 'If it was necessary to access the code, it could be done. But it is not an easy procedure. Both me and the IT guy need to access the system to allow it and there are several steps involved.'

'Just to be clear, you are saying it can be done?'

'Yes, but to be equally clear, it's not easily done.'

'So how many times has it been done before?'

'I reckon that's about as much as I'm going to say now, thanks, Jack. I don't like the direction these questions are taking. I've been nothing but co-operative and now you're trying to twist things. You want the truth? Rusty is a dead set loser. All his life he's had people try to help him and he's thrown every opportunity to the wind. If he hadn't skipped school and crashed my try-out at the grammar school that scholarship would have been mine. I would have had the opportunity to play in the NRL. But no, not only did Rusty take it from me, he completely wasted the opportunity he was given! He threw away the chance of a lifetime just for the hell of it. And now he's destroying my livelihood and I'm not going to stand for that. I'd like you to leave now.'

Jack was already packing his briefcase. 'I'm sorry, Cameron, I have to ask these questions if Rusty has any chance of a fair trial. I'm not accusing anybody; I just need the facts.'

'Like hell you're not accusing. I'd be careful if I was

you, Jack, Rusty has a way of dragging people down with him.'

Knowing when to call it quits, Jack snapped his briefcase closed and left the office without another word.

The house was quiet when Jack got home. It was swimming day, he realised, glad for the opportunity to kick back for half an hour or so before the busy evening routine began. The drive to Sydney was tiring, especially when he had already put in a full morning at work first. And, he was still trying to process what Cameron had said. While Jack had asked the questions with his sights set on Sebastian as the suspect, Cameron had clearly taken it that he was the one under scrutiny.

Dropping his briefcase in the study, Jack sat down at his desk for a moment, trying to gather his thoughts. He had never really considered Cameron to be a suspect. It just seemed a stupid move from a successful businessman and at the initial interview Jack had sensed what he thought to be a genuine motive to help an old friend who needed a leg up to make his way back into the world.

Hearing about the scholarship from Cameron's side, however, had raised a couple of red flags. Although seemingly nonchalant when he had first mentioned it, Jack could clearly see the resentment Cameron held against Rusty was still alive and well. And, in fairness, that was understandable, to some degree. Not only had Rusty swooped in and casually taken something Cameron believed to be his, but worse still, he had squandered it for no apparent reason. But the true tell had been in rage Cameron later exhibited when he had called Rusty a loser. It was well-controlled rage, but it was real and, in that moment, Jack glimpsed the teenage Cameron, pondering how he might have achieved a childhood dream if only his idiot mate hadn't ruined it for him.

Another thing to consider was that Cameron had the means to track Rusty's actions. Many employers used hidden cameras to keep tabs on their staff and nobody would be better equipped to do this than the CEO of a security company. It would explain how Cameron potentially knew which items had Rusty's prints on them.

Jack sighed. He knew he should be excited that he had finally come up with a firm suspect and a motive. But, on the other hand, it added further complications and new questions to answer. Twenty years was a long time for someone to hold a grudge. And, was a teenage grudge really a strong enough reason to potentially sabotage your own successful business? If so, it was a calculated and deliberate scheme that spoke of a vengeful person and Jack really wasn't sure that he could see that in Cameron Melville.

Shaking his head, Jack headed for the lounge room where he could hear the TV.

'Hey, Dan,' Jack said, loosening his tie as he sat down on the nearest armchair.

'Hi,' Danny replied. 'You don't mind if I watch TV, do you?'

'No, not as long as you put in a good day's work first.'

'I did, I swear.'

'That's what I like to hear.' Pulling his tie off altogether, Jack leaned back into the armchair as an idea formed in his mind.

'How about your day? How was Sydney?' asked Danny.

'Busy and tiring. Now I just have to work up some energy to get on to some internet searching tonight.'

'That's easy as.'

'Yeah, for you it is. I'm not as nimble fingered.'

'What do you need to search for?'

'Any newspaper articles about Rusty. I'm sorry I was cranky the other night, but you opened my eyes to how much stuff is out there. I got annoyed because I hadn't factored in how much time I will need to spend finding all that. Lucky I'm used to managing with not much sleep.'

Danny nodded absently, his eyes still on the basketball game he was watching. But Jack knew him well enough to see that he was deep in thought. And, if he had played his cards right, he would soon be able to offload the tedious internet research.

It took a couple of hours, but the offer finally came through at eight o'clock. Danny had put the boys to bed to let Jack get to work sooner and eventually appeared at the dining room table when they were asleep. He sat down and opened his laptop, then looked over at Jack without saying anything.

'You need something?' Jack asked, without looking up.

Danny hesitated a moment before asking, 'Do you want some help with the internet stuff?'

'Well yeah, but you've got your school work to finish first.'

'I've done everything for today. That's why I was watching TV before.'

Jack nodded slowly. 'All right, that would be great.'

'I only want to help you, not him.'

'I don't care what your motivation is, help is help.'

'What do you want me to do?'

'Okay, part of being Rusty's defence means that I need

to know anything that's out there in cyberspace about his previous crimes. I want you to find any articles and print them. Keep a record of the dates as well.'

'All right.' Although he was clearly not going to show any enthusiasm, Danny quickly got to work, scrolling through sites on his laptop, keeping one eye on his phone at the same time.

Happy with his small victory, Jack got on with his own work. He just hoped there wasn't too much out there for the prosecution to get hold of and use to their advantage. Until Danny had shown him how easily newspaper articles showed up online, this was something he hadn't been too worried about.

'There's one here about an organised theft ring at Grammar they reckon he might have been part of,' Danny said fifteen minutes later.

'What? When was that from?'

Danny scanned the laptop screen. 'I dunno, like the *nineties*.'

Coming around to Danny's side of the table, Jack peered at the screen. 'How did you even find that?'

'Easy. I just went to the Sunset Shire Museum website. We went to the museum on a school trip and they told us they got a government grant a few years ago, to set up the website. Part of that was digitising all the old newspapers and making them searchable by name and topic. We had to use an old story to do an assignment, so I already knew how to search it. It's a pretty amazing website.'

'Great work mate, that's exactly the kind of stuff we need to know about. If you can find it, so can they.'

Danny shook his head. 'I can't believe he was stealing stuff at school.'

'I don't reckon he was. He told me he left because he knew they would accuse him of it anyway.'

'And you believe him?'

'Yeah, I think I do. He's not into burglary.'

Danny was quiet as he clicked on print and continued scrolling through the list of articles. 'Here's one about him winning the scholarship in the first place.'

'Send me the link will you, so I can read it myself.'

The first thing that struck Jack when he opened the webpage, was the striking resemblance Danny bore to the baby faced Rusty, whose image filled the front page of the *Sunset Point Sentinel,* dated almost twenty years ago. The second was the difference in his eyes. In the photo, Rusty had the exuberance and arrogance of youth; now those same eyes were hard and wary, worn down by the path his life had followed since then.

Danny too was staring at the photo. 'He could be *me*!'

'Yeah, I know. It's like you're learning in biology, genetics is a crazy thing sometimes.'

'Including being a criminal?'

'Dan, come on, we've been over this. Becoming a criminal is not a genetic thing.'

'Well, Rusty's brother is a criminal too, doesn't that show something?'

'Yes, it shows that a child's most prominent role model is their same sex parent.' Jack realised his mistake as soon as the words left his mouth.

'Awesome.'

'No, no,' Jack backpedalled, 'that's only true when the child is in constant contact with the parent. You can't emulate someone if you never see them.'

His attention was focussed on the article on the screen

as Danny nodded absently and said, 'He must have been a pretty good player to get a scholarship; their rugby team has been top three for about fifty years.'

'Yeah, by all accounts he was. There you go, that's something positive you inherited from him, your sporting talent.'

Danny just shrugged.

'Come on you both won sporting scholarships, doesn't that tell you something?'

'I guess it tells me he was better than me because his scholarship was real.'

Jack's heart skipped a beat. 'What do you mean *real?*' he asked, careful to keep his tone neutral.

'Well, Grammar didn't make him pay any fees, whereas my *scholarship* is actually just someone besides my parents footing the bill.'

Thrown by this but determined not to show it, Jack probed first without making any admission. 'Who told you that?'

Danny looked at him and shook his head. 'You always say I'm not dumb, but underneath you think I am.'

'I'm just asking you a question, Danny, who told you that?' Jack did his best to keep his anger in check but inwardly he seethed at Tamara. She had promised faithfully that she would not reveal the truth about him paying Danny's school fees.

'Nobody told me, I worked it out for myself.'

Jack wasn't about to be bluffed into an admission. 'Dan, I'm not even sure what you think you've worked out.'

'I saw a letter at Jim's house one day. I wasn't snooping or anything, it was just on the table. I saw my name on it so I had to read it, just to make sure I wasn't in trouble or something. I don't know why you didn't just tell me from the start.'

Jack sighed. 'We didn't tell you because, well, I more than Jim, didn't want you to feel like you were under any kind of obligation to me. There's no strings attached, I just want you to get a good education. Just think how different Rusty's life could have been if he'd stayed at school.'

'I still don't get why you do so much for me. I really do appreciate it you know, but it worries me too.'

'Why does it worry you?'

'Well, what if something happened to you? Like if you got sick and couldn't work or even if you died? I'm not saying you will, but you know, one of the guys at school, his dad got killed in a car accident and they had to sell their house and everything.'

'Dan, I started my career in wills and estate planning. Trust me, my will is a thing of beauty and I have more than adequate life insurance. You would be looked after, don't worry.'

'But what about your family?'

'They're more than provided for.'

'I still don't get it.'

'All right, I'll spell it out. You're like a son to me and I want to help you reach your full potential.'

Averting his eyes for a moment, Danny started doodling on a piece of paper. 'Isn't it a bit weird to think of someone else's kid like your own?'

'You're asking the father of an adopted child that?'

'Oh man, no, no, I didn't mean like Sam…'

'It's okay, Danny, you're not the first to ask the question. Look, for whatever reason you came into my life when I really needed a change in direction. Meeting you

165

literally changed me. Call it the hand of God, or fate, or everything happening for a reason, but I honestly believe you were meant to be part of my life. As for the other question, if you'd asked me ten years ago, I would have been sceptical about the bond you can build with someone else's child but I've realised it's entirely possible to have that connection.'

Danny was quiet for a moment, as he digested this. 'So, then maybe you were meant to be the one to help Rusty. Because if you didn't know me then you would never have heard of him.'

'That's right. I wouldn't have done it for anyone else.'

'And you really don't mind? I still feel bad.'

'I'm in too deep to mind now. And I believe Rusty has been framed.'

'You really believe he was framed?'

'Yes, I do, and we need to find out why and who by. This case has certainly opened my eyes to some of the inadequacies of the legal system.'

Danny turned his attention back to his laptop. 'Then I guess we'd better get back to work.'

Chapter Fourteen

Jack's Tuesday was in the nightmare category. His first mediation meeting did not go to plan. In fact, it went so wrong, Jack was forced to remove one of the parties from the room before physical violence erupted. It wasn't unheard of in his specialised line of work, but he hadn't needed to actively referee warring parties for a long time. Then, one of his subsequent clients chose to stage a sit in until her particular demands were met. Sorting out that situation left Jack almost an hour behind schedule for the rest of the day. It was only when he was hurriedly tidying his desk before heading home at five to six that he found an envelope stamped "Personal" in his In tray. Ripping it open, Jack read the contents, then scrunched the letter into a ball and pitched it into his confidential shredding box.

The carefully worded document from Mengel and Associates in Manly made it clear that Cameron Melville would not be available to answer any further questions without legal representation at a mutually convenient time for both parties. Jack didn't blame Cameron for protecting himself legally, it was exactly what he would advise his own clients to do, but it was another complication to deal with. Furthermore, it was a fitting end to his day from hell.

Hoping for some sympathy on the home front, Jack instead walked into a scene of chaos. Sam and Joshua were bickering at the kitchen table, each with towels draped around their necks. A bottle of shampoo sat next to them. Detritus from afternoon tea was still on the kitchen bench and there was no evidence that dinner had been started. Erin appeared then, with a whimpering Chloe on her hip, and Jack could see by her expression that he wasn't the only one who'd had a lousy day.

'Thanks a lot for being so late,' she said. 'Chloe is getting a tooth and has been cranky all day and then Sam came home with head lice. Upon further inspection, Josh has them too. It's taken me two hours to get the stuff in their hair and Chloe has been crying the whole time,' Erin said. 'You can have her for a while now.'

Dropping his briefcase near the door, Jack reached out to take his daughter. 'Come here, Bubby,' he said. The younger of the twins by ten minutes, Chloe was generally calm and placid, but tonight she was definitely not her usual self.

'No! Mummy!' she wailed as Erin attempted to unwrap the toddler's arms from around her neck.

'It's all right, I've got her,' Jack said, prising Chloe's arms free and putting her against his shoulder.

'Where's the milk?' Erin asked. 'I've been waiting for it to make macaroni cheese. It's the easiest thing I could think of for dinner.'

Although Jack had a good poker face, he could never conceal a guilty expression.

'Are you kidding? You didn't get it? I asked you this morning and texted you two hours ago. I don't know why it's so hard to get a bottle of milk when there's a Coles a few doors down from your office.'

'I really am sorry, but nothing went right today. I meant

to grab it at the servo on the way up the hill. I'll go now and take Chloe with me.'

'Yeah, good luck getting her into the car when she's like that. I'm sorry you had a bad day, but so did I and I've got my own work to get done tonight. One of our deadlines got changed and everyone has to pitch in or we'll lose the contract. I couldn't get anything done this morning when Mum was here because Chloe was so clingy.'

Jack exhaled sharply, while attempting to calm Chloe, who was still whimpering on his shoulder. 'I'll get something delivered for dinner,' he said. 'You should have told me about your work thing.'

'I would have if you'd called to tell me you were going to be late. You're not single any more, remember?'

'All right, point taken. I need to work on that.'

Erin's expression softened. 'Yeah, you do, but I'll forgive you this time if you get dinner sorted. Can we make it Thai?'

Jack nodded as he scrolled through the contacts in his phone. 'My thoughts exactly. I'm just in the mood for a green curry. After we eat, you go and work and Dan and I will get the kids to bed.'

'All right.'

Two hours later, the house had been restored to order and three of the children were in bed. Chloe, however, was still attached to Jack. Only half asleep, she was quiet as long as he kept still and didn't attempt to put her down in her cot. Giving up on that idea for the moment, he made himself as comfortable as he could at the table and attempted to get some work done before bed.

'Getting teeth must hurt,' Danny said, as he flipped

169

half-heartedly through his biology textbook.

'Yeah, it's no picnic. Poor little thing. How was your day today?'

'Boring. I had to read, like, fifty pages of biology about plants and now I've got to write a report about it.'

'Well, they might sound boring, but humans couldn't survive without plants.'

'I know, but it doesn't make this stupid report any easier.'

'Just get stuck into it Dan, there's no other way.'

They worked in silence for a while. Jack was happy he and Erin had recovered from their little spat and that she had the peace of the studio to work in. Tucked under the house, the studio was a perfect place to compose without interruption. When he had bought the property from an aspiring musician who'd liked the idea of a rural getaway, but hadn't been able to afford the repayments, Jack had long term plans of converting the sound-proofed studio into a media/games room. But seeing Erin's eyes light up the first time he had showed her his house had altered that plan. They had soon realised it also doubled as a perfect nap room when the twins were tiny and they had gratefully accepted help from anyone who offered. Jack shook his head at the memory of those first few months after the twins were born, when he and Erin had traded shifts upstairs and the studio had been a silent oasis in the desert of sleep deprivation. Looking down at Chloe, he smiled at her cherubic face. What was it about sleeping children that bought everything into perspective? No matter how hard those first few months had been he wouldn't trade them for anything and was often wistful that the girls were growing up too fast.

Reaching down, Jack gently placed a hand on Chloe's forehead, relieved to find the Panadol had kicked in and her fever had subsided. She had started snoring gently too, which meant she was finally in a deep enough sleep to put into her cot. Easing himself up from the table, he gently lowered her to a horizontal carry that would let him put her into bed with the least movement.

Danny looked up. 'Are you putting her down?'

'Yeah, I think it'll work this time.'

'I just realised I need to print something but it's about forty pages. Do you reckon you've got enough ink? I can get you more tomorrow.'

'Just use the laser printer. It's on the left side of my desk.'

'Okay, thanks.'

Chloe went down easily this time, rolling onto her side and not stirring as Jack tucked her in. After checking Charlotte was still covered, he turned off the lamp and half closed the door and went across the hallway to check on the boys. Joshua was curled in a ball in the centre of his bed, the covers awry and his hair unusually flat due to the headlice treatment. Moving him back on top of his pillow and pulling the covers up, Jack got a strong whiff of eucalyptus. At least these days treating nits didn't involve metho or other caustic chemicals he thought, as he absently scratched his own head. Sam was a much neater sleeper and looked like he hadn't moved since Danny put him to bed. Relieved that he had managed to uphold his end of the deal for the evening, Jack decided on a quick shower before facing some more work.

Jack was surprised to hear the TV when he walked back

downstairs. Although he hadn't officially banned Danny from television on weeknights, it was an unspoken understanding that he wasn't at liberty to put the TV on unless all his work was done first. Considering the length of the biology report he was supposed to be writing, Danny had clearly given up on the idea of at least getting it started tonight. Frowning slightly, Jack walked into the lounge room to find Danny sprawled on the couch watching South Park.

'Hey, Dan, what are you doing?'

'What's it look like?'

Jack's heart lurched as he recognised the same attitude he had struck when this whole mess started. 'Don't be rude, mate. Why aren't you doing your schoolwork?'

Danny didn't reply for a moment and then sat up suddenly. Looking over at Jack he shook his head in disgust. 'I can't believe you did that.'

'What did I do?'

Danny waved a sheet of paper at him. 'I found this on the printer.'

'You're upset that there was a piece of paper on the printer?'

'It's not just a piece of paper. It's a receipt. For a dental plate.'

Although he did his best to remain outwardly calm, Jack's heart started to pound. 'What's wrong with that?'

'I'm not a stupid kid.'

'I agree completely.'

'Yeah, you say that, but you still think you can do things and I won't notice.'

'I don't know what one thing has to do with the other.'

'I know you're getting *his* teeth fixed. Don't lie!'

Jack met Danny's furious gaze for a moment then dropped his eyes. 'Okay, fine, I've arranged to get Rusty's teeth fixed. I'm just not sure why you have such a problem with it.'

Danny launched himself to his feet and stomped out onto the veranda. After a moment's hesitation, Jack followed.

'Seriously, Daniel, what's wrong?'

'Don't call me that!' he shouted.

'Come on, buddy, talk to me.' Jack walked towards Danny.

Danny shook his head, fury evident in his rigid posture. 'I should never have told you about him! He's a deadbeat and he's screwing everything up. You're spending time on his stupid case that you should be spending with your family. You got home really late tonight and Erin was so mad at you. I heard you arguing.'

'We argued because I forgot to get the milk. Trust me, Danny, that had nothing to do with you or Rusty. I just had a horrible day with my other clients. And, for the record, I *always* forget the milk despite how many times Erin reminds me. I can't tell you how many late-night milk runs I make to the servo.'

But Danny kept speaking as if he hadn't heard a word. 'You're spending your own money getting his stupid teeth fixed! What does Erin say about that?'

'She's fine with it. It's just a plate, not porcelain implants or specialised cosmetic reconstruction.'

'You still shouldn't have done it!'

'Danny, come on, calm down.'

'No, I will not calm down!' Danny said, shaking his head.

173

'Danny, please don't get so worked up. It's okay,' Jack said, putting a tentative hand on the teenager's shoulder.

After swatting his hand away, Danny shoved Jack in the chest. It wasn't hard, but it shocked Jack all the same.

'Danny,' Jack warned, taking a step closer. There was no response from Danny, so he took another step. 'It's going to be all right, mate,' he said calmly.

When Danny lifted his arms, to push him again, Jack was ready and grabbed his hands.

'Leave me alone!' Danny yelled, attempting to pull away.

With Danny's wrists secured a vice grip, Jack shook his head. 'No, we need to talk about this.'

After another unsuccessful attempt to escape, Danny crumpled against the wall and a tear rolled down his face. 'It all just sucks,' he mumbled.

'It does,' Jack agreed, releasing Danny's hands.

Danny's face crumpled and more tears leaked from his eyes.

'Dan, it's all right,' Jack assured him, placing a consoling hand on his shoulder.

'No, it's not,' Danny said, roughly swiping the tears away. 'It's so *not* all right.'

Acting on instinct, Jack took a step closer and gathered Danny into a hug. It felt a bit strange, now that physically their roles had reversed, but for just a moment, Danny let go and allowed himself to be embraced. Sensing when he was about to pull away, Jack took him by the shoulder and gently steered him back inside and sat him on the couch. Then he headed into the kitchen and grabbed a bottle of water out of the fridge. While Jack waited a few moments for Danny to compose himself, he shot a quick text to Erin, asking her not to come upstairs just yet.

Danny still looked like he wasn't in the mood for talking, but this time it was in a withdrawn and sad way rather than the defiance he had displayed earlier. Jack handed him the water and took a seat next to him on the couch. He waited while Danny opened the bottle and took a long drink.

'I'm sorry if I upset you by organising this for Rusty, but there was no ulterior motive I promise. I don't feel any sense of obligation on your behalf…' Jack paused for a moment, choosing the right words. 'Seeing Rusty in that place, I don't know, Dan, it's a pretty cruel old life where you don't have a proper set of teeth. Not to mention your dad will make a better impression with a jury if he looks respectable.'

'What happened to his teeth?' Danny asked.

'I don't know, I didn't ask.'

'He must look so dodgy without them.'

'Well, he's only missing three, but, yeah, it's not a great look.'

'Who loses their teeth, anyway?'

Sighing, Jack paused for a moment before speaking. 'Danny, I'm going to be totally honest with you.'

Setting his water on the coffee table, Danny announced, 'I think I need a beer.'

Jack's head snapped up and he swivelled to look at Danny. 'Mate, I'm not sure what you're allowed to do at home but I really can't let you drink on my watch.'

Danny burst out laughing. 'You're so gullible! I hate beer, I had to empty enough stinky beer cans when I was a kid to last me a lifetime.'

Shaking his head, Jack sighed in relief. 'You brat,' he said and left it there, steering clear of Tamara yet again, while thinking about Rusty and his mother. Maybe she had been the same, absent when it suited her, but still the apple of her son's eye. Talk about history repeating itself.

Danny was still chuckling when he picked up his water again and Jack used the opportunity to get a positive conversation started. 'Like I said, mate, I'm going to be totally honest with you. When I first met Rusty, I felt the same way you do. I thought he was a loser, a petty career criminal who had been justly punished for breaking the law. My initial aim was to make sure he got a fair trial and hopefully a reduced sentence. I freely admit I was only doing it for you, not for him.'

Keeping his eyes fixed on the water bottle, Danny made no comment.

'You know what, Dan? Most people in jail don't just wake up one day and decide to break the law. It's generally a long progression from a bad childhood, lack of decent role models, mixing with the wrong crowd and so on.'

'Yeah, but he's old enough now to know right from wrong.'

'I know, and I agree he has to take responsibility for the crimes he has committed, but I really don't think he did this. He copped his punishment and plead guilty for the other stuff he did, so why would he lie about these robberies and say he didn't do them?'

Danny shrugged. 'Because that's what loser criminals do.'

Jack exhaled loudly. 'I genuinely feel sorry for him. He infuriates me a lot of the time, but that doesn't mean he doesn't deserve to get justice.'

'He sucks as a father.'

'Rusty was just a kid when you were born, not much older than you are now. He and your mum weren't in a very solid relationship and his own family was no kind of example to follow. He had no idea how to be a good parent. For what it's worth, I think he was willing to give it a try to start with, but then his efforts got thwarted and he just gave up.'

'It's great to know your dad gave up on you.'

'He didn't give up on you, he gave up on trying to deal with your mum. Relationships and marriage can be difficult. And parenting has a steep learning curve. I was twenty years older than Rusty and had everything going for me and I still struggled initially. Some days I still do.'

'Yeah, right. You're an awesome dad. You don't have to pretend to make me feel better.'

'I'm not pretending, Dan, I'm being honest,' Jack said. 'As much as I wanted to be a father, the initial reality was more challenging than I expected. It was hard work and I felt like I didn't know what I was doing. I struggled with not being able to keep things on schedule or make firm plans. It was Erin who guided me through the minefield and showed me that I had to become comfortable with some level of disorder or we would both go crazy.'

Danny lay down on the couch again. Jack took this as a good sign, as he had come to realise that talking with a teenage boy about serious topics was often best done without being face to face. He even remembered that some of the best conversations he'd had with his own father had taken place while they were engaged in some kind of activity.

Jack's patience was rewarded when Danny finally spoke again. 'Okay, just say he is innocent; then how can you prove it?'

'Well it's pretty tricky. If someone framed him, then it

would probably be someone who has a vendetta against him. In Rusty's case, framing him was all too easy because he did silly things like touch what he wasn't supposed to and leave cigarette butts lying around.' Jack decided not to mention Cameron at this point, to void creating any false hope before he had considered everything further.

'Yeah, cigarette butts are, like, one of the biggest polluters on earth.'

'That's right, they are,' Jack agreed. 'I'm glad you kids today aren't stupid enough to smoke.'

'Nah, we go straight onto dope.'

Jack looked over at Danny, but couldn't read his expression. He wondered if he should open that can of worms. But, before he'd decided which way to jump, Danny said, 'Don't worry, I'm not a dopehead.'

'That's good to know. Please keep it that way.'

'Yeah, yeah,'

'Anyway, back to Rusty and your question of what we can do. I've already started going through everything with a fine-tooth comb and I'll keep at it until something shakes loose. I'm not saying the police did anything wrong, they just followed a carefully laid out trail that was designed to lead them directly to your dad.'

'Don't criminals have lots of enemies?'

'Yeah, some do, but Rusty isn't that kind of criminal. That's why it's so strange he's been framed. He's not a bikie, or into drug dealing or organised crime. I reckon he has just made some stupid decisions on the spur of the moment. He was genuinely trying to make a fresh start when all this happened.'

'You honestly believe that?'

'I do.'

'I reckon I should help you then. Every night.'

Jack shook his head. 'Schoolwork has to come first.'

'I'm on top of it now. If I really focus during the day, I'll easily get it finished. As weird as it sounds, I liked helping you last night. It was cool that there was something I could do better than you, that was really useful.'

Nodding slowly, Jack thought for a moment. 'All right. I'd love some help. But if your schoolwork slips, it's no deal.' Jack lifted his arms and crossed them like contestants did on the game show.

'I know.'

'Okay then. I reckon we call it a night and start afresh tomorrow.'

'Sounds like a plan.'

Chapter Fifteen

Too tired to face a swim the next morning, Jack hit snooze several times before finally forcing himself out of bed. Erin was still sound asleep, having not come up until after one, and Jack hoped Josh and the twins might sleep in too, leaving him only to get Sam organised for school and himself ready for work.

His efforts were rewarded with a sleepy but heartfelt smile when Erin appeared in the kitchen at seven forty-five, holding Charlotte on her hip. 'Wow,' she remarked. 'School lunch packed and Sammy in cleaning his teeth with five minutes to spare.'

'You don't have to sound so surprised.'

'I'm not surprised, I'm impressed. You had a pretty late night yourself. Is everything all right with Danny?'

'Yeah. We had a bit of a blow up but it kind of worked out for the best.'

Erin put Charlotte in her high chair and gave her a leftover square of toast from Sam's plate. 'So, you guys are okay?'

'Yeah, we're good,' Jack said, leaning down to kiss Charlotte on the head.

'Dadda,' Charlotte responded, wiping her hand on his sleeve.

'Don't do that, Char,' Erin said, reaching over to brush the sticky crumbs off Jack's coat. 'We don't want to mess up Daddy's lovely outfit.'

Jack stood with his hands outstretched and gave a feigned hurt expression. 'What's wrong with my trusty old grey suit?'

'Nothing, really. It's just an interesting choice considering it's about twenty years old and looks like it came off the rack at Target.'

'It's nineteen years old and I got it from Roger David, thank you very much.'

Erin laughed. 'You forgot to pick up your dry cleaning yesterday, didn't you?'

'It might have slipped my mind.'

'Lucky you've always managed to snag this back out of the Vinnies bag and that you haven't gained much weight since your twenties,' Erin said, as she clipped a bib on Charlotte.

'It's a bit of a sentimental favourite. I wore it the first time I made a court appearance.'

'Fair enough, but I reckon you need the red tie with it,' Erin said, disappearing into the laundry. She returned a few seconds later and waited while Jack removed the green tie he had so carefully chosen, before expertly knotting the red one for him. 'Much better,' she said, patting the tie. 'You look perfectly respectable. Just not quite as dapper as usual.'

Jack laughed as he pulled Erin into a hug. 'It'll have to do for today. Sorry about yesterday. Did you get everything done last night?'

'Yeah, we did. I'm sorry too, I shouldn't have jumped down your throat.'

'We're all good then. Take it easy today, let the kids

watch too much TV.'

'That's not a bad idea. It's a shame you can't do the same.'

'I'm going to fake a headache and avoid the staff meeting this arvo. That'll do me.'

It was a much calmer household that evening when Jack and Danny settled themselves at the dining table. Skipping his meeting allowed Jack to get home an hour earlier and he had taken the boys for a play outside before getting all of them bathed and in their pyjamas before dinner. It wasn't a guilty conscience as much as an act of goodwill on Jack's behalf, a tangible sign he was making an effort after yesterday. Although Erin was tolerant, and coped much better than he did with household calamities, Jack didn't like to take advantage too often. He had promised her that family life would not suffer at the hands of his career and he had to follow through on that promise.

Before they got started, Jack gave Danny an edited version of events thus far, trying to paint Rusty in the best possible light. It took some poetic licence to achieve this, but Jack was still resolute in his efforts to eventually have the two of them communicate in some way.

Danny listened thoughtfully when Jack told him about the sole password Rusty had used. 'You might not believe this, but I actually agree with him. Making up new passwords all the time, and remembering them, is a pain in the butt.'

'Yeah, I think we can all sympathise with that. And it might be one of the few things the jury will be on his side about.'

'Are you allowed to tell me this stuff?'

'Yeah, I told Rusty I was going to discuss it with you.'

'And he didn't mind?'

'No, he's okay with it. You can't tell anyone else though, of course.'

'Who am I gonna tell? I don't want anyone knowing my father's in jail.'

'You know I can set up a meeting with him if you want.'

Danny shook his head. 'Nuh. I don't want to see him in a prison cell.'

'It's not in his cell. We meet in a private meeting room.'

'I don't want to go to a prison. Ever.'

'All right, all right,' Jack said. One thing at a time, he reminded himself before assigning Danny the task of getting Google Earth images of each of the properties that had been robbed.

They worked in silence for the next ten minutes, each focussed on their own task.

It was Danny who spoke first. 'Who's Alison?' he asked, looking up from his laptop.

'Beats me. Why are you asking that? I thought you were gathering those images for me.'

'I'll do that in a minute. I just put Rusty's password into this website that exchanges letters for numbers based on the phone keypad. It's supposed to help you choose more secure passwords. I just did it backwards and Alison is the one of the top hits. There are other words too, but I don't reckon they'd be ones that he would use.'

Grabbing his iPhone, Jack navigated to the keypad. 'You mean like 2 is ABC, 3 is DEF?'

'Yeah exactly. When you substitute the numbers and add the N you get Alison.'

Jack worked through each number of the password,

confirming what Danny had just told him. Rusty's password spelled Alison. 'You don't know anyone called Alison? No family member?'

'No. I don't know Dad's family.'

Jack just nodded and made no reference to the fact that Danny had just called Rusty Dad. 'I'll ask him next visit,' he said eventually.

They went back to their own tasks. First, Jack wrote the name Alison on his notepad before he resumed reading the internet search pages that Danny had printed out on Monday night.

Once again it was Danny who broke the silence. 'Found her!'

'What? How?'

'Don't blow a gasket, but it's your old favourite, Facebook.'

'Dan, if it helps me get this sorted, I'll thank the guy who invented Facebook personally. Just tell me how you worked it out.'

'Easy. You said Rusty uses the same password for everything, so I logged into his Facebook account.'

'Don't you need a username or something for that?'

'You use your email address. I saw Rusty's on that client form. I tried it and it worked. He doesn't have many friends but one of them is called Alison. She's *really* pretty, so I'm not sure why she's his friend.'

'Pretty women often go for the dangerous type.'

'I should change his status to incarcerated.'

Jack couldn't help but smile, then tried to look stern. 'Danny, that's not nice. And I'm not totally comfortable with what we're doing here.'

'You're not doing it, I am. Blame the kid if you get in

trouble.'

'Good point. All right, what's her surname?'

Danny studied the screen. 'Um, Melville. Alison Melville. Hang on, Melville, isn't that the boss guy's last name?'

Jack resisted the urge to bang his head on the table, as he recalled the framed picture of a beautiful woman on Cameron's desk and the way Cameron had instructed his secretary to "remind Ali that lunch is at one". Yet again Rusty had neglected to mention vital information and he was back to square one.

'Yeah, it's his name,' Jack said finally, trying not to let Danny see how annoyed he was. 'I have a feeling that Alison is probably Cameron's wife.'

CHAPTER SIXTEEN

After a challenging morning at work on Thursday, Jack was in a decidedly no-nonsense frame of mind when he drove through the main entrance to Regent Park. Taking the last bite of a stale muesli bar that had done little to satisfy his growling stomach, Jack scrunched the wrapper and stuffed it in the empty coffee cup in the centre console. That being his third latte for the day, he sincerely hoped he might feel more alert by the time he got inside the facility.

Circling the main parking lot, Jack banged his hand on the steering wheel when he saw all the spots were full. 'You've got to be kidding me!' he growled and nudged his car up over the gutter and followed the rough track to the gravel overflow lot. It too was nearly full, and he almost missed the space on the far right. Slamming on the brakes so hard he created a cloud of dust, Jack threw the car in reverse and backed into the spot, not caring that he was crooked and probably too close to the car on his left. Upon exiting the car, he slammed the door and remote locked it over his shoulder as he strode up to the buildings.

The afternoon sun was hot and Jack's face was flushed by the time he entered the main office. Hearing the door bang, the receptionist looked up, and did a double take. 'Is everything all right, Mr Nolan?' she asked. 'You're looking a little flustered.'

As much as he wanted to say, no, everything is not all right, I've been saddled with a non-paying client who loves playing games and I thoroughly resent having to squeeze in an unscheduled visit to get information he should have already given me, Jack remembered his manners and took a second to compose himself before answering. 'I'm fine, thank you,' he said. 'It's just a bit of a walk from the outside parking lot.'

'Yes, it is quite a trek. There's a management meeting on today, that's why the main lot is full.'

'Right,' Jack replied.

Sensing there would be no polite chit chat today, the middle-aged woman slid the sign-in form over the counter and buzzed for a guard to escort Jack to the meeting office.

Although he didn't say a word when Rusty swaggered into the office, Jack's rigid posture, crossed arms and tight jaw spoke volumes. Clearly on the back foot, Rusty turned to watch the guard leave, apparently wishing he could follow him out the door. Never one to back away from a stare down, however, he took his time seating himself before raising his eyes to meet Jack's.

Jack got right down to business. 'What's the go with Alison?'

Denial was Rusty's default position, but he was so caught off guard by Jack's question, his attempt to look surprised was dismal. 'Alison?'

'Just don't bother, Rusty. I know your password spells Alison. I know Cameron's wife is Alison. I don't like coincidences at the best of times, but when two facts like that jump out at me I get very concerned.'

'Who told you?'

'Your smart kid worked it out. He cracked the code on your generic password, then logged onto your Facebook account using said password, and there she was.'

'And now you're gonna say "I told you so" about the password.'

'You just said it for me. However, I'm glad you did tell me your password, otherwise I would never have known about Alison, would I?'

Rusty shrugged. 'Probably not.'

Jack resisted the urge to roll his eyes. 'Well, come on, what's the story with Alison Melville?'

Although clearly not happy about answering the question, Rusty finally did so. 'We used to go out when we were kids.'

'Kids as in twelve, thirteen…?'

'More like sixteen, seventeen.'

'How long did you go out?'

'Well, it was kind of on and off but maybe two years all up.'

'Okay, even at that age, two years is a fairly significant relationship.'

'I guess so.'

'So, who broke it off?'

'She did.'

'Any particular reason?'

'She started going out with Cameron when I got a job on a fishing boat.'

'And how did you take that?'

'How do you reckon? I was so pissed off. She kept on and on at me to get a proper job and make something of myself. And then when I did what she asked, she did the dirty on me.'

'So, did you accept defeat quietly or try to even the score in some way?'

Rusty stared down at the tabletop for a moment and then up at the small barred window before answering. 'I slashed Cameron's bike tyres, knocked down the fence at his house, and cut the phone line.'

'Anything else?' Jack said, unable to hold back his sarcasm.

Rusty shook his head. 'Nothing criminal.'

'Just tell me.'

'I started going out with Tamara, which as we know, was not a good move.'

'How does that relate to Cameron or Alison?'

'Tamara was Alison's best friend and she and Cameron had dated for a while.'

Jack massaged his temples, attempting to vent his frustration and annoyance without resorting to angry words. When he finally spoke, his tone was quiet and measured. 'So, the relationship you had with the mother of your child was based on revenge?'

'Pretty much.'

Jack drew a series of 3D cubes on his notebook, taking his time before speaking again. 'How long were you together before she got pregnant?'

Rusty shrugged. 'Not that long, maybe three months.'

'And how did you react when you found out?'

'Believe it or not, I was actually kind of excited. I've always liked kids and I liked the idea of being a better father than my dad ever was.'

It took Jack a moment to process this information. It wasn't what he'd expected Rusty to say. 'You were prepared to give the relationship a go, then?'

'Yeah, I was. Tamara will probably deny it, but I was. I kept working on the boat and gave her all the spare cash I could. But it was never enough for Tamara. Like I told you, she always thought she was too good for me. I reckon she wanted a bad boy boyfriend to shock her parents and her friends but she didn't see me as a long-term prospect.'

'You don't think she deliberately got pregnant?'

Rusty shook his head. 'No, definitely not. She was really shocked and upset. For a while there, I didn't even think she was going to keep the baby.'

Jack was actually making notes now, even though the information he was collating was not directly connected to the case as far as he could tell. He would make a timeline later, but for now he knew he needed to be methodical and keep emotion out of the equation. Yet again, he marvelled at how well Danny had turned out given his less than ideal conception and lonely childhood with a mother who apparently resented his impact on her life.

'So, by your own admission, you and Tamara were not love's young dream and you broke up just after Daniel was born?'

'Yeah.'

'Am I to take it that you never got over Alison then, if you continue to use her name as your password almost two decades later?'

Rusty glared at him for a moment in a way that was so like Danny that Jack almost laughed. He held back his smile though, returning Rusty's stare. 'Just answer the question. All I'm doing is drawing a conclusion from the information in front of me.'

'Well, it wasn't like we never hooked up again, we did, a couple of times. But in the end, she saw Cameron as a better bet. He stayed on at school, he was respectable, he had a normal family and I was just a loser.'

The notes filled almost a page now and Jack made sure his notepad was well concealed behind his briefcase, not wanting Rusty to read what he had written. 'You didn't answer my question about getting over Alison. You still have a thing for her, don't you?'

'I guess so. Have you seen a picture of her? She's really hot.'

Jack nodded. 'She is a very attractive woman. Is that the only reason you couldn't get over her?'

'I dunno, she just got under my skin. She drove me a bit crazy, but I liked it. You know how some women can do that to you?'

'Yeah, I know,' Jack agreed in a rare moment of solidarity between them. He turned the page of his notebook and kept writing. 'So, when you hooked up again, as you put it, I take it she and Cameron were still together then?'

'Yeah.' Rusty gave a half smile, as if to invite a moral debate, but Jack ignored it.

'Do you think he ever found out?'

'Nope.' Rusty maintained his combative expression.

'And you didn't do anything else to antagonise him or to alert him that you and Alison were fooling around behind his back?'

'Nuh. After I got interrogated by the cops for property damage seventeen years ago, I never spoke to Cameron again until just before I started working for him.'

'You didn't get charged?'

'Nope, they couldn't prove it was me.'

'So, in the intervening years you didn't attempt to

192

contact Alison in any way, even though by your own admission, you still weren't over her?'

'No, how could I? She and Cameron moved to Brisbane and then to Sydney. I had no idea how to get in touch even if I wanted to.'

'Until Facebook.'

'Yeah.'

'So how did you become friends on there?'

'She sent me a friend request.'

'Would Cameron know that?'

'Yeah, he would be able to see it on her friend list and mine.'

'Do you think he was upset by it?'

Rusty shook his head. 'No, not at all. We laughed about it when he invited me for that first drink and agreed we'd just been stupid kids. They've been married for twelve years, so I guess their relationship is pretty secure.'

'You are saying there is nothing untoward in your friendship with Alison on Facebook?'

'No. Lots of old school friends friend each other on there.'

Jack paused in his writing for a moment. 'Is there anything else you need to tell me about Alison?'

'No, there's not. What else could I have to tell?'

Chapter Seventeen

It felt like he had barely closed his eyes all night. But it wasn't for lack of trying. Between counting backwards from one thousand, tensing and relaxing every muscle in his body and chanting "sleep is coming" to himself, Jack had been at the point of getting up to watch some of his backlogged Survivor episodes, when he had finally drifted off at about three. And now he was awake at five thirty on Saturday morning, even though he didn't need to be. Savagely plumping his pillow, Jack rolled onto his other side and drew the doona up around his chin, willing his eyes to close again, but it was no use. After ten minutes, he decided he may as well get up.

Flinging the covers back, Jack shivered in the cool morning air. Feeling around on the chest of drawers for his fleece, he knocked the pile of work papers, that he had spent hours sorting, to the floor. Perfect! Finally unearthing the fleece, he pulled it on, but realised it was on inside out when he tried to zip it up. Yanking the jumper off again, Jack turned it right way out and shoved his arms back in as he slipped out of the bedroom, closing the door behind him.

Stumbling down the stairs in the dark, his bare foot landed squarely on something sharp at the bottom. 'Argh!'

he growled, kicking the small plastic block across the lounge room. Why was there always Lego on the floor? Navigating into the kitchen, Jack flicked on the light switch and wrenched open the cabinet above the bench. He selected one of the large mugs, and slammed the door shut, wincing as the bang echoed in the quiet kitchen. As he filled the kettle, he forced himself to take a deep breath and calm down.

Finally, Jack had the smoking gun he had been searching so desperately for, a motive to explain why Cameron might sabotage his own business to exact revenge on an old adversary. The previous night, Jack had waited until Danny went to bed and then logged onto Rusty's Facebook account. Although he often feigned ignorance, Jack was internet savvy and had no problems getting on to the site. But seeing what was in the message folder had ignited a fuse of fury within Jack like he couldn't remember feeling for a very long time.

Concerned about the amount of coffee he had been drinking lately, Jack opted for a cup of tea. He heated some milk on the stove while the kettle was boiling and poured the warm milk in the mug first, then the water and finally the tea bag. Erin found his tea ritual amusing, but it was the only way Jack drank it, having learnt the tradition from his father.

His father.

Looking down at his tea, Jack felt the familiar stab of pain that still gripped him on occasion. Even though his dad had been dead more than ten years, Jack still missed him so much it hurt sometimes. Wrapping the rug from the couch around himself, he went out to sit on the veranda. A favourite spot to enjoy breakfast in summer, they rarely ventured out once the mornings got chilly, as the sun did not warm the veranda during the cooler months. Wrapping his hands around the warm mug, Jack stared out at the beautiful morning vista of the range and sipped his tea.

Leaving a note for Erin, Jack left the house at six thirty. The children were still sound asleep and would hopefully allow their mother a bit of a lie in. And Danny would keep the boys amused when he got up. Jack felt bad taking off so early, but it would be hard to act normal and he didn't want to inflict his cranky mood on everybody else.

Pulling into the carwash, Jack drove into one of the manual bays and fossicked in the centre console for some two dollar coins. He climbed out of his car, deposited three coins in the machine and pocketed the rest of the coins, before removing the spray hose from the wall. Washing his car always calmed him down. Jack didn't know why, but clearly something about the rhythmic motion of sponging the soap over the car surface and the physical exertion of applying a coat of wax connected with the right part of his brain to restore some semblance of calm.

The manager appeared as Jack was buffing off the last of the Turtle Wax. 'We've got a special on the auto wash this week,' he said. 'You could have saved yourself the trouble.'

'I like to do it myself,' Jack replied, happy that he had managed a civil response.

'Yeah, I'm a bit like that too,' the man said. 'You have a good day now.'

'You too,' Jack said, knowing that he wouldn't.

Erin texted him while he was eating breakfast at Angie's. *Are you okay? Saw the teabag in the rubbish.*

Jack smiled before replying. Tea was his comfort drink, usually only consumed when he was in need of some emotional sustenance. *Yeah I'm good. Sorry for bailing but Rusty is doing my head in and I don't want Dan to know.*

Ah, that explains the tossing and turning?

Sorry ☹ Just couldn't slow my mind down.

It's okay, just woke a couple of times when the blankets disappeared.

Sorry again. You are the light of my life.

☺ I love you as big as the sky.

Jack's heart swelled. Josh said it to them all the time, but it sounded even more special coming from Erin.

Ditto. See if you can keep Danny busy. Don't want him to worry.

I'll get him to take the boys to soccer. Drive safely.

Always.

Rusty's expression was guarded when Jack entered the office, having realised that an unscheduled meeting this early on a Saturday was not a good thing. And, if that was not warning enough, Jack's uncharacteristic scowl should have told him just how the meeting was going to play out. Still, Rusty couldn't resist poking the bear. 'Well, if it isn't Perry Mason himself,' he said. 'In a hoodie, no less.'

Dumping his briefcase on the table, Jack stayed standing. 'You're lucky I'm not the violent type, Rusty.'

Leaning back in his chair, Rusty folded his arms and gave an impatient sigh, signalling that he was not going to ask what the problem was.

'Let me tell you something about myself,' Jack said, enunciating each word carefully as he planted his palms on the desk, then leaned forward to look his client in the eye.

198

'I'm pretty easy going as a rule. I like to stay calm and assess things before losing my cool. But let me tell you something else. If you push me hard enough, I'll push back.'

Rusty's gaze flickered around the room before glancing back at Jack. 'What did I do?'

'More like what didn't you do.'

'Stuffed if I know.'

'You didn't tell me the whole story!'

Rattled by Jack raising his voice but determined not to show it, Rusty held his ground. 'What story?'

'You and Alison. You neglected to mention that you were, in fact, having an affair with her at the time of the robberies.'

While disgusted with Rusty for having an affair with a married woman, that wasn't what bothered Jack the most. What made him so furious was that, once again, Rusty had hidden the information, clearly expecting that Jack would not find out. And he had done this while knowing that Jack was desperately searching for a motive for someone to frame Rusty. He had allowed Jack to waste a huge amount of time trying to build a defence out of thin air. And, undoubtedly, he was still going to try and deny it.

'Affair?'

'Don't even bother, Russell. You know we've accessed your Facebook account. The messages are right there.'

'The messages don't say anything about an affair.'

'No, they don't. But I'm really good at reading between the lines. So let's stop wasting time.' Finally, Jack pulled his chair out and sat down but he didn't open his briefcase. Instead, he folded his arms and fixed Rusty with a hard stare.

Rusty stared back a moment, then shrugged. 'All right,

fine. Busted I guess. And I didn't tell you because it's got nothing to do with why I'm in here.'

'How do you know that?'

'Because she's going to leave him.'

'You're a fool, Rusty, an absolute fool. No, you're not dumb, you're not stupid but you're a fool because you can't see what this means.'

'What does it mean?'

'It means you've given Cameron the perfect opportunity to set you up! For what it's worth I do believe you. I don't think you committed those robberies and I reckon you were framed but we're never going to prove it. If you'd just done your job you could have come away with a qualification and had a chance at a future and a decent life. But, instead, you take up with your boss's wife. So not only have you messed up your own life again, you've messed up your son's life because he's so ashamed of you that he started sabotaging his own future because he thinks it's going to happen anyway.'

'Why would he think that? Unlike me, he's got people helping him stay on the straight and narrow. He's got everything going for him.'

'Teenagers don't have the wisdom of adults. They get these crazy ideas in their head and it's really hard to convince them otherwise. They make stupid, impulsive decisions and get themselves into trouble.'

'Don't let him do anything dumb.'

'Believe me, Rusty, I'm trying, but your poor life choices are not helping.'

Rusty leaned forward and pounded the heel of his hand on his forehead. 'You reckon Cameron framed me, then?'

'Yeah, I think it's quite possible, but like I said, we're

never going to prove it.'

'But we were so careful! He couldn't have found out.'

'Well, apparently, he did.'

'Unbelievable.'

'Oh, you better believe it, Rusty.'

'So, what can we do now?'

'Not much, but rest assured I will see this through because I told Danny I would. Yeah, I called him Danny. You know why? Because I've been more of a father to him that you ever have, so I have the right to call him by the name he prefers to be called.' Jack shook his head. 'How that kid has turned out so normal is beyond me given the way his parents carry on.'

'I knew you didn't like Tamara.'

'Yeah, that's a perfect, childish reply and I did not say that I dislike her.'

'No, you're far too perfect for that, aren't you?'

'I'm not saying I'm perfect, I know I'm not. But I reckon if someone was trying to help me I might just listen to them.'

'I am listening. What are my chances of beating this?'

'I will do my utmost for you, Rusty, but in my professional opinion I reckon you should be planning for another little stint inside. I hope Alison finally comes to visit you after all the trouble she's caused.'

'I don't get why the cops can't bust Cameron if you've got a motive.'

'Because there is no physical evidence! He was already fingerprinted to eliminate his prints on the control units and nothing came up. He's got a clean criminal record, not so much as a parking ticket. I'm sure he could get himself an alibi for the days in question. A jury would struggle to comprehend why a very successful businessman would sabotage his own company over a teenage grudge about a girl. His own legal team would take great delight in shooting that theory down.'

'What if Alison testified?'

Jack shook his head. 'You really think she's going to stand up in court and admit she was having an affair with you? Given that she hasn't sent you so much as a postcard, let alone come to visit you at any point over the past four months, I'm not liking your chances, Rusty.'

'What about the messages?'

'They prove nothing. I picked up on it because I've spent my career looking beyond the obvious, but to an average person there's nothing concrete to prove you were doing anything more than meeting for "coffee" in your own words.'

'The whole legal system is so screwed up.'

'Like I said, Rusty, you played right into Cameron's hands.'

Parking at the bottom of the driveway, Jack skirted around the lower boundary fence and on to the walking trail that led up to the ridge. He wasn't dressed for a hike, but nor was he ready to face everybody at home yet, so jeans and t-shirt would have to suffice. He had already texted Izzy and offered her fifty dollars for the afternoon if she would help Erin with the kids. She had eagerly accepted and said she would bring a friend. Jack was fairly certain this was to check out Danny, but as long as Erin got a bit of a break he didn't see the harm in it. If Danny was anything like his father, he would no doubt enjoy the attention of two girls.

Jack relished the feeling of the autumn sun on his arms.

His dad had often taken him for a hike on a Saturday afternoon, declaring it to be the answer to all life's problems. Having faced a few major personal and work challenges in his time, Jack knew that not everything could be resolved by a walk up to the ridge, but it certainly helped restore some equilibrium. He thought more about his father as he walked. They had been the best of friends, always. Maybe that was why he was so driven to help Rusty, so that he could give Danny one thing that money couldn't buy, a genuine father/son relationship. Jack couldn't imagine how his own life would have been without his dad's steady, guiding hand. He had inspired Jack to study law, recognising in him the right blend of intelligence and compassion for people and the desire to make a difference in the world.

Patrick Nolan's sudden death remained as one of the hardest things Jack had ever been through. Knowing he could never again speak to his dad, or share a handshake, or a hug had seemed beyond comprehension. At the time, he was already reeling from Christine giving him the flick, so he filled every spare second of his time with work to numb the pain. Working himself to the point of exhaustion became Jack's coping strategy. It wasn't sustainable, of course, but it had given him purpose when his world collapsed.

Making it to the top in half an hour, Jack stood on the ridge for a long time, willing the pent-up fury to leave him. He had to keep going with Rusty's defence and he would be unable to do so if he stayed this angry. It took a while, but eventually he started to feel a bit better, as well as physically exhausted. Finding a smooth expanse of flat rock, Jack sat down and rested for ten minutes before heading back.

Knowing he had well and truly slacked off with his parenting duties for the day, Jack got back into dad mode as he drove up the driveway. The sight of the boys running to the back door to greet him hit him like a stab to the solar plexus. He didn't think there was ever a time his father hadn't been there for him, and here he was spending the day wrapped up in his own stuff, neglecting his duty as the co-leader of his family. Leaning down, Jack let Sam and Josh climb onto him for a hug then deposited them in the lounge, with the promise he would be back in a moment to take them outside to play. He then went to find Erin.

While Izzy and her friend Hannah took the girls for a walk to the shop, Erin was sitting on the veranda, enjoying the afternoon sun. Pulling her to her feet, Jack enveloped her in a hug. 'I'm so sorry, Eri. I don't know why I let myself get so caught up in things that take me away from you guys.'

Erin hugged him back, leaning her head against his shoulder. 'I was pretty mad when you didn't show up for lunch, but you did redeem yourself by sending Izzy over. She's so great with the kids. With Hannah here as well, I've actually had time to read this three-week old magazine.'

'How did Danny enjoy the attention?'

Erin laughed. 'He went roller blading with Xavier again. The girls were a bit put out that he wasn't here.'

'I can imagine,' Jack said. Breaking the embrace, he sat down on the outdoor lounge, extending his legs and pulled Erin down beside him. They sat in companionable silence watching a flock of sulphur-crested cockatoos converge in a nearby tree before Jack spoke again. 'I'll try and do better next week, I promise.'

'Babe it's okay. You're doing it because you care so

much about Danny. He was part of your life before we were and I don't expect you to do anything except your best. You don't know how to do things any other way.'

'I know I shouldn't let Rusty get inside my head, but he has to be one of the most frustrating individuals I've ever met. It's taken all this time for him to *finally* get what we're up against. If he'd just told me everything at the start I might have had time to come up with some kind of plan. As it stands now, I don't think I can do anything for him.'

'Is it that bad?'

'It's really not good. I'll give Julia a call later. She might be able to suggest something.'

Erin leaned over to kiss him. 'We all love you as big as the sky. Never forget that.'

Looking over to see the boys running towards them, Jack swallowed the lump in his throat. 'How could I possibly forget?'

Feeling like he should make amends, Jack insisted that Erin go to the cinema with her sisters that evening. Izzy's school was having a fundraiser and while it wasn't a movie Erin particularly wanted to see, she didn't have to be convinced very hard to have a night out. It wasn't until after she left that Jack realised Danny might have plans of his own for the night. He and Xavier might well have cooked up something more exciting to do than feed and bathe four children, who were not keen to go to bed.

'Hey, Dan, if you want to do something with Xavier, it's fine,' Jack said, catching Charlotte mid leap as she bounced on the couch.

Ensconced on the floor with the boys playing Hungry Hippos in what had become a nightly ritual, Danny shook his head. 'I can't leave you here by yourself.'

'I know it doesn't look like it, but I can manage if I have to. I've done it before. I don't want you to miss out on any fun.' Chloe was bouncing on the couch now and Jack could only grab her after wrapping his legs around Charlotte to keep her still.

'This is fun.'

'Well, there's fun and there's fun. But seriously, go if you want to.' Picking the girls up, Jack deposited them in the play pen for a moment while he caught his breath.

'I don't want to. Xavier's doing something with his dad.'

'All right, just offering.'

Relieved to have an offsider, Jack didn't push the issue and between the two of them they finally managed to get all four children to sleep, if not in their own beds. Loving how cute the girls looked snuggled up in his bed, Jack left them there for the moment, while he picked up Joshua and took him down to his room. Tucking him in, Jack kissed him on the cheek then sat on the side of the bed for a moment, smoothing back his soft, springy curls, amazed that this perfect little human being belonged to him. As time consuming as they were at this age, Jack wanted to hold on to this time for as long as he could, dreading the day when his children would no longer see him as the centre of their universe. And, despite still being angry with Rusty, Jack couldn't help but feel sorry for the man in the prison cell who had missed all those years with Danny, when father/son bonding was so important.

He headed back downstairs and found Danny engrossed in *The Magic Faraway Tree* with Sam asleep beside him. 'Great book, hey?' he said, sitting down in the nearest recliner.

Danny blushed a little, then smiled. 'I just wanted to find out what happened when the land moved away from the hole in the cloud and the kids were still trapped there.'

'You don't remember the story?'

'I never read it before.'

Jack didn't respond, knowing he couldn't really say anything without conveying how he felt about Danny's parents. Flicking on the TV, he channel surfed for a moment, finally settling on Frasier. He had always enjoyed the show and realised now it should inspire him and give some hope that fathers and sons could be reunited even if they had little in common.

Exhausted after his sleepless night, Jack was dozing off when he heard Danny speak. Blinking to try and focus, he sat up straighter in the chair. 'Sorry, mate, what did you say?'

'I heard what you said to Erin before.'

'When? As she was leaving?'

'No, when you were out on the veranda. I was putting your bike away down in the equipment room. You said you can't help Rusty.'

Jack sighed. 'I was tired and fed up. I only said I didn't *think* I could help him. But I'll get over it, Dan. I'll attack it again and I'll come up with something.'

'Forget it, Jack. Just give it up before you waste any more time on him. I've been thinking about it a lot and I've decided I don't want anything to do with him. I don't even want to know if he stays in jail or not. He's never going to change and I've messed up your life enough.'

'Danny…'

'You can't change my mind. I'll finish my school work and go home and I promise I'll keep up from now on.

You're right, it's not genetic to become a criminal.'

'Danny, please, we've come so far.'

Shaking his head, Danny got to his feet. 'Seeing you with your kids and Xavier with his dad, I realised Rusty is never ever going to be that kind of father. I always had this fantasy he would come back one day and we'd have that kind of relationship normal people do. But I'm kidding myself. I was just a mistake and I was never important enough for him to even make an effort to get to know me.'

Biting his tongue so as not to reveal some home truths about Tamara, Jack shook his head, trying to come up with something that would change Danny's mind.

But the moment had passed and Danny was already walking towards the stairs. 'I've had an awesome time staying here, so I can't be sorry about that. But I am sorry you've wasted your time.'

Knowing when to give up, Jack stayed silent and resisted the urge to throw something very hard and very far.

Chapter Eighteen

Up early again the next day, Jack formulated a plan for the morning as he made himself a cup of tea. He hated feeling angry and, while he didn't want to be the bad guy, he knew he had to bring matters to a head. Until a month ago, he had barely given Danny's father more than a passing thought. Now his whole life seemed to have been taken over by Russell Anderson and not in a good way.

Enjoying some solitude while the rest of the household slept, Jack drank his tea and read the paper, savouring the opportunity to catch up with what was happening in the outside world. He felt bad about taking off again this morning, but time was getting critical now and Erin *had* agreed he had to do what he had to do. Besides, he could soften the blow by getting breakfast ready.

By the time everybody else woke up, Jack had bacon and a batch of French toast in the oven, the table set and had even cleaned up his cooking mess. Seating himself at the head of the table, he supervised the twins, allowing Erin to enjoy her breakfast in peace for a change. She was on to him, though, and raised her eyebrows as he stacked the dirty plates into the dishwasher.

'As much as I loved all this, I'm assuming you're pre-empting a guilty conscience?' she said.

'I know I'm constantly apologising lately, but Danny

and I have got an important errand to run,' Jack said softly. 'I promise it won't take too long.'

'It's fine, actually. The girls and I decided last night that we're hosting a barbeque today. The others are coming over around eleven.'

'Really? Now I feel even worse.'

'Don't worry, Mum and Arianne are coming over to help soon.'

'You're sure? I could probably put it off until later, but I want to catch him off guard.'

'It's okay and thanks for breakfast.'

'My pleasure.'

Danny was surprised but grateful when Jack made it clear he didn't want to talk about Rusty that morning and suggested a driving lesson instead. Eager as always to cruise around town in the Audi, Danny had a quick shower and was ready ten minutes later. Despite being so busy, Jack had managed to squeeze in several lessons over the past two weeks and had actually enjoyed the process more than he imagined he would. Today was going to be a bit different, though.

After doing their usual circuit, Jack instructed Danny to continue past the main street of town. 'This road leads out to the highway,' Danny said, as he pulled to a stop at the traffic lights.

'Yep, it does. You're ready to give it a go now. It's four lanes and it will be quiet this time on a Sunday morning.'

'Okay, if you reckon I can do it.'

'You can definitely do it. As long as you listen to me, you'll be fine.'

Needing no further urging, Danny proceeded through

the lights and out on to the highway on-ramp. He had picked up the technical skills of driving easily, not complaining when they had practiced gear changes for two hours straight or had driven the same block twenty times, so as to perfect take off and stopping. Danny definitely was a hands-on type of learner and Jack did appreciate that academic work didn't come naturally to him. Yet, he'd proven he could do it when he put his mind to it.

It was a nice morning for a drive and Jack allowed himself a moment to appreciate the scenery as they motored along. The highway to Sydney was picturesque, passing through rolling hills and green fields as it headed south east. It was one of those surreal moments when Jack glanced over at Danny driving his car. The first time they had gone for a drive together, Danny's head barely reached the top of the seat. Now he needed to adjust the headrest up to accommodate his height.

'What?' Danny asked, feeling Jack's gaze.

'Nothing, just reminiscing. I didn't envisage the day you'd be driving me around.'

'Yeah, it is kind of weird. It's an awesome car to learn in though.'

'True. It certainly beats the old Cortina I learnt to drive in.'

'What's a Cortina?'

'Now you're making me feel ancient. It was a popular Ford model back in the day.'

Danny nodded, then rolled his eyes as another car passed him. 'It really sucks that I can't go over ninety.'

'Yeah, it does a bit. But rules are rules. Ninety is fast enough for now.'

'Where are we going anyway?'

'To a little café up the road a bit.'

Fifteen minutes later they arrived at the tiny village of Begonia, named for its thriving flower fields. Now owned by a major Sydney florist, however, the community no longer benefited from its commercial success as much as they once had. Like many other small towns that had been bypassed after highway improvements, Begonia was a shadow of its former self and consisted mainly of the usual café, pub and general store/post office as well as a few other small businesses.

Directing Danny down the main street they finally came to a stop at the Meeting Place Café. Pulling out his wallet, Jack handed Danny a twenty-dollar note. 'Wait for me here,' he instructed.

Danny stared at him. 'What? Where are you going?'

'To see a man about a dog.'

'I don't even know what that means.'

'Dan, just bear with me, okay? I'll explain soon.'

Unsnapping his seatbelt with more force than necessary, Danny opened the driver's door. 'What am I supposed to do here?' he said, before getting out of the car and looking around.

Jack exited the car and walked around to the driver's side. 'There's an internet café, three live sports channels and a huge range of sports magazines. Take your pick.'

'How long are you going to be?'

'Not long. I'll be back soon,' Jack said, climbing into the driver's seat.

'See ya,' Danny said, making no effort to conceal his annoyance.

'Yep, I'll be right back,' Jack said before pulling out from the curb.

Securing a three-hour day-release pass for Rusty had not been too difficult. Given his general good conduct, and the fact that he would be escorted by a guard in a prison vehicle, it was as simple as completing the paperwork. Jack had actually set it in motion the first week he had visited Regent Park, hopeful that Danny might want to see Rusty. Knowing they had a regular Sunday transport for family visits to the Meeting Place, he had managed to get Rusty on today's list. The Meeting Place was a prison initiative, largely staffed by ex-inmates or those on work release, and was used as a meeting place for inmates on day-release.

Jack's stomach churned as he drove to the back street where the inmates were unloaded. While he didn't think Rusty would try anything, the realisation that he was temporarily responsible for a prisoner ratcheted Jack's blood pressure up a notch. Sitting in his car, he waited while four men of varying ages were unloaded, noticing that they had been given different shirts to wear. Jack wasn't sure whether this was to appease the family members they had come to meet or the townspeople, but he had to admit that seeing Rusty in a checked blue shirt made him seem less intimidating than when he was wearing prison garb. Realising that he had no clue how this whole situation was going to pan out, Jack opened his door and walked over to greet his charge.

Given that Danny had no idea where Regent Park was or that a day release pass was even possible, his surprise was genuine when he spotted his long-lost father. Jack did feel some guilt about getting the kid there on false pretences, but, on the other hand, he knew if he had told him he never would have come. The look on Rusty's face was telling, he actually looked unsure of himself, and for Jack it was confirmation he did genuinely care about his son. Anticipating Danny's reaction, Jack was ready to avert his attempt to escape and quickly sat next to him, blocking off his exit from the booth he had parked himself in.

'I'm not talking to him!' Danny said, twisting in his seat to face the end of the booth.

Jack motioned for Rusty to sit down, but Rusty remained standing, assuming a combative stance. 'I thought you said he wanted to see me.'

Adopting the more forceful tone he'd used on his last visit to Regent Park, Jack pointed to the seat on the opposite side of the booth. 'Sit down.'

Surprisingly Rusty did as he was told.

'All right, I'm a *little* bit sorry that I had to deceive you guys, but, at the end of the day, I had to take action because I can't do this anymore. You two dragged me into this situation and, believe me, I have tried my hardest to be the voice of reason and work some kind of miracle, but all I've been given is the run-around.'

Rusty glared at him but obviously thought better of making a smart comeback.

'This is not a good situation, I completely agree. But we've got to work with what we've got and I'm at the point where I'm exhausted from doing all the heavy lifting. So, from now on, you guys have to do your part. Rusty, that means you need to lose your attitude and help me, instead of dragging me backwards and acting like I'm putting you out by trying to defend you. As for you, Dan, it means you need to make an effort with your dad. If you genuinely didn't care, nothing about this would have upset you. I didn't put myself and my family through this whole ordeal

214

for you to just say, "Forget about it". We're way past the point of no return now.'

Danny did not respond in any way but Rusty nodded.

'All right, let's get specific. Danny, I'm going to start with you. Considering you just wrote an assignment for RE discussing the phrase "Judge not lest ye be judged", I have to assume you have some knowledge of forgiveness. Yeah, your dad has made some massive mistakes and has not lived a life of virtue. But you're not perfect either and, at some point, you have to cut Rusty a break and accept his past and try to encourage him to create a better future. You're a big boy now and you're old enough to deal with this.'

Catching Rusty's smug expression, Jack pointed his finger at him. 'And, as for you, Rusty, if you want a relationship with your son, then you need to man up. I know your own childhood wasn't good and that you had nobody to show you how to be a good father, but you're well and truly an adult now. You know how the world works and what you have to do. Take responsibility for your own actions and make a plan for a better life.'

Danny had turned around by this stage but was crouched at the far end of the booth, being careful to avoid looking at his father. Perched at the other end of the booth on the opposite side, Rusty was stealing looks at Danny every now and then. Their physical likeness was striking and Jack realised that Danny's new sibling would have close to the same age gap as he and Rusty did.

'We're not leaving here until you have talked,' Jack said. 'I've got plenty of stuff to keep me occupied and I'll be in the corner over there so don't even think about trying to leave. Especially not you, Rusty.'

'Yeah, I was totally going to make a run for it.'

Danny's only reaction was a muttered, 'Loser.'

Rusty gave Jack an imploring glance but Jack was beyond sympathy. 'You're the parent here, Rusty and this is not a mess of my making. Start talking.'

With that he turned and walked over to the corner to claim the big table near the window.

The trip home was silent. Jack drove, not wanting Danny behind the wheel when he was upset and/or distracted. In truth, he couldn't tell how the kid was feeling. After a slow start, father and son had eventually spoken. Jack was too far away to hear what was being said and, to be honest, didn't really want to know, but he had looked up a few times and seen some sort of conversation taking place. Now Danny was using his fall-back and feigning sleep to avoid conversation. Jack didn't mind, as he wasn't in the mood for talking anyway.

In reality, he wasn't sure he should have forced the issue, especially when Danny had made it clear he didn't want to speak to his father. Although, if Jack wanted to split hairs, Danny had never said he didn't want to speak to Rusty, he'd said he didn't want to visit him in prison. Yep, that is a pretty flimsy defence, Jack thought, as the meaning behind Danny's words had been clear.

Glancing over at Danny, Jack realised he wasn't faking it, he was asleep. There was no way he would deliberately let his head droop forward the way it was now. Jack hoped he hadn't pushed Danny too far and damaged their friendship. Yet, it was a risk he felt he had to take. Sure, it had been brought about by frustration, but sometimes heightened emotions push you into doing things you wouldn't otherwise do.

But, it was too late for second thoughts, and they would just have to live with the fallout. Jack turned the radio up, hoping the Sunday talkback show might distract him.

As it turned out, the impromptu family barbeque helped to diffuse the situation. They arrived home to find cars in the driveway and a house full of Erin's relatives. When he had first met Erin's family, Jack had found such get-togethers intimidating, but now he genuinely enjoyed them. Having such a small extended family himself, he relished the sense of togetherness and especially loved watching the cousins play together. It amazed him how they could throw a party on the spur of the moment, but it always seemed to work out okay, with everybody bringing something to eat and plenty of offers of help for the hosts.

Jack found Erin in the kitchen, putting the finishing touches to a garden salad.

'Oh, you're back. How did it go?' she asked.

'I dunno, to give you my considered professional opinion. Dan wasn't happy about it, but they did end up talking. Whether or not it was a productive conversation has not been disclosed.'

'Right. Well, Xavier is here, of course, and Mitch too, so Danny can hang out with them.'

'Yeah, that's good,' Jack said, grabbing a party pie off the tray Erin had just pulled out of the oven. 'In fact, it's more than good because Danny and I can avoid each other easily in this mob.'

'Is it that bad?'

Finishing the pie in three bites, Jack shrugged before reaching for another.

'You and your party pies.'

'They're so good.'

'You can make an excuse if you want, say you've got work stuff to do.'

'No, I'm all right. But just give me a job where I can be super busy without having to make chit chat for a while.'

'You can marinate the chicken and then it will be time to clean the barbeque. We haven't used it for ages. I think I saw cobwebs on it the other day.'

'Sounds like a plan.'

The last of the guests departed around three o'clock, except for Erin's brother, Luke, who helped Jack clean the barbeque. Luke asked if it would be okay for Danny to join Xavier later for pizza and a movie.

'I know he's meant to be studying every spare second, but I thought a few hours off would be okay,' Luke said, as he brushed the last of the accumulated charcoal off the main plate.

'Yeah, that's fine,' Jack agreed, happy to keep Danny occupied, and secretly relieved that he wouldn't have to face him at the dinner table that night.

'It's great to have Xavier spending time with someone who I know won't lead him astray,' Luke said, rubbing some oil into the plate. 'Danny's parents have done a great job with him, they must be really proud.'

Jack forced himself to nod. All Erin's family knew about Danny was that he was a friend of Jack's. They assumed the connection was with Danny's parents and he'd never told them otherwise. He didn't consider it lying, given that it was to protect Danny. They knew his parents weren't together, but not much more than that. 'Yes, he's definitely a child to be proud of,' Jack finally said, gathering up the paper towel and the last few barbeque implements.

Luke nodded. 'For sure. Don't worry I'll drop him home by about ten.'

'No worries. Thanks for helping me do this.'

'No probs. You know me and barbeques. And, just quietly, I think Erin wanted me to give you some tips about how to keep this one schmicko between uses.'

Jack nodded. 'All right, point taken. I'll look after it better from now on, I promise.' The deluxe barbeque had been a wedding present from Luke and Jack had noticed how his brother-in-law often checked on the state of it, seemingly alarmed when Jack gave it only the barest of cleans after use, then did no maintenance until it was required again.

'Hey, Jack, I'm not telling you what to do, but these guys, they go so much better when you give them a bit of love, you know?'

'Yeah, I'm hearing you. Thanks for taking Danny for the night.'

'No worries at all, he can come over anytime he likes.'

While the boys watched Toy Story on DVD that night, Jack and Erin played chess. Both self-confessed chess nerds, they loved to play together when they got the opportunity. The girls had gone down easily, so they had set up the board as soon as the movie started. Sometimes when the lag between games was getting too long, they had been known to arrange babysitters for a few hours and play on their travel set at a café in town.

'Luke gave me the rundown on barbie maintenance,' Jack said, as he studied his pieces.

'Please don't be offended. He always mentions how it

needs to be oiled after use and all this other stuff and I thought it would just be easier if he showed you, rather than you hearing it second hand from me.'

'I'm not offended. He's right, I do neglect the barbeque. I don't deserve to be a barbeque owner.'

'It's not quite that serious. You haven't gone past the point of no return yet.'

'That's good to know.'

They looked at each other and smiled, happy to just be hanging out together and relaxing.

By nine thirty they had migrated to the couch, each holding a sleeping child as the credits rolled. Sam, in particular, had always been a cuddly child, especially when going to sleep. Jack and Erin often wondered if it was to do with losing his parents so young, if the need to be held was somehow reassurance that he was safe and loved, despite being orphaned at ten months old. They had told him of his adoption as soon as he was able to understand and he was a happy, well-adjusted child, but Jack and Erin were vigilant in case any kind of emotional distress were to surface. It was impossible to imagine their family without their eldest child, yet Jack still felt a sadness when he thought of Erin's friends, Eve and Toby, who never got the chance to see their child grow up. He wondered, too, if they were happy with him as Sam's adoptive father. Being so close to Erin, they had consciously chosen her as their son's guardian when making their will, but they hadn't known him.

As she often did, Erin read Jack's thoughts as he gazed intently at Sam, sleeping in his arms. 'Eve and Toby would totally approve of you,' she said.

'I hope so. I don't know, all this stuff with Danny and his dad, I'm wondering if I was right to force the issue.

Maybe he's just better off without Rusty in his life.'

'It's too late to second guess now. Besides, you are an amazing judge of character. If you thought Rusty was going to be a negative influence, you would never have brought them together.'

Jack sighed. 'The lines are so blurred with Rusty. He has some character flaws for sure, but underneath it all he's a kid from a bad home who had to find his own way in life. I reckon if he'd had the chance he probably would have been an all right father. I can't say anything to Dan, as he's got such rose tinted glasses when looking at Tamara. He doesn't understand she was a big part of the problem.'

'Danny showed me some recent pictures of her. She looks totally different. She really has got the pregnancy glow.'

'Good for her.'

Erin picked up the remote and turned off the TV, before facing Jack. 'Okay, I'm going to play devil's advocate here. I get how you feel about Tamara and I pretty much feel the same way.'

'But?'

'She was seventeen when Danny was born. He was unplanned with some loser guy she wasn't that serious about. While all her friends were out having fun, she was a single parent with very little support. It had to be really hard. This time around she's in a good place. She's got a life partner, she's older and wiser and she had the luxury of planning this baby. It's a completely different experience.'

'It doesn't make up for Danny's formative years though. If it wasn't for Jim and Gloria I hate to think where he would have ended up.'

'I know, I get it. But at least she's making a change now.

Better late than never.'

'Yeah, okay. Meanwhile she's still mother of the year in Danny's eyes while I'm the bad guy for forcing Dan to see his father who Tamara deliberately kept away.'

'Danny will come around. He idolises you.'

Jack shook his head. 'He used to. I reckon it's worn off these days.'

'No, he still does. He just doesn't tell you anymore.'

'You really think so?'

Erin nodded. 'One hundred percent. You're an easy person to idolise.'

Jack smiled as his heart swelled. 'You honestly are the light of my life.'

The back door opened and Danny came in. Glancing into the lounge room on his way past he merely nodded and mumbled, 'Night', not breaking his stride as he headed for the stairs.

'Good night,' Jack and Erin echoed.

Jack raised his eyebrows. 'I'm not feeling the love.'

'It will be okay,' Erin assured him. 'Now let's get these guys to bed.'

CHAPTER NINETEEN

Jack skipped his swim and left early for work the next morning. He wasn't feeling quite as stressed, he decided, as he flipped open the blinds in his office and set his coffee down on the desk. So much of his head space had been taken up with coming up with potential reasons for someone to frame Rusty, and now he actually had a motive, the weight had lifted a bit. It was getting down to legal manoeuvring now and that was something he could do. Whether it ended up in a good result for Rusty was another matter, but he would leave no stone unturned. All that could wait until tomorrow, however. Today was about getting his own backlogged work finished before he started eight days of annual leave.

Despite his busy day, Jack thought about Danny a lot. He texted Erin a few times to check how things were. She assured him Danny seemed okay and was acting normally, although he didn't seem to be doing much school work. Jack didn't worry too much about that, he was down to his last two assignments and they were well underway. It was now the school holidays, after all and the kid did deserve a break after working so hard the last few weeks. Jack contemplated again whether he had done the right thing in bringing together father and son the day before, but still believed it was the right move. Danny had always had a

223

stubborn streak and didn't like to back down when he had taken a stand about something. So, it was as much that as the whole criminal thing, Jack assured himself as he reached for the last documents in his In tray.

It was nice to leave his office with a clean desk that afternoon, knowing he had a break from the daily grind. Jack's position officially gave him seven weeks of annual leave and he tried to work public holidays in where possible to make them go a bit further. They hadn't made any plans for these Easter school holidays, which was just as well, given how much more work he had to do in preparation for Rusty's trial. Jack had moved on from being annoyed at losing valuable leisure time, now he was drifting towards mild panic about getting everything done. But working under pressure was his specialty, so he would just have to go with it.

Jack entered the house quietly. Slipping in through the back door he found Erin reading a magazine at the kitchen table, a cup of tea in her hand. Leaning down to kiss her, Jack put a finger to his lips.

'He really seems fine,' she said softly. He's in there now playing Hungry Hippos with the boys. Mum and Dad have taken the girls for a walk. They're training for the hill trek at the triathlon festival.'

'Great idea. Pushing that double pram up the driveway is hard enough, they'll be ready to conquer Everest after coming back up Range Road.'

'What are you going to do?'

Jack set his briefcase on the table and loosened his tie. 'I reckon I'll shamelessly use the boys as a buffer. You know, just burst in and say hello. He can't totally freeze me out in front of them.'

'No, that's true. He didn't speak ill of you today, which was encouraging.'

'I'm assuming he didn't speak of me at all.' Jack pulled his tie off and undid his top button.

'Uh, no, he didn't.'

'No surprises there. Oh well, here goes.'

Jack never tired of the welcome reception he received when his children spotted him each afternoon. The shouts of 'Daddy's home!' always touched his heart and he had perfected the art of having all four of them climb over him without getting strangled or tackled to the ground. Not having heard him come in today, Jack had the luxury of watching the boys play for a moment. Seeing Danny so engaged with them was moving and he stood there mesmerised for a minute, before Sam spotted him.

'Hi Dad!' he called, too involved in the game to perform his usual effusive greeting.

Josh, however, was willing to abandon his hippos. He clambered up onto the couch and leapt into Jack's arms in one fluid move. 'I missed you, Daddy!'

Jack squeezed him playfully and kissed him on the head. 'Me too! Did you have a good day?'

'Yeah, it was fun! Danny took us swimming.'

'Wow, that sounds great. Did you say thank you?' Jack addressed the question to Josh, but kept his eyes trained on Danny, who, as yet, hadn't turned around.

'We didn't need to say thank you,' Sam explained. 'Danny likes taking us swimming.'

Jack walked around the couch and sat down on one of the recliners. 'Is that right, Dan?'

Danny shrugged. 'Yeah, of course.'

'Did *you* have a good day?' Jack set Josh down so he could re-join the game.

'Yep.'

'Are you going to start speaking to me again?'

'I wasn't not speaking to you.'

'Well, you weren't seeking me out for conversation.'

Danny sighed in response, but finally turned around to face Jack. 'I'm still a bit mad at you, but I kind of understand why you did it.'

'I was out of options, mate, so I just did what I thought was right.'

'I know you would never do anything bad on purpose, so I guess I have to believe you.'

Touched by Danny's words, Jack decided to push the envelope a bit further. 'Talk about anything interesting?'

Danny raised an eyebrow, letting Jack know he wasn't totally off the hook. 'Maybe it was personal.'

'I meant generally, not specifics.'

'It wasn't as bad as I thought it would be. He's kind of funny in sarcastic way.'

'Yeah, he is,' Jack agreed.

'We're not best buddies all of a sudden, just because we've talked once.'

'I know and I don't expect that. But sometimes when you've been estranged from someone the first meeting is always the most awkward. When I'm working in family mediation, sometimes the hardest thing is to get warring parties to meet. After that you've got somewhere to go.'

'Yeah.' Danny turned back to the game and Jack headed to the kitchen, deciding not to push things too far too soon.

When Danny didn't appear at the dining room table that

night, Jack considered moving into his study. It would be easier to leave everything set up in there and it was quieter too. Yet, he couldn't bring himself to do it. Their nightly ritual had become a high point of his day and, he had to admit, he would feel a bit lonely working away by himself in there, even though he normally loved the solitude. Not prepared to confront Danny about his reasons for absenting himself, and knowing how much he still had to do, Jack put his head down and got to work.

Finally appearing downstairs at nine thirty, Danny loitered around the lounge room for a while and headed into the kitchen. A few minutes later, Jack was genuinely surprised when Danny arrived at the table holding two mugs of hot chocolate.

'I thought you could use this.' Danny set one mug next to Jack and took a seat opposite him.

Looking up, Jack smiled. 'Thanks, Dan, this will really hit the spot.'

'How's it going, anyway?'

'It's going. Exactly where I'm not sure, but I'm plugging away.'

'I think I need to tell you something, but you have to promise not to get mad.'

'Mad? How often do you see me get mad?'

'Hardly ever. But you did the other day when you found out about the messages. Dad said you ripped his head off.'

Jack took his glasses off and twirled them by the stem. 'That's an exaggeration. But yes, I did speak my mind.'

'I think you scared him a bit.'

'I don't know about that. He looks like he'd be pretty hard to scare.'

'Why did you get so mad about the messages? I looked

at them, and they were just about meeting for coffee sometimes.'

Jack thought for a moment. Rusty had asked him not to tell Danny about the affair and he had agreed it was best kept confidential. He wouldn't go back on that promise, but he had to give Danny something, or he'd get suspicious. 'It wasn't the content I was mad about,' he said, finally. 'It was the fact that he didn't tell me about them before. He hides information from me all the time and it wastes a lot of time when I have to go digging for it.'

Taking a sip from his drink, Danny nodded thoughtfully. 'That would be annoying.'

'Okay, Dan, I'm assuming Rusty has disclosed something you think I should know. Tell me, please. I won't get mad. I expended my yearly supply of anger the other day so I won't lose it, I promise.'

'Well, he said that maybe you should check out Alison.' Danny met Jack's gaze tentatively.

'Alison?'

'Yeah.'

Knowing he had to keep his word, Jack exhaled as quietly as he could and clenched one fist and then released it. 'All right, why does he think we should check her out?' he said, wondering if it was too late to go to the car wash.

'Well, he was thinking about it, and he said that maybe Alison only got back in touch to set this all up.'

'But why would she do that? As I understand it she was the one who called it quits back when they were seventeen. Why would she want to get back at him?'

'She did break it off first, but they got back together a few times later on.'

'I know, Rusty told me that when I was reading him the

228

riot act.'

'Well, the very last time they broke up, it was Dad who ended it because Mum was pregnant.'

Jack nodded slowly, still clenching and unclenching his fist. 'Right. Well I suppose that does make sense. If Alison was undecided about which guy she wanted to end up with, finding out her best friend was pregnant to the guy she ultimately liked better must have come as a shock.'

'If she liked Dad better, why did she stay with Cameron?'

'Oh, I reckon it was the old head versus heart dilemma. Cameron could give her everything she was supposed to want like security, respectability, and a solid and stable future. But clearly your dad was the one she really loved back then, even if he wasn't such a great prospect by societal standards.'

Danny shook his head. 'It's awesome to know you were a mistake created by two people who didn't even really like each other.'

'Ah, Dan, I know it's not ideal. But, on the other hand, it is what it is. I reckon your parents did like each other at the time but it was probably a relationship that would have just run its course if you hadn't come along. And, as much as you can be sad about that, on the other hand you can't regret it. Without Rusty, you wouldn't be you. You're only the person you are because of that one in however how many billion genetic combination that came from your parents.'

'I never thought about it like that before.'

'I have and that's why I can't be upset about it. That's not to say you don't need to make sure you don't make the same mistake, though.'

229

Danny rolled his eyes. '*I know*! I heard you the first hundred times you told me about being responsible. I'm not planning on being a teenage father.'

'Good to know you're listening.'

Danny made a face and concentrated on his drink.

'I'm forgiven, then?' Jack couldn't resist asking.

'All right, I forgive you. But, like I said, Rusty and I aren't best friends. The only reason I talked to him at all was because he kept going on about what a great guy you are.'

'*What?*' Jack spluttered, almost dropping his drink.

'He told me I needed to listen to you and stay out of trouble. Which is a bit much coming from him.'

Jack was still processing Danny's first statement. 'Well, maybe. But, on the other hand, he's trying to make sure you don't make the same mistakes he did. Isn't that a good thing?'

Danny shrugged. 'I guess.'

'You don't have to be best friends. I just want you to talk to each other a bit.'

'We'll see what happens. But for now, are we going to check out Alison?'

Jack stifled a smile at the use of *we*. He thought for a moment before replying. 'Well, it can't hurt. If Cameron did do it, he was far too smart to leave clues. Maybe if it was Alison, she may have been a bit more careless,' said Jack. And, because she had clearly been in some of the homes with Rusty, she might have seen him touch things, Jack thought, his pulse quickening as he contemplated these facts. 'All right, Dan, you can really help me with this. I've got to keep going on what I'm doing because the court date is looming, but you have my permission to let loose on your laptop. Cyber stalk her and find out all the info you can.'

'Awesome. I'm on it.'

Awoken by a wandering Josh at one thirty, Jack resisted the urge to let him climb into bed with him and Erin. They had gone through a bad phase with Sam, even resorting to seeking professional advice, and had learned it was always best to settle the child back in their own bed.

'Come here, Joshy,' he whispered, pushing back the covers and scooping Josh up. Jack stumbled out of the dark bedroom, glad when he got to the hallway, where a small night light gave off a muted glow. After settling Josh back into his bed and patting him until he fell asleep, Jack headed back down the hallway but paused when he noticed the door to the guest bedroom was open. He leaned in to close it, in case Danny might want to sleep in, and stopped. Danny's bed was empty.

Jack slipped down the stairs and then could see that the light over the dining room table was still on and Danny was sitting there, working on his laptop, with his earphones in. At ten thirty when Jack had said good night, Danny assured him he was going to bed soon. Either he was up to something untoward or he had stumbled across some important information.

Padding across the wooden floor, Jack stopped behind Danny and put a hand on his shoulder as he leaned down to look at the computer screen. Danny reacted as if he'd had a bag of ice cubes poured down his back.

'Holy shit!' he cried, jumping violently in fright. Looking up to see it was only Jack, he relaxed a little, putting a hand to his chest. 'Man, you scared the life out of me!'

Jack held his hand out in a calming gesture. 'Sorry, Dan, I'm really sorry. I didn't mean to startle you.'

Danny pulled his headphones out of his ears and shook his head. 'What are you doing up?'

'Returning a wandering child to bed. What are *you* still doing up, more to the point?'

'Sorry, I just got so caught up in all this. I reckon Dad's onto something with Alison.'

'Why?'

'She's a real estate agent. And all the places that were robbed are managed by the company she works for.'

Jack pulled up a chair. 'Are you serious?'

'Yeah. They're all rentals. I never realised that.'

'Neither did I.'

'The real estate company, Olsen and Wilson, have undertaken a major security upgrade on a lot of their properties. I'm guessing Cameron got first go on the contract because of Alison or maybe he suggested it in the first place to promote his company.'

'Either scenario is quite possible.'

'Not only that, Alison has been the liaison for the whole security upgrade project. She's the one who visited each property and set everything up.'

'Wow.'

'Pretty suss, hey?'

'Majorly suss. How did you find out all that?'

'Well Facebook was the first port of call. She posts a lot of stuff both on her personal page and the company page. They've also got a blog on their website and they've written quite a few posts about how they are taking better care of their customers and all that stuff by having more secure properties. There were also some community newspaper stories about the company and how Alison is their rising star. Apparently, Olsen and Wilson just took over an LJ Hooker franchise that went belly up and she made sure it all ran smoothly.'

Jack looked at the laptop screen. 'Well, it looks like we're on to something then, doesn't it?'

'Yeah, I reckon.'

'All right, great work, Dan. Seriously, this is amazing. But how about you call it a night? We'll get back on to it tomorrow.'

'Yeah, I'm going. I just need to finish downloading the Windows update.'

'Oh, the big one?'

'Yeah. If the laptop hibernates it pauses the download and times out. It's nearly finished.'

'Okay, good night then. Get some sleep. And thanks again.'

'No worries.'

Chapter Twenty

When Erin came downstairs the next morning, she found Danny asleep on the kids couch. Wrapped up in the Thomas The Tank Engine doona that the boys had made a cubby out of the day before, he was quite a sight to behold. Working as quietly as she could, Erin had gotten as far as boiling some water for tea when her phone buzzed with a text message.

Creeping into the lounge room to retrieve her phone from the coffee table, she noticed that Danny had woken, obviously startled by the vibration on the wooden surface. Looking at her through bleary, unfocussed eyes, it took him a moment to realise where he was.

'Sorry, Danny,' Erin said, 'I didn't mean to wake you.'

'No, no, I'm sorry. I didn't mean to crash down here. I was downloading something and I thought I'd just lie down for a second.'

'It's all right. I'm just concerned you probably didn't sleep very well on that couch. It sinks a bit at the back.'

Stretching under the doona, Danny shook his head slowly. 'I totally crashed. I don't reckon I would have noticed if it was a bed of nails.'

Erin laughed. 'Well it's not quite that bad. But you

should have stretched out on the big one, it's much more comfortable.'

'I didn't want to put my feet up on your good couch.'

'Don't worry about that, the rest of us do. Can I get you a cup of something? Tea or coffee?'

Extending an arm out and feeling the chilly morning air, Danny pulled the doona tighter around himself. 'A cup of tea would be nice, if that's okay.'

'Of course it is. I'm making one for myself before the kids appear.' Erin disappeared into the kitchen for a moment and returned with two steaming cups. 'You take milk and sugar, right?'

Danny nodded and sat up, repositioning the doona so it was draped around his shoulders. 'Thanks,' he said, reaching out to accept his tea.

'You guys were obviously on to something last night. I know I had an early night, but Jack is still dead to the world. He's usually the first one up,' Erin said as she sat down on the other couch.

'We think it might be Alison. We found lots of stuff that connects her to it.'

'Wow, that's a bit of a change of course.'

'Yeah, totally. We're going to follow it up more today.'

'That's good news, right? Jack thought it was all over.'

'Yep, we hope so.' Danny took a long drink of his tea before speaking again. 'I'm really sorry how all this has affected your life.'

'Don't be silly, we love having you here. Even though it's not the best of circumstances, having you visit has been great.'

'Are you sure?'

'Of course I'm sure. You're always welcome in our

home.'

Danny's cheeks flushed. 'Thanks. I really mean it.'

They chatted easily for the next ten minutes. Although Erin hadn't known Danny as long as Jack had, she too had developed a deep affection for him and liked getting to know him better. She also enjoyed hearing stories about Jack before she had known him.

'What was the deal with the skateboarding accident when he broke his wrist?' she asked, making herself comfortable on the armchair.

'I told him not to go down the hill. But he was trying to act cool, you know, and totally lost it on the turn. I'd never heard him swear before then.'

Erin laughed. 'You should hear him when he steps on Lego with bare feet. I was sure there was more to it than him tripping over the board on flat ground. He reckons it still hurts when it rains.'

'If he'd practised a bit more, he would have been fine. Considering he'd never done much skateboarding he was pretty good at it. I know I pay him out a lot, but it's like he's good at everything he tries. I wish I was like that.'

'Jack is very intelligent and, yes, he is good at most things he tries, but he's got his weaknesses too. He's definitely not musical or artistic. His singing voice is very average and he can barely draw a stick figure.'

'Now I know why we've never done Sing Star or played Pictionary.'

'Trust me you never want to be on his team in Pictionary,' Erin said with a smile.

'How about his dance moves?'

'He's actually a pretty good dancer. You have to drag him onto the dance floor but he holds his own once he's there.'

'So, no other things I can dis him about?'

'No, I think I've probably said enough for now. The thing to remember is that we've all got our own talents, Danny. You're an amazing athlete and you're great with your hands, either of those things will take you a long way in life.'

'I guess so. But I've got to finish school first, right?'

'Absolutely. It will open so many more doors for you.'

Danny was telling Erin about the time he and Jack got matching haircuts when Jack appeared, wrapped in a tartan dressing gown and with football socks on his feet. 'Just for the record, the hairdresser said it looked cool,' he said, with a pointed look at Danny.

'I never said it didn't,' Danny replied with a grin.

'Danny was telling me about Alison,' Erin said, taking another sip of tea.

'Yeah, Alison. The more I think about it, the more I think she's good for it. In fact, I've come up with a plan to get a copy of her fingerprints.'

Danny finished his tea with one last gulp and set the cup on the coffee table. 'Really?'

'Yes indeed. I hope you two are up for a bit of acting.'

'Us two?' Erin asked, looking sceptical.

'Yep. I can't risk being part of it, but she hasn't seen you guys.'

Pulling the doona tighter around himself, Danny raised an eyebrow. 'What do you want us to do?'

'If you will kindly make me a cup of coffee, I'll tell you.'

The silver Mercedes coupe with the Olsen and Wilson logo on the door sped down the suburban street and screeched to a halt outside a modest three-bedroom house on the outskirts of Sydney. Expecting to see the poised and elegant Alison Melville featured on the company website, Danny and Erin watched in surprise as she emerged from the car in jeans, boots and a pink t-shirt. The glorious long hair she flaunted in all the publicity shots was pulled into a ponytail, partially tucked under a Nike cap.

Having been forced to bring Jack's car because he needed the Odyssey with all four child seats, they had parked further down the crowded street. The house they were viewing, although fully renovated, was at the lower end of the price scale. Posing as a single parent, Erin decided that pulling up at the house in a nice car might raise suspicions.

'You reckon she slept in?' Danny said. They had been waiting about ten minutes and had almost been at the point of calling to see where she was.

Erin shook her head. 'No. She's too good at what she does for that, but something obviously happened.'

'Will we walk up and point at our watches?'

'No, let's not be nasty. We want to get on her good side.'

Alison was clearly flustered when she opened the door. 'Hello, Rebecca, is it?'

Erin nodded and smiled. 'Yes, Rebecca Malone. But you can call me Bec.'

'Sure. Nice to meet you, Bec. I'm so terribly sorry to be late and looking so ridiculous.'

Erin smiled politely. While Alison might not be looking her normal glamorous self, she was far too attractive to ever look ridiculous, even with a cap on. 'No problem at all. Rough morning?'

'The worst! We had a major flood in one of our unoccupied properties at six this morning. I went out there thinking it would take only an hour or so, but it ended up being one disaster after another. You can imagine how hard it was to get a plumber out there on short notice. And to top it off my phone battery died after you rang, so I couldn't call the office to get someone else to come out here to do this viewing.'

Erin smiled again, thanking their lucky stars for the dead battery.

Alison cast her eyes down to the bottom of the steps where Danny was standing, eyes glued to his phone screen, a Bondi Beach cap and mirrored sunglasses hiding most of his face.

'Oh, this is my son, Leo.' Erin rolled her eyes and shook her head in an exasperated fashion.

Alison smiled sympathetically. 'Hi Leo,' she ventured.

Danny glanced up for a second. 'Hi,' he muttered.

Erin rolled her eyes again. 'He's got opinions on everything our new house should have, but do you think I can get him interested in viewing properties?'

'Teenagers hey?' Alison said, leading the way into the house.

'Come on, Leo,' Erin called from the doorway.

Danny slouched up the stairs and followed them into the house, eyes still on his phone.

No matter what Alison may have done in regards to having an affair with Rusty and possibly framing him as a thief, she was an excellent real estate agent. Showing them around the house, she pointed out all the good points as well as the flaws and remained a pinnacle of professionalism at all times. She politely rebuffed Erin's attempts to derive personal information and did not try any hard sell tactics. She just imparted the relevant information about the house and waited patiently while Erin viewed each room.

As much as Erin was quite enjoying the charade, she soon realised they had a major problem. Due to her lateness, Alison hadn't had time to set up the bottles of water, pens or notebooks that featured on the photos on the company website. Obviously staged for viewing, the house was stark and sterile, with nothing on the benches or any of the surfaces. Their plan to get fingerprints from a pen or water bottle was dead in the water.

'Do you have a business card?' Erin asked, as they concluded the tour back in the lounge room.

'Of course,' Alison replied, opening her briefcase and proffering a plastic card dispenser.

'Thanks,' Erin said wearily, taking a card from the top of the pile.

Danny surprised them both by saying, 'Hey, Mum, have you got a baby wipe?'

Shooting him a puzzled glance, Erin reached into her bag and pulled a wipe from the travel pack she carried everywhere.

Taking the wipe, Danny proceeded to thoroughly clean his phone screen.

Erin rolled her eyes again. 'He can keep that clean but you should see his bathroom.'

Alison laughed. 'Well the black tiles here would hide a lot of grime.'

'That's very true. I'm quite interested, but it will all depend on finance. You know how banks are with single parents.'

'Yes, I hear it can be quite a challenge to get a loan

these days.'

Realising there was nothing more she could do without raising suspicion, Erin extended her hand. 'Thank you so much, Alison. I will meet with the bank and see what I can wangle. As I said, I'm quite interested.'

'You're very welcome and all the best with the bank. Call me anytime if you've got any questions.'

Danny finished cleaning his phone and handed the wipe back to Erin.

'Gee, thanks,' she said drily.

'Can we get a photo before we go?' Danny asked.

Erin raised her eyebrows, her surprise genuine. 'What, a photo of you and me?'

'Yeah. I want to put it on Facebook.'

'What? After paying no attention for the last half hour, you want a picture?'

'Yeah, I haven't updated my status all day. It's a nice house and it will impress my friends.'

Smiling apologetically Erin said to Alison, 'Sorry, do you mind?'

Ever professional, Alison returned the smile. 'Sure, no problem.'

Pulling off the cover, Danny handed his phone to Alison. 'It works better without it,' he explained. 'You need to hold your finger right on the button for a second so it can focus.'

Still not sure what Danny was doing, Erin stood next to him and smiled uncertainly while Alison took several snaps.

'Thanks,' he said, when Alison was finished. Dropping his phone in his jacket pocket, he led the way out of the house.

'Thanks again, Alison,' Erin said, 'I'll be in touch.'

Giving a friendly wave she followed Danny down the stairs.

'No problem, I'll await your call.' Alison waved back, and then headed inside.

They didn't speak until they were back in the car. After settling into the driver's seat Erin turned to look at Danny. 'What was with the photo?' she asked. 'Your charade of indifference was perfect until then. I was worried she was going to catch on.'

'Fingerprints,' said Danny. 'We didn't get any. It was the only thing I could think of to get them.'

'Oh, right! Of course. Quick thinking. So that's why you cleaned the screen and took the cover off?'

'Yeah. I was hoping you'd have a wipe.'

'I always have wipes. I might forget my phone or my lipstick, but never the wipes.'

They both smiled.

'Do you reckon you got any good prints?' Erin asked.

'I think so. I tried not to touch it when she handed it back. But her hands were all over it.'

'Yeah they were. Well done, Leo.'

Danny nodded. 'It was actually kind of fun.'

'I know. I got right into it.'

They looked at each other and laughed.

'All right,' Erin said, putting the key into the ignition. 'We'd better get back and rescue Jack. After that birthday party, the kids will be full of sugar and climbing the walls.'

Grinning mischievously, Danny cocked an eyebrow. 'Really? In that case I say we have lunch first.'

Erin grinned back. 'Yeah. Let's have lunch.'

Jack was hard at work on his laptop at the dining room

table when they got home. Surrounded by piles of paper and blissful silence, he looked up and smiled as they walked in. 'Hi. I was wondering where you guys got to. How did it all go?'

Ignoring his greeting, Erin stared in surprise at the empty lounge room. 'Okay, where have you stashed them?'

'They're asleep.'

'All four of them at the same time?'

'Yeah.'

'I don't know how you do that! I'm lucky to get the girls down together.'

'They ran themselves ragged at the party and I took the long way home. Sam held out the longest but even he was nodding off once we wound up the range.'

'In that case, I think I might have a nap too,' Erin said, dropping her bag and sinking down onto the couch.

'Hey, no sleeping until you tell me what happened. Do you reckon you fooled her?'

Danny sat down opposite Jack at the table. 'We totally fooled her and I got some fingerprints,' he said, pulling the phone from his pocket and holding it with a tissue.

Jack listened excitedly as Danny and Erin recounted the events of the morning. 'Awesome Dan,' he said when they explained the phone tactic. Using the tissue, Jack deposited the phone into a zip lock bag and sealed it. 'You took the sim card out, didn't you?'

Danny shook his head.

'No worries, I'll get some gloves in a minute and take it out. I've got a spare phone you can use until they lift the prints.'

'Okay,' Danny said.

Over the course of their respective careers, Jack and

Inspector Dieter Schmidt had occasionally traded professional favours if both thought it was legal and ethical to do so. Having made a quick call to his friend that morning, Jack knew the fingerprints would be taken care of quickly and confidentially.

Erin kicked her shoes off. 'How long will it take to get the prints?'

'I don't know. The main thing is getting them into the system so they can be compared. Dieter can get it done quickly, but then we've got to get the investigating detectives to consider this new info. That might take time. It's got to be done the right way.'

'But isn't the case coming up soon?' Erin asked.

'Yes, it is. But we can only do what we can do for now.'

'All right. I really am going to have a quick sleep. All this acting has worn me out.'

Jack made a quick visit out to Regent Park in the late afternoon. It was fortunate they were fairly relaxed about legal appointments, Jack thought, as he pulled into the near empty car park. While regular visiting hours ended at four, he was allowed to visit as late as eight pm, as long as he called ahead first. At this point he was pretty much on first name basis with all the office staff so the access procedures had become quite streamlined.

Already sitting in the meeting room when Jack arrived, Rusty greeted Jack warily, unsure of the reception he would receive after their last couple of meetings. But, having worked most of the anger through his system and knowing that staying mad at Rusty would not help either of them, Jack decided to call a truce.

'Okay, Rusty, let's just focus on the here and now,' he

said, laying his briefcase on the desk and sitting on the other chair. 'Please tell me there is nothing else I should know about your little dalliance with Alison.' Jack eyed him closely as he uncapped his pen.

Rusty shook his head. 'There's nothing else. She used to meet me at some of the rental houses when the tenants worked to unlock the house and let me in. She would then call the tenant and confirm they were at work and assure them she was supervising the installation.'

'That's what they're calling it these days, is it?'

'You're a real smart arse when you want to be, Mr Solicitor.'

'Takes one to know one.'

'I agree it was dodgy, but it was the easiest way to meet and we made sure we covered our tracks. And it's not like I didn't do my job properly.'

'There's some pretty big shades of grey there, but hey, let's not rehash that. I guess for the moment I'm more interested in why you think Alison would want revenge.'

'It's like I told Daniel. I don't think she ever forgave me for Tamara getting pregnant. Her and Cameron have been trying to have a baby for a few years now and I reckon it's stressing her out.'

'I'm fairly certain that having an affair with an old boyfriend is not the prescribed way to deal with that.'

'Now you're just being a smug bastard. I bet you don't talk to your other clients like that.'

'My other clients pay me by the hour, so they don't waste time debating everything I say.'

Rusty was about to respond, but knowing when to cut his losses, just shook his head instead.

'Back to Mrs Melville,' Jack said. 'Do you believe she's

vindictive enough to do that to you?'

'Yeah, I think so. I mean, she can be sweet and kind, but you don't want to mess with her. She can be hard as nails when she wants to.'

'Did you ever smoke around her?'

'Yeah, I did. Outside, of course. She's not a regular smoker, but she always cadged one or two off me when we met. And she packed the butts up and took them with her,' Rusty said, his face changing expression as he realised how calculated that action was.

'Did you ever touch valuable items when she was there?'

'Yeah, a couple of times. She didn't like me doing that.'

'As a highly regarded real estate agent, I should hope not.'

'And the smart arse is back.'

Jack ignored that comment. 'So, Alison has definitely not visited you or had any contact since your arrest?'

'No, nothing, I swear.'

'Well, we think we've got some prints, so if we can convince the police to take another look you might, and I stress might, just get lucky.'

'How is it lucky when the stupid cops got the wrong guy in the first place?'

'They only got the wrong guy because you left yourself wide open. You also got lucky because your son knew someone who could actually help you.'

Rusty stared at the tabletop for a moment. 'Thanks for getting Daniel to meet with me. He's an awesome kid.'

'He is.'

'I reckon it's all because of you.'

'No, I can't take all the credit. Jim and Gloria Stewart

are the ones who've done most of the hard yards and, as much as you might not like Tamara, she must have done something right.'

'Yeah, whatever. I remember the Stewarts. Their son Jeremy was in my class at primary school.'

'They're good people. They were keeping an eye on Daniel long before I met him.'

'I guess I am lucky then, aren't I?'

'Yeah, you are.'

CHAPTER TWENTY-ONE

Although it was difficult to remain focussed on Rusty's trial preparation, Jack forced himself to keep at it over the following days. Morning swims with Danny helped him start the day in a good frame of mind and he generally managed to squeeze half an hour of work in before the kids got up. Depending on the day's activities, there were other windows of time when he could sneak to his study, or occasionally the music studio for a while, if he needed total peace and quiet.

Jack tried not to get his hopes up too much about the fingerprints. There was no guarantee that there would even be usable prints on the phone, and the detectives on the case may not even consider new evidence at this stage. Having done himself no favours with his behaviour during and after his arrest, they might not be particularly sympathetic towards Rusty. And Jack knew he would probably feel the same way if the circumstances were reversed.

Amidst all the technical trial prep, Jack found himself thinking about Rusty's mother a lot. It concerned him that he and Danny had apparently had the same kind of maternal influence and he felt he needed to explore their relationship further, if for no other reason than to work out a way to get Danny to see Tamara in a more balanced light.

Holed up in the silence of the studio on Wednesday morning, Jack dialled Gloria Stewart's number. After exchanging pleasantries and updating her on the case, he explained why he had rung. Gloria listened carefully, then paused for a moment before answering.

'As much as I trust your professional judgement, Jack, I beg to differ on your comparison of Tamara and Eileen. As we know, Tamara did leave Danny to his own devices a lot and that job she had at the pub was more about meeting men than earning a living, but Eileen, she was more of a victim of circumstance.'

'How so?'

'Well, times were different then as you know. There was more of a stigma about divorce and broken families, especially in a small town, which is probably why Eileen stayed in the marriage. She had to work two jobs to keep food on the table and pay the rent, because her husband certainly didn't earn any kind of honest living. They weren't glamorous jobs she had either. She worked the morning shift down at the fish markets and then did cleaning for several local businesses at night.'

'Right.'

'She was a hard worker too, everyone said so.'

'But she must have known that leaving the boys unsupervised could only lead to trouble.'

'Maybe, but at least she knew they'd be fed and have a roof over their heads if she worked. It probably seemed like the lesser of two evils.'

'True enough,' Jack agreed.

He was still thinking about what Gloria had told him when he went to see Rusty that afternoon. Spending the first half hour of his visit confirming that all the affected properties were rented through Olsen and Wilson, Jack also managed to pin Rusty down on the issue of his password. 'Do you think it's possible that Alison could have seen you enter your password at any of the places in question?' he asked, eyeing Rusty intently.

Rusty wouldn't meet his gaze. 'Yeah,' he agreed. 'I definitely didn't tell her but she was there and might have snuck a look more than once.'

Obviously expecting to be chastised for this admission, Rusty was thrown by Jack's next question.

'Tell me about your mother,' he said.

'My *mother*?'

'Yeah.'

'What's she got to do with any of this?'

'Nothing. I'm just interested, that's all.'

Apparently relieved at the change of topic, Rusty gave the closest thing to a genuine smile Jack had witnessed from him. 'My mum is awesome,' he said, his tone softening and his whole demeanour changing. 'No matter what kind of scrapes I've got myself into, she's always stood up for me. I've been telling her for years she should leave Dad and have a nice life for herself, but she never listens.'

'So, you're still in regular contact with her now?'

'Yeah. I've always been in contact with her. Ever since I left home she's written me a letter once a week, regular as clockwork. That's how I knew who you were when you showed up here.'

It was Jack's turn to be completely thrown by the conversation. 'You knew who I was?'

Rusty nodded. 'Of course. You were the big hero at Sunset Point who saved the Beach House. Like every other man and his dog up there, Mum thinks you're the best thing since sliced bread.'

Jack clenched the edge of the table with both hands, looking down for a moment and then snapped his head up to glare at Rusty. 'If you already knew who I was,' he said, slowly and deliberately, 'why didn't you say something? Why'd you make it so hard for me to even help you?'

'I didn't want you to have the upper hand.'

Still bewildered, Jack shook his head. 'I hate to break it to you, Rusty, but given that you're the one in jail, I was always going to have the upper hand.'

'Yeah, but at least I got the opportunity to see you squirm a bit. You're so out of your comfort zone in here, it's entertaining to watch.'

'That's really very childish.'

'Yeah, it might be, but it's all I've got and you still don't understand, do you?'

'I guess I don't.'

'Let me ask you something, Jack. If you were not allowed to see your own kid and then you heard all about this guy, who everyone thinks is awesome, come and do all the things you should be doing for your son, but you can't, because you're not smart or rich and you've screwed up your life, do you think you'd like it? And then, just to make it even worse, what if this guy was the only one who might be able to get you out of jail? Do you reckon you'd greet him with open arms?'

It was Jack's turn to avert his gaze. The defensive responses were right on the tip of his tongue – he hadn't deliberately taken Rusty's place with Danny, he was only trying to help, and Rusty should have tried harder to stay in touch, and shouldn't have had an affair with a married woman and gotten himself into this mess – but he couldn't bring himself to say them. Finally, amidst all his bluster and abrasiveness, Rusty had cut though the maelstrom of what had brought him to this point in his life and revealed his deepest insecurities.

And, for the first time, Jack understood where his client was coming from.

* * * * *

Thursday morning brought with it a dense fog that encased the valley, hiding the town below. As he stood out on the veranda, drinking a cup of tea, Jack thought about how appropriately the scene matched his headspace – hazy and unclear which way was up. His last conversation with Rusty had clouded his thinking, blurring the boundaries he had set about pursuing the case without getting emotionally involved. While Rusty's actions had indeed been childish, Jack couldn't help admiring him for playing the only card he had to play. And, as much as he didn't like to admit it, he was embarrassed that his own demeanour had been so easy for Rusty to see through. So much for acting like he had it all under control.

Although he was at his desk by eight o'clock, the silence of his study proved claustrophobic after a while, so Jack headed out to the lounge room to see what the kids were up to. With Josh and the twins still engrossed in Play School, Jack sat down to help Sam with his new Lightning McQueen puzzle. Caught up in sorting the dozens of similar looking pieces, it took a moment for Jack to process that the siren blaring in the background was not coming from the TV, it was actually his phone. Danny had changed the ring tone again.

Jumping up, Jack grabbed his phone from the couch and immediately swiped the screen, when he saw it was Dieter's number.

'Hey, Jack,' his friend said, in his usual laconic fashion.

'Dieter, how are you? We've all been sweating on your results.'

'Well, I've got some good news. We got a nice set of prints. There were a couple of Danny's too, of course, but he did a good job cleaning the screen so well first. Those phone screens pick up the prints nicely.'

Jack let out a breath he didn't even realise he was holding. 'That is amazing news. Thank you so much.'

'No problem. But we're not home and hosed yet. I'm going to have to finesse this and it might take some time. Your client has got some pretty impressive form and he hasn't exactly been co-operative throughout the whole process.'

'I know. I completely understand what you're saying. But if you can convince them to have another look…'

'I'll do everything in my power.'

'Coming from an inspector that means something.'

'Yeah, but I still have to tread gently.'

'Understood. Thank you again. I owe you big time.'

'It'll even out sometime. Besides I am genuinely invested in justice being done.'

'I know you are. Just let me know when you know something.'

CHAPTER TWENTY-TWO

The next twenty-four hours crept by agonisingly slowly. Both Jack and Danny were on edge, but put their nervous tension to good use. Danny finished his last assignment and even made a rough plan for the next term's assessments. Jack put up a new swing set in the back yard and spent a whole hour pushing the girls, who refused to get off until he promised to take them swimming. With the boys away at an overnight sleepover with Sam's biological grandparents, the house seemed too quiet and each of them yearned for the chaos of Sam and Josh running around, to distract them from thinking about the elusive fingerprints.

Jack allowed himself to daydream briefly about the way he would speak to the press when Rusty was released from custody. As much as he genuinely preferred to stay out of the spotlight, he was not averse to positive publicity when truth was upheld and justice prevailed. Jack certainly didn't want to rub Cameron's nose in it and would be circumspect when pressed for closer details. Despite everything, he genuinely liked Cameron Melville. No doubt some smart journalist would ask if he was considering making the move to criminal defence, to which he would reply, unequivocally, no. While Jack was glad his training had provided him with the skills to mount a successful defence, and negate the need to go to court, it had also reinforced to him that the direction his career had moved in had been the right one for him.

It was hard to know how Cameron would play the whole thing. No doubt he would attempt to keep it out of the press altogether. The media attention had been big when it all happened, raising many questions about home security systems and the companies that installed them. But given that Rusty's trial date was months away, it had soon lost steam. Most of the public probably wouldn't even remember it. So, unless the robbery victims made a big deal about it, Jack assumed it would all be dealt with very quietly.

They still hadn't heard anything when Jack went to pick up the boys that afternoon. Sam's grandparents, Harvey and Maureen, lived twenty minutes away, allowing them regular access to their only grandchild. Although only biologically related to Sam, they had grown to love Sam's step-siblings as well, giving the kids another set of grandparents. Whenever Harvey and Maureen came to visit, they would lavish Joshua and the girls with equal affection and always insisted Josh come too when Sam went to stay at their house.

Jack hadn't even lifted his hand to knock before the door was opened and Maureen embraced him with a warm, motherly hug. 'Hello, Jack! Please come in and have some afternoon tea.'

Catching a whiff of the delicious smell of home baked biscuits, Jack needed no further urging. Glancing into the lounge room and seeing Harvey in the midst of creating a Lego village, with the boys eagerly helping him, Jack felt the tension of the last few days melt away. This was what life was all about, he realised.

It was hard to believe his first meeting with this warm and loving couple had happened under the tensest of circumstances. Devastated at the sudden loss of their only child, Maureen and Harvey were determined to contest the wills of their son and daughter-in-law, that clearly stated custody of Sam was to go to their closest friend, Erin. Although at that time he no longer specialised in wills, Jack occasionally took overflow cases. Having ticked "will dispute" on her client form, Erin was referred to Jack and arrived in his office in a highly-stressed state, desperate for legal advice. She was so upset that Jack didn't have the heart to tell her that he had no experience with child custody. Besides that, he was intrigued with the situation, as well as Erin herself, and thus decided to take the case on.

'What kind of coffee would you like?' Maureen asked. 'We've got this new machine and I love showing it off.'

Seating himself at the kitchen table, Jack said, 'Um, latte thanks.'

'Coming up.' Maureen placed a plate of jam drops on the table. 'Have some,' she said.

Jack took one, savouring each bite of the delicious biscuit while Maureen made the coffee. 'Thanks so much for having the boys stay over,' he said. 'I hope they behaved themselves.'

'Don't be silly. We love having them stay and of course they behaved themselves. They've got such beautiful manners.'

'We do insist on that at home, so it's good to know they do it away from our nagging.'

Maureen smiled. 'Of course Sammy is our own flesh and blood so he's that tiny bit more special, but oh, Jack, we adore that curly haired scallywag too. With those beautiful eyes of yours and the way he chats nonstop, he's impossible to resist.'

'Scallywag is a good way to describe Joshua,' Jack agreed with a smile, reaching for another biscuit. 'And, yes, he is impossibly cute. The chatting can wear a bit thin at bedtime though.'

Maureen nodded. 'Yes, I know how that goes,' she said, with a distant smile.

'Does Sam look like Toby at that age?'

'Yes, very much so. He's a little bit taller and thinner, but otherwise just like him.' Maureen smiled proudly this time. She set Jack's coffee on the table and made herself a cup.

It was so good to see Maureen in such a good space. Those months after the accident had been agonising for everybody. Jack had recognised the devastating grief Maureen and Harvey were experiencing and knew their actions were motivated by a desperation to keep hold of the only piece of their son they had left. His immediate strategy had been to put the brakes on the will dispute, allowing everybody to grieve, and he had also facilitated a temporary joint custody arrangement. As Jack had hoped, time, and the day-to-day reality of caring for a young child, had softened Maureen and Harvey's stance and they had come to see that Toby and Eve's decision had been the right one. It had been a life changing experience for everyone involved, but Jack still felt he had gained the most, the wife and family he had longed for, as well as a meaningful career refocus.

'Penny for your thoughts,' Maureen said, sitting down with a cappuccino.

Jack smiled. 'I don't know; I was just pondering how

unorthodox, yet beautiful, this whole situation is.'

Reaching across the table, Maureen grasped his hand. 'Yes, I know. To lose our son, but gain three more grandchildren.' She shrugged. 'It's not what you would ever choose, the loss I mean, but then it's hard to imagine not knowing those precious souls you brought into our life.'

'It's like Sam is this amazing little conduit.'

'We always knew he was special.'

'About as special as they come.'

'So,' Maureen said, patting Jack on the arm, 'Do you think you'll have any more children?'

Jack smiled wearily. 'I'm pretty sure we're finished. Ecstatic with what we've got, but happy to call it a day.'

'Four is a good number. Even.'

'Yeah, it is and I reckon we've already won the fertility lotto twice, considering how hard it is for some people to conceive at the age we did.'

'Yes, that's true. You were definitely blessed.'

'We know it. Great coffee by the way.'

'Thank you. I worked in a coffee shop for a while, so I know my way around the machine. I've got some bikkies to take home too.'

'Thank you, we won't say no. And now I'd better gather up the boys and give you your peace and quiet back.'

'Trust me, there's such a thing as too much peace and quiet.'

Jack picked Danny up at the Aquatic Centre on the way home. He had opted to do a squad session there for training purposes and to keep busy. As Jack expected, Danny looked exhausted when he climbed into the front passenger seat. Despite that, before they set off, he turned around and touched knuckles with the boys who were secured in their car seats in the back. 'Hey, boys!' he said.

'Hi, Danny!' they chorused back.

Settling into the seat, Danny put his seatbelt on and leaned his head back against the head rest.

Jack smiled. 'Hard enough for you?' he asked as he pulled out onto the main road.

'I'm wrecked!' Danny replied. 'Who is that guy anyway?'

'That's Andre. He's a former Soviet champion. Just quietly, I reckon he thinks our training methods are a bit soft here.'

'Yeah, totally. We had to do a two k IM.'

'What? Ten laps of each stroke?'

'Yeah. The butterfly nearly killed me.'

'Well, you said you wanted a good workout.'

Danny made a face and shook his head. 'I hope you've got some Deep Heat at home.' Turning to the back again, he smiled at Sam and Josh. 'Did you have fun at your sleepover?'

'Yeah!' the boys said.

'Nanna made us bikkies,' Sam said.

'Bikkies?' Danny's eyes lit up.

'They're on the floor down there,' Jack said. 'But don't go too crazy, they're Erin's favourite.'

Helping himself to two jam drops, Danny checked his phone before speaking again. 'Are there another set of grandparents?' he asked softly.

'Uh, sort of. I don't think Eve's father was ever really in the picture and her mother is what you might call a free spirit. She lives out in the wilds of Tasmania and doesn't really stay in touch. We're happy for her to have as much contact as she wants, but so far it's been pretty minimal.'

'Oh, right. And Eve didn't have brothers and sisters?'

'Apparently there is a half-brother, but he's much younger, about twenty I think. Eve had left home before he was even born.'

'Do you think it will be weird for me being so much older than my brother or sister?'

'No, not at all. I reckon you're going to be a pretty hands on big brother.'

Jack was surprised when Erin came out to the garage to greet them. She always missed the boys when they were away, but not so much that she dropped everything to say hello the second they arrived. When she reached over and opened Jack's door, he began to get worried. What's happened? he wondered, his heart starting to pound.

'Where's your phone?' Erin asked.

'My phone?' Jack had to think for a second. He had turned it to silent before he went into Harvey and Maureen's house, thinking it was set to vibrate. But obviously it hadn't been. He reached into the lower pocket of his cargo pants, pulled the phone out and pressed the home key. There were seven missed calls. Three were from Erin and four from Dieter.

Meeting Erin's gaze, Jack's eyes widened. 'Did he say anything…?'

Erin shook her head. 'You know Dieter, he gives nothing away. But he sounded pretty keen to speak to you, I think that's why he tried the landline as well.'

Even though he was relieved there was nothing wrong at home, Jack's heart continued to pound. Now that the moment of truth had arrived, he wasn't sure he actually wanted to know. As tense as waiting was, there was always that element of hope. Having the results meant that hope was either realised or extinguished. Taking a deep breath, Jack pulled the keys from the ignition and climbed out of the car. He was reaching over to open the back door and get the boys out when Erin grabbed his other arm. 'I'll do that. You go and call Dieter.'

'Okay.' Jack took another deep breath and turned to Danny. 'Dan, can you give Erin a hand here?'

Clearly equally anxious, Danny nodded. 'Yeah, yeah, I'll help.'

Heading out to the back yard where he knew it would be quiet, Jack navigated to his contacts and tapped Dieter's number.

It seemed to take forever for Dieter to answer and when he finally did, he asked Jack if he'd mind being put on hold for a moment. 'Sure, no worries,' Jack said, not meaning a word of it. Feeling like a cat on a hot tin roof, he paced the paved barbeque area for several minutes, growing ever impatient. Who'd be a criminal defence lawyer? he thought as he nudged Sam's soccer ball with his foot. Give me complex mediation issues any time, in preference to this stressful suspense.

When Dieter finally came on the line, his tone was bland and unhurried, as usual. 'Jack, good to finally get hold of you.'

'Yeah, I'm so sorry. I had the phone on silent, forgot to switch it back.'

'No probs, I just wanted to talk to you before I head into a major task force meeting in about five minutes.'

'Right. Have you got some news?'

'Uh, yes. Yes, I have.'

'Okay.' Jack's heart was in his throat now.

'Well, the good news is the investigating officers are willing to have another look at it. I've got an appointment with them tomorrow.'

'Great, that's good, right?'

'Yeah, it is. The bad news is that Cameron Melville is pressing further charges of trespass and break and enter. It appears Rusty jumped the fence at the Balmoral office one morning and gained unauthorised access to the office through a window.'

'When was this?'

'Months ago, when he worked there, he had an early job and had forgotten something from the workshop. Rather than call Cameron, he let himself in by somewhat dubious means. I think it was all fine and dandy at the time, but it looks like you've touched a nerve somewhere and Mr Melville is putting the screws in. They've got it on CCTV, so there's no denying it. And, of course, for the jury it's not much of a leap from breaking into your workplace to entering homes you've previously worked at.'

'This just gets better and better.'

'It can be par for the course in criminal cases.'

Exhaling, Jack tried to gather his thoughts. 'So, you haven't heard back about the prints then?'

'No, not yet. Sorry, I shouldn't have rung so many times when you're on a knife edge. I'll call you the second I hear anything.'

'Thanks. I'll make sure my phone is on.'

'Good plan. Talk to you soon mate.'

'Yep, catch you later.' Hitting the red disconnect icon, Jack bumped his fist against his forehead, then kicked the soccer ball so hard it sailed over the pool fence and landed right in the deep end.

Jack's first thought on hearing about the extra charges was to storm out to Regent Park and read Rusty the riot act for being so stupid. After a long, hot shower, however, he calmed down somewhat. There was no point worrying about the charges until they heard back about the prints. If, as hoped, the prints put Alison in the frame, the extra charges would go from being a major issue to a minor one, especially given that nothing had been stolen from the workshop.

Although it was too late to organise baby sitters so he could take Erin out to dinner, Jack did his best to create a cosy night in. After getting the girls down early and leaving Danny to put the boys to bed, Jack and Erin enjoyed a leisurely game of chess, a glass of wine and some interesting conversation not related in any way to Russell Anderson.

'How about a game of Pictionary?' Jack suggested after packing up the chess board.

'What?' Erin replied, puzzled. They didn't have Pictionary.

Jack feigned a hurt expression. 'Danny took great delight in consoling me for my complete lack of artistic talent. I'm not so sure I like the two of you having cosy little chats about me.'

Erin laughed. 'It wasn't deliberate character assassination. I was just making a point about individual strengths and weaknesses.'

'Well, whatever you said hit the mark. He's all enthused about school since you told him how important it is. Never mind the years I've spent pleading and cajoling him to put the required effort in.'

'Oh, poor Jack,' Erin said, reaching across the table to pat his hand. 'You know how it is, kids don't listen to the adult who does the hard yards. Just like Sam refuses to have a banana when I make his lunch but when Dad says it gives him energy he takes it. Or how Joshy screams blue murder when I wash his hair but doesn't even blink when you do it.'

Jack laughed this time. 'All right, fair point. I'll do anything to get Danny through to graduation day. Maybe you can send him encouraging messages on Facebook.'

'Maybe I can.'

They grinned at each other across the table.

'I like it when you're on holidays,' Erin said.

'Me too, it's a real treat to just hang out at home.'

Switching on the TV, they came across Planes, Trains and Automobiles and laughed so hard Danny came down to see what they were watching. Scoffing at the storyline at first, he nevertheless sat on the kids couch, ostensibly to play with his phone, but was soon engrossed in the movie and stayed until the end.

'I can't believe I just watched such a lame movie,' he said, as the credits rolled.

'Hey, come on, Dan, it may be dated, it may be a bit corny, but it's not lame. It's a classic,' Jack said.

'Yeah, sure it is.'

The three of them chatted a bit longer, comparing favourite movies and enjoying the respite from the stress of the court case. Jack couldn't believe how much more relaxed he felt and decided it was a good omen going forward.

Then his phone rang.

Dieter didn't mince his words.

'It's not her,' he announced without fanfare.

Jack was stunned. '*What?*' he said, jumping to his feet

and walking down the hallway.

'I'm sorry, mate, Alison's prints don't match any of the samples we took from the evidence, or the plastic box they were stored in.'

'You're sure?'

'One hundred per cent. Every piece of stolen property was printed. As you know Rusty's prints popped up on several items and we eliminated the property owners, Cameron and now Alison. She's clean, we can't touch her.'

Slipping into his study, Jack shut the door and slunk into his chair. 'Please tell me this is a nightmare and I'm going to wake up! I was so sure we had something.'

'Welcome to my world. Detective work is one step forward and five steps back a lot of the time.'

'So, the investigating officers probably won't be so receptive now, huh?'

'Well, it's pointless if I don't have anything to show them. I really am sorry, Jack, for what it's worth I thought you had some traction there. Unless you can conjure me up another suspect and put them at each of the crime scenes, I haven't got anything to compare the unknown prints with.'

'So, there are definitely unidentified prints in the mix?'

'Yeah, but like I said, unless you can directly link someone...'

'I know, sorry, it's not your fault.'

'Sincere apologies for ruining your night.'

'All good and thank you for your help anyway.'

'Anytime.'

Two a.m. saw Jack lying in the hammock in the back yard, kneading his temples to soothe the pounding in his head. The hammock was one of his favourite thinking spots, although he didn't often make use of it at this time of morning. If he wasn't so gutted, he would have been enthralled with the spectacular stars on display. Taurus was clearly visible as was Orion and the Southern Cross. Burrowing under the sleeping bag he had dragged out with him, he tried to formulate the options he would put to Rusty the next day.

The first option, obviously, was to continue with the not guilty plea and use the teenage grudge defence. Although Alison was apparently in the clear, Jack still wasn't convinced that Cameron hadn't had some hand in the crime – either because of the rugby scholarship or because he had found out about the affair. It was a hard one to call because bringing up the affair was not going to win Rusty many points with the jury. Yet, on the other hand, it might sway some of them on the grounds of motive for Cameron. But then there was the Danny angle and, although not likely, it was possible that Cameron did not know of the dalliance and this plea would almost certainly wreck his marriage. All in all, it was a sordid and messy defence, even though it was apparently the closest to the truth.

A much weaker option for the not guilty plea was to go with the unknown suspect defence, concentrating instead on explaining away the evidence and trying to establish reasonable doubt. Although likely to cause the least collateral damage, it was also the least likely to succeed.

The final, and less appealing path, would be to plead guilty and ask for a rehabilitative sentence. Jack knew he could probably get Rusty kept on at Regent Park and have him put through a work training program. The end result would be a solid chance at getting a proper job upon release and, with time served, the sentence would not be excessive.

It went against everything that Jack believed in, though, and he hated the idea that falsely admitting guilt to work the system might actually be a better option than fighting for the truth to be upheld. The other issue with the guilty plea was that Rusty might not be granted a rehabilitative sentence and could end up back in one of the bigger prisons.

As a shooting star streaked across the sky, Jack shook his head. 'I reckon it's going to take more than a wish upon a star,' he said, taking a long, last look at the sky before climbing out of the hammock and heading back inside in search of some Panadol.

Chapter Twenty-Three

Despite being fortified with two square meals and a proper coffee from Angie's, Jack's stomach was in knots as he drove to Regent Park the next afternoon. Having already procrastinated the morning away, he knew he had to rip the band aid off and tell Rusty the bad news. Casting his mind back to how indifferent he'd felt upon their first meeting, it was hard to believe his feelings had changed so much. While the jury was still out about how he felt about Rusty as a person, Jack empathised with his frustration at being held accountable for something he didn't do, and being completely powerless to do anything about it.

Rusty actually took the news better than expected. But then again, he'd been in and out of the system half his life and probably never held out any great hope that the cards would fall his way.

'So, we're back to square one then?' Rusty asked, folding his arms and exhaling loudly.

Jack couldn't meet his gaze. 'Yeah,' he said. More like square none, he thought.

'Well what's the go, then? I take it there's no other rabbits to pull out of the hat?'

'No, unfortunately I'm all out of rabbits,' Jack said, before explaining the options he had formulated the night before.

Rusty listened intently and thought for a moment before speaking. 'You reckon I should plead guilty, don't you? Just get it over with.'

Jack shook his head. 'I can't make the decision for you. And, for the record, I don't think that. I don't believe a citizen of this country should ever have to cop a punishment for something they haven't done. But, in saying that, you have to look at your options and decide if you want to take a punt. That guilty plea could get you the best end result.'

'If it wasn't for Daniel, I wouldn't give a stuff. I'd get you to put it all out there, no matter how ugly or how embarrassing it might be for Alison.'

'I would agree with that.'

'That's because I reckon you care about Daniel as much as I do.'

Jack nodded.

'I named him after my little brother you know. He would only answer to Daniel, never Danny.'

Jack's eyes widened. 'I didn't know you had a younger brother.'

'Daniel was born when I was six. I loved that kid, more than I'd ever loved anyone I reckon.'

Honing in on the fact Rusty had said loved in past tense, Jack just nodded, waiting for more information.

'Everyone adored Daniel. He was just that kind of kid. Even Dad had a soft spot for him, and that's saying something.'

Jack nodded again.

'You probably won't believe me, but I was a good kid back then. Even though I was only little, I knew Dad was dodgy and my big brother was going down the same path. I didn't want to be like that and I didn't want Daniel to either. So, I used to really keep an eye on him, you know, try and be a good influence. Mum used to sit the two of us down sometimes and say how proud we made her.'

'Everyone likes to please their Mum.'

'I didn't mind looking after Daniel, he was such a good little buddy. He used to go everywhere with me.'

'Uh huh.'

'One day I came home from school and Mum was crying. Daniel hadn't been feeling well for a while so she had taken him to the doctor. Turned out he had leukaemia. The poor little guy had to go to hospital and have all these horrible tests and chemo and stuff. He never complained, just took it all in his stride.'

'That's awful, Rusty.'

'Yeah, it was awful, the worst kind of awful you can imagine. The chemo didn't work, he just got sicker and then he died from an infection. Just like that. Four years old.'

Jack swallowed the lump in his throat. 'I'm so sorry to hear that. I can't imagine how hard it must have been.'

Rusty shook his head again. 'Things were never the same after that. Mum kind of gave up on everything for a while there and Dad, well you don't want to know about Dad. I never knew anyone could drink that much rum and still remain upright.'

'I don't know what to say, Rusty. I had no idea.'

'Not many people do know. We never talked about it much afterwards and I gave up on the idea of being a good kid. Didn't seem to be much point when something like that could happen anyway.'

Just to be doing something, Jack twirled his pen slowly on the desk, at a loss as to how to respond.

Eventually Rusty spoke again. 'Even though it was an accident and all, I really was happy when Tamara told me about being pregnant. It kind of made up for my little brother. No matter what she says, I wanted to be part of Daniel's life. Now he's all grown up and I missed the boat.'

'There's still time to be a good father. You've just got to get yourself together and make a go of things. Think about what your little brother would want you to do.'

Rusty was silent for a moment, apparently swallowing back tears. Jack was silent too, unsure how to deal with this unexpected turn of events.

'He'd be ashamed of me now, I reckon,' Rusty said, his voice faltering.

'Only you can change things, Rusty. Just make the decision and go forward in a different direction.'

The guard stuck his head in the room then, easing the tension a little. 'Are we all good in here?'

Jack spoke for both of them. 'Yes, fine, thank you.'

Rusty was quiet as Jack talked him through the finer details of the guilty versus not guilty plea, not making the usual smart comments or being obstructive.

'Like I said, it's up to you,' Jack said, as he packed his briefcase. 'And you'll need to make a decision soon. I'm very good at what I do, Rusty, but I honestly don't know if I can win this for you. Circumstantial evidence can be a killer.'

'Thanks for trying anyway and doing it for nothing and all. It makes me realise how special my son is when someone would do that for his loser father.'

'Thank you for telling me about your brother. I'm so sorry you had to go through that, and I know it must have been hard to talk about it.'

'It still hurts all these years later; you know?'

'I imagine the pain would never truly go away.'

'I can't believe I stuffed up my chance to be a good dad. I swore I'd do a better job than my old man.'

'Daniel might be physically grown up but he still needs a father.'

'I reckon you've done a pretty good job at that.'

Jack shook his head. 'No, I've never tried to take your place, and I am working really hard to convince him to have a proper relationship with you. He's just stubborn, like his old man.'

'Probably not the best trait to inherit.'

'No, but it means he's not giving up and neither am I.'

Rusty just nodded in reply and Jack packed the last of his things and left him sitting alone in the room, hoping he might score a few more minutes of solitude before being transported back to the common room.

Rusty's revelation replayed in a loop in Jack's mind all the way home. His chest constricted as he thought about the ten-year-old boy who had lost his baby brother, with no kind of support to help him through the ordeal or going forward. He was touched that Rusty had shared that information with him, although it added another layer to what was an already tangled and twisted situation.

Jack could never remember feeling this conflicted about the right way forward in a court case. One of his greatest talents as a solicitor had always been his ability to not only plan strategy, but also a very honed instinct about how a case was likely to unfold. Right now, those instincts had deserted him, and he was almost as clueless as the first day he had read the paperwork.

Slowing down for a red light as he drove through town, Jack decided to head to the gym for half an hour. While his knee injury ruled out running on hard surfaces, he was allowed to use the treadmill and, right now, he needed to run, so as to block out the chaos in his mind for a while. Back in his twenties and thirties Jack had never acknowledged than he ran to escape his own head, but, in hindsight, that's exactly what he had done. And it was why being forced to stop running had been the catalyst for changing his life so significantly.

Driving up the driveway at four thirty, Jack tried to ignore the heavy, clawing sensation in his stomach and the pain in his legs. Sure, the run had helped, but not enough. Steeling himself, he walked into the house. Judging by the sound of running water, Erin was bathing the girls while Sam and Josh were playing trains in the lounge room. It was a beautiful moment of brotherly companionship but today it didn't make Jack smile, like it usually did. Instead, he let his mind entertain the thought of losing one of his kids. It was so horrific to contemplate that he couldn't even stop to greet the boys, heading instead for the solitude of his study.

Leaving the light off, Jack closed the door and lay down on the couch in the corner. With the blind down the room was dark, which suited him just fine. Squeezing his eyes shut he imagined himself dropping into a black crater, totally invisible from the world. He had been here before, although not for a long time and he never imagined he would go back. Not when things were so different now.

After a while, Jack knew he had to pull himself together, but just couldn't summon the required effort. Get a grip! he thought as he dug the heels of his hands into his eye sockets and cradled his forehead with his palms. He could hear activity outside, the boys running up and down the hallway and the murmur of voices. Jack groaned as realisation dawned. Erin's parents had arrived for dinner. That wasn't a bad thing per se, but it did mean he would have to face them and he wasn't sure if he could do it.

Jack wasn't sure how long he lay in the dark, but, as was inevitable in a house with seven occupants, his solace was eventually broken. He had already ignored a text from Erin asking how much longer he would be, but his car was in the garage so he knew they would eventually realise he was home. As it happened, it was Danny who discovered him. He wandered into the study, flicked on the light and went over to the desk to grab a ruler, then jumped violently in fright when he noticed the figure on the couch.

'Jeez, Jack, you scared me! What are you doing in here?'

Still overcome with emotion, even more so seeing Danny there and remembering Rusty's sad revelation, Jack couldn't bring himself to speak. Holding his hand out in a *wait a second* gesture, he just shook his head.

'Jack?' Danny was alarmed now, his eyes darting between Jack's face and his surrounds, apparently looking for something that might explain his state.

Finally, Jack managed to talk. 'I'm okay,' he murmured.

'You don't look okay. You're freaking me out.'

'It's all right. I just need a minute.'

'Can I do something?' Danny was clearly torn between wanting to help but also not wanting to witness whatever was happening.

'No. I'm okay, really. Go back outside, Dan and turn the light off please.'

Casting him one last look of concern, Danny did as he

was told.

Knowing how much he had frightened Danny, Jack wasn't surprised when the door opened five minutes later. Erin's movements were unhurried and quiet and she left the light off as she walked over to the couch and perched on the edge. She didn't speak right away, instead she gently placed her hand on Jack's chest, allowing him to grasp it. When she finally spoke, her voice was soft. 'What's wrong?'

Jack exhaled loudly. 'Everything,' he mumbled. 'No matter which way I look at this, we're done for. I've achieved nothing beyond forcing Danny to see his father against his wishes, and now he's going to witness him being sucked back into the prison system. I gave Rusty and Danny false hope that we might beat this and it was all for nothing. I've neglected you guys and, today, Rusty told me the heartbreaking story of watching his little brother die of cancer. His name was Daniel.'

Erin's other hand flew to her mouth. '*What?*'

'I'll tell you about it later.' Jack cradled Erin's hand in his, amazed how much calmer he felt just from that simple gesture. She was the only person in the world he had let see him like this and probably the only one who could talk him off the ledge.

'All right, I'm going to be the annoying voice of reason here,' Erin said. 'I seem to remember the first time I came into your office, looking like a total wreck and blubbering for a solid hour, you told me no matter how catastrophic legal problems seem, there is *always* a way forward.'

'First of all, you didn't look like a wreck, you looked good enough that I would have told you anything to get you to come back. And, secondly, that was back in my personal injury days. Those cases are much more black and white.'

'Babe, you are honestly the smartest person I know. There is a way to do this and you're going to work it out. I seem to remember another thing you said to me. You said that as long as your lawyer is truly invested in the case, their training and expertise will allow the truth to be upheld, always.'

Jack chuckled softly. 'Again, that was to get you to come back.'

Erin hit him playfully. 'Come on, you meant it and I one hundred per cent believe that of you. I wish I could help you somehow, but I'll do everything I can to give you the space to get it done.'

'But you shouldn't have to.'

'Jack, just go with it, okay. I've got people to help me and as long as you make a few cameo appearances during the day, the kids will cope. There's an end date to this, so we just have to tough it out.' Although the couch wasn't really wide enough for two, Erin lay down beside Jack and wrapped her arms around him.

Tracing the contours of his wife's face, Jack kissed her, a long and lingering kiss that conveyed everything he felt about her. 'Thank you,' he whispered, finally.

'You're going to do it.'

'I wish I believed that right now.'

They lay there for another few moments until the sound of Josh yelling, 'Mummy! Why are you hiding?' at the top of his voice transported them back to reality.

By the time dinner was over, Jack had regained some equilibrium. A case was never over until closing arguments and he was nowhere near that yet. And, as much as he had initially struggled to face everybody at dinner, it was exactly what he needed. You just couldn't be a sad sack when you are with small children. In addition, Jack genuinely liked his in-laws, so being in their company was an enjoyable way to spend the evening. Not to mention the fact that having a meal prepared for you, the mess cleaned up afterwards and the kids put to bed was a treat to be savoured.

Clearly relieved that Jack seemed to be his normal self again, Danny asked if it was all right if he went to the movies with Xavier and Mitch.

'Sure, mate,' Jack said. 'Just make sure you take your key.'

'Yep, no worries.' Danny was already off and running up the stairs to get changed.

'We'll drop him off,' Evelyn said, as she packed the serving dishes into a box.

'Would you?' Jack asked. 'That would be great.'

Erin's father Malcolm smiled knowingly. 'Give it a few years and you'll be driving the fanciest taxi in town,' he said in his usual understated way.

'So I keep hearing,' Jack said with a smile, not wanting to entertain that thought just yet. Having Danny here had given him a glimpse into the future and he was determined to focus on being present with his children in these precious young years, before home for them became just a place to eat and sleep.

Malcolm and Jack chatted easily for the next few minutes while they waited for Danny to come back down. A former building inspector for the local council, Malcolm was a quiet but interesting man, for whom Jack had a lot of respect. Although initially taken aback at the way his father-in-law had questioned Jack's intentions, due to the way he and Erin had met, Jack soon realised it was only out of concern for his daughter and could not fault him for that.

'I don't know the whole story with young Danny and I don't need to,' Malcolm said now, as they watched the teenager put his shoes on. 'I just wanted to say that I can see your influence on him. You should be proud of that.'

'In what way?'

'He's very well-mannered and chivalrous. Those things will take him a long way in life.'

'Well, yeah, I hope so.'

'He's willing to give things a go too, boys need that trait. Otherwise they just stay inside and play video games all day.'

'That's true. He has his moments, like any kid, and he acts like he's not listening a lot of the time, but I think some of what I say to him gets through.'

'Of course it does.'

Jack watched fondly as Danny stopped to check his appearance in the hall stand mirror. He wasn't really shaving yet but Jack had left some aftershave in the bathroom and he caught a good whiff of it as Danny headed into the kitchen. Maybe he'd have to give him a heads up about how much to use.

Jack had just waved the visitors off when he heard a dog barking - inside. Tracing it to the kitchen, he shook his head when he realised it was his phone ringing.

Erin looked over at him. 'Aren't you going to get that?' she asked, as she dropped an empty milk bottle in the overflowing plastic tub under the sink.

'No. It's that same telemarketer,' Jack said. 'One day they're going to get the message, I'm not answering.'

'Great ring tone.'

'Danny keeps switching it. I don't know how he does it without my password.'

'He just waits until you put your phone down and walk away when the screen's still active. I saw him pick it up before.'

'I'll have to make sure I turn the screen off then.'

'Don't tell him I told you.'

'As fond as I am of that kid, I'm glad he's gone out.'

'Oh really, why is that?' Erin smiled at him, a smile that still captivated him after five years together.

'Let me think … the kitchen is spotless, the toy sweep is done *and* the kids are asleep. You want to join the dots?'

The smile again, playful but heartfelt. 'Hmm, maybe we could start sorting our receipts for tax time.'

Jack laughed. 'Well, as exciting as that little chore is, I was thinking more of an early night.'

'Is that right?'

'Yep. It's a great idea, don't you think?'

'You do have some good ideas.'

'So, are you coming?'

'Okay, tell you what, if you put the recycling out first I'm totally up for an early night,' Erin said, with a smile.

'Deal.' Jack grinned.

CHAPTER TWENTY-FOUR

When Jack first started doing Surf Patrol, he had joined the North Bondi Surf Life Saving Club. Fresh from two months of professional lifeguard training at Sunset Point, he wanted to keep his skills sharp and therefore chose one of the busiest beaches in the country. It had been an amazing experience. He had never imagined that so many people could occupy one patch of sand, or that surf conditions could turn treacherous so quickly. Compared to the occasional rescue at Sunset Point, at North Bondi the lifesavers could perform dozens of rescues per shift. Jack spent a happy six seasons at the North Bondi club, but once the twins were born, due to practicalities, he transferred to the Misty Bay Surf Life Saving Club. Situated just north of Sydney, it was a much smaller club, but the sense of community was just as strong and the commute time was less than half of that to Bondi. The thriving little town reminded Jack of Sunset Point, as did the beach, protected as it was between two headlands. As much as Bondi had challenged him to improve his surf skills, he had never completely lost his fear of big waves and liked the fact that Misty Bay rarely saw anything that he couldn't handle.

Initially, Jack had decided to miss his last patrol of the season, feeling every spare second should be spent on Rusty's defence. But after the events of the past few days, a patrol shift was exactly what he needed. As anybody who had spent a quiet Saturday afternoon standing on a beach for five hours knew, time really did seem to stand still when the only thing you were required to do was watch the ocean and the people in it. Having never spent so much time away from the beach before, Danny was more than willing to join him. In fact, they arrived an hour early to get in some board paddling time before the shift started at twelve.

Danny carefully examined Jack's racing mal board once they arrived at the club. 'Wow, it's a nice one,' he said, running his hands over the smooth paintwork and lifting it to test its weight. 'Trust you to get a custom made Kracka.'

Jack opened his locker and stowed his bag inside. 'You know me, Dan, if I'm going to buy something I like quality. I'd gladly let you use it today, but it's only rated to eighty kilos. I reckon you'd be pushing that, right?'

'Yeah, I'm more like eighty-five.'

'No worries, there are a few decent club boards you're welcome to use.'

Once they headed out into the water, Jack realised it wouldn't have mattered if he'd only been able to offer Danny an old door to paddle on. Like any kid who had come up through Nippers, and had spent hundreds of hours out on the waves, Danny was poetry in motion on a board.

Since his early introduction to the big rescue boards back at Sunset Point, Jack had worked hard to improve his skills. And he was very competent now, in fact one of the more skilled club members. But he didn't have Danny's effortless grace, or his ability to roll or pop at a second's notice, or to read the surf and know exactly how to respond to get the best possible ride. While the waves were only moderate today, there was an occasional random set big enough to cause Jack to hang back, whereas none caused Danny even a moment's pause. After one such set, Danny checked his watch as he sat out the back, waiting for Jack to paddle up to him. 'You could have totally gotten through that set. The rip did all the work for you and your board is so light.'

Jack manoeuvred himself to a sitting position. 'I know. In theory, I totally understand timing and looking further out to see what's coming, but as soon as I see a really big one looming large, I hang back instead of powering through.'

'I wouldn't have said that last set was really big.'

'Your big and my big are two different things. Trust me, Danny, you don't know how much easier it is when you learn something as a kid. Just be grateful you won't have to learn from scratch in your thirties or forties. Board paddling doesn't come so naturally to me.'

'Kind of like me and maths?'

'Yeah, kind of like that.'

'Okay, I see what you mean. But compared to what you were like when you first started, you're pretty awesome now.'

'Yeah, I have my moments, although I still have some pretty spectacular wipe-outs. But I genuinely do enjoy it these days. Although I'm not much of a surfer, I agree when surfers say there is something about the ocean that takes you to another place altogether. Even just sitting out here like this is amazing. If everybody did it, I reckon the collective stress of society would halve in an instant.'

Danny smiled and nodded, although Jack wasn't sure if he was really agreeing, or just pretending to, so he didn't have to listen to some kind of philosophical speech. Danny was still young enough to think that being in the ocean every day was just something that he did, he didn't look beyond the fun and social aspect. Nor did he realise how lucky he was to have grown up with it as part of his life. There wasn't much point telling him that, though, so Jack just enjoyed the moment of solidarity with him before they eventually headed back in.

Like Jack expected, as a guest patroller, Danny was a big hit with his patrol team. The teenage members bonded with him immediately, offering to show him around and find him a spare uniform, and the older members were similarly intrigued.

'Jeez, Jack, where have you been hiding him?' Patrol Captain, Kevin asked, having watched Danny out on the board.

'Queensland,' Jack said. 'He's just visiting.'

'Shame,' Kevin replied. 'We can always use someone of that skill level. Does he compete?'

'Yeah, a bit. He's more into rowing at the moment, so I don't think he gets in enough training for podium finishes beyond Branch.'

'Makes you sick, doesn't it, when they're that good without proper training?'

'Uh huh. Believe it or not he was actually my first training partner.'

Kevin cocked an eyebrow. 'Go on.'

'Long story. I'll tell you about it when we hit the four o'clock slump.'

'Good idea. In the meantime, I might get you down on the south flag to start.'

'Sure thing,' Jack replied, picking up a foam tube and making his way across the soft sand.

Standing at the water's edge, Jack cast his eyes out onto the water. Although it was getting close to the end of the patrol season, being school holidays, it was still busy in the water. The campground adjacent to the beach was packed with holidaying families determined to enjoy the last snatch of summer, before beach swimming became too chilly. Fortunately, the weather was holding, even though Easter was so late this year.

Not for the first time, Jack pondered the knee injury that had forced him to take up swimming, which had then led him to Sunset Point, lifeguarding and ultimately to Danny. Were they all just random events or had fate pushed him in the direction he was always supposed to go? And, following that logic, was he destined to be the person to somehow turn Rusty's life around? If so, it seemed a heavy burden to carry, but one he was going to have to live with.

Caught up in his thoughts, it took Jack a moment to register that a family group had started drifting away from the patrolled area. Jack blew his whistle and held his tube to the left, directing them back between the flags. Relieved when they complied immediately, Jack gave himself a mental shake for letting his attention drift. Taking a few steps down into the water, he made a conscious decision to turn off his analytical mind for the next few hours and focus solely on the job at hand.

Jack didn't protest when Danny offered to drive home. His ongoing tiredness often hit hardest in the late afternoon and he was relieved to let Danny negotiate the back roads in the fading light. Attending patrol had been a good decision that forced him to focus on something other than Rusty's case for a few hours. He had loved sharing it with Danny too. Although they were both surf lifesavers, they had never patrolled together before. Jack was chuffed when Danny had ditched his new friends for an hour to hang out with him, first on a roving patrol in the ATV and then on the north flag, sharing the easy conversation and companionable silences patrol lent itself to.

The first part of the trip home was silent too, with Danny concentrating solely on several tricky hill starts and learning how and when to engage high beam on the unlit road out of town. Danny didn't speak until he hit the first flat section of road, clearly relieved to be able to relax a little more. 'When do I have to be back at school?' he asked.

'Term starts on Tuesday week, doesn't it?'

'Yeah. But isn't the trial like the week after that? Shouldn't I hang around for it?'

'No, definitely not. School is your priority. I'll worry about the trial.'

Danny didn't respond for a moment, apparently deep in thought as he gripped the steering wheel. 'I was just thinking about Dad being there by himself. I kind of feel bad for him.'

'That's really thoughtful, Dan. But, don't worry, I'll be there with him the whole time. Maybe your grandma will come down for it, they seem like they're pretty close.'

Danny seemed surprised by this. 'Seriously?'

'Yeah. She writes to him every week. Do you know her?'

Danny shook his head. 'No, not really. I kind of remember meeting her once or twice when I was really little, but then Mum and her had a fight about something

286

and I guess she stopped caring.'

'I don't reckon she stopped caring, I suspect it was more like she was trying to keep the peace,' Jack said, biting his tongue to hold back yet again about making a comment about Tamara.

Not wanting to lose the sense of equilibrium that being on the beach had given him, Jack decided not to work that night. After the kids were in bed, he and Erin sat down to watch TV, but she was soon asleep, worn out after a trip to the zoo with the cousins. Nudging her to lie down, Jack covered her with the fleece rug and gazed at her, content to watch her sleep. Erin was the matching bookend of his world and it was hard to remember his life without her in it. Yet, they had taken the scenic route to find each other.

Jack and Erin had attended neighbouring girls/boys high schools, had overlapped two years at Sydney university and had even been in Europe the same summer, but neither had heard of the other until the day Erin walked into his office. Initially, they had regretted not meeting earlier, but they more they talked about it, the more they realised to change any of what went before would mean they wouldn't have what they did now. For Jack, even if they'd still had Josh and the twins, the idea of life without Sam and Danny, was unthinkable. And, while there were many life experiences he wouldn't want to repeat, he knew those same experiences had shaped him, made him a better person and, ultimately, a better husband and father.

Erin stirred then, groaning as she realised she had fallen asleep on the couch, again. 'I swear this thing has got a sedative sewn into it. What are you thinking about?' she asked, noticing Jack's pensive look.

'You, mainly.'

'Really?'

'Yeah, really. It makes a wonderful change from Rusty.'

'You're so nice.'

Jack smiled. 'I try.'

'Really, Jack. The reason you're caught up in this whole mess is because you're a genuinely caring person.'

They smiled at each other tiredly. Then one of the girls started crying.

'I'll go,' Jack said.

'Thanks,' Erin murmured, her eyes drooping as she snuggled under the blanket again.

Jack leaned down to kiss her on the cheek before heading upstairs.

CHAPTER TWENTY-FIVE

Jack was up at five am the next morning. Ignoring the lure of the paper outside the back door, he made himself a coffee and headed into the study. Setting the oversized mug down, he cleared off his desk, stacking all the amassed notes and paperwork on the floor. He then placed a fresh notepad in the centre of the blotter, as well as his favourite blue and red pens, and a new green highlighter.

It was time to go back to basics.

During his first year at uni, one of Jack's lecturers had been injured in a car accident and they'd had a substitute lecturer for the remainder of the semester. Jack could still remember the incredulous looks of his classmates as the elderly man in an academic robe had limped into the lecture hall, hunched over his walking stick, then made a point of switching off the microphone and the overhead projector that most teaching staff favoured back in the eighties. Casting a steely glance at the ninety students spread all over the two hundred seat classroom, the lecturer had advised them if that they wanted to hear what he had to say, they would need to move in closer. Surprisingly, all had complied, sensing Professor Alwin Moore was not somebody to be trifled with.

Professor Moore lived up to his reputation as a crotchety, old-fashioned academic and Jack had received his lowest ever passing grade in that subject, but he had never forgotten the obvious love of law the old man possessed, nor his deep and complete understanding of how it worked. One of the things Professor Moore had pounded home was the need to start every case with a completely clean slate, then build it piece by piece, verifying every piece of information yourself. Only a lazy solicitor relied on the work of others, according to Professor Moore.

Bearing this in mind, Jack segregated the paperwork signed over from Legal Aid and stacked his own notebooks on the small filing cabinet adjacent to his desk. Picking up the blue pen he wrote Rusty's full name, date of birth and the date of his arrest on the top right of the page. Setting his pen down, he focussed on the information for a moment in a meditative way, consciously bringing his mind back to the starting point of the case. The silence of the house was just what Jack needed to undertake this exercise properly. After five minutes, he grasped his coffee cup with two hands, took a long drink, and then picked up his pen.

By mid-afternoon Jack had made no great breakthroughs, but he had had a few small victories. The first of these was the validity of the boot prints. Having verified that Rusty's work boots were the highest selling brand in the country, with tens of thousands of pairs in circulation, Jack knew he could dispute the prints as reliable evidence, given that the unit block where the prints were found had two other tradesmen living there, one who wore the same size and style as Rusty.

Secondly, he was confident the cigarette butts could be explained satisfactorily, given where Rusty smoked and where he disposed of them.

Thirdly, Jack had realised that the stolen property with Rusty's fingerprints on it came from two units in the same block, which had installations on the same day. Jack wasn't quite sure what to make of that. It could simply be a coincidence, but, then again, out of seven properties with installations on various days, why were those two the only ones that had stolen property directly linked to Rusty?

It was tedious, time-consuming work, but Jack had to give it to Professor Moore. Even though he was meticulous in his own work standards, Jack acknowledged there were things he had overlooked and facts he had taken as absolute, without personally verifying them. Setting his pen down, he took off his glasses and stretched, then headed out to the lounge room.

As much as Jack appreciated Erin taking the kids over to play with their cousins to give him some peace and quiet, he felt a twinge of loneliness as he lay down on the couch for a moment. He tried to ignore the pang of resentment he felt towards Rusty for taking up precious family time, reminding himself that it was all for Danny. And, more than that, it was a genuine miscarriage of justice, something that every lawyer should be outraged about.

Checking his watch, Jack thought for a moment. He'd had enough of being cooped up in his study for the time being and, as unappealing as another visit to Regent Park was, it was probably the best way to spend the rest of his afternoon. It was difficult to motivate himself to move though, especially when the couch was so comfortable and his eyelids were so heavy. *I'll just lie here for a moment,* Jack thought, rolling onto his side and pulling the fleece throw rug over himself. *A fifteen-minute power nap is all that I need.*

A fifteen-minute power nap turned into a deep slumber, interrupted only by his phone vibrating on the coffee table. Bolting upright, Jack ran his hands through his hair and squinted in the afternoon sun that was streaming into the lounge room. Picking up his phone, he was shocked to find he had slept for over an hour. The message was from Erin, asking how his day was going and checking if it would be okay to head home soon. A super productive day, he thought wryly, glad she couldn't see him.

Yep, good day. I'm heading out to Regent Park, so house is all yours, he texted before lying back down. Jack had read somewhere that staying in the position you were in when you woke up helped you to remember your dreams. He couldn't remember exactly what, but he had been dreaming about something just before he woke up. And it was niggling at his subconscious.

Jack stayed there another five minutes, but whatever it was had disappeared into the depths of his brain and if he stayed on the couch any longer, he would go back to sleep. Hauling himself to his feet, Jack stretched and yawned, then headed upstairs to get changed.

Rusty's slumped shoulders and downcast eyes said it all when Jack arrived in the meeting room and took his seat. He mumbled a faint greeting in response to Jack's hello. It took Jack a moment to notice there was something different about Rusty and he smiled to himself when he realised what it was.

'You got your teeth fixed,' he said.

'Yeah,' Rusty grunted.

'Do they have a dentist here?'

'Nah, they take you into town and you get stared at in

the waiting room as if you're going to take hostages or something. Then the dentist tells me I must have friends in high places to get bumped up the list so fast. As if. It was hardly worth the effort of it all.'

Yeah, you're welcome, Jack thought. No thanks necessary. Although, of course, Rusty didn't know he had arranged it. Determined to remain upbeat, he smiled.

Rusty didn't reciprocate, he just sat motionless, looking at the floor.

Jack could understand why Rusty was flat but it was a complication he didn't need. Although he couldn't believe he was thinking it, Jack wished for a return to Rusty's signature belligerence, anything that would put the fight back in him for what was to come. There was an awkwardness about the silence in the room and Jack felt a need to fill it.

'How has your weekend been?' he asked, realising as soon as he spoke, what a stupid question it was.

'It's been fantastic. We got to watch the Shawshank Redemption on TV last night.' Rusty might be down but he hadn't lost his sarcasm.

'They let you watch that in here?'

Rusty shook his head. 'The clowns running this place probably didn't even realise what it was about.'

Jack was about to defend Regent Park as one of the better prisons in the system, but didn't bother. 'I've had a few small victories, although nothing of any great substance. Probably the best is the boot print, we can definitely shoot that one down as evidence.'

'Awesome.'

Let it go, Jack thought. He doesn't realise that you just spent all day picking dozens of pages of evidence to pieces.

'You don't remember anything unusual about the two units in the same block on West Avenue? That's where the stuff with your fingerprints was from and they were both Olsen and Wilson rentals.'

Rusty thought for a moment, then shook his head. 'I did up to five installs a day. They've all merged together in my head, especially because I was unfamiliar with the area.'

'So, you wouldn't remember off hand if that was an occasion you met Alison?'

'No. She didn't come out to every O and W property.'

'When exactly did you start seeing her?'

'Mid September.'

'Well, the time frame fits. I'll have to look into that angle a bit further.'

'Whatever.'

Jack exhaled. 'At what point did Cameron offer you a job?'

'About a month after we caught up the first time. He just rings me out of the blue one day and says he's got an opening for an installer, if I was interested.'

'And this was an unsolicited offer? You hadn't asked him, even jokingly, if there were any jobs going at his company?'

'Nuh, no way. It would have been embarrassing for both of us.'

'So how did you take it when he made the offer?'

'I thought he was kidding. I laughed.'

'But you soon realised it was a genuine offer?'

'Yeah. He started talking about training and uniforms and I was like, whoa, he's serious.'

'All right, that's good. It shows Cameron could have had an agenda. We can use phone records to prove he called you.'

Rusty nodded.

'How did you fit into the office? Were the other staff pleasant?'

Rusty's expression darkened. 'All except that little shit Sebastian.'

Jack looked up sharply. 'What?'

'Sorry, pardon my French.'

'No, no, I don't care what you called him, I want to know why.'

'Because that's what he is. Always looking at me like I was something that got stuck on the bottom of his shoe.'

'Did he say something to you?'

'No, he never did, but I could tell what he thought of me. I reckon he was the one who sprung me the day I climbed in the window. It was no big deal, I just had to pick up an extra keypad. But when I get back from the job he told me Cameron wanted to see me, all smarmy like. He was the one who had access to the security camera footage.'

Jack's heart was pounding now. He kicked himself for dismissing the Sebastian angle so easily. 'So, when you spoke to Cameron, he knew what you'd done?'

'Yeah. He was actually cool about it; I mean he told me not to do it again but he didn't make a big deal about it. Well, not until now, anyway.'

Jack rested his elbow on the table and massaged his forehead with his fingertips, contemplating the two different ways that sons of criminals had turned out. 'All right, Rusty,' he said eventually. 'Believe it or not, you just gave me a big boost with that little snippet. I never knew you had an issue with Sebastian.'

'I wasn't hiding it; I mean I hadn't even thought it…'

295

'It's fine. I didn't ask you.'

'What, you reckon it could be Sebastian?'

Jack shrugged. 'Possibly. Don't get your hopes up too much, but I'm going to get that son of yours to cyber stalk him and we'll see just what we come up with.'

'Hey, all good with me.'

For the second time in twelve hours, his phone woke Jack. As a rule, he didn't sleep with it anywhere near him, but he had been so exhausted at midnight that he dropped it on the floor as he crawled into bed. Grabbing the phone and flicking it to silent, Jack squinted at the screen. Danny. What the hell? Rolling out of bed, he stepped into the en suite and closed the door before swiping the screen.

'Dan?'

'Hey Jack, sorry to wake you but I thought you'd want to see what I found.'

'You're still up?'

'Yeah.'

'All right, I'm coming down.'

Using the light of his phone screen to navigate, Jack headed downstairs. Danny was still seated at the dining room table, an empty container of Turkish Delight ice cream next to him. Jack held his hands out in a *what gives* gesture.

Danny shrugged. 'Sorry. You said to let you know if I found anything.'

'Yeah, I know, but why didn't you just come and wake me up?'

'I didn't want to, like, interrupt anything. You went so nuts about privacy that other time.'

'Trust me, Dan, the only thing you're interrupting at

two am is sleep. But, thank you for being considerate, I appreciate that.' Surveying the table, Jack added, 'Have you even moved in the last two hours?'

'Only to get the ice cream. Sorry, I ate it all.'

'That's fine. What have you got?'

'Well it seems that Sebastian is quite the social media guy. He's got Facebook and Twitter and he's always posting stuff.'

'That's good. Anything jumping out?'

Danny nodded. 'He and Alison seem to be pretty good buddies. There's all these pictures of them having Friday drinks and out clubbing.'

Jack sat down. 'Really? Alison goes clubbing?'

'Yeah, weird hey?'

'Why is that weird?'

'Well she's old, like over thirty, and she's married.'

'Mate, I know when you're sixteen anything above twenty seems ancient, but there's no age limit on clubbing and married people are allowed into clubs too.'

Making a face, Danny said, 'All right, fine. It just seems weird when Cameron isn't there too.'

'That's a good point. This is great stuff, Dan, but you didn't wake me at two in the morning just for this, did you?'

Danny held up a finger. 'No, there's one picture here I want you to see.' He scrolled through Alison's posts and found the image he wanted, then spun the laptop around so Jack could see the screen.

Pushing it back a little so he could see it more clearly, Jack studied the picture. Apparently taken at a bar or restaurant, the photo showed Sebastian and Alison arm in arm with huge grins on their faces, each holding a champagne glass aloft. Knowing he must be missing something, Jack stared at the picture, willing the elusive secret to jump out at him. It didn't and he finally admitted defeat. 'You got me, Dan.'

'Look at the caption.'

Jack peered at the screen again. 'Revenge is sweet.' Sitting up straighter, he met Danny's gaze. 'Now we're getting somewhere,' he said, as his heart started to race.

'Check out the date,' Danny said.

'November tenth.' Although he was beyond tired, Jack felt like he'd just had a double espresso. November tenth was the date of Rusty's arrest.

'Good?'

Jack nodded. 'Yeah, it's a start. Let me think a minute. The arrest took place at about five fifteen. This was obviously later that night. Is there a time on there?'

'Well, it was posted at nine twenty-six. That doesn't mean it was taken exactly then, but normally if you take a picture on your phone and post it you do it around the same time.'

'True. Well, in any case, it was obviously taken at night, so the time isn't super important.' Jack hunched forward for a moment, willing his brain to focus. How had a petty criminal, apparently doing his best to go straight, gotten himself tangled up in this whole mess? And how had he ended up defending him? It would seem all bets were off now in regards to leaving Alison out of the picture.

'How do you reckon Sebastian and Alison cooked this all up anyway?' Danny asked.

'Who knows? The fact that they socialise together seems to suggest they are reasonably well acquainted. Alcohol loosens tongues. They obviously had a common goal to get back at your dad.'

'You can tell your policeman friend, can't you?'

'Yeah, I can. But I've got to get more details and evidence.' Jack skimmed his fingers across the track pad, looking at the other photos and reading the comments. A lot of it was nonsense, just random comments from people on a night out, but then he clicked on a link that led back to Alison's work page and another series of posts. He tuned Danny's excited chatter out as he read further, his heart sinking as reality hit. Sighing, he pushed the laptop away, as if to distance himself from the information it held.

Eventually Danny noticed the change in Jack's demeanour. 'What's wrong?' he asked.

'It's not what it looks like. The company Alison works for had a sales contest with another company. The other company won the first time, so Alison's company called the second contest the revenge round. As you can see, they won. The prize was a bottle of Moet champagne, which is what Alison and Sebastian are drinking in the photo. If you look more closely in the picture, you can see the bottle.'

'But why is Sebastian celebrating? He doesn't work with Alison.'

'Like you said, they socialise a lot. He was there and he had a glass of her expensive champagne.'

'Are you sure? It just seems really suss given the date and all.'

'I know, Dan, but I think that's just a coincidence. Look, I'm not closing the door on it, as I reckon the fact they know each other is a major red flag, but this just wouldn't stand up in court.'

Danny's defeated sigh said it all.

'Thanks, Danny, for all this, I really, really appreciate it and I reckon tomorrow when we've both had some sleep we can take another look at it. But for now, let's go to bed.'

Closing his laptop, Danny pushed his chair back. 'Yeah, all right.'

CHAPTER TWENTY-SIX

Jack slept late the next morning. The curtains were tightly drawn, but he could tell by the level of light in the room that it was well after his planned wake up time. He was sure he had set his alarm for six, but either he had turned it off while half asleep, or Erin had. It wouldn't be the first time. Hearing the muffled sounds of the kids running around downstairs, Jack felt a deep gratitude to Erin. She was so capable, and so accommodating. When this was all over, he was going to either take her away himself, or send her on a girls' weekend, depending, of course, on what kind of babysitting arrangements he could make.

Throwing the covers back, Jack was about to sit up when he had a flash of insight. What had he just been dreaming about? He rarely remembered his dreams, although the experts insist that everybody dreams every night. Resuming his sleep position, Jack willed his brain to relax and go back to where it had just been. Once again, he couldn't make it happen. He could sense it, almost pounce on it, but each time Jack reached out, it skipped out of his grasp. The relaxation technique worked, though, it fact it worked so well he went back to sleep.

The next time Jack awoke; it was to the sensation of a convoy of trains travelling along his right leg. 'Good morning, Joshy,' he said, shifting his bleary-eyed gaze to the middle of the bed, where Joshua had stationed himself and his trains. Although he and Sam were great playmates, Josh liked to do his own thing as well, and often sought Jack out, not always to actively play with him, but just to have him nearby. Jack had spent many an hour working in his study with Josh driving trains around his feet. It was precious time and sometimes he had to remind himself to just enjoy it, like now.

'Hi Daddy. Why are you sleeping all day?'

'I'm just a bit tired this morning. Where is Thomas going?' Jack asked. Joshua got a great kick out of taking his trains off track, often driving them over furniture and other household items, not to mention humans.

'It's not Thomas, its Edward.'

'Sorry, where is Edward going?' Jack rubbed his eyes. In his defence, both trains were blue.

'Up a very big mountain.'

Jack smiled. The kid had an imagination all right.

It was after eleven by the time Josh had wrapped up the game to his satisfaction and Jack had showered and dressed. Heading downstairs, he smiled resignedly at the sight of the bomb-site lounge room. He and Erin had given up tidying after every activity and found it easier to do a clean sweep each evening. It was hard to remember how empty the house had once been, how silent.

Chloe spotted him first. 'Up, Dadda!' she said, launching herself at his legs.

Jack picked her up, gasping as she gave him a strangling neck hug. 'Hey, Bubby, not so tight,' he said, prising her hands apart.

If Danny's body language was anything to go by, he was

still glum that last night's research hadn't been what he hoped. Reclining on the couch with Josh by his side, he was half watching Thomas The Tank Engine, as well as playing on his phone. Sensing Jack's presence, he looked up briefly and gave him a half-hearted smile. Jack nodded in return. There wasn't much more he could say at this point.

Sam and Charlotte were hard at work creating things with play dough. This in itself spoke volumes about how Erin's morning had gone. As much as she appreciated the educational and fun benefits of play dough, she hated finding tiny bits of it strewn throughout the house. It was usually only offered as an outside activity, and not very regularly. Jack could hear her in the laundry now, apparently working her way through the exploding dirty clothes basket.

Chloe was strangling him again and yelling in his ear. 'Swim, Dadda!'

Jack looked outside. It was a greyish kind of day and there was a stiff breeze. Plus, he'd just had a shower. But, on the other hand, he had just used up all his shirking household and childminding duties credit and expending excess energy in the pool would pretty much guarantee that at least the younger three would have an afternoon nap. And Erin would have an hour to herself while they were in the water. So, in the interests of a happy-ish wife, and maybe an hour or two of peace to continue scoping out the Sebastian angle, a swim might be just the thing.

As expected, Josh and the twins crashed right after lunch, as did Danny, his very late night finally catching up with him. A fellow puzzle lover, Erin worked on a one-hundred-piece jigsaw with Sam on the dining room table. It was their special thing to do together. Jack sat next to them, painstakingly scrolling through Alison and Sebastian's Facebook profiles. Although he still had no desire to join the social media revolution, Jack was coming to understand how people got caught up in it and how easy it was to turn into a voyeur, with so many people willing to share so many of their life experiences. He even found himself heading off on several tangents, clicking on one profile and then another, not all of it related to Rusty's case.

'Any luck?' Erin asked.

Jack flinched, then relaxed when he realised that Erin's eyes were still focussed on the pile of puzzle pieces in front of her. He had strayed off the path again, looking at family photos of Alison's sister, that really had no bearing on what he was supposed to be doing. 'Uh, no, not yet. I'm just so flummoxed about what people put on here.'

'Yeah, some people go way overboard. They make it easy to be cyber stalked.'

'Have you ever cyber stalked someone?'

'Of course. I mean if it's there, it's there. It's not like I'm *hacking* into their stuff.'

'True. Who have you checked out?'

Erin shrugged. 'The usual. People from school, Sam's friend's parents, the new kindergym coach, people from work.'

'I never knew that.'

'Well, considering you don't like Facebook, I didn't think you'd be interested. Lots of people look up their exes or their partner's exes.'

'You looked up Christine, didn't you?'

Erin averted her eyes. 'Maybe I had a quick look.'

'Did you make any great discoveries about her?'

'Nah, not really. Our kids are cuter.'

'Of course they are.'

Erin still didn't look up.

'I can't erase her from my past,' Jack said.

'I know.'

Exhaling as quietly as he could, Jack changed the subject. 'Thanks for letting me sleep in today.'

'You needed to. You were exhausted when you got to bed then you were up again half the night. I can always tell when you're zombie tired because you talk in your sleep.'

'Really?'

'Yeah, a lot. You were having a full-on conversation with yourself last night.'

Jack took his hands off the laptop keyboard and looked over at Erin. 'What was I saying?'

Erin shrugged. 'I don't know, lots of mumbling about photos.'

'I guess I was probably just thinking about this.'

'Yeah, but you were saying that before you went downstairs too.'

'Maybe I was having some psychic insight.'

'That must have been it. Although, come to think of it, I'm sure I heard you say something about my birthday and Tiffany jewellery.'

Jack laughed. 'Now why would I be dreaming about that?'

Erin poked out her tongue and they grinned at each other before going back to their respective tasks, making the most of the silence.

Shifting camp back into his study would have been the practical course of action, but Jack opted to leave his computer out on the dining table. He wasn't really getting anywhere with Facebook, anyway, and he didn't want the kids to think he was ignoring them. In between setting up a cubby, building an impressive train track and giving some horsey rides, he even managed to view the last album in Alison's extensive photo collection. Considering this was undertaken with Charlotte on his knee, playing with the bezel on his watch, and Josh parking trains on every spare surface of his laptop, it was a major achievement.

Still despondent that his great discovery had led nowhere, Danny was slouching around playing with his phone, and took it pretty hard when Jack shook his head. 'This is so dodgy. I reckon they're totally guilty.'

'Sorry, Dan, it's innocent until proven guilty. There's no proof in any of this.' Jack reached over to pick up his phone, which had just buzzed with a message. Studying the screen, he laughed at the image of the grumpy bear face Danny had sent him. When he looked back to his computer screen, he was alarmed to see that Josh had abandoned his trains and was randomly striking keys on the keyboard. 'Joshy, no!' he said, louder than he meant to. Somehow, Josh had scrolled through the photos on screen and "Liked" one of them.

Upset at Jack's tone, Josh's lip wobbled and Charlotte chose that moment to start kicking her brother, which led to a retaliatory shove. 'Sorry, buddy,' Jack said, pulling Josh's hands away from the laptop and placing Charlotte out of harm's way on the floor, 'but you know you're not supposed to touch Daddy's computer.'

'What did he do?' Danny asked, coming over to the table.

'I think he liked a picture. Can we reverse that? I mean Rusty isn't supposed to have Facebook access right now.'

'Yeah, it's all good,' Danny said, sitting next to Jack. 'We can just unlike it again.'

Unhappy about being put on the floor, Charlotte burst into tears and tried to climb up Jack's leg. 'Up, Dadda!' she cried.

'All right, Char,' Jack said, hefting her up again at the same time Josh claimed both knees for himself.

'Off Dosh! Off!' Charlotte said, grabbing a handful of her brother's hair.

'Ow!' Josh screeched. 'She hurt my hair!'

'You guys,' Jack said, shoving his chair back to keep them out of Danny's way and releasing Joshua's curls from Charlotte's surprisingly strong grip.

Having done what he needed to, Danny glanced over at Jack. 'Do you want me to shut this down for now?'

Still attempting to wrangle the two children on his knee, Jack nodded absently. 'Yeah, all right … no, wait a sec. No! No!' He yelled so loudly that everybody stopped and stared at him.

Danny froze, his hands hovering just above the keyboard. 'What?'

The surge of adrenalin was so strong that Jack could barely speak. 'Please, don't lose that photo! That's it! That's it!'

'What's it?' Danny said, his hands still frozen mid-air.

'That's the photo that's going to prove Rusty is innocent!'

Jack had actually seen the photo before, on Alison's Facebook page, but, somehow, he had missed that little detail. An apparently insignificant little detail when viewed from a distance, but very significant when you zoomed in on it. He had a flash of déjà vu and realised that this was what he had been dreaming about these past few days.

Ensconced in his study, Jack again trawled through the Facebook photos. It was different this time though, this time he had a purpose, he knew what he was looking for. Finally, he felt like he was on to something.

The unnamed woman was in several pictures. Going by the fact she was in a photo labelled "staff drinks", she apparently worked at the same real estate agency as Alison. Did that mean she and Alison were in cahoots? Or perhaps the woman and Sebastian were co-conspirators? If so, how? And, more importantly, why?

Jack hovered over each picture the way Danny had shown him, to see if any tags showed up to help him identify the mystery woman. Frustratingly, none did. He was about to call Danny in again and see if there was another way to track the woman through Facebook, when he realised there was a much easier way. Opening a new browser window, Jack navigated to the Olsen and Wilson Real Estate website, then through to the staff profiles. He found her at the bottom of the second page. Her name was Nikita Blair. Nikita Blair, Jack thought, trying to remember where he had heard the name before. Reading through her brief bio offered no obvious clues. Nikita had joined the O and W team a year ago and had recently been promoted to agent. Studying her picture proved similarly futile and Jack was sure he had never met her. Nikita wasn't a stunner like Alison, but she was attractive, with bright red hair cut in a pixie crop and funky, black-rimmed glasses. She looked to be in her mid-twenties.

Looking away from the screen for a moment, Jack wrote the name on his blotter. The act of doing that annoyed him slightly and then he remembered. The LinkedIn email! He had dismissed the invitation from Nikita Blair to join her LinkedIn network, an invitation he assumed had come as a result of him speaking at a recent conference, but clearly that wasn't the connection after all. Excited, but bewildered, Jack scratched his head. Who on earth was Nikita Blair and why had she attempted to connect with him just a couple of weeks earlier? It was a concern, actually. This whole thing was murky enough without him personally being drawn into the fray.

Looking at the name again, Jack recalled the night he had dismissed Danny's efforts at cyber stalking Nikita Blair and the comment Danny had made about her changing her name. Jumping to his feet, he ran to the door and flung it open.

'Danny!' he yelled. 'Can you come in here a sec?'

Apparently startled by the uncharacteristic urgent tone, Danny was there in a matter of seconds. 'What is it?' he asked. 'Is something wrong?'

Doing his best to stay calm, Jack explained what he was looking for. Needing no further prompting, Danny seated himself in front of the laptop and got to work. In two minutes, he had the required information up on the screen.

'So, you do know her after all?' he asked.

Perching himself on the edge of the desk Jack nodded. 'Well, I know who she is. The name I had was obviously a nickname, short for Nikita.'

'But she changed her last name too,' Danny said.

'Yeah, well, Blair is her middle name, so she simply dropped off her surname.'

'Why would she do that?'

'To stand out in the crowd? Perhaps she thought Smith

was a bit mundane.'

His pulse was racing now and Jack knew he needed to channel his nervous energy, rather than scattering it in a multitude of directions. After thanking Danny for his help, Jack asked him to go back and watch the kids for a bit longer so he could make a call.

Returning to the O and W website, Jack clicked on Nikita's list of properties and selected the one closest to the city. Then he picked up his phone and dialled Julia's number.

CHAPTER TWENTY-SEVEN

The open house was a hive of activity when Julia arrived at nine. Heading straight into the kitchen, she smiled in relief at the sight of the bottles of water and Olsen and Wilson pens lined up neatly on the bench. Grabbing a water bottle by the lid, Julia shoved it into her bag before selecting a pen. Waiting until Nikita was busy talking to another viewer, Julia surreptitiously wiped the biro clean and slid it into the zippered pocket of her Lorna Jane hoodie. To act the part of a potential buyer, she took a quick walking tour of the house. It was nice enough, she supposed, but Julia really wasn't a fan of compact bedrooms, or tiled floors for that matter. Besides, the house was too big for the block, kind of like a size twelve squeezing into a ten. Heading back into the kitchen, Julia picked up a flier and was so preoccupied studying the comparative values of the neighbourhood, she got a fright when Nikita spoke to her.

'What did you think?'

Julia held a hand to her chest. 'Sorry, you startled me. Um, yeah, I like it. I really like it. But I have to talk to the bank. Can I call you direct with an offer?'

'Sure! Of course. Let me just get you a card.'

'No!' Julia said, a little too forcefully. 'Um, I mean you can just write your number on the back of this.' Turning the flier over, she reached into her pocket and extracted the

311

pen, glad that she'd worn the hoodie with the thumb hole that allowed her to keep most of her hand covered.

'All right.' Nikita took the pen and wrote a landline and mobile number, then drew a smiley face and wrote her name underneath.

'Thanks heaps,' Julia said, accepting the pen back in a way she hoped didn't look suspicious. 'I'll hopefully give you a call this afternoon.'

Jack met Julia at her office. Still dressed in her exercise gear, she struck a noticeable contrast in the seriously upmarket office. Jack had worn a suit himself so he didn't look out of place. Although she hadn't lingered at the house and had used Google maps for the fastest route back to her office, the traffic had been manic and Julia was now running late for a management meeting.

'The stuff is in the bag over there,' she said, kicking off her runners and peeling off her socks. 'She handled the pen and quite possibly the water. I kept my paws off them as much as possible but I've done the print card for you. It's in the bag too.'

'Thanks a billion, Jules. I owe you like you wouldn't believe for this.'

'Always happy to help my favourite cousin.' Julia unzipped her hoodie and tossed it on the floor.

'Seriously, I'm forever in your debt.'

Julia pulled out a hand mirror and slicked on some lip gloss. 'Don't mention it. We're all working for the common good.'

'I can't believe I dismissed Danny so easily with this. I could have saved myself a lot of time.'

'But there was nothing to suggest she was in any way

involved. You know what law is like, lots of boring details for once occasional breakthrough. Sorry I can't chat about it more, I've gotta run. Let's catch up soon and could you please close the door on your way out so I can get changed?'

'You got it,' Jack said.

* * * * *

Although the twenty-four hour wait for the print confirmation was just as painstaking, this time Jack possessed a quiet confidence that the prints would match.

And they did.

Dieter was impressed. So much so that his voice actually conveyed his excitement that things had worked out this time. 'I must admit, Jack, that I thought you were on a hiding to nothing with all this. But you always were the determined type.'

Jack nodded, although of course Dieter couldn't see it over the phone. 'Yeah, I like to think I'm determined. But I've got to admit that I thought we were pretty cooked.'

'Run me through it again. I'm still a bit unclear how you put it all together.'

'It was the bag. The red Coach handbag that was missing from the box of recovered stolen items. I was always sure a male hadn't stolen it, but seeing that Cameron reimbursed the young lady, it kind of got overlooked after that.'

'I don't even know what a Coach handbag is.'

'My point exactly! I'll tell you my war story one day, but suffice to say I had prior knowledge and I'd studied the picture of it. It was a special edition, so it was quite distinctive.'

'And this woman had the same bag?'

'Yeah.'

'That's still a bit of a leap.'

'True, but the fact she worked in the same office as Alison and was at a gathering with Sebastian was ringing some pretty big alarm bells. I didn't see any evidence of her wearing the missing necklace though.'

'Oh, you wouldn't have heard. The home owner found it, so it's no longer listed as missing.'

'Great. That's one less thing to worry about.'

'So, you worked all this out from Facebook?'

'Yep. I'm a social media hater but hey, it's obviously got its uses.'

'Was Nikita tagged in the photo?'

'No, but I found her on the company website and then tracked her through Facebook. That's where I discovered the name change.' Jack felt a bit guilty at the use of I, when it was really Danny who had worked it out. But, then again, he had eventually come back to the information of his own volition.

'That's pretty sound investigating, Jack. You thinking of crossing to the dark side, joining the cops?'

'No thanks! I'm awed at what you guys do, but it's not for me. I'm signing off anything criminal after this one.'

'Yeah, I don't blame you. I'm just heading over to see the investigating officers now. You going to go over and tell your buddy at Regent Park?'

'Yep, I'll head over in a bit. Yet again he's got some explaining to do.'

For the first time ever, Jack actually enjoyed the drive out to the prison. Somehow the highway surface seemed smoother, the flower fields more cheerful, the sky a more perfect shade of blue. It could also be the fact that it was hopefully one of the last times he would need to make the trek.

Rusty was waiting in the meeting room when Jack bounded in. Apparently in the grip of a head cold, he greeted Jack with dull, watery eyes before making a grab for a tissue from the box on the table and sneezing violently into it.

Making a mental note to douse himself in anti-bacterial gel on the way out, Jack set his briefcase down on the table and smiled.

Rusty frowned back at him. 'What are you grinning at?' he said, before launching into a violent coughing fit. Jack didn't know whether it was the cigarettes or the cold, but it was a scary cough that sounded like it needed medical attention.

'You seen a doctor about that?' he asked.

Rusty shook his head. 'Nurse looked me over. Reckons it'll pass in a week or so. Half the place is down with it.'

'Right. Well I guess that's one of the disadvantages of communal living.'

'Yeah, you got that right. But I'm guessing you didn't come here to talk about that.'

'No, no, I didn't. I'm here to talk about Kit.'

For the second time since he'd known him, Jack managed to catch his client completely off guard. 'The real estate chick?' Rusty asked, lowering his gaze.

'Yes, as you well know. I need the whole story this time.'

'I answered your questions about her when you asked,'

Rusty said defensively. 'I told you about the lock and I admitted I asked her out.'

'But you neglected to tell me a lot of other information.'

'What information?'

'Stop stalling, Rusty. Tell me everything about your association with Kit Smith.'

'Well, like I already told you, I asked her out for a drink when she sorted out the flat. She said no and I thought, oh well, you win some you lose some. Anyway, a few weeks later I'm out at this bar and she comes up to me, all friendly like. Tells me she's not at work now and she's glad we bumped into each other. A few drinks later I'm back at her place.' Rusty shrugged. 'Typical one night stand I thought. Then she started calling me and we went out a few more times. It was fun for a while but she's one full on gal. She wanted me to go shopping in the city and to all these fancy restaurants. It was costing me a packet and it just wasn't my scene. Plus, by that time I'd met up with Ali anyway.' He shrugged again. 'I told Kit it was over and she seemed to take it all right.'

'You sure about that?'

'Well, yeah. She cried a bit, but all girls do that when you break up, right? I never spoke to her again.'

'Did you ever smoke at her place?'

'Um, yeah. Outside.'

'Why didn't you tell me that Kit works at the same real estate office as Alison?'

'I didn't see the point. I don't think they even knew each other back then. It's a big company and Kit was still working out of the former L.J Hooker office.'

'So, you're saying Alison never mentioned Kit, or Nikita as she is now calling herself? She never said she was having any issues with her?'

'Nuh. We didn't really talk about work stuff.'

Resisting the urge to ask Rusty what they *did* talk about, Jack pushed on. 'By the same token, Kit didn't mention Alison?'

'No. She didn't even move to the main office until after we broke up.'

'Did Alison know you'd been dating Kit?'

'No. I didn't want Kit to get in trouble for dating a client.'

'So, did you arrange little rendezvous with Kit while you worked too?' Jack asked.

Rusty shot him a death stare. 'No, I didn't. It was all above board,' he said.

'I need the truth, Rusty. I really don't care what you got up to, but if she came and visited you at work I have to know.'

'I said no. Jeez, how many times are you—' His voice trailed off.

Jack eyeballed him. 'What?'

'It really wasn't anything dodgy, but there was one time Kit came out on the bus to meet me at a job. We were going to a concert and if I'd had to go back and pick her up from her place we would have been late. The lady whose unit it was had to duck out and Kit came inside for a minute.'

'Did you touch stuff?'

'Yeah, I was showing off, you know? I told her what I'd picked up at the other unit I'd done earlier that day too.'

Jack nodded. 'The two units in the same block. Right. So, Kit could have gotten your password when you left?'

Rusty shook his head. 'No, I made her go and wait in

the van before the lady got back. And no, I did not tell her my password.'

'Think Rusty, this is really crucial. We've got Kit's prints on the stolen property, and we've got her in possession of a piece of unrecovered stolen property. We have an explanation as to how she could have gotten your cigarette butts and how she knew what items would have your prints on them. But what we really need to work out is how she got your password.'

Rusty seemed genuinely perplexed by this turn of events. 'But why would Kit stitch me up? We were never that serious and I broke up in person, it wasn't like I texted her or just stopped returning her calls.'

'I'm not being facetious when I say that is commendable, Rusty, but there's something we're not getting here. Did you ever talk about passwords, just generally?'

Rusty reached for another tissue and blew his nose before answering. 'Maybe, nothing I remember. I might have told her I used the same one for everything, but I didn't tell her what it was.'

'All right, I believe you. I guess I'll just have to try and bluff it out of her.'

Rusty shook his head. 'I can't believe Kit did this. What did I do to make her so mad?'

'I don't know Rusty, but I'm going to talk to somebody who just might.'

Chapter Twenty-Eight

Jack chose one of the cafés on Circular Quay as the meeting place. Danny and Xavier had come for the ride to the city and were eager to go exploring on their own. Living so close, Xavier was familiar with Sydney Harbour but it was Danny's first visit. Jack watched his eyes widen as he got his first proper look at the iconic harbour bridge and Opera House.

Xavier was ready and willing to play tour guide. 'Come on, Dan, I'll show you round.'

'Okay, that's all right isn't it, Jack?'

'Yeah, of course, off you go. Here's some money,' Jack said, pulling out his wallet and extracting a fifty-dollar note.

Xavier's eyes widened this time. 'Wow! Fifty bucks.'

Jack smiled. 'By the time you guys have some lunch and take a ferry ride there won't be much of that left.'

'Thanks, Jack,' Danny said.

'Off you go guys. Keep your phones on, right? And text me every hour.'

'All right,' the boys chorused, before scampering into the crowd.

She was already seated in the café. Dressed in a beautifully cut turquoise and black dress, the woman was stunning, even from a distance. Jack watched as she flicked her long auburn hair over her shoulder and reached into a black Prada clutch bag to check her phone. She's probably wondering where I am, Jack thought, watching for a moment longer as she tapped her foot, clad in an elegant black stiletto, on the bar at the bottom of the table.

Up close she was even more beautiful, her skin as smooth as porcelain and her eyes a bewitching green. Despite himself, Jack couldn't help but stare, just for a second. Gee, Rusty, you were definitely punching above your weight with this lady, he thought.

'Alison?' he said as he approached, although of course he knew it was her.

'Hello, Jack,' she said, with a cool nod, making no move to extend her hand to shake. 'I won't say I'm pleased to meet you because I'm really not. Take a seat.'

Jack sat down, feeling like he'd just been chastised, even though he had no reason to. Rusty was right, she was as hard as nails. 'Can I get you something?' he asked, picking up the menu and studying the overpriced coffee blends on offer.

'Espresso,' she said, resting her hands on the table. They too were elegant, with long tapering fingers and perfectly manicured nails. Her engagement and wedding rings gleamed in the ray of sunlight that was dancing across their table. Having twice purchased an engagement ring, Jack knew there was some serious money in the simple but stunning diamond setting on Alison's third finger. Clearly Cameron had been successful enough in his business to afford such a ring, but Jack got the feeling Alison would have had it even if her husband needed to go into great debt to acquire it.

Jack signalled the waitress and gave their order, feeling

Alison's cool gaze upon him as he did so. What was with this woman? She was making him feel completely inadequate, even though he too was dressed to kill in his newest Hugo Boss suit, a blue silk tie, the gold dress watch he wore only on special occasions and his best cufflinks. He had even squeezed in a haircut that morning.

'That was Rusty's son you were with before, wasn't it?' Alison asked, arching an eyebrow.

Wondering how she'd seen the boys when she was already inside, Jack didn't answer for a moment.

'I saw you walking down Pitt Street fifteen minutes ago,' Alison said.

Frowning, Jack met her gaze. 'How did you know who we were?'

'I looked you up on your firm's website, as I'm sure you did me.'

Averting his eyes, Jack did his best not to blush as he thought about just how many pictures of Alison he had studied in the past few days. Nodding, he examined his hands a moment before speaking again. 'Yes, that's Danny. How did you know?'

'Because he's Rusty eighteen years ago. Definitely more clean cut, but otherwise a carbon copy. I'm assuming he's the link in all this? How you came to be involved?'

'Why do you say that?'

'Because there's no other way Rusty would have the means to acquire legal representation of your calibre.'

Jack's face showed his surprise at the compliment.

'Besides, I read up on you and what you did at Sunset Point. Tamara still lives there, so I'm assuming you met Daniel up there somehow.'

Jack nodded his confirmation, then launched into an

321

overview of the case and what had led him to this meeting. As he spoke, Alison's face remained impassive and, if she was rattled by what she was hearing, she didn't show it.

'Why would you assume I have any part in this?' she asked, when Jack finished speaking.

'I don't believe you were *actively* involved in framing Rusty,' Jack said. 'But I'm certain Nikita doesn't like you. That, and the fact that you have both been involved with Rusty in recent months, is too much of a coincidence.'

'What makes you think Nikita doesn't like me?'

'I've spent a lot of time in courtrooms over the years and have become pretty good at reading body language. There are several group photos on your company blog with you front and centre and Nikita in the background.'

'There's no malice in that, I'm one of the senior staff, she's our newest junior.'

'It's not that, it's the way she's looking at you, even the way she's positioned her body in the opposite direction to you that makes a statement.'

For the first time, Jack saw a flicker of unease in Alison's expression. 'That doesn't prove anything,' she said.

'I don't need proof. I'm sure if I asked around your office I'd get all the confirmation I need.'

'No, don't do that.' Alison's face showed a hint of fear this time, as she suddenly realised how this situation could quickly unravel her carefully constructed life.

'Then you'd better tell me what you know.'

Alison exhaled, then looked over sharply at Jack. 'You're not recording this, are you?'

'No.' Jack held his phone up, showing the recording function was not activated.

'She had pictures of Rusty and me together. I don't

know how, well, I think she was sort of stalking him by the sound of it.'

'But didn't you only meet during work hours? Wouldn't she have been at the office?'

'Cam was away one weekend and I went over to Rusty's place. Given how far away it was from where we live I didn't think there was any chance we'd be spotted.'

'So these pictures…'

'They weren't anything salacious, but we were holding hands in one, hugging in another.'

'Nikita blackmailed you?'

'Yes, she did. I got her fast tracked to agent, even though she should have put in a couple more years as a property manager. Fortunately, she is very good at the job, so it didn't raise too many questions.'

'And she promised not to tell Cameron?'

'Yes. I assured her if she ever did her career in the real estate industry would be finished.'

'So why did she still go after Rusty then?'

Alison shrugged. 'To get back at both of us I suppose. I never took her to be quite so vindictive.'

'Did you suspect her at any time?'

'No, I really didn't. Rusty has always been a loose cannon, I just thought he'd gone back to his old ways.'

Feeling much more in control of the conversation now, Jack leaned back a little in his chair. 'I've got to ask you, Alison, why risk everything for an old boyfriend? Believe it or not, I actually like the guy, but you're right Rusty *is* a loose cannon. He's politically incorrect, he's abrasive, and he skirts around the truth a lot. He's not the kind of bloke you could take to a fancy dinner party. I'm just a bit bewildered how this has all come down to two intelligent, professional women fighting over a man you would never want to take home to your parents.'

For a moment, Alison fixed her gaze on the uneaten chocolate tipped biscotti that had arrived with her coffee. 'I can live quite happily without him in my life if I don't know his whereabouts, but if he's around I have this compulsion to be with him. It's like smoking. I know it's not good for me and I never buy a packet myself, but if someone offers me one I can't resist.'

Jack nodded. 'What about Cameron?'

'Cam is the man I want to grow old with, and hopefully have a family with. I love him and our life together. But Rusty, well, he was my first love and those feelings never completely die.'

Jack nodded again, although he didn't agree. His first true love had pretty much ripped his heart out and jumped up and down on it. But then again, he was the dumpee, not the dumper, like Alison. They had all the power and no doubt viewed things differently.

'So why didn't you visit Rusty at Regent Park?'

'I thought he'd done it, you know, I thought he'd tried to wreck Cam's business. Why would I visit him?'

Jack wasn't sure he believed that explanation but didn't press the issue. 'Well, Alison, there is an innocent man in jail at the moment and you had a hand in putting him there, however unintentionally. If you read up on me, you know I'm a mediation consultant these days and my focus is keeping things out of the court system. I've come up with a draft proposal that will get Rusty out of jail, prevent Nikita from going *to* jail and stop the media getting hold of any of the juicy details.'

'That sounds too suspiciously good to be true.'

'No, it's not, it's all legit and, trust me, Nikita is not getting off scot free. But you know how it goes, there's no such thing as a free lunch. I will need your help in getting Nikita placed at another real estate agency and, most importantly, I'll need you to get Cameron to drop the latest charges. Can you do that?'

'Yes.' Alison was back to being brisk and businesslike now.

'All right. We've got somewhere to start then.'

Wanting to catch Nikita completely off guard, Jack called her to enquire about the same house Julia had viewed. 'I'm looking to move to Sydney,' he explained, 'and the real estate industry is such a jungle. I just thought I'd give you a call and save some hassle. I realise it's probably a bit unprofessional, using a contact from a work case and all, but I get the impression you don't mind bending the rules on occasion.'

'Oh yes,' Nikita gushed. 'I'm quite a rebel at heart.'

'I don't suppose you could fit me in today?' Jack wheedled. 'My next meeting just got cancelled, so I'm a free agent all afternoon, all evening if it comes to that.'

'Normally I'd say no way, but for you, Jack Nolan, I will cancel a couple of other appointments. My evening is wide open too.'

'Fancy that.'

'Yeah, I quite agree,' Nikita said with a giggle. 'Will two thirty work?'

'Perfect. I'm really looking forward to meeting you.'

'Same! See you there.'

After checking in with the boys and directing them to catch the three o'clock train home, Jack grabbed a quick sandwich and a coffee and headed out to the house. Julia was right, he thought, it did overfill the block. He took a moment to straighten his tie and remove his wedding ring before stepping out of the car. Then he grabbed his jacket from the backseat, slipped it on and buttoned it and quickly reviewed his reflection in the window. Not too bad, he decided, even if Alison hadn't succumbed to his charms.

Nikita greeted him at the door. 'OMG, Jack!' she said, 'Hugo Boss and cufflinks? You are a man who knows how to dress. *And* you drive a black Audi. I might just faint.'

Glad that the window tinting hid the child seats in the back, Jack shrugged casually. 'Well my motto is if you earn it, you deserve to spend it.'

'I *love* that motto!' Nikita gushed, holding out her hand to shake.

Jack squeezed her hand gently for just a moment more than was appropriate for a first meeting, while giving Nikita an appraising glance. 'I already like what I see,' he said, looking intently into her eyes.

Reluctantly releasing his hand, Nikita stood back to let Jack in, returning the gaze in an openly suggestive manner.

One of the things Jack loved best about working in law was the opportunity to study people and their behaviour, especially when they were not aware they were being scrutinised. He had to give it to Nikita, her sales pitch was first rate, but the way she maintained and intensified the flirty banter as the viewing progressed was decidedly unprofessional. She took great pains to point out the double shower and Jacuzzi in the en suite as well as the intimate dining nook where you could host a romantic dinner for two.

When they arrived back in the lounge room, in a low

and husky tone, Nikita asked, 'So what do you think?'

Jack nodded thoughtfully. 'It's not bad,' he said. 'Not very kid friendly though.'

Nikita giggled and shoved Jack playfully on the arm, giving his bicep a quick squeeze as she did so. 'Kids? You are a man who thinks ahead. This could just be a starter property.'

'Oh, I'm not thinking ahead; I'm talking about the kids I've already got.'

'You've got kids?'

'Yeah, four of them.'

Her mouth dropped open. 'Four?' she said. 'Really?'

'Yep, two boys and two girls,' Jack replied. 'What, you don't like children?'

'It's not that I don't like them, but four? That's a handful.' Shuddering a little, Nikita stepped away from Jack and positioned herself near the kitchen bench. 'There's a flier here with all the specs and some neighbourhood comparisons,' she said, an insincere smile pasted on her face. 'It's a good price point for this area.'

Jack walked over and picked up a flier, pretending to study it for a moment before looking at Nikita again. 'When you were together, did Rusty tell you he had a son?' he asked, eyebrows raised.

Her face paling, Nikita stared at Jack. 'What?' she asked, blinking rapidly.

'You know, Rusty, the guy you went out with a few months back. The one who's in jail for burglary.'

Nikita's right eye started twitching. 'I told you I don't date clients,' she stammered.

'I know what you told me, Ms Blair, but you made an exception for Rusty didn't you?'

As Jack expected, Nikita did not capitulate easily. At first, she expressed outraged denial, then defensiveness and finally succumbed to floods of tears when she realised she had been well and truly sprung. Between the sobs, Jack managed to confirm that she had been following Rusty on the weekends and on some week days when she had property viewings and thus an excuse to be out of the office.

'How did you know where he would be?' Jack asked, handing her his handkerchief.

'I put a tracking app on his phone when we were together. He's so clueless about that stuff he didn't even know it was there,' Nikita sniffed, dabbing her eyes with the hanky.

'Why would you do that?'

'I didn't want him sneaking down to the pub with his friends when he could be with me instead,' Nikita said. 'At least with the app I could check where he was and bust him if he was lying.'

Widening his eyes in disbelief, Jack stared at Nikita. 'That seems pretty extreme for a casual relationship.'

'It wasn't casual to me.'

And therein lay the problem, Jack realised. Nikita had trouble accepting that Rusty just wasn't that into her. 'So,' he said, thinking on his feet, 'you lurked around the properties he was working at so you could get his password, didn't you? That's very calculated Nikita.'

Nikita shook her head rapidly, apparently outraged at this suggestion. 'No! That's not what happened. I followed him because I wanted to see him. I used to take videos of him working to watch later and that's how I accidentally got his password.'

Jack couldn't hold back his sarcasm. 'Oh, well, that makes it okay then.'

Realising she might have said too much, Nikita's bottom lip started to quiver. 'I'm really in trouble, aren't I?' she cried, dabbing her eyes, before bursting into tears again.

Jack managed to quell the hysterics when he explained the lifeline he could offer her, that is, a placement at another real estate agency (with a two-year probation period) as long as she completed three hundred hours of community service and a first offenders program staged over eight consecutive weekends with strict attendance conditions.

'What if I can't do it?' she asked. 'I'm going to Bali in a couple of weeks.'

'Then you'll be arrested and at the mercy of the court system. You'll have to pay for your own defence and you won't have somebody like me to help you learn from this mistake and move on with your life. I strongly suggest you postpone your trip to Bali.'

'I don't see why *I* have to move to another agency. Olsen and Wilson are the new heavy hitters in Sydney Real Estate and I want to be a part of that. Why does bitch-face *Alison* get to stay there?'

Jack sighed. 'Nikita, you are the one who committed a serious crime, not Alison. All Alison did was steal your boyfriend. As morally reprehensible as that may be to you, there's nothing illegal about it. And she didn't even know that Rusty had been going out with you.'

Nikita pouted but eventually nodded. 'All right,' she sniffed.

'This isn't a free ride, Nikita, it's a one-shot opportunity that you're extremely lucky to have been given. Make no mistake, you will need to be on your best behaviour and successfully complete all modules of the course, including the counselling. You'll be strictly supervised and if you miss any of your program sessions, you will be arrested.'

'Why are you helping me like this?'

'Because I don't want to see a bright, ambitious young woman like you end up in jail for a stupid, impulsive action. Trust me, you don't want that on your resume.'

Nikita's bottom lip quivered again. 'I've never done anything like that in my life but I just really loved him, you know? It can make you do crazy things.'

Jack nodded tiredly. 'Yes, it can. But if I can offer you some free advice, you're going to have to learn to be a lot less crazy the next time you get dumped.'

Chapter Twenty-Nine

It wasn't the Ritz, but as far as budget accommodation went, The Palms Motel on the outskirts of Millvale was clean and comfortable. Pulling up in the front car park on Easter Saturday morning, Jack looked across at his passenger, relieved he had agreed to stay there.

Although under no obligation to undertake any kind of rehabilitation process now the charges had been dropped and he had been cleared, Jack had convinced Rusty that it was his best option going forward. Calling in a few favours, Jack had managed to get him a place in a six-month program that combined a bush setting with a variety of outdoor tasks ranging from growing the food they ate to constructing and maintaining the buildings on the site. Upon successful completion, they would be given a pathway into specific work training. Jack had planted the seed of undertaking a trade apprenticeship of some kind, but for now he was just happy Rusty had agreed to this first, important step. Best of all, the program was in Queensland, less than an hour's drive from Sunset Point. With every second weekend free, it was a gradual way to maintain the fledgling father/son relationship that had started to grow over the past couple of weeks.

Appearing a little shell shocked at the idea of being a free man again, Rusty followed Jack into Room 18 without comment. With no bus seats to Queensland available until Sunday morning, and wanting Rusty to stay well clear of Sydney (and Alison), Jack had booked him a room in town. It wasn't until they were inside that Rusty seemed to snap back into the moment. 'Don't I have to check in or something?'

'No, that's all done. One night with breakfast included. Free Wi-Fi in the main foyer and the smoking corner is over behind the courtyard.'

'Right. How much do I owe you? There's the bus ticket too.'

Jack shook his head. 'It's on me. A little welcome back to society present.'

Rusty dropped his bag on the floor and sat on the bed. 'Thanks, mate. Are you sure? I mean, I don't have much spare cash on me now, but I can get it back to you later.'

'I'm sure. It's not exactly city rates out here.'

Rusty nodded. 'I appreciate it.'

There was a small round table near the window. Jack pulled out one of the chairs and sat down. 'On the topic of cash, just letting you know that Cameron deposited your last two weeks pay and your severance package into your account yesterday.'

'You're kidding.'

'No, I'm not. He didn't pay you the payday after you got arrested and, given that you were let go without notice, that meant he owed you another three weeks wages plus accrued holiday leave. It was in your employment contract.'

Rusty shook his head. 'I never even read that thing. But that's not what I'm confused about. Why's he paying me at all? It's not like I was going to go after him for it.'

Jack shrugged. 'Apparently he's a decent person and a

fair businessman. By the way, I didn't ask him for it either. I did approach him about giving you a reference but that was an email conversation. I was pretty floored about the payout too. It's a shame you won't be able to stay friends because he seems to be one of the genuine good guys in the world.'

'A bit like you, hey?'

Jack shrugged again and smiled. 'If you say so.'

'Do you reckon he knows about me and Ali?'

'I honestly don't know. Given that they still seem to be together now, possibly not. But you've got to leave that alone, Rusty. Erase her out of your life. Defriend and block her on Facebook and cut the cord. She'll always have you on a string otherwise. Besides all that, Cameron doesn't deserve to be cheated on. Nobody does.'

Rusty nodded slowly. 'Yeah, I know. I don't reckon I'll ever get another woman who looks as good as her though.'

'Seriously, Rusty, she's bad news. You don't seem to have a problem attracting women, so I'm sure you'll find someone else.'

Rusty didn't answer. Instead he reached down and opened the front zipper of his bag. He pulled out an envelope and walked over and handed it to Jack.

'What's this?'

'Just read it. I'm going to have a smoke.'

After Rusty left the room, Jack examined the envelope. It had been on quite a journey, first to Rusty's parents' address in Queensland, then his previous address in Parramatta and finally to Regent Park. Given the amount of crossing out and the tiny, almost illegible scrawl of the last forwarding, Jack was impressed it had finally landed in Rusty's hands. The envelope had been neatly slit open – by the prison Jack assumed – and it only took a second to

333

extract the contents. Inside was a handwritten letter and, as Jack unfolded it, a photo slipped out. Holding it up, Jack studied it, his brow creasing as he did so. At first glance he thought it was a photo of Danny as a young child, but upon closer examination, he realised it wasn't. The boy in the photo had a freckled complexion and his hair was a lighter shade of brown. And he wore a school uniform that Jack didn't recognise. It was clear that he was Rusty's child though, having the same strong resemblance to his father that Danny did.

Jack stood up and opened the curtain to allow some light in. The handwriting was small and, without his glasses, he squinted to read it. He scanned the two pages and discovered that the boy in the photo was called Julian and he was eight years old. His mother, Vanessa, had met Rusty at the Sunset Point Surf Club on New Year's Eve nine years ago. They had apparently enjoyed a brief holiday fling with no expectations of an ongoing relationship from either of them. Initially, Vanessa had decided not to tell Rusty about his son, happy to raise Julian on her own, but had come to realise, as he was growing up, that he deserved to know his father. It was an open and honest letter, asking Rusty if he would like to become part of his son's life.

Jeez, Jack thought, is this guy ever going to stop surprising me?

Rusty looked different when he came back in. Not just physically different in his civvies, but unsure of himself. It was clear that he valued Jack's opinion, or he wouldn't have shown him the letter, so Jack knew he had to play it just right. Despite that, he couldn't help but smile when Rusty looked at him questioningly.

'What are you grinning at? This is pretty heavy duty,'

Rusty said.

'I know. I'm not making light of it. I was just thinking that Daniel's gone from being an only child to having two siblings in a very short space of time.'

'Yeah, weird hey? Daniel said Tamara has a bun in the oven. But seriously, do you reckon I should get in touch? Vanessa might not be so keen once she knows where I've been the last five months.'

'I can't tell you what to do, Rusty but this woman sounds pretty genuine. You said you wanted a chance to be a good father and this could be it. As for the last five months, you can tell her that the charges were dropped when it was proven that you didn't do what you'd been accused of. Of course, you will have to tell her about your past, but on the other hand, you can tell her you're about to undertake a training program and potentially gain a trade. It sounds like she's single and still holds a candle for you.'

'You reckon?'

'Yeah, I do. Like I told you, I'm very good at reading between the lines.'

'She was a great girl. Not high maintenance like Kit.'

'And she lives over in Rosethorn which is close to your training campus and close to Danny. It would be good for the brothers to meet. Danny is great with kids.'

'I reckon I'd like Mum to see both of them. She hasn't got any other grandkids.'

'I think you should definitely do that. I'll always be sad my mum never got to meet her grandchildren.'

'Do you reckon I could see Daniel again before I go? Would he want to?'

'Yeah, I reckon he would. Tell you what, come and have dinner with us tonight.'

'You mean it? I don't want to scare your kids or anything.'

'You're not that scary, Rusty.'

Flush with funds after his unexpected payday, Rusty took a cab up to the Nolan residence. When he opened the door to let him in, Jack did a double take. Dressed in dark denim jeans, Converse shoes and a long sleeved, button up checked shirt that hid his tattoos, Rusty scrubbed up very well. He'd had a haircut too and his full set of teeth really transformed his appearance. You would never know he'd done time, Jack thought.

Rusty laughed. 'Amazed I look so fancy hey?'

'Well…' Jack hedged.

'It was Kit. She took me shopping and made me buy this stuff. She tried to make a new man out of me. I've got to admit it does make you feel different when you look the part.'

'That's true,' Jack agreed, standing aside to let him in.

'Went to the chemist too,' Rusty said. 'Got on the patches.' He patted his right bicep.

'Oh, good on you. Hope you can kick the habit.'

'Yeah, me too. Durries cost a fortune out in the real world. Besides, I don't want my kids getting any ideas.'

'Kids, hey? You going to meet Julian then?'

'Yep, I reckon I might if Vanessa gives the green light.'

'That's great.'

It was an enjoyable night. Given that he'd been the one to extend the invitation, Jack insisted on organising the meal himself. He retrieved a homemade lasagne from the depths of the chest freezer and put it in the oven, and rounded out the meal with a Greek salad from the deli in town and some garlic bread from the supermarket. It was simple fare, but tasty enough to have everyone reaching for second helpings. The boys accepted Rusty at face value, excited to meet Danny's dad. Jack was glad they were too young to have to know the full story. On his very best behaviour, Rusty was quieter and much less forthcoming with his opinions than usual. He accepted the offer of a beer, but sat on it for most of dinner, sipping it slowly from the tall glass Erin had poured it in. Apparently still not completely on board with being pals with Rusty, Danny was quieter too, but clearly impressed with the way his wayward father was conducting himself in polite society.

Jack did his best not to get too excited about the way they were chatting together. It was only the first step in a long journey of getting to know each other. Still, it was an encouraging start and Jack could honestly say he had done all he could to facilitate a new relationship going forward. There was a good chance Rusty might quit his program and drift back to his old life, the statistics weren't on his side, yet Jack had a sense of hope that he was in the right mind frame to finally clean up his act.

Jack walked Rusty down the driveway to wait for his cab. It was an unusual moment between the two men, more or less on equal footing now that Rusty was out of jail and no longer requiring the services of a solicitor.

'You don't have to wait,' Rusty said. 'They said it could be up to fifteen minutes.'

'I don't mind, I always enjoy an evening stroll. I also wanted to see how you felt about the whole Kit situation. I'm sure it seems unfair she escaped jail while you had to spent half a year in there.'

Rusty shook his head. 'I wouldn't wish it on anyone, let alone a young girl like her. Don't get me wrong, I'm glad she's still having to pay her dues, but, no, I'm not that bitter about it. Truth be told, there were other things I didn't get sprung for over the years, so it was probably kind of fair all up.'

'I'm not even going to ask about that. I don't want to know.'

'Don't worry, I'm not planning on telling you. I reckon you know more than enough about me already.'

'True that.'

'You're a lucky bloke having children who love you, a nice wife, a great house.'

'I am lucky. Luckier than most.'

'I'd forgotten how good it is to sit around a table with a family at dinner. It wasn't until I became friends with Cam as school that I found out that's how normal people lived. His family weren't well off by any means but they used to sit at the table and talk to each other every night. I thought it was really cool.'

'Sounds like Cameron has always been a good friend to you.'

'Yeah. Like you said it's a shame we can't stay mates.'

'Yep.'

'Thanks for giving all this to Daniel. It's all I ever wanted for him, you know, to have a normal life with people who care about him.'

'I'm happy I've been able to help give him that.'

'I reckon I owe you much more than the motel room and the bus ticket. There's the school fees and all the other stuff you've got for him over the years. The stuff I should have been providing for him. He told me all about it.'

Jack shook his head. 'The only thing you owe me is making a genuine go of the rehab program. If you do that, consider all debts repaid.'

'I meant what I said yesterday, you are one of the good guys of the world.'

'Anyone can be a good guy, Rusty, you've just got to want to be.'

Rusty exhaled and looked down at the ground for a moment. 'I know I don't deserve to be proud of Daniel seeing that I haven't done anything to contribute to his upbringing, but I am. I can't believe he's my kid. When I think of how messed up Tamara and I were…'

'Rusty, don't worry about it. It is what it is. You're in a position to be part of his life now, so grab it with both hands.'

'Tamara isn't going to like it.'

'I'll talk to her. In any case, Danny is old enough now to choose to spend time with you if he wants to.'

'That's true. He's got my number.'

The lights of the cab came into view. Rusty extended his hand. 'Thanks, Jack, for everything. I know I was an arsehole most of the time but I appreciate all you did. If it wasn't for you I'd still be sitting in there for the next year at least.'

'You're welcome, Rusty,' Jack said, returning the handshake. 'I won't argue that you weren't the easiest client, but it's been good for me, personally and professionally. Make a go of the program and see if you can make it work with Vanessa. She looks like a good prospect.'

'Yeah, I reckon she is.'

'I'll be in touch, regularly. I mean that.'

'Good. You'll keep me on my toes.'

Jack and Erin rounded off the evening with some star gazing on the veranda. Remembering his promise to treat her to a surprise for being such a good sport through the whole drama, Jack had something in the works, but decided to hold off telling Erin just yet.

'Believe it or not our life can go back to normal,' he said, putting an arm around her shoulder. 'No more late night strategy sessions or weekends out at Regent Park. And no more fake house viewings.'

She snuggled in against him. 'You're going to miss Danny though. We're all going to miss him.'

'I know. I don't even want to think about him leaving.'

'I knew you'd work it out for the best for Rusty, though.'

'It was a hairy ride. I honestly did not think we'd ever see this day.'

'So do you reckon you'll change direction again and get into criminal defence?'

'Not you too! No, I don't want to do that, seriously. But I'm certainly willing to facilitate more pro bono work, try and find some clients who don't know how to access the legal system when they need it.'

'That's a great idea. One of the things I love most about you is how kind you are.'

The screen door opened. 'Oh, sorry,' said Danny. 'I didn't mean to…'

'It's all right, Dan, we're just talking,' Jack said. 'Come on out.'

Danny surprised them by coming up behind and extending an arm around each of them. 'I just wanted to say

I really, really, love you guys. Like seriously. I can't thank you enough for everything anyway, but to have my dad sit at your dinner table and you acting like he's totally normal, it just spun me out. You're the most awesome people ever.'

Seizing the moment, Jack turned around and enveloped Danny in a proper hug. 'We love you too, mate, you're our fifth child. You're always welcome here. And never hesitate to ask for help. Ever.'

'I won't.'

'And, by the way, your dad *is* totally normal.'

Danny stepped out of the hug and raised his eyebrows. 'I guess we'll see about that.'

CHAPTER THIRTY

Easter Sunday was a glorious autumn day, the sky a denim blue and the temperature warm, with just a hint of chill. The stained-glass window depicting the last supper was a sight to behold at ten o'clock mass, with the light streaming in at just the right angle to highlight the beautiful artwork. Given that they usually only made it to Sunday evening mass, it had been a long time since Jack had seen the window in it's full glory.

It was certainly a day to be joyful, Jack acknowledged as he surveyed the colourful Easter banners at the front of the packed church, his heart full to have so many family members together. As well as Erin's extended clan, Julia was there too with her husband and three daughters. She had also brought her parents, Jack's aunt and uncle. It had been a spur of the moment invitation, extended yesterday afternoon, but they had happily accepted, excited at the chance to catch up. With Danny not being Catholic, Jack had assured him he didn't have to come, but he had, telling Jack it would be a bit lonely to stay at home by himself and, besides, Sam and Josh had created a complex seating plan with Danny slotted in between the two of them.

It was hard to believe the rollercoaster ride they had been on since that first meeting with Danny's principal. If

Jack had known what lay ahead he would have had serious doubts about taking Rusty and all his baggage on, but, like many things in life, it was better not to have known in advance. Thinking of Rusty, Jack figured he should be on the bus heading up to Queensland and hopefully a new, positive chapter in his life.

It was good for the soul to stop and reflect. With the twins being held by Grandma and Izzy, Jack took the opportunity to still his mind for a moment, offering a prayer of thanks for all that he had and thinking of his parents, as he always did. They would be so happy for him, so proud of the family he had created. Looking at Sam on his right, Jack thought of Eve and Toby, hoping they too were proud of the little boy they had left behind. Sensing Jack's gaze, Sam turned and smiled. Reaching over to ruffle his hair, Jack smiled back, remembering a conversation they'd had in the car on the way to school a few weeks before. 'If my other mum and dad are in heaven,' Sam had said, 'and that's where your mum and dad are too, do you think they know each other?' Choked up by the innocence yet wisdom of the question, it had taken Jack a moment to answer. Looking in the rear-view mirror to where Sam was sitting in the back seat he had nodded and answered, 'I reckon they definitely do, Sammy.'

It was a hectic, yet wonderful day. Glad that he had learned not only to cope with, but also to enjoy, hosting big family get-togethers at his house, Jack let himself relax and enjoy the chaos. With food aplenty and enough chocolate to sink a ship, everybody seemed to be having a good time, especially the hordes of children ranging from the twins up to Danny and Xavier. With pretty much every toy they owned strewn somewhere around the property and the basketball hoop a popular spot for the big kids, it was a scene that spoke of good old-fashioned fun.

Having led the lunch clean up duties, Jack and Julia took the opportunity to relax and found a space on the veranda to sit and chat.

'You know, you've inspired me,' Julia said, taking a sip of wine.

Jack raised an eyebrow. 'What? You mean my blind leading the blind defence strategy?'

'No, not that. Although, like always, you somehow came through. Just like uni when you swore you failed but ended up on the dean's list.'

'Seriously, Jules, this situation was more good luck than good management, but I am intrigued as to how I've inspired you.'

'The whole pro bono thing. I mean, we all talk about it when we start out, but how many of us actually do anything for free?'

'Not many. I didn't until Erin came along. Of course, that wasn't so much pro bono as me doing the majority of the work in my own time, but it was when I fully realised what a game changer proper legal representation can be. Don't get me wrong, Legal Aid is an amazing service, but when it all comes down to billable hours, some people just miss out. We should work on something together, maybe try and involve some other law firms.'

'I'd like that. We don't do enough stuff together any more. As much as those first few years at McDonald and Wright were hell on earth at times, I loved working with you. I still miss it sometimes.'

'Yeah, me too. Come and stay for the weekend

sometime and we'll put our heads together.'

'Good plan. The end of this month should work.'

'I'll put you on the calendar. We could set up the tents in the yard and have a camp out.'

'Perfect,' Julia replied. 'Oh, by the way did you work out who sent the newspaper article to Danny?'

Jack nodded. 'Yeah, I did and it's fine. Nothing sinister, it was—'

A posse of children interrupted their conversation. 'Hey, Dad, you said we could go for a swim after lunch and it's after lunch,' Sam announced. 'So, can we please go now? Please? Please?'

Joshua leapt onto Jack's lap and planted a hand on each side of his face. 'Please, Daddy? Please?' he wheedled, pushing his face so close they were nose to nose.

Laughing, Jack pulled him into a hug. 'All right, you can go and I guess that means you need me to come with you, right?' he asked looking at the assortment of cousins assembled around him.

'Yes!' they chorused.

Julia smiled. 'Looks like you've got your work cut out for you. Want me to come too?'

'I would indeed.'

CHAPTER THIRTY-ONE

It felt like longer than five weeks since Jack had been in Sunset Point. It was the same as always, simple in its beauty and unhurried to a fault. Given that Sam's school had an extra week of holidays due to a building renovation project, Jack had extended his leave and they had all flown up with Danny on Easter Monday morning. Excited to have rented the Beach House at such short notice, Jack dropped off Erin and the kids there first, before driving Danny home.

Danny was clearly surprised when Jack turned off the ignition and got out of the car, but said nothing as his friend followed him up to the front path. Having not been up close to the house for several years, Jack was amazed at how much the one story Besser block building had changed. The exterior had been rendered, the roof painted, new gardens planted at the front and, as Danny had told him, the garage was in the throes of being transformed into a new master suite.

When Tamara walked into the lounge room, Jack did a double take. Erin was right, she did look totally different to the Tamara he used to know. The brassy blonde hair had been replaced by a much subtler shade of brown and her angular cheekbones had softened considerably. Then, of course, there was the baby bump. She had probably only gained five kilograms, but it suited her, changing her whole

347

appearance dramatically.

'Danny!' she exclaimed, striding over to engulf him in the kind of hug only a mother can give. It was amusing to watch, with her being so much shorter than Danny, but there was nothing contrived about it, nor any mistake about Danny's enthusiastic return of the embrace. 'We missed you so much!' she said, holding him close for another moment, before standing back and looking at him. 'I think you've grown taller too.'

Jack wasn't sure if it was the pregnancy hormones or absence making the heart grow fonder, but in that moment, his opinion of Danny's mother altered. For the first time, he saw unadulterated mother love, rather than what he had always perceived as indifference or sometimes even borderline emotional neglect. Then again, perhaps he had continued to judge Tamara too harshly for her transgressions many years before. Like Erin had said, she was young and inexperienced at life when Danny was small. Maybe she had grown into motherhood as she matured. Better late than never. Besides, Danny loved her unconditionally, and at the end of the day, that was all that really mattered.

'Hi Jack,' she said.

'Hello,' he replied. 'You're looking well.'

'Thanks,' she said. 'I feel really good.'

'Where's Colin?' Danny asked.

'Out in the garage. Go out and say hello, he's missed you too.'

Danny headed outside and Jack took the opportunity to have a quick word. 'Tamara, I know it's not any of my business, but I think it's really important that Danny keeps in touch with Rusty. I don't know if you heard he's moved back up this way and Danny is conflicted, because he knows how you feel about him.'

Tamara stared at him for a moment, then shrugged. 'I don't mind if he sees him. Colin has been in my ear about it for ages now and I guess he's right. As long as I don't have to socialise with him, then it's fine, I guess.'

'I'm glad you agree. On that note though, I think you and Rusty need to make a bit of an effort with each other. Just be aware there might be occasions when Danny wants both of you there, like his school graduation. It will cause him huge stress if he thinks you'll claw each other's eyes out. Surely you can be civil.'

Another shrug. 'I suppose so.'

'Do you really hate him that much?'

Tamara sighed this time. 'No, not really. I was just so mad at him about everything back then, it kind of became a habit. Danny is so much like him now it reminds me of Rusty at that age. We had some good times together before I got pregnant.'

'You can't regret it, though, not when Danny's such a great kid.'

Tamara didn't respond for a moment and Jack felt his hackles rise. Surely that wasn't a hard question to answer? It wasn't until he looked at her more closely that he saw the tears in her eyes.

'Sorry, I didn't mean to upset you,' Jack said.

'It's all right. Pregnancy hormones,' Tamara sniffed. 'You're right, I don't regret it now, not one bit. He's a beautiful boy.'

'He is.'

Danny walked back in and Tamara and Jack both looked at him so intently, he stopped in his tracks. 'What?'

he asked.

'I was just asking your mum if you guys will come and have dinner with us one night while we're at the Beach House.'

Danny's eyes lit up. 'Yeah, we'd love to, right, Mum?'

Tamara nodded and smiled gratefully at Jack. 'Yes, that would be nice.'

CHAPTER THIRTY-TWO

It was the best of weeks.

Autumn in Queensland was mild, as always, and beach conditions were perfect. Jack couldn't remember the last time he had felt so relaxed. In fact, it was probably the last time he had holidayed at the Beach House, he thought, as he watched Sam and Josh splash around in the shallows and the twins dig in the sand with their beach toys. Erin was out and about somewhere, probably at the day spa, Jack decided. Not that it mattered. His job was to get up early to make breakfast, then gather the kids up and let them loose on the sand while Mummy slept in and caught up on some R and R.

Early afternoon saw them all enjoy a nap, and then it was socialising for the rest of the day. Gloria and Jim were frequent visitors and Danny would drop around after school. The dinner with Tamara and Colin had gone well, further softening Jack's opinion of Danny's mother. A genuine diamond in the rough, Colin was solid and loyal and had clearly been the catalyst to Tamara's transformation. For the first time since he had known Danny, Jack felt he could step back a bit from the supervisory role he had always played in his life. While he had never minded doing it, it was a relief to know Danny's parents were now on the same page as him.

Things were on track with Rusty so far. He had arrived safely, checked into his accommodation and was currently undertaking an orientation week. Jack knew it wouldn't all be smooth sailing, that Rusty would no doubt struggle with conforming and would need to curb his distrust of authority figures. But then again, most the men in the program were in a similar place, having been recent prison inmates, so surely there were procedures in place to cope with that. It was a solid, well-established program that had a good success rate and Jack had done all he could in leading the horse to water. It was up to Rusty to make the most of it.

* * * * *

Jack was surprised by the house. As he drove along the street, he assumed it would be the ageing weatherboard cottage with peeling paint and a front lawn that was more knee-high weeds than grass. Stopping at the curb, he checked the number on the letterbox and realised he was wrong. The house he was looking for was two doors further down.

He parked the rented Tarago and looked more closely at the house. It was no palace, just a simple brick bungalow, but it was certainly no dump either. Traversing the nature strip, Jack let himself in through the wrought iron gate and walked across the neatly mown front lawn. Well-tended flowerbeds lined the sides of the front yard and several miniature trees in pots were arranged along the front wall of the house. Parked in the carport at the side was a gleaming white Daihatsu Charade. Good, that meant she was likely to be home.

His knock on the front door was answered quickly and

Jack tried not to gasp out loud at how tiny the woman was. It was hard to believe she could have produced such a tall son. 'Eileen?' he asked tentatively, worried he might, in fact, have the wrong house.

'Yes, I'm Eileen. And you're Jack. Jack Nolan.'

'That's right,' Jack replied, taken aback not because she knew who he was, but that she didn't seem surprised to see him.

Eileen grasped Jack's hand. 'I've been hoping each day you'd drop by and you timed it well because Barry is off fishing, so we can talk in peace. Come on out the back and we'll have some morning tea.'

Jack nodded and stepped inside.

The interior of the house was dated but immaculately neat and the paved area at the back was a cosy space, perfect for entertaining. Within minutes Jack had a cup of tea and a slice of fruit cake in front of him. Eileen sat opposite him, her own tea in a matching china mug. Although her hair was completely grey and her face heavily lined for a woman who wasn't yet sixty, Eileen's lively green eyes softened her appearance.

'Thank you for getting Russell out of prison,' she said. 'I know he's no angel, but he's a good son underneath it all and I knew he'd never have anything to do with robbing houses. I fretted about it for so long, then it occurred to me that there was someone who could help him.'

'I didn't put it together until the other day. You sent Danny the newspaper article and later rang me, pretending to be from the school, didn't you?'

Eileen nodded. 'Yes, I did. I'm sorry to have deceived you, but I didn't expect Daniel to react the way he did to

353

the story from the paper. I thought he would get straight in touch with you. When I heard he was acting up at school, I was beside myself and thought I'd really mucked everything up. I knew that if I could get you up here, you'd make it right, somehow.'

Smiling wryly, Jack shook his head. 'I'm flattered, Eileen, but I have to tell you, this was a challenge like no other I've encountered in my career. Why would you put so much faith in me?'

'You're one of the best in the business, of course I put all my faith in you.'

Jack was about to explain the many facets and specialties in law and how his lack of experience in criminal defence could have harmed Rusty's chances of a favourable outcome rather than enhanced them, but realised it didn't matter. Eileen was a mother determined to help her son, Jack had a law degree and his friendship with Danny meant he would take on the case for free, so, for Eileen, there was no question that Jack was the man for the job. 'I'll be honest with you, I would never have volunteered to take Rusty on, but I am truly happy that I did help him.'

'I'm sure you've heard all about my husband, Barry, and my other son, Darryl. It pains me to say it, but for them, crime is almost an addiction. It's like they are lured to it even when there's an honest way to do something. But Russell, like I said, he's a good man at heart. He just needs some firm direction.'

'Well, hopefully he's getting plenty of that now.'

'Yes, I think he is. He rang me yesterday and said he's getting along well.'

'Danny is really looking forward to meeting you again. I never realised you'd kept such close tabs on him, I'm so happy you've been on the periphery of his life even if he didn't realise it.'

'How could any grandmother ignore a grandchild? I'm not bitter at Tamara, heaven knows I've been judged enough not to judge another woman, but it did make me sad at times that I had to go to such lengths to catch glimpses him of. I think I'll burst when I get to speak to him in person, hug him and feed him, do all the grandmother things.'

'He is an amazing young man. I'd gladly keep him if I could.'

Eileen smiled. 'There aren't enough words to thank you for all you've done for him.'

'I don't need thanks for something that gives back so much more than I put out.'

They talked for an hour. Eileen spoke honestly about the pain of losing her third son and the hard slog back to a semblance of her former self. 'It's true what they say,' she said. 'The pain never really goes away, but you do learn to live with it.'

Jack grasped her hand for a moment, knowing there was nothing he could say to soften that sad reality.

Eileen excused herself for a moment, to freshen the teapot, and the conversation became easier then, with each trading family anecdotes. It gladdened Jack to hear that Barry and Darryl were both out of trouble at that time, having discovered deep sea fishing as a shared hobby.

'I'm not completely naive, mind you,' Eileen said. 'I'm sure they don't pay any attention to bag limits or fish size or even the zones they're allowed to fish in, but being out there on the water stops them getting up to anything untoward on dry land. It's brought me a lot of peace.'

Wrong again, Jack realised as they continued to chat. He had pegged Eileen as a victim, a down trodden woman who had let life beat her down. But she was far from that. Eileen was a survivor who had used her wiles to do her best for her family. Initially, he been a little concerned about Danny meeting her but that fear, he now realised, was entirely misplaced. Eileen would only enhance her grandson's life.

All too soon it was time to go. It seemed perfectly natural to enfold Eileen in a hug as they said goodbye, even though they had only known each other an hour.

'I'm sure we will meet again, Jack,' Eileen said. 'I'll write you a letter every now and then to keep you up to date with what's happening.'

'I'd love that,' Jack replied. 'Next time we're up this way you can meet my family.'

'I can't wait,' Eileen said with a smile.

* * * * *

Jim and Jack had fallen into the routine of going for a paddle each afternoon while Gloria and Erin took the kids to the park. Like Danny, Jim was a natural on the board, easily able to power through the waves in the surf zone and then continue at speed out on the flat. I hope I'm as fit as him in twenty years, Jack thought on his last afternoon there, trying to ignore the pain in his hamstrings and lower back as he did his best to match Jim's pace. Finally, the older man slowed and then stopped, dropping back to a sitting position and using his legs to turn the board back around to face the shore. 'You could never get sick of this view,' he said, looking back at the distant beach, his face showing his contentment and how at home he was out on the ocean.

Jack paddled up alongside him, doing his best not to let the relief at stopping show on his face. 'Very true,' he agreed, sitting back on his haunches for a moment before dropping his legs down into the water.

'I can't believe I'm saying this, but I'm glad you got Rusty back up here. I know I've told you he was nothing but trouble when he was a kid, but you're right, he never had any kind of example set for him,' Jim said. 'Barry never did an honest day's work, and never made any attempt to bring his sons up right.'

'Eileen told me that Barry has discovered deep sea fishing.'

'Yes, he has. I think we're all a bit wary that he's working some kind of angle, scamming someone along the line, but for now it all seems on the up and up.'

'I've got to admit I was surprised by Eileen and Barry's house. I assumed they would live in some dingy rental.'

'Well, they always did, but Eileen inherited her aunt's place a few years back and has been savvy enough to keep the title in her name only. Everyone was so happy for her, to finally have a bit of security in her old age and, just quietly, I reckon it's pulled Barry up a bit, knowing Eileen's in charge now.'

Jack smiled at the further confirmation that Eileen was no victim. 'Danny is going to see her this weekend. She's so excited.'

'She'll be tickled pink, I reckon, to finally be able to properly interact with him. And there's another kid you said?'

'Yep, there is. I'm not sure how that's all going to pan out yet, but Rusty is definitely keen to make a go of fatherhood this time.'

'I don't know how you do it, Jack, but you've got the Midas touch. First you save the Beach House for us, then you get Dan back on the straight and narrow and reform his no-hoper father. You're quite the fixer.'

Jack shook his head. 'Let's not count our chickens just yet. Besides, I just pulled all the threads together. Danny was actually a really big help too; I couldn't have done it without him. As much as I can say it was an experience I never want to repeat, there was a major silver lining and it makes you wonder if it wasn't all meant to happen this way.'

'Well, you only have to sit out here for a few minutes to realise there are much bigger forces than us at play in this world.'

'You've got that right. But, like I said, let's not get ahead of ourselves. There's every chance this could all go pear shaped.'

'Yeah, it might. But, at least right now, there's every chance it won't.' With that Jim resumed his kneeling position and leaned forward, digging his arms into the water and moving forward at the same brisk pace he'd led them out with.

Bracing himself for the physical challenge ahead, Jack knelt on his board and followed him in.

About The Author

Helen McKenna lives on the Sunshine Coast in Queensland. She has a Bachelor of Arts degree from the University of Queensland and has worked in banking, local government and as a biographer. As well as writing, she currently works in learning support and as a swimming coach. The Third Time* is her third novel and is a sequel to one of the stories in The Beach House.

* The Third Time was previously published as Third Offence.

Helen loves to hear from her readers, so please feel free to drop her a line:

Email: info@helenmckenna.com.au
Website: www.helenmckenna.com.au
Facebook: www.facebook.com/HelenMcKenna.Author
Twitter: www.twitter.com/helenmckenna_

All paperbacks are currently available directly from her website and all titles are also available as e-books at the major retailers.